Titles by Robin D. Owens

HEARTMATE
HEART THIEF
HEART DUEL
HEART CHOICE
HEART QUEST
HEART DANCE
HEART FATE
HEART CHANGE
HEART JOURNEY

Anthologies

WHAT DREAMS MAY COME
(with Sherrilyn Kenyon and Rebecca York)

Heart Fate

Robin D. Owens

BERKLEY SENSATION, NEW YORK

THE BERKLEY PUBLISHING GROUP
Published by the Penguin Group
Penguin Group (USA) Inc.
375 Hudson Street, New York, New York 10014, USA

Penguin Group (Canada), 90 Eglinton Avenue East, Suite 700, Toronto, Ontario M4P 2Y3, Canada
(a division of Pearson Penguin Canada Inc.)
Penguin Books Ltd., 80 Strand, London WC2R 0RL, England
Penguin Group Ireland, 25 St. Stephen's Green, Dublin 2, Ireland (a division of Penguin Books Ltd.)
Penguin Group (Australia), 250 Camberwell Road, Camberwell, Victoria 3124, Australia
(a division of Pearson Australia Group Pty. Ltd.)
Penguin Books India Pvt. Ltd., 11 Community Centre, Panchsheel Park, New Delhi—110 017, India
Penguin Group (NZ), 67 Apollo Drive, Rosedale, North Shore 0632, New Zealand
(a division of Pearson New Zealand Ltd.)
Penguin Books (South Africa) (Pty.) Ltd., 24 Sturdee Avenue, Rosebank, Johannesburg 2196,
South Africa

Penguin Books Ltd., Registered Offices: 80 Strand, London WC2R 0RL, England

HEART FATE

A Berkley Sensation Book / published by arrangement with the author

PRINTING HISTORY
Berkley trade paperback edition / September 2008
Berkley Sensation mass-market paperback edition / December 2010

ISBN: 978-0-425-23821-9

BERKLEY® SENSATION
Berkley Sensation Books are published by The Berkley Publishing Group,
a division of Penguin Group (USA) Inc.,
375 Hudson Street, New York, New York 10014.
BERKLEY® SENSATION and the "B" design are trademarks of Penguin Group (USA) Inc.

PRINTED IN THE UNITED STATES OF AMERICA

10 9 8 7 6 5 4 3 2 1

To all my readers.
Thank you.

Characters

Note: All previous heroes and heroines are HeartMates.

Lahsin Burdock D'Yew, GrandLady D'Yew: Heroine of *Heart Fate,* married to Ioho Yew at fourteen, now seventeen (Fam Strother).

Tinne Holly: Hero of *Heart Fate*, Second son of Passiflora and Holm Sr., will inherit the Green Knight Fencing and Fighting Salon (Fam Ilexa).

Ioho Yew: GrandLord T'Yew, husband of Lahsin.

Taxa Yew: Daughter of T'Yew, his Heir.

Holm Holly (Jr.): Hero of *Heart Duel*, HollyHeir, warrior (Fam Meserv).

Lark Holly: Heroine of *Heart Duel*, FirstLevel Healer (Fam Phyl).

Passiflora Holly: Mother of Holm Jr., Composer.

Holm Holly (Sr.): GreatLord, HeartMate of Passiflora, working to be Captain of the Councils.

Genista Holly: Wife of Tinne Holly.

Cratag Maytree: Chief guard of the Hawthorns.

Saille T'Willow: Hero of *Heart Dance*, FirstFamilies Great-Lord and premiere Matchmaker.

Ruis Elder: Hero of *Heart Thief*, a Null who suppresses Flair, Captain of the starship *Nuada's Sword* (Fam Samba).

Ailim Elder: Heroine of *Heart Thief*, SupremeJudge of Druida, telempath (Fam Primrose).

Rand T'Ash: Hero of *HeartMate*, jeweler, armorer (Fam Zanth).

Danith D'Ash: Heroine of *HeartMate*, animal Healer, verifier of Fams (Cat Princess).

Straif Blackthorn: Hero of *Heart Choice*, premiere tracker of Celta. Cousin to Tinne Holly (Fam Drina).

Mitchell Clover Blackthorn: Heroine of *Heart Choice*, HeartMate of Straif.

Holly/Blackthorn Family Tree

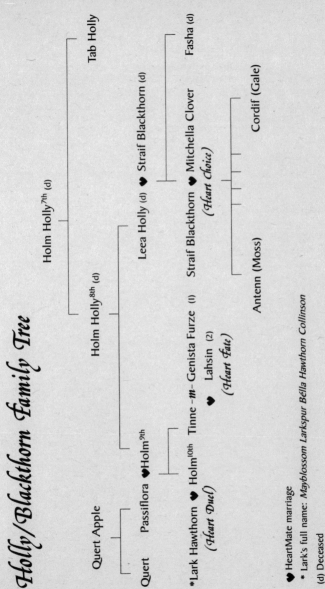

Tab Holly

Holm Holly⁷th (d)

Holm Holly⁸th (d)

Leea Holly (d) ♥ Straif Blackthorn (d)

Fasha (d)

Straif Blackthorn ♥ Mitchella Clover
(Heart Choice)

Quert Apple

Passiflora ♥Holm⁹th

Quert

Antenn (Moss)   Cordif (Gale)

*Lark Hawthorn ♥ Holm¹⁰th Tinne –m– Genista Furze (1)
(Heart Duel)   ♥ Lahsin (2)
                                          (Heart Fate)

♥ HeartMate marriage
* Lark's full name: *Mayblossom Larkspur Bélla Hawthorn Collinson*
(d) Deceased

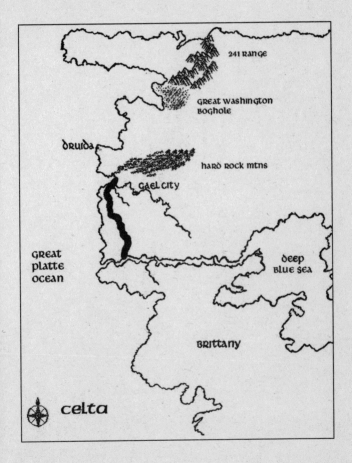

241 RANGE

GREAT WASHINGTON
BOGHOLE

ÒRUIÒA

HARÒ ROCK MTNS

GAEL CITY

GREAT
PLATTE
OCEAN

ÒEEP
BLUE SEA

BRITTANY

CELTA

One

DRUIDA CITY, CELTA
406 Years After Colonization,
Winter, Before Dawn

Lahsin slid through the shadows of T'Yew Residence,
escaping. Her husband. His Family. Her life. She was as un-
obtrusive and light-footed as a mouse. But she was used to
being mouselike in this place since the very beginning of her
marriage to the master, FirstFamily GrandLord T'Yew, at
fourteen.

He hadn't ordered her to his bed tonight. She didn't know
why, only blessed the fact. She couldn't expect him to miss
another night of rutting this week, and she was sure her
Passage—the fever dreams that would free her Flair, her psi
powers—would come soon. Passage would debilitate her.

She'd heard that Second Passage came like a fickle
storm—first a strong wind and a spattering of rain, then dying down, then hitting with awesome force. Now at seventeen, the first dizzying eddy marking the start of her Second
Passage had swept over her just yesterday. She thought. She
hoped.

Because with the first indication of Second Passage, a
Celtan was legally an adult. She could legally go, now, and
didn't have to endure an underage marriage.

She *would* go. Despite the vows they made, despite the
physical connection made during sex, she wasn't completely
bound to T'Yew. Because she'd been wed at fourteen she

could escape. She prayed that the laws had not changed since the old book she'd found was published.

Most Noble children didn't leave their homes when they were seventeen, but closer to twenty or twenty-two, if ever. Usually there was plenty of room for them in great houses.

But she wasn't a child, and this huge echoing castle was constricting her, stealing her air every minute. She could do *nothing* right in their eyes, T'Yew's and his daughter Taxa's. They often told her she was incompetent, helpless, *useless*. So she'd decided. To. Just. Leave.

Her fingers barely touching the cold marble of the wide bannister, she trailed them down, keeping track of her progress, counting the sweeping steps.

She should check on T'Yew. Her Flair was erratic and fluctuated in strength, but he and she were bound by sex and other links. She sent a spurt down the mental tie she kept as thready as possible.

He snored in his bed, that huge, horrible, Master's bed in the huge, horrible MasterSuite. Some woman was with him— the new servant from a distant branch of the Yews, here to work in the Family Residence.

Good luck to her, because she was good luck to Lahsin. If her luck held, she'd be away from Druida City and north to Alfriston before the Yews and her own Family, the Burdocks, realized she'd run away. They wouldn't look north. There was no reason for her to go in that direction. No Family holdings, and the land was cold and rough. Once they searched Druida, they'd continue southward, to Gael City.

Alfriston was a long two-days' walk away. She'd make it, she hoped. She *had* to be there, find shelter and work before her full Passage started and she'd be vulnerable for days. So far there had only been a half septhour of torment, enough to accelerate her plans to escape. She'd been useful to T'Yew as she was, after only one Passage, but if her Flair bloomed strongly, as both Families anticipated, they'd never let her go.

If they caught her, her life would become worse. They'd keep her in nauseating depressFlair bracelets all the time except when they wanted to use her. It wouldn't just be a punishment. Like the hours in the dark dungeon. Like her husband's sweaty body straining and forcing into her.

Don't think of that, of him! If she did, panic would fill her and the terror would paralyze her. If she considered what they might do to her, she might simply shudder to death in horror.

And what would they say publicly when they discovered she was missing? That she was mentally deficient? That she needed a loving home, loving arms to support her during her Passage? She had to clamp a hand over her mouth to stifle the bitter laugh, hold still a moment until it passed. And that cost her.

So close to escape, her blood was pounding in her veins in anticipation and fear of discovery, and she knew by the soft quarter chiming of the antique clock that she was behind schedule. She'd planned on being through the entry hall and to the side door by now. Instead she was at the bottom of the stairs, facing the front door. She blinked, trying to make out the shapes of the few elegant pieces of furniture, the doorway to the right that would lead to the correct corridor.

Do you leave, then, D'Yew?

She flinched, froze in her tracks. It was the voice of the house itself, the great Residence, speaking in her mind. Of course she should have expected it to feel her movements, but she thought she was beneath its notice.

I leave. My Second Passage comes. A thought occurred and giddiness swirled through her. A witness! The Residence was a witness! *You are my first witness*, she spoke to the house in her mind as well as in low, hissing words. "I, Lahsin Burdock, repudiate this marriage to Ioho Yew, GrandLord T'Yew. I, Lahsin Burdock, repudiate this marriage to Ioho Yew, GrandLord T'Yew. I, Lahsin Burdock, repudiate this marriage to Ioho Yew, GrandLord T'Yew." As she said the words, several tiny spiderweb threads linking her to him shriveled.

I hear you, the Residence replied coldly. *I no longer recognize you as D'Yew. You are no longer mistress of this house.*

She snorted at that. She'd *never* been mistress of this Residence. Would the Residence rouse T'Yew? Taxa? Anyone else in the household? Not that anyone would help, all the servants were Yews, and they all would try to stop her. They knew Ioho liked her under his thumb.

But I do not let you leave. You are a wretched thing, but T'Yew wants you.

A whimper caught in her throat, rippled from her. She wouldn't give up. She grabbed her bundle and stumbled toward the door. The Residence didn't send even a tiny glow to the lamps to light her way.

She tested the door. Locked. A chuckle came in her brain, the Residence itself, playing with her, having too much fun to call T'Yew or Taxa. She muttered the password couplet and the physical locks snicked open. All the doors and windows had excellent spellshields, as was common to FirstFamilies.

No choice. She'd always had a little Flair for spellshields, now she'd have to gather what she could, along with her courage, and test it. She *would* leave, even if she tempted death by trying to teleport, something she hadn't mastered. Again her mind scrabbled, spellshields or teleportation?

I do not let you leave, the Residence taunted. *I do not let you leave or steal from the Family.*

Flinching, words stuttered from her. "I don't have much. Only some clothes, old clothes, nothing jeweled. My, uh, the skycrystal necklace T'Yew gave me for my wedding. Before we married. He gave it to me, when I was Lahsin Burdock. It's mine." She wet her lips. "Some food. Bread and cheese and furrabeast travel sticks. I, uh, missed several meals lately. This food would have been given to me when I was, uh, D'Yew."

You have gilt.

"Only a few coins. You know the NobleCouncil sends me a little monthly allowance. My Family gave me a dowry." Just a token and less than the bribe T'Yew had given them. Did she forfeit that to T'Yew? She didn't know. She nearly moaned.

You have the Family marriage bands. Cowardly runaway thief.

She'd nearly forgotten them. Gathering all her wispy Flair, she said the Unbinding Words she'd secretly learned and memorized. The armbands fell off and clanged on the marble threshold. Lahsin started.

I'm no longer D'Yew, have nothing D'Yew would have. Let me go!

No.

The timer chimed again. Too late, too late, dawn was coming.

Worse had come to worst. She set her sack down, placed both hands on the door, and leaned against it.

What do you do, little no-Yew? Another snide chuckle.

She couldn't let the house distract her. Was that a creak of a floorboard overhead? She had to get out.

Screwing her eyes shut, she *willed* her Flair to come. It *had* to come. She sent all her desperation into calling it.

It hit her like a sizzling wildfire. She saw, heard, touched, *tasted* the spellshield, knew the weaving of its fabric. Yanked it apart.

OUT! She didn't know if she screamed aloud or not. She couldn't tell because the Residence itself was screaming.

POP! She stumbled back at the force. All the shields were down. Every single one. Gone from all windows, all doors.

In fact, all the windows and doors themselves were gone. The double front door fell outside before her in slow motion.

Lahsin felt the Residence shudder, implement emergency procedures to protect the Family and itself and raise a weathershield, drawing on all its stored energy.

It was too busy to hinder her now.

Appalled at what she'd done, unsteady on her feet, she snatched up her bag and stumbled into the night, which was graying into day, circled around the front door, the major door to the estate. She'd leave as she'd come. That felt good. Felt right.

Outside, she saw a glittering scarf of stars with one of the waxing moons caught in its shining swath, Cymru moon. Oh, she was nearly gone!

She ran.

Ran down the gravel path of the glider drive. Ran around the curving road, still in sight of the house through the bare winter trees. Ran and ran and ran to the front greeniron gate, which she struggled to shove open only enough for her and her bundle to squeeze through. No spellshield here, either.

The whole estate? She'd blown the spellshields for *the whole estate*? Blinking and shaking her head, she decided she didn't know how she did it, but it was done. Now she was escaping, leaving those behind defenseless.

No, Ioho and Taxa and the Residence and her other tormentors would *never* really be defenseless. Never vulnerable. Never beaten.

Her nervous laugh began ugly, then picked up a note of exhilaration.

She was out! Out of the estate by herself for the first time in three months!

And she was no longer D'Yew.

Almost.

She had to repeat her repudiation of the marriage to three neutral parties, three entities with no interest in her—not her Family or intimate friends or lover or HeartMate—before she was free. She felt the narrow mental bonds she had to T'Yew loosen.

Clouds swept away from the second moon, Eire. She saw the road and knew where to go.

But she was too close to the estate. She breathed deeply and ran some more, ever faster, ever freer! Soon she *would* be free of all hideous Family obligations. She'd never go back. Never, ever. Not to her Family—she only trusted her older brother—and not to the Yews.

She thought she'd die before she'd be forced back. T'Yew would punish her if she fell under his hand again. There'd be blows and the horrible thrusting of his body into hers.

The Burdocks and the Yews, both warped Families. She would never be part of that again.

She ran down the wide road past FirstFamily estates. All FirstFamilies were warped. Her blood sang with excitement, with freedom.

Until she ran into a large, solid man who grabbed her as she rocked on her heels.

She hadn't even made it out of Noble Country.

*T*inne was up early. As usual, he hadn't slept well. He sat at his desk, working on the Green Knight Fencing and Fighting Salon's books, when tapping came at the door. Thankfully, his time with papyrus was short now that he was no longer HollyHeir. He was back into the second son slot—Heir to his G'Uncle and the Salon.

"Come!" he called.

His wife walked through the door, and at the pallor of her face, the refined slenderness of her once voluptuous curves, a pang arrowed through him. Things had not been right between them since they'd lost their unborn child. He'd tried to reach her . . . but she turned more to her own Family, blaming his for the mishap. As was right.

But she wouldn't speak of their loss. Nothing he did comforted her. If she wanted to attend a party, he took her out but they hadn't made love for a long time. They hadn't even had soulless bouts of sex for months. They couldn't connect emotionally anymore. He'd changed, too, become more somber, less impulsive than he'd been. Not the man she'd married.

More, he'd forgiven his parents for breaking their Vows of Honor that had cursed the Family and led to her miscarriage. She hadn't been able to do so. Bitterness lined her fair face. She hadn't wanted to live with her own Family, but hadn't wanted to live on the small country estate that he owned. She seemed to both love and hate T'Holly Residence. She found no peace.

He stood, forcing a smile, and waved to the comfortable chair in front of his desk. It wasn't often she came to see him when he was in his den. They didn't spend much time together.

She wore a gauzy sea green gown that shimmered with silver sparkles. Real silver, he knew from the bill. The dress emphasized the beauty of her blond hair, deepened the color of her eyes. There were smudges under those pretty eyes. He frowned and started around the desk. She raised a hand. "Please, sit."

Humming wariness infused his muscles, making them tense, heavy. He dropped back into his chair.

Unusually still, she folded her hands in her lap, another rare gesture. Tinne's gut twisted.

"I want a divorce."

The emotional blow knocked him breathless. He fell back into the soft leather squabs of his chair. He opened his mouth but no words came. He shut it, his mind reeling for some response. Finally he croaked, "There is no divorce for First-Families."

"There never has been." Genista's mouth trembled, and she swallowed. "But I asked SupremeJudge Ailim Elder to have legal people craft a law." She gestured, and it was beautiful and graceful as always, but with none of the verve she'd had before . . . before. "I don't want to retire to separate Households and live that way, still bound together." Her eyes were damp but steady. "I don't want to be bound to the Hollys."

No physical blow had ever been harder. He couldn't breathe.

"I've followed all the steps for divorce that the other classes have. All the horrible tests of body and mind and spirit that proves a marriage is over.

"Also the SupremeJudge thinks that additional measures are necessary to ensure that a FirstFamilies marriage is not dissolved too lightly. She suggests having the SupremeJudge and three FirstFamilies Heads of Households agree that the marriage is broken. I arranged that as well."

He could barely process this. Silence reigned as he tried to keep his mind from the shattering pain. Finally he forced from a dry throat, "Who agreed to this terrible action?"

"SupremeJudge Ailim Elder; D'Sea—the mind Healer; T'Heather—the FirstLevel Healer; T'Willow—the matchmaker."

Genista drew out a sheaf of papyrus from the sleeve of her gown and placed them carefully on the table. "All my test results. The formal documents for divorce. Everything is in order. All my personal items have been 'ported to my Family's Residence, and I'll teleport myself as soon as I leave you." She glanced at him, away, then back again, flashing him a smile that held no humor. "I was cowardly, but not too cowardly. I left a message in your parents' and brother's and G'Uncle Tab's cache about the divorce and the procedure—my tests. You will have to be tested, too. Your Family will be notified when they wake."

She was too far ahead of him. He couldn't keep up. He stared at the white pages. They should be red with blood.

The corners of her mouth turned up. He sensed the smile was as forced as his own had been. "Come now, Tinne. You know we married for other reasons than love."

"I love you." The words he hadn't said for a long time rushed out of him now.

She shook her head. "I don't think so." She bit her lip, swallowed hard. "We were excellent lovers in bed, connected sexually more than anything else. I came to love you, and I think you loved me. Once. But we can't go back to who we were . . . before."

Despite her words echoing his thoughts, he protested. "We can try again. Counseling."

"That didn't work before. It won't work now. We've grown apart."

Anger flamed. He narrowed his eyes.

Now she raised both hands, palms out. "Please don't fight this, Tinne."

Another blow. Fighting for what he wanted was second nature for a Holly.

"The scandal," he croaked.

She shrugged. "If the Hollys cared about scandal, they shouldn't have stirred one up and kept it boiling for the last few years by refusing to mend their broken Vows of Honor."

He stared at his hands—competent with sword, knife, blazer, yet helpless to keep his wife. "I can't even recall how long it has been since a Noble Lord or Lady has divorced."

"Eighty years." Her words were stilted. "That's what Judge Elder said." Genista's slender fingers tipped with pink tinted nails came into his narrowed vision as she waved at the papyrus. "The conclusion is that a divorce would be best for me."

Failure ate his gut.

"Don't," she whispered, and he felt the small link between them cycle with grief, as always. But this was different. He wrenched his gaze up to hers.

Tears filled her eyes and trickled down her face. "It's *not* your fault. You *didn't* fail, or at least no more than I. If there is failure, guilt, it's a shared thing. But we ... we ..." She withdrew a softleaf from her sleeve, wiped her tears, and blew her nose. Then she straightened and lifted her chin.

"I'm not the same woman you married. I can't go back to being that person, and I can't continue to be with you and not be reminded of my loss."

She met his gaze. "You must also be mentally and emotionally evaluated before we can continue with the divorce—the seven tests. I've set up appointments for you later this morning, since I thought you'd want this done as quickly and cleanly as possible." Her smile was sad. "If your tests show that you love me deeply, we will try grief Healing again. But I don't think that will happen."

He hated this. Hated that she might be right. Hated that she knew him so well and could slice him so deeply.

Genista rose from the chair and walked to the door. She stopped with her hand on the latch and glanced over her shoulder, appearing much less anxious than when she'd entered. "Tinne," she said in nearly a whisper, "I know you have a HeartMate."

"She's wed," he said automatically.

"And she's seventeen, isn't she? Has she had her Second Passage?"

He shrugged. "I don't know." He'd never spoken to Genista about his HeartMate and didn't want to now.

Her smile was as sad as her eyes. "You have strong Flair, so she must as well. You'll link with her during her Passage. I'd rather not be around when that happens."

"My fault again," he croaked.

"No, once-my-dear." One of her shoulders rose, then fell. "It's destiny. We had our time together, and it was good, it was wonderful." She turned away. "But when times turned bad, they were tragic. I haven't been able to rise above that tragedy, and I can't, if I remain wed to you."

Blow after blow after blow. In all his life of daily sparring, of deathduels, he'd never felt so pummeled.

"I'd like a new start. In a new place. Gael City, probably. Find your love and claim her."

Impossible.

His wife opened the door and left without a backward glance, closing the door with a final, quiet push.

Tinne stood and marched stiffly to the bathroom, where he puked his guts up.

Two

♥

*T*he man was large, tall, and broad. Rough-looking with scars on his face. That alone told Lahsin he wasn't Druida City born. She bounced off him, and her weak knees might have buckled if he hadn't grasped her upper arms. She wouldn't be able to get away from him.

His brows came down. "Now who are you?"

She didn't really know, but said, "Lahsin . . . Burdock." She didn't think she wanted her birth name, but she wanted Yew even less.

He looked up and down wide dawn-empty Bountry Boulevard. She sensed he wasn't exactly sure where the Burdock Estate was and whether she was near it.

One side of his mouth quirked up. "Returning from a night out?" His fingers gentled on her arms, then dropped.

"Yes, yes," she babbled, hitching the knot of her bag up her shoulder. "Clothes, you know. My timer is broken." She waved her arm that had her perfectly good timer under the warm cloak. At that moment the sun rose bright enough to show the colors he wore. "You're a Hawthorn," she blurted.

He inclined his torso. "Cratag Maytree, a guard in T'Hawthorn's household." He shook his head slowly. "But I don't think you should be out here on your own, even as early and deserted as it is. P'raps I should see you back to your Residence."

She pinned a bright smile on her face. "I'm perfectly fine." She waved again, and the sleeve of her cloak slipped down. Black bruises from Yew's fingers showed on her wrist.

Cratag looked down at his own fingers and flexed his hands, and Lahsin stared at his hands, too. Cratag's fingers could fit on the bruises. He was a bigger man than Yew, but her ex-husband had large, blunt fingers that didn't go with the rest of his carefully cultivated aristocratic appearance.

The heat of humiliation burned her cheeks.

Cratag put a meaty hand on her shoulder, again gently, and his squeeze was small and comforting, like he knew his strength and used it carefully.

"You want to press a case for assault?" he asked softly. "Report this to the Druida guardsmen? I know an honorable one."

She shook her head frantically. She had to be going. Now. Sooner than now. *Transnow.*

Voice even quieter, he said, "You don't have to be afraid of me. And you don't have to be afraid of whoever did this to you. As you noticed, I'm a Hawthorn guard, and I'm close to my Head of Household, GreatLord T'Hawthorn himself. He who was Captain of all the Celtan Councils last year and the year before. I can take you to him, you can tell your story. Commoner or Noble, he'll see that right is done and you're protected."

She felt her eyes get wider and wider, and her heart thumped so hard and fast that she thought it might break through her chest. Talk to another FirstFamily Lord? No, no, no! They all stuck together. No one would listen to her. No one would believe her. She wanted nothing to do with FirstFamilies, or even Nobles, ever, ever again.

Wanted nothing to do with men for that matter. If this Hawthorn guard had been female . . . but that was just a silly wish. A distracting thought, when she'd better get her fear under control, now. She swallowed, dipped a curtsy. "No-thank-you-very-much."

His eyes narrowed, his tone roughened. "I'm going to give you some advice, GentleLady. If the man you were with put those marks on you, he's not a good man. No matter how good a lover he is, he's not a good man, and he won't treat you right.

Probably not any woman right. So you don't go back to him. You leave him. You hear what I say?"

She nodded violently.

They stared at each other. He lifted his hand from her shoulder, raised it.

And she flinched again.

Everything about him got even slower as he scratched the scar on his cheek. He took a couple of paces back, and the breath she'd been inadvertently holding shuddered out.

There was more scrutiny on his part. Enough so she realized that he had very little Flair and was depending on sight and experience and body cues, or whatever.

"GentleLady," he said so abruptly and in such a low, dangerous rumble that she jumped, dropped her bag, and scooped it up without her gaze leaving him. He could still stop her. Such a big man could do anything with her he wanted. The new day and all the threat it would bring wound her fear and tension tighter.

He put his hands in his trous pockets. She noticed he wore working trous, not the fancy, blousey Noble trous that used a lot of material to proclaim the worth of the wearer. And he stepped back several more paces. Far enough that if he lunged at her, she should be able to get away.

"GentleLady," he repeated.

The sun was definitely over the horizon now, and she glanced around. T'Yew Residence wouldn't be stupefied for long, would soon give the alarm. She'd already lost too much time. She knew none of the town gates well enough to teleport to them, if she could 'port. She'd be caught.

"Listen to me!" he demanded.

It was enough to have her jump again, but this time her fingers clenched over the cloth knot of the bag.

"You're sure you won't put yourself under my protection? I'm an honorable man, I promise to help you."

She didn't know she had enough breath to laugh, but she did. Her eyes stung, and she sniffed loudly. All very rude.

He nodded. "Very well. Looks like you're in trouble, maybe I can help another way. Have you heard of FirstGrove? It's a sanctuary for those who need one."

"A myth," she said, her voice higher and shakier than she wanted.

"A sanctuary," he repeated. "Find a door, and it will open and protect you."

Again she was snorting laughter, shaking her head.

"You must have heard that Ruis Elder hid there. It exists. I was there myself, my first few days in Druida. Afore I knew that T'Hawthorn would acknowledge me as Family and take me on as a household guard. A deserted estate, like many old ones, this one is lost within the city." He tilted his head, jutting his chin. "It lies northeast." His nostrils flared as he sniffed. "It smells green. The greenest place in Druida. Look for the sign of BalmHeal, the Family who took care of FirstGrove." Then he turned his back.

Lahsin just stared at him for a long, long moment, until she saw his spine stiffen, like he was going to turn or move again.

A shrieking alarm split the air. T'Yew Residence! She knew that sound.

The Hawthorn guard spun.

Lahsin bolted.

Northeast.

And prayed to the Lady for signs of BalmHeal.

*T*inne let the hot waterfall pulse over him. He hadn't been able to go to his bedroom where he and Genista had made love so often.

That hadn't been the only place, of course. They'd been sexually crazy after their marriage. There wasn't a room in his suite or hers where they hadn't mated. Even here he kept his eyes closed. How was he going to live in these rooms?

He was dressing in his sitting room when he heard echoes of his Mamá's musical voice outside his door, uncommonly shrill. Obviously she and everyone else now knew of his failure.

"Tinne? The Residence told me you were up. We think we should have a Family meeting."

"The white room in five minutes. Talk to you then," he said.

A few minutes later he entered the room, glad he'd chosen a different place than the one most often used—the green room, where he'd brought Genista to announce their marriage.

This confrontation was going to be bad, one of the worst

things he'd ever faced. After many years his father, T'Holly, had finally achieved his dream of being Captain of the First-Family Council and thus All Councils. The whole Family—except Genista—had been making the social rounds last year, discreetly campaigning for T'Holly.

If Tinne and Genista's marriage was found to be shattered and Tinne actually went ahead with her wishes for a divorce—his gorge rose again, and he forced it down—it would be the first divorce in the FirstFamilies in all the years on untamed Celta.

The scandal would be huge, would smear the Family reputation and honor for generations. A tarnished Family had to fight harder to survive.

The scandal would definitely put an end to T'Holly's dream of being Captain for more than the past year.

Tinne kept telling himself that he'd live through this but still doubted it.

He stopped inside the door, but didn't sit. Everyone was there, his parents, his G'Uncle Tab, his brother Holm, and his sister-in-law, Lark. They all sat stiffly, faces various shades of impassivity, eyes various shadows of shock.

"Genista said she'd left messages for you explaining that she has requested a divorce." He waved, and the documents that had been on his desk were 'ported to a table. He hadn't touched them, didn't ever want to touch them. Let the Family look at them if they wanted. "Here are the documents, the results of her seven tests and the legal forms from the SupremeJudge."

The faces of his relatives blurred. His eyes couldn't focus. He didn't care. "I have acceded to her wishes to undergo the testing regarding whether to dissolve the marriage. Naturally I hope my tests will reveal that we can reconcile." Was that his own voice, so cool and composed while his belly felt like it contained writhing snakes?

"But if we can't reconcile, there will be a divorce."

Shock swept through his Family like a tidal wave. Tinne felt each blow as his relatives understood what he'd said. His father aged in seconds.

All sweetness vanished from his Mamá's link, which filled with a terrible hurt. She was hurting because he did.

He couldn't bear that pain, so he angled his body away from her. He glanced at his G'Uncle Tab, a second father, his teacher, the man he would succeed. Tab's expression had so-lidified to impassive stone, his eyes flattened. Tinne had no trouble believing this man had faced the dangers of the sea.

Swallowing hard, Tinne slid his gaze in the other direction toward his brother Holm and Holm's HeartMate, FirstLevel Healer Lark. They sat thigh to thigh on a twoseat, Holm's arm around her shoulders. Their link was so strong that he could almost see it. Stronger even than his parents'. His brother held himself in a deceptively casual manner, but his muscles had tensed. His heart, too, welled with grief. Grief that Tinne hurt, that this would hurt the Family for a long time to come.

Tears trickled down Lark's face, and she linked hands with Holm.

The Residence spoke quietly. "D'Sea, the mind Healer, is here for Tinne's testing."

Saved! He no longer had to speak to his Family, didn't have to suffer with them. Let them discuss this, figure out Family policy through the terrible scandal. He suspected he had only enough courage to survive the next few days of testing.

He turned on his heel, opened the door, and went through, closing it on his stricken Family. He met D'Sea at the tele-portation pad. She was a small, middle-aged woman with a heart-shaped face and blue green eyes. She was formally dressed in a long tunic of velvet panels, light blue alternating with dark. Her full trous, bloused and cuffed at the ankles, showed midnight blue. Her hands were tucked in her oppo-site sleeves, which were long and square, holding pockets.

"Merry—" She stopped the standard greeting, cleared her throat. "Greetyou, GreatSir Holly."

Tinne inclined his head. His whole body was stiff. "Greet-you."

D'Sea didn't meet his eyes. "You know that your . . . wife . . . consulted Healers to undergo the tests determining that your marriage was damaged beyond repair and you should divorce."

"Yes."

"I received notification that you also agreed to take the seven tests."

"Yes."

She dipped her head. "Very well. I had to have in-person

confirmation from you." She glanced at him, and Tinne sensed her Flair. "You are under no mind control."

"No."

A sigh issued from D'Sea. "Very well, the Healer, Grand-Lord T'Heather, and I will be overseeing your testing." She hesitated. "Unless you want your sister-in-law, Lark—"

"No!"

"Very well."

Every time she said that, Tinne knew she meant differently. She wanted this no more than he. She didn't like the breaking of a marriage. Especially a FirstFamilies marriage. She stepped onto the teleportation pad, and for the first time her aqua eyes met his. "We will teleport to T'Heather's personal Healing room in his Residence for the testing."

Tinne didn't want to say an empty "very well," so he nodded. Nor did he want to go to testing, he wanted to pound out his feelings on his drum.

She held out her hand, and he took it. Her fingers were cool and dry. She sent him the image of a room he'd never seen before, a circular room with padded pale pink walls, and windows that let in bright sunlight. "On three. One. Two. Three."

And they were there.

The moment he arrived, a comforting warmth enveloped him, seeming even to reach inside him and touch his heart to ease the hurt. Great Flair lived in this room, and Tinne was glad of it.

"Welcome, Tinne," said T'Heather. The man looked more like a farmer, with large-knuckled hands, than the best Healer on Celta. He gestured with one of those big hands to a chair. Though the chair looked like the most luxuriously comfortable chair available, one that would conform to Tinne's body, he tensed.

"The testing's beginning now?"

T'Heather jerked a nod. "Best finish this miserable task."

A corner of Tinne's mouth quirked up. "Good to know my fate's in the hands of a sensitive Healer."

T'Heather speared Tinne with a brown gaze. "Your lady—" Tinne flinched.

Now T'Heather cleared his throat. "Genista Furze—"

Her birth name hurt worse. "Just get on with it." Tinne's

nostrils quivered. "Most of all, I want it done." He stalked to the chair and sat. Long and softly padded, the back rose above his head, the leg rest was longer than his feet. The chair arms were padded, too. The chair tilted back, and Tinne's stomach clutched. It was harder to fight when off his feet, but not impossible.

T'Heather clasped his hands behind his back, stared at Tinne with brown eyes. "Divorce is not acceptable in our culture, and we don't make it easy."

Nothing about that morning had been easy, and Tinne hated being here.

"A person in a divorce must endure seven tests regarding their mental, emotional, and spiritual state, particularly regarding their spouse. Each test is designed to probe whether your marriage is sound or . . . not."

Tinne didn't want to listen. Didn't like knowing that Genista had already been through the tests and their marriage was already judged unsound.

T'Heather scowled. "D'Sea, as mind Healer, and I, as First-Level Healer of Celta, will be testing each aspect of your being. These tests are based on the seven energy pulses that we Healers study. The matchmaker, GreatLord Saille T'Willow, will also test the relationship itself. We will use various tools."

Why couldn't it be a fighting pattern? Twenty patterns? Tinne knew how to master, win those. He knew how to take physical blows, rise above the pain of aching muscles, stinging slaps, bruises, and broken bones—

"Tinne!" T'Heather roared, his gaze was hard.

He bared his teeth. "Just get on with it."

D'Sea stepped forward, her eyes fathomless. "We can stop this process at any time. Genista requested it and wants the divorce, but we all know that the most common solution to a dysfunctional Noble marriage is simple separation."

"For life," Tinne said.

She nodded, concern shadowing her eyes. "For life."

"But if I fail these tests, my marriage is truly dead. There's no hope of making it work."

"There is really no 'failing,' the tests simply show us what is," she said.

"But that's what the tests determine, that my—our—marriage is dead."

D'Sea opened her mouth and closed it, sharing a glance with T'Heather. "That is what the tests determine."

"You're too tense," T'Heather said.

Tinne didn't answer, couldn't seem to relax his muscles. Not good.

D'Sea sighed and came toward them, holding a goblet. "A calmer, to distance your emotions until we test your heart-soul."

"Why don't we do the physical examination first?" T'Heather said. "The Hollys are a physical Family. It will release some of his frustration. Save the first day of emotional testing until tomorrow."

Frowning, D'Sea said, "I don't know . . ."

Tinne drank. It wasn't nasty. Weariness eased his muscles a little. He closed his eyes, let the black-and-white flashes behind his eyelids flare and fade. "Nice to know you Healers have a good procedure."

T'Heather frowned. "I've never done divorce testing. Isn't supposed to happen in FirstFamilies. Hardly legal."

"Don't blame me, I'm here because of Genista. I'd like another round of trying to mend my marriage." But as Tinne said that, he wondered if it were true. He'd tried so hard already, he might have given all he could to Genista, especially since she wouldn't, or couldn't, give back. He felt scoured out.

The chair tilted and rose until he was upright. He opened his lashes to see T'Heather squinting at him and D'Sea walking toward him, with something that glowed brightly with violet light. Tinne's stomach jumped. "What's that?"

"An object that will show your spiritual health, especially with regard to your relationship with your wife."

Tinne hunkered down. The shock of Genista's request that had propelled him forward into action was wearing off, and he was faced with the reality of what he was doing. Having every fliggering part of him scrutinized and measured. With no secrets. Completely vulnerable.

He didn't like it but what were his options? With typical Holly impulsiveness he'd already committed himself. His pride wouldn't let him retreat.

D'Sea put the pouch on his head, and he got a slight shock, then it was nearly too hot to bear. The odor of lotus drifted around him.

"I want you to close your eyes and relax. Think peaceful thoughts, visualize a high mountaintop."

The room's light dimmed around him. He set himself the task of breathing evenly, centered himself, and definitely did *not* think of a high mountaintop. The one time he'd been in a mountain range, he and his brother had been in mortal peril. He thought of a hilltop instead, warm and sunlit in the summer, round and covered with long, fragrant grass.

"His spirit is fractured," D'Sea said.

"Pretty nasty black jagged streak," T'Heather said.

"Thank you," Tinne replied courteously.

"Genista had such a streak, too, not surprising, since they'd lived in a cursed household for several years," D'Sea said.

A lightning bolt struck Tinne's hill. He said, "The curse was lifted last year."

"Not soon enough to prevent irreparable hurt—to Genista, to you, to your marriage," T'Heather said bluntly. He turned to D'Sea. "You're the mind Healer, should we probe the streak of negative energy?"

"If it were a physical wound, wouldn't you?" she asked.

"Yes." T'Heather grimaced.

Three

❖

At first the pain was small—a tugging and pulling at him inside, like someone had gotten his guts in their hands. He endured. Then he thought cold hands poked at his very heart, and he could barely breathe through the hurt. When they finally snagged his nerves and zinged his whole system with lightning, he arched and fell out of the chair and onto the floor. He welcomed the bruise on his cheek because that was hurt he understood.

He panted to catch his breath. He *hated* falling. Gritting his teeth, he rocked to his hands and knees and flung himself back into the chair. T'Heather leaned over him. Gentle fingers skimmed Tinne's cheek, and it mended.

"Sorry," T'Heather said. His expression went from concern to pity.

Tinne couldn't face that and looked aside. His gut tightened as he flashed back to the time when he was in the starship *Nuada's Sword* and had a kidney removed.

This had been worse.

And it was only the first test of seven.

D'Sea wasn't there.

"That's one of the worst," T'Heather said. His shaggy gray brows lowered. "Can you go on?"

"Of course." Tinne forced words from a dry throat.

The brows went up enough to wrinkle T'Heather's forehead. "Get up and walk for me."

Feeling like an old man, stretching muscle by muscle, Tinne stood. He wanted to hobble hunched around the room, but couldn't show such weakness. He rolled his shoulders, shook out his legs and arms, then walked around the room. This close, he could see that the creamy pink walls had a faint pattern of pale purple heather sprigs. He might have liked it, once.

"Well enough," T'Heather said gruffly. "We've scheduled three today and three tomorrow, with the last and the physical on the third day."

Swallowing, Tinne said, "Couldn't we get it down to two days?"

T'Heather shook his head. "I wouldn't recommend four tests today." His smile was an upward twitch of his lips. "One tests your 'heart energy,' and that's bound to be rough." He hesitated. "The lady took five full days for the tests, moving as quickly as possible. It's a rugged examination schedule. Divorce testing is supposed to be grueling." He eyed Tinne consideringly. "But if you want it in two . . . I've never known a tougher group than the Holly men." T'Heather shrugged. "What say we do three tests today and the physical? Then we'll attempt to finish four tests tomorrow."

He glanced at the timer. "This first examination lasted a septhour and a half, but D'Sea and I believe that the spiritual energy is the one most affected by the curse."

D'Sea walked in, looking pale, strained, and serene. "I don't know why you and Genista never consulted me," D'Sea said. "I could have helped."

"Genista doesn't care to talk about our loss." He didn't either. "We did go through some marriage counseling." Short and spectacularly unsuccessful.

"She didn't say much to us during the examinations, either," T'Heather said.

"I want to finish this testing in two days," Tinne repeated.

D'Sea raised her eyebrows and glanced at T'Heather.

He nodded soberly. "Three energy examinations and the physical today. The last four tests tomorrow."

D'Sea searched Tinne's face, her gaze probing. "Very well."

Tinne said, "What's next?"

"Examination of your Flair," T'Heather said.

Scrutinizing another very important aspect of his life. "Right."

D'Sea went to a worktable and messed with herbs and pouches. Tinne settled into his fighting stance and practiced a basic pattern. His body moved better, getting back to normal.

"Please resume your seat," T'Heather said.

Tinne checked the state of his clothes. Dry. Wrinkled. Didn't smell too bad. He wished he wore fighting garb. He went back to the chair, sat, breathed, and pretended to relax.

"Regarding the last test results, since it doesn't seem as if you want to have individual consultations with me as a mind Healer . . ." She waited, but Tinne said nothing, so she went on. "The best way to Heal your spiritual energy flow is to participate in meaningful Family rituals, meditate every day, and schedule time each week in the Holly HouseHeart. I will send the last recommendation to your father, so he is aware of your needs."

Tinne's breath left him noisily. "If you insist."

"I do."

He liked the HouseHeart, wouldn't mind spending time there, but being in the rest of the Residence would be difficult, especially if his entire Family—including the entire staff— would be watching him after this. Which, of course, they would.

A divorce.

A major scandal.

A major hurt.

"Some communion with nature would be good," D'Sea said.

"It is winter," T'Heather said drily.

"A mild one so far," D'Sea said.

"Snowstorm's coming today," T'Heather said, nose twitching.

"Oh. The Hollys have a plant room and pool, that should suffice." D'Sea filled an indigo blue pouch with herbs.

T'Heather gestured, and the lights dimmed. Tinne's chair tilted back.

"The pack will go on your brow. Get comfortable. Close your eyes. Visualize a starry sky," T'Heather said.

Like mountaintops, the words *starry sky* brought terrible

memories of shooting unwillingly through space. Tinne let himself say a mental curse word, figured all of these tests would slice him to the very marrow. Then he steadied his breathing and went back to his hill. This time he was lying on his back, looking at the intersecting galaxies, the bright stars, the twinmoons. His hand was in Gen—No. He was alone. *Lonely.*

Jasmine and mint comforted him, as a velvet pouch was set on his forehead. It helped him fight the loneliness and prepare for the worst. Which would come.

*L*ahsin hurried through the streets of Druida as inconspicuously as possible. There were too many people who could notice her.

As soon as she'd left the big estates of Noble Country and wended her way into the city, the streets became more crowded. She kept zigzagging into shadows whenever she saw someone. Middle- and low-class folk were going to work. How she wished she was one of them! But she trusted no one.

Her plans were wrecked. Every gate of the walled city would have been notified she was missing. She couldn't leave Druida anytime soon. Tears leaked from her eyes, made her cheeks cold.

Soon she was hopelessly lost. All she knew was that she was going north. Her only comfort was that if she didn't know where she was, no one might be able to find her.

Not much reasoning, but her ties with her Family were small—T'Yew had seen to that. Her connection to him was broken, and no one else of the Yew Household had wanted to know her well enough to have any Family links to her.

She couldn't be found that way.

She prayed that what she'd heard a couple of days ago was true and the FirstFamily GrandLord who was the best tracker was out of town on a mission.

She snuffled, dug in her coat pocket for the small mound of softleaves, drew one out, and wiped her eyes and blew her nose.

A while later she stopped in the deep alcove of a door of a deserted building. Feeling foolish, she sniffed. Old brick, dust. She turned west and inhaled again—the sea. She moved back to check the north—cold, wind, a storm coming. She shivered and took a step outside the door and looked northeast. One last large breath . . . at the edges of the mixture of humanity, stridebeasts, food, gliders . . . the scent of growing things. Green. She drew in a shallow breath, and as she did, a low thump came into her mind associated with the green smell. She strained her ears and her mind, but it didn't repeat.

So she pulled her cloak around her and went back out onto the streets, keeping her pace to the brisk walk of those around her. Going northeast to the smell of green. The streets turned smaller and older, but busier because many people lived over their shops. It was a part of the city she'd never been in and didn't recognize. Both interesting and scary.

Then she caught it again—the low thump. She waited again. Nothing.

Someone called to her, trying to sell her something, she thought, and she turned—again northward—into the first alley she came to, then she took turns at random. A third time the thump came to her mind, and she finally realized what it was, the heartbeat—living, growing beat—of a garden.

Finally she came to the end of a small corridor between buildings, into a little hollow tangled with plant stalks. The brown stems were thick enough to be impassable on each side, and there was a six-meter wall in front of her. Beyond it branches of even taller trees thrust into the sky.

She shivered, thinking it was a good thing this winter was milder than last year, or she'd have been forced to find shelter by now. Even so, her Flair weathershield was spotty, sometimes warming her hands but leaving her face open to the chill, sometimes making her feet clumsy, cold blocks. But her energy and Flair were waning. Too much lack of sleep. Too much fear. Too much unknown.

"Who's there?" asked someone, sounding nervous.

Lahsin sidled with silent feet along the wall, saw a low opening in the thick brush, and dropped to her hands and knees to shove her sack before her and move inside the low animal path.

Heavy feet crunched dried, dead leaves, then came low mutters, then receding footfalls and silence.

She huddled against the wall. It was warm. It had appeared to be of the excessive height and armored brick that ringed an estate, but could it possibly be the side of a building? Carefully, she sent her mind probing for others.

She found an abundance of plant rhythms, but no other minds. A small sigh trickled from her. She was getting stiff. It wouldn't do to linger in this little, scruffy nest. And she was hungry. She had to find a safe and private place to eat and plan how she was going to escape from the city, from her husband—her former husband.

He would be very, very angry.

Just the thought of him and the hunt for her had her moving again, continuing to crawl through the underbrush next to the warm wall along the animal path. It was larger than cat-sized, and there weren't that many feral cats, and even fewer dogs, as dogs were prized as pets.

As soon as she realized she heard little rustlings in the back of her mind, she stopped, listening. Verdant plant life. Not the barely pulsing beat of the bushes she was pushing through, but plants on the other side of the wall. Huge old trees, some Earth trees, some Celtan, some hybrid. Their life signatures nearly mesmerized her. FirstGrove?

She strove to recall what she'd learned in grovestudy as a child. The place had been the first grove planted and tended by the colonists. The site had contained the first HealingHall, natural Healing springs that had been augmented by a hundred years of Healers. That HealingHall had become so exclusive to the highest Healers and Nobles that those visiting it had dwindled, then the secret had been lost.

Lahsin began moving on hands and knees again. Whether this place was the lost garden or not, she didn't know, but the wall was warm, and the wind outside the bushes had risen, cold and cutting. She'd had enough of cold and cutting.

After a while of crawling, the bushes arched high enough for her to stand and hurry down the path, spending more Flair to keep her movements quiet. Soon the weak sun shot blue white rays through the gray clouds that added a smidgeon of warmth. She was more aware that she could use her Flair to keep quiet or keep her warm, but not both. She'd expended too much energy and Flair this morning, shattering the T'Yew Residence's spellshields and windows and running away.

The wall curved gently, and she followed and finally saw an indentation ahead. A door?

She heard the stomping of feet and crunching of branches ahead of her.

She scuttled, then stopped at the sound of voices and put her hand over her mouth to quiet her ragged breathing. "That pidyn-suckin' fliggerin' sonofa-blerk Winterberry. Swaggerin' inta our gatehouse an' tellin' us to walk—walk!—to Northgate lookin' for some stup of a lil' girl who got herself lost. I was just ready to sink my teeth into a cinnamon glazed doughround."

"Sloegin, he said 'patrol' between here and Northgate."

Lahsin was caught in an awkward crouch. The door in the wall was just two meters from her. She could see it now, a small, square door. If only she were there! Branches had formed a thicket around the door, but were much thinner beyond it. She could see the colors of the Eastgate guardsmen's uniforms. If she could see them, they could see her . . .

"Patrol," Sloegin snorted. "That's walkin' our asses off this whole quarter a' the city! Ya think Winterberry went ta Southgate an' Northgate? No. He only came ta us and we're the only ones doin' this search."

"I heard that on ancient Earthan, the guards patrolled in gliders," the second man said.

The first smacked the second on the head. "Gliders? My ass. Gliders are for more important things than findin' a little girl-wife." He smacked his lips. "The old man liked 'em young 'n' tender."

"Those FirstFamilies are weird. Always said so."

They were coming closer. Lahsin used precious Flair to fashion a no-see-me spellshield around herself and wondered if it worked. She'd only heard of the new no-see-me spells and had practiced crafting this one by herself. It demanded considerable Flair, so she slowly straightened and leaned against the wall.

"Did you hear somethin'?" the second guard asked.

"Dunno."

There was silence except for their breathing.

"Gettin' cold, snow's comin' t'day or t'morra." There was more boot stomping. "My feet are cold. Nothin' but big plants here. Pro'bly got big thorns."

Another snort from the first one. "You afraid'a that shadow beast they talking about?"

"Ain't no shadow beast, some big tomcat, mebbe. Don' believe nothin' 'bout no big beast at all."

"Yeah. This trashy strip runs quite a way atween the wall and the backs'a those buildin's."

"Mostly deserted, those buildin's. Don' know what might be livin' in or 'round 'em."

Lahsin couldn't keep the spellshield up, it was slipping, but the door was shrouded by tall bushes and set deeply into the wall. She ran and fell into the dark corner of the door.

"That was def'nitely a sound," one guard said loudly. "The beast?"

"Thought you said you didn't believe in the beast."

"Changin' my mind. Should we 'vestigate?" He sounded nervous but determined.

"Yeah."

Fumbling, Lahsin found the door handle and pressed the thumb latch. Nothing. *Oh, Lady and Lord, oh, please, please, please*, she prayed. Sensing the strong shields—more like force fields—set in the walls, she fiddled with them. She'd always been good with shields. *Lady and Lord, please, I need in—*

"Guess we better look down there, 'least 'til it narrows."

"Them plants are too high, too wild."

I need in now! Tears streaked down her face. She breathed through her mouth. *Lady and Lord, in!*

The door opened, and she plunged into a tangle of bushes.

"What's that?"

"Nothin'. Nothin's here," the second man said loudly.

Lahsin watched with wide eyes as the door swung silently shut. On the back was a plaque that caught the sun and read, "BalmHeal." She slumped in relief.

There came thrashing beyond the door, the crackling of bush branches and swearing.

"You said the guards used to patrol in gliders?"

"On Earthan, yeah."

"Guy at Northgate owes me. Might wangle the gate glider."

"Yeah? Can't go no farther. Sure looks like a place where that shadow beast might lurk. Look, gotta rip in my coat sleeve. Nasty plants."

"Yeah, you're a reg'lar sophisticated city boy."

"Glider."

"Sounds good."

Lahsin ran down a twisting path, showing patches of stone underneath the overgrown ground cover, and through a couple of tall, mazelike hedgerows, in, in, in.

She stopped, panting, when the vista spread out before her.

The measure of a garden is its beauty in winter, and this one was glorious. Or had been glorious once upon a time. A pool of irregular curves lay before her, wide and long enough to swim in. Steam rose from it in fragrant drifts. It was bordered with crafted white marble. A couple of bays were obviously made for Healing specialities—a headrest of stone filigree, a round curve that looked like it had an underwater seat. Wooden benches were grouped in threes around the pool, some set in stone, some in the ground. An arbor and a small garden shed were near.

A whimper fell from her lips. Best of all was a deep curve of land jutting between two rounds of the pool. It was a mound of emerald green permamoss. Surely the last bit of green in all of Druida. Permamoss was used in bedsponges, and the soft springiness and the color called to her. She walked to the green, set her sack down, and stretched out. Yes. Perfect.

The humid warmth drifted over her from the pool. Mist covered her, enveloped her, wrapped her.

All was quiet. There was no sound except the natural movement of leaves, of water lapping at the sides of the pool. The moss beneath her smelled herbal and comforting and drained her lingering anxiety. Her bruises and aches eased.

She let the grayness of the mist thicken into sleep.

T*inne thought he'd lost a few pounds already, expend-*ing Flair, running patterns between the tests to keep himself going.

Next his relationship with Genista would be examined. Since he'd requested two days of testing, the Healers had decided to change the order of the examinations. They probably knew he was trying to deny his failure in his marriage.

D'Sea and T'Heather had left. Saille T'Willow, the matchmaker, was conducting this test. Saille was nearer to Tinne's own age, no gray in his chestnut hair. He was new to his title, and understanding softened his blue eyes.

"I need to walk around," Tinne said. He preferred to be moving between the actual tests. If he sat in the chair, he'd try to relax, then pain or anger would sweep him, and his body would prepare to defend him from threat.

All the threat—and blows—had been mental and emotional, and he wished he'd gone through a week of hard fighting with his G'Uncle Tab instead.

Saille T'Willow crossed to the desk where he'd placed a case upon his arrival. "Please feel free to walk around."

The window had been lightened and revealed a smattering of large snowflakes drifting down. Tinne paced the room, loosening his muscles, did some stretches, and saw Saille eyeing him.

Saille murmured, "I need to sign up for exercise at the Green Knight."

Considering him, Tinne said, "You look in good condition."

"Thank you." Saille hesitated. "I have already formally allied with the T'Holly Family—with your father and brother. I would ally with you, too."

This took Tinne by surprise. He was a SecondSon, his descendants—his mind grappled at the thought of having no descendants, then gave up. "My Family is close. Alliance with them is alliance with me."

"Nevertheless, I would ally with you and your G'Uncle Tab." Saille sat behind the small desk and unrolled a thin, flexible pad of compressed permamoss in a dark, forest green color. He opened the velvet bag and poured out some runes made of pottery fired a deep green with the incised symbols in real gold.

They were different than most runes Tinne had seen. Instead of individual glyphs they had single and double lines, forks, and branches, as if they'd connect into patterns.

"Pull up a seat," Saille said.

Relief washed through Tinne. He found a regular chair and sat.

Saille gathered the runes and held them in his hands. "We ask the blessings of the Lady and Lord in this consultation. May all that is revealed here be for the greatest good of Tinne Holly and Saille Willow." Glancing at Tinne, he continued.

"Hold your hands over the pad on the desk, then I want you to find your center."

Tinne rubbed his hands to hide the fine trembling of his fingers. Saille dropped the runes into Tinne's cupped palms.

The pieces of pottery tingled, but Tinne used that to take him to a place deep within himself. The still place, his center.

"When you are ready, we will proceed." Saille's voice was low and soothing.

Tinne closed his eyes and cleared his mind, imagined the pale green light of a forest morning, his favorite image based on a spot at Tab's small country estate. He welcomed the lack of thought and emotion, sank deeper into the serene peace. But he couldn't quite let himself escape. Someone else was near. Someone who wanted something from him, a link to the outer world with all its heavy burdens. A word escaped his lips, "Ready."

"Think of your wife, Genista, and your marriage."

Tinne's fingers spasmed over the runes, his hands cracked open, the pottery clattered to the pad.

He opened his eyelids. Even to him the pattern looked ugly and jagged and was definitely in two different parts that didn't seem like they could ever align.

A jolt of pain shot through him as he considered the runes more closely. The runes appeared as if there had once been a pattern, bold and vibrant, and the very skewing of it hurt his heart. He studied Saille's face instead and found it expressionless, but his mouth had thinned.

Tinne's insides clenched. His back had tensed, he sat straight and focused on steadying his hands. Saille picked up the runes, his breath expelled, his fingers trembled. The man curved his hands over his prized tool—surely something he'd crafted himself—and chanted several couplets, then scowled. Apparently he didn't feel that was sufficient to cleanse the runes—was the energy so negative? Tinne winced, breathed deeply, and shoved the edges of depression away.

Saille opened his box, sprinkled herbal water on the runes, and replaced them. He took another small embroidered bag and tipped it, streaming runes Tinne knew, with proper symbols of gold and backs of deep metallic red. Again Saille blessed them, then gave a halfhearted smile. "Ready?"

Again Tinne found his center. He lingered a while in the

pale green, moved even deeper to where the glade was dappled with sun and the leaves rustled a little, changing the light. Finally he said, "Ready."

"Think of sex."

Again his hands clamped and broke apart, the runes hit the pad, this time accompanied by a guttural sound Tinne wished he could call back. Opening his eyes, he saw a pile of red-backed runes, no glyphs showing. Precariously atop the pile was one rune gleaming with a gold sigil that Tinne knew. "I'm not impotent!" He shoved from the chair, turned his back on Saille, but knew his red neck would show his humiliation.

"There are other meanings to the rune," Saille said in his professional voice. Tinne heard the clicking of the runes, then muffled sounds as they went into the velvet pouch. Thank the Lord and Lady that was done! "I would say that you have suppressed sex and are frustrated."

Because it was the truth, Tinne said nothing.

"There are three more questions we could ask, but I don't think they are necessary, do you?"

"Anything to get this over with," Tinne muttered.

"Please, sit."

Before he turned, he surreptitiously wiped his forehead with his arm, letting the sleeve absorb dampness. Then moved to the edge of the chair.

"The next part of the examination will test your sexuality. I've conducted many HeartMate and wife findings, so anything you might experience I've seen before."

"You mean orgasm."

Four

❦

That's right, orgasm." Saille smiled, and Tinne didn't trust it. The smile was more charming than his Mamá's or brother's when they were being devious.

Tinne *hated* these tests, and to be told that the next one might induce a sexual release just so he could be studied shivered his bones. His heart was simply torn. He wanted Genista and his marriage—but he wanted them the way they were in the past, before the loss of the baby, and that simply would not happen. That life was gone forever, and the pain of it lingered.

But to divorce—that would smear his and the Family's reputation for generations in many ways—from losing clients at The Green Knight to having other Families preferring not to marry into the Holly Family.

But to insist Genista remain married to him and bound to his Family when she didn't want to—no. Not an honorable choice.

All he knew, now, was that he wanted these tests *over*.

Tinne smiled back, a ferocious smile, mocking the insincere one Saille had given him.

Saille shook his head. "Very well, you are not pleased. I can construct the next examination to take place privately."

Heat rose to Tinne's face. "Thank you." His nerves twanged, and he banished thought and controlled the fear the best way he knew how, executing the last, most difficult fighting pattern. When he'd finished and was breathing hard, Saille walked in front of him and bowed; as he would after sparring, Tinne bowed back.

Then Saille gestured to the comfortchair, which was tilted back and hovering two feet above the ground. Tinne winced but climbed back into it. He hated it more than the starship lifepod, and that had been the worst experience of his life.

Until Genista had come into his rooms this morning.

The windows darkened and the light dimmed more than it did when the Healers did their tests.

"Just relax," Saille said.

"I've heard that too often this morning."

"I'm sure. Could you hold this please?" Saille handed Tinne a memorysphere, empty and ready to record. Bad enough that he was being tested, but to have his emotions recorded was horrible.

"I'll be writing my report immediately after we're done," Saille said. "The memorysphere will be destroyed in two septhours, maximum."

"Promise?" Tinne asked thickly. The orb was throbbing under his fingers, a drum rhythm he often played, sending him again to that still center of himself.

"I promise," Saille said. "Close your eyes and center yourself."

Tinne did. This time he went deep. To the forest at midday, light and shadow dancing on an emerald bed of permamoss where he lay, watching the leaves, the peeks of deep blue sky. Everything was wonderful here. A sigh escaped him.

Saille's voice slipped into Tinne's world, but didn't disrupt it. "I want you to think of love. More, I want you to know love, experience it."

Tinne distantly heard a door close.

Think of love. The words dropped like floating leaves in a breeze upon Tinne. The air of the summer's day enveloped him.

Love. His mother was the first scene, her cradling him as a child, which segued into scene after scene of his boyhood. More of her came, the scent of her, his love for her that was returned. His father joined her.

His father—images, feelings, of just his father and him in the fighting salons. His respect and love for his father.

Holm, his brother. How proud he was to be the brother of the gilded HollyHeir Holm. So dashing and bright and charming. Holm who even let him win in a few of their fighting lessons, Holm's surprise and hoot of laughter when Tinne had beaten him fair and square.

All the mixture of loving Family memories, far and recent past, the strong link that had been broken and mended to be even more powerful.

Except for Genista's.

Genista. The sexy, fun beauty men panted after. The woman whose Family disapproved of her and didn't understand. The sizzling glances, the unexpected vulnerability in her eyes when he'd asked her to marry him. It had been a marriage of convenience, but he'd kept all his promises. He had learned to love her, worked hard at the marriage, had thought of only her as his mate, and forgotten his HeartMate.

Love for the unborn child within Genista. His child. The hope of the Holly Family, which was lost, so soon after.

Clouds had scudded over the trees, blocking the sun, darkening the sky. It must be raining, because his face was wet.

Genista. That was both Saille's voice in his mind and Tinne's sad internal murmur of her name. She was receding. He'd tried to keep her close, pull her near, but she wouldn't let him.

Rejection. Hurt. More pain. A shielding of his own emotions against her.

Think of love, experience love. Another urging by Saille that had Tinne rolling to his side on the moss, letting its softness cushion him. The sun was back, highlighting tiny pastel flowers in the emerald carpet that was just beginning to bloom.

And he wasn't alone. There was another, a girl not quite a woman. Naive and innocent in many ways. An instinctive wave of tenderness swept from him to her. She was sad, too, hurt, too. The rain had touched her.

He didn't look at her closely, didn't even pull her name from the depths of him that he'd closed off. But he took her in his arms.

Love. Yes. This was love, the holding and being held. Having someone's body fit your own, giving you strength when you were weak, sharing.

The good moments before inevitable heartbreak. It rained. Then rain turned to snow.

* * *

*A*t first *Lahsin's dreams were vague. Then anxiety peaked* and she was running, running, running, just as she really had. She tore her clothes and scratched her skin as she plunged into a thicket, but the thorns grew around her, shielding her, keeping her safe. When she turned to face the wall, there was not one, but a choice of three doors. Each different. One a rectangular light blue stone door with a white marble surround, the middle a pointed arch of gnarly wood with hanging green vines, the third less a door than a white, shining portal.

As she shifted from foot to foot trying to make a decision, the gray mist got heavier, and she descended further into sleep.

After a while, as she lay dreaming, the weather warmed and strong arms encircled her, tender arms urged her close to a man's muscled body. She sighed and smiled. Gentle hands stroked her, palms with tough skin, not the pampered smoothness of T'Yew's. They touched her hair, smoothed. Arms holding her close.

The scent of man rose to her nostrils, and she wrinkled her nose. No. She didn't want a man. Not now, not ever. But he was against her, his arms around her, his feet tangled with hers.

No! She thrashed, trying to escape. The arms let her go. Not enough. She couldn't breathe. Heat throbbed through her. Hot, hotter, hottest. Too hot. She was burning! She screamed.

And swallowed water.

She flailed her arms and legs, felt water—hot water—drag at her sodden clothes. She coughed. The water wasn't unpleasant.

But the disorientation and fear were.

She shook her head, and the cold slap of wind sobered her. Though she knew the springs were warm around her, chill bit deep, and she shivered with cold and could almost feel her lips turning blue. She saw nothing, blinked, still nothing.

She mewled and spit out water, yet the taste of herbs stayed on her tongue. The sound of her own rough breathing, the pounding of her heart caught her attention.

Breathe. Center.

Slowly the coldness ebbed, being replaced once again by the hot water, until she thought it would sear her skin.

Fever. Chills.

Finally she understood what was happening. Another incident of spiking Flair. A precursor of her Second Passage.

She bit her lip, and the small pain cleared the last of the fog from her brain. She discovered she'd been right, she was in the hot springs Healing pool. In FirstGrove. Safe, for now.

Her hair was plastered to her head, but she was standing, not swimming. She'd moved to where the water hit her just below her breasts. Chill air was beginning to penetrate the mist of the pool. The wind was rising again. Was snow on the way as one of the guardsmen had predicted?

Neither of the men had sounded very knowledgeable about anything. Perhaps he was wrong.

A strange rumbling-grunting drew her attention.

Once again that morning she kept perfectly still.

They'd been right about the beast.

Five

❧

The creature was huge. *No, that was her fear magnify-*
ing it. Large. Doglike, though she hadn't seen many dogs;
none that looked like this, large with a long muzzle and sharp
teeth and gray matted hair and big, mean yellow eyes. It
stood on the mossy peninsula projecting into the pool where
she'd lain. It moved a little, and she saw that one of its back
legs was crippled, like the bone had broken and healed all
wrong.

Her heart began thumping hard again, her breathing
quickened, and she made no effort to regulate them.

Could the animal have pushed her into the pool? Or had
she rolled in herself, in the throes of the little Passage fugue?

Keeping its eyes on her, it lowered its nose to a heap on
the ground.

Lahsin took a few steps back, considered swimming to the
other side of the pool or the far end. Then her heart gave another jolt as she realized what the dog-thing was investigat-
ing. Her bag! It tore at her sack, pawed at it, found her food,
and gobbled it down.

"No!" she shouted. It stared at her and growled, still eating.

She hurried to the rim of the pool, now waist level, and
sent a spume of water at the dog. Only a small spray hit it. A
louder, threatening growl.

Helplessly, she watched it rip all the softleaves from the food she'd packed and eat it. She could count its ribs, and it looked scrawny and crippled, so she knew it was hungry, starving perhaps. But that was all her food!

She didn't dare lever herself out of there, not when she'd be wet and vulnerable, so she splashed toward the steps about two meters away from the mossy area and climbed the few stairs.

The dog lifted his snout, growled again, then awkwardly backed away from her sack and the pool. She watched it disappear into the brush beyond an arbor.

Then she discovered she was shivering in the winter air.

Snow began to fall. Fast. In big, fat, icy flakes.

*S*lowly Tinne rose from the trance. Slowly, because he knew that once he reached full consciousness, emotional pain would attack like a ravening wolf, and he'd have to force his tired brain to think.

But his eyelashes lifted, and as they did, the room brightened from dimness to the pearl gray of a winter's day. Snowfall obscured the landscape. He longed to return to his summer afternoon in the forest. He blinked and swallowed hard and must have made some noise, because Saille glanced up from the desk where he was writing and smiled at Tinne. "You're back."

Saille rose and picked up a glass filled with water and sprigs of mint and brought it to Tinne. "May I have that?" He nodded at the memorysphere.

Tinne handed it to Saille, noticing shifting wisps inside it—green, gray, white. There was no red for lust, and Tinne was infinitely relieved that he hadn't had a sexual release.

He had no doubt T'Willow, the premiere matchmaker on Druida, knew Tinne had been whirled into a dream of his HeartMate instead of Genista. That the dream had had no sex.

That Tinne couldn't even think of Genista and sex anymore.

He finally admitted that was the true sign that his marriage was ruined.

Saille's expression saddened. "I'm sorry."

Tinne didn't meet his glance. "Genista." He had to stop and clear his throat. "Genista was right. Her tests, and now mine. So far they reveal that we are no longer a couple."

"It's rare that I see a splintered marriage. Those who have one don't come to me for help, though they should."

Tinne snorted, muttered, "You and D'Sea."

"I prefer couples happy in their marriage, yes." Saille smiled again. "Especially now that I'm so happy in my own HeartBond."

Narrowing his eyes, Tinne studied him. It hadn't been easy for Saille T'Willow to find and win his HeartMate. He'd even sent his HeartGift circulating with minimal shields throughout the city. Just the idea of rough fingers handling his Heart-Gift made Tinne shudder. Saille had also overcome the results of his lady's kidnapping and attempted murder.

"Was it worth it?" Tinne asked.

With lifted brows, Saille said, "Was everything I suffered last year worth the delight of the HeartBond? Yes. Of course." Since the man's face had lit with pleasure, Tinne figured it wasn't just a line of patter to reassure clients.

Saille sent him a direct look. "You may learn that yourself."

Of course Saille knew Tinne had a HeartMate, many in the FirstFamilies circle knew. Knew she was wed to another. Knew he'd wed another. Fated to be apart.

But this man would know who she was just by looking at Tinne. It was part of Saille's Flair.

A soft tap came on the door, a low voice. "You done?"

Saille sent a last commiserating glance at Tinne, said, "I'll see you later," and opened the door.

T'Heather tramped in, followed by D'Sea.

"Yes or no?" asked T'Heather.

Saille stiffened. "I'll send you my full report later."

But the Healer exuded authority. "A quick generalization now would help us."

"Yes, the marriage is beyond repair," Saille said. He inclined his head to T'Heather, then to D'Sea, and left.

More tests.

More pain.

*L*ahsin's will nearly broke.

Cold, alone with a feral animal, no food, no shelter. What was she going to do? When had she ever spent a night outdoors? A few summer nights in the manicured garden at the country estate, in the children's section, completely safe.

She had no food, perhaps enough gilt for supplies that would last a few days. She couldn't imagine creeping out of this place to steal in the city. She'd never be good at that, she'd be caught. Would the garden let her in if she were a thief?

Her stomach rumbled, emphasizing her problem. She shut down the panic. She would manage. She'd escaped, hadn't she?

Blinking away snow that stuck to her lashes, she squinted, blinked again, recognized the corner of a garden shed. She straightened her shoulders, gritted her teeth, tucked her hands in her opposite armpits, and struggled out of the pool.

With cold, stiff fingers she picked up her belongings—the pouch with her gilt and the necklace, her clothes—and shoved them in the sack. She shook out her hooded cape and drew it on, but it was damp and not much help against the wind and cold.

She thought she saw another building, perhaps a tower, in the distance beyond the snow, but she was too cold already to explore. If she caught her ankle in a hole and broke it, fell to the ground, and lay while snow covered her, what would happen? Would the power of FirstGrove prevent her from dying? She didn't know and certainly didn't want to find out.

She headed toward the garden shed. Hadn't she heard an old story about someone living in a garden shed? T'Yew had snorted, his lip had curled, he'd said it showed the nature of the man, that he would never match the greatness of his FatherSire. He was a disgrace to his title. A FirstFamilies Lord, then, but whoever he was, he'd survived in a garden shed. Lahsin would do no less.

Maybe it would have some food. She couldn't hope for a no-time, a food storage unit that kept food exactly the way it was placed inside, but there might be dried vegetables. She could survive on dried vegetables.

This place was very old, perhaps there was an antique kitchen garden run as wild as everything else. And there was the hot spring for water. Herbs and plants for tisanes she could make that would strengthen her.

First she had to get out of the cold. She shambled to the small building, each footstep hard, because she couldn't quite feel her feet.

She circled the shed twice, thrashing through underbrush, before she saw the door indicated by a handle and hinges and a small crack. The building wasn't large, about three meters square. How could she unlock the door? She sensed it wouldn't simply open for her as the door to the garden had. A long, rumbling growl made the hair on the back of her neck rise. Centimeter by centimeter, she slowly turned her neck to the left. Sheltering under the overhang of the roof corner was the beast.

It growled again. Praying and sending an *open*! spell, Lahsin pressed the cold, cold latch and shoved quick and hard, and fell into a musty-scented place. She turned and slammed the door shut.

Then she slid down the wall. Just getting out of the cold and wind made her feel better. Feeling came back to her feet, first in stinging prickles, then true pain, and she gritted her teeth and moaned between them.

She wondered what spells the shed might have. "Light," she said, and the grime on the one small window lessened. A very weak glow came from a ceiling spell. Not much.

"Heat," she said. Nothing, not even the tiniest brush of Flair to indicate a spell embedded in the building.

Shivering, she stripped and spread out her wet clothes. Lady and Lord knew how long it would take for them to dry. Then she tried another spell, a simple one. "Dry!" A small warmth fluttered around her halfheartedly. It was the very last of her Flair for septhours, but it might be enough to do the job by evening.

She chose a corner to huddle in. The cold wasn't *too* bad. The whole garden seemed warmer than the rest of Druida. She would survive. Tomorrow, if the snow wasn't too deep and her clothes had dried—or she'd managed to gather a little more Flair to dry them—she'd explore. With a garden this big, there would be other structures. She wouldn't have to stay in the shed.

There might even be a house. Or a Residence. She wasn't ready for that, but she would just have to overcome her dislike of a Residence. They didn't all have to be wretched personalities like the Yews' or condescending like the Burdocks'. If she'd had to live centuries with Yews like Ioho and Taxa, she'd have turned nasty, too. An awful thought.

As the day wore on, she dozed and woke periodically. She thought of the garden and what she'd seen and how she might live here and tend it. A pretty dream.

Now and then she heard the click of claws outside, and then the light faded from the window.

She knew the animal—*was* it a dog?—hovered outside in the cold, close to the warmth of the door. It didn't whine, didn't growl. Could she possibly trust it? If she let it in, would it hurt her?

She'd seen its ribs, how it had torn into her food, and she couldn't get the idea out of her head that it was waiting for death.

Could it possibly be sentient? *Beast?*

Silence.

Shifting a little to get more comfortable, she stared at the window, wondered if she deluded herself that she could see stars.

Hear you. The mind touch startled her. It was gruff. Resigned. Maybe there was a touch of a whimper.

Forming an image with her words, Lahsin sent, *I will let you in. You stay away from me. We both survive.*

This time the quiet was like the animal was considering. Then a rush of desperation came at her. Not her own, but like what she'd felt.

What had allowed her into the garden.

I agree, the beast said. *We do not hurt each other.*

I agree, Lahsin echoed. *We do not hurt each other.*

Wondering if she was being too stupid, too softhearted, or just learning to be a more courageous person, she rose and opened the door.

Snow whirled in, the beast came, too, nearly dragging itself. She didn't help it.

I am a dog. It looked at her with the eyes that she recalled were yellow, and it was too dark to read its expression.

She watched as it settled itself, waited. Eyeing the dog, Lahsin figured the best way either of them would get some peace was if she left the door open a scrawny-dog-sized amount so he could leave and not pounce on her in the night.

She went back to her corner, arranged her clothes as a bed, and nibbled her lip, wondering what the best way to bespell the corner for warmth would be. If she had enough Flair.

At T'Yew's she'd practiced only minor Flair, turning on lights, housekeeping her own room. Yew's daughter and the Residence itself had managed all the great spells necessary to run it. Just as YewHeir had had the MistrysSuite. But Lahsin didn't want to think about that. She'd gotten her own small room after a couple of months of sharing the MasterSuite with Yew, when he'd wanted a more mature, knowledgeable bed-mate. One that wouldn't shiver and hide or vomit after sex.

She shook her head hard. Even this corner in this forgotten garden was better than what she'd come from, and she cherished it. Drawing in a big breath, she centered herself and gently prodded her Flair. There was nothing on the surface, but deeper inside her—it was like an oncoming thunderstorm. You knew it was big and dangerous, but it was also exciting. Surely she'd manage to sustain herself during the fever fugue of Passage. She hadn't heard of anyone going crazy or dying from it lately. Those were probably all old stories.

She sat and spread out the ripped sack and all her belongings. Not even a crumb of food. She looked at the long, angular tears in the sack, wondered if she could mend them. Perhaps. Frowning with concentration, she smoothed the cloth bag out. A tiny, hard lump was in the corner.

She fumbled through the tear, snatched at it, a little herbal pill flecked with red. She'd found only one in an open packet in a dusty corner of the pantry when she'd gotten the travel sticks. The herb was supposed to give energy. She stared at it, shivered. Could it stir her Flair? She needed Flair to keep the shed warm through the night.

Just thinking about a heat spell made her colder. Finally, with a shrug, she took the pill and laid it on her tongue. The sweet, spicy cinnamon tasted good and she let it melt away.

As she'd hoped, her Flair rose, evenly, filling her with sweet power. She hummed in delight.

She needed warmth in the night. How could she get it? The shed didn't have an inbuilt heating spell. She thought back to her grovestudy days, when she'd learned to build on other spells or on nature.

Other spells. The shed had preservation spells that would keep her heat Flair going once she set it in place. Closing her eyes, she felt the shed, what its walls had experienced through the seasons. Winter, like now, chilling the stone and riming it with frost.

Summer, never stifling, but the sun's light penetrating the small window in the opposite corner, warming the walls, trapping the heat until well into the night. That was it! Remembrance of summer days.

She crafted a simple couplet, spoke it, and knew it worked, even drying her clothes! She grinned until she saw the dog sitting near the door, muzzle withdrawn from its teeth, eyes narrowed. Did she dare stay here with it?

A personal shield, she thought she could do that. After all, she'd broken all of the shields on Yew Residence, she should be able to craft one. She did, with a Word, and it seemed so easy she didn't know whether she trusted its strength. So she walked over to a large pair of pruners. The dog growled and inched away from her, more toward the door.

I won't let you hurt me, she sent to the dog. Wouldn't hurt to talk to him, would it? And since she'd used so much Flair she was now too tired to care whether that made sense or not.

She nudged her clothes around in a nest so they looked halfway comfortable and settled herself down, keeping a loose grip on the meter-long pruners. Just before she slept, she met the dog's yellow eyes, and he said mentally, *I said I would not hurt you. I am taking shelter just like you.*

I won't hurt you, either, she sent, but she kept her gaze on him as the physical discomfort of sleeping on wadded clothes atop a stone floor faded and her eyes drifted closed. Her very last thought was that she was free.

Without food in winter, but free.

*A*fter the tests that evening, Tinne took a chance and teleported directly to his waterfall stall. Before he stripped off his clothes and sent them to the recycle bin, he contacted the Residence and issued a "Do Not Disturb" request for all communications systems and the sigil to be applied to his door.

He didn't want to see anyone or listen to anyone, and most definitely he didn't want to do any more fliggering talking. He turned up the heat, flow, and noise of the waterfall, so it was all he experienced—a torrent of cleansing white water bubbling over him, though he sensed people tiptoeing outside his door. His Mamá, his father, his brother. Lark, his brother's wife and the Holly Healer, *didn't* show up, but since T'Heather was her MotherSire, Tinne figured the man would have talked to her. Thankfully the rest of his Family honored his wishes.

He let a gentle spell dry him as he staggered in the early winter darkness to his bed and fell facedown on it.

The soft rumble of a purr wafted to his ears, and a cat—his hunting cat, Ilexa—stepped onto his back, kneading his stiff muscles. He grabbed the corner of the spread, pulled it over his lower body, and grunted. "Greetyou. Nice to see you after all these years." Not that he was seeing her, his face was mashed in a feather pillow and he'd closed his eyes. But somehow just having her back loosened a tight knot inside him.

I returned because you need me. The cat spoke in obviously female tones.

It was the last thing either of them said for several moments as she worked on him. Finally as he was sinking into sleep, he opened one eye to see her curl in her regal cat bed on the floor. Mutated from Earthan cheetahs, the sturdiest feline that had adapted to Celta, her coat was golden with beautiful brown markings. But she appeared a little ragged. He'd always pictured her as elegant and deadly. *Thank you for leaving the wild for me, Ilexa.*

Of course I would. Wild is too hard, anyway. No good food. No warm shelter. No FamMan.

A corner of his mouth curved up. "So you've decided to return and be my Fam."

"Yesss," the cat said. *Residence and Family no longer cursed.*

"My parents fulfilled their Vows of Honor over a year ago," Tinne mumbled.

Took time for rotten Flair smell to vanish from Holly land.

"Oh." Then sleep claimed him.

*T*he next morning Tinne awoke with the awful anticipation that doom was about to crash down on him. Then he remembered and doom fell, flattening his spirits before he rolled from his bedsponge.

He lay there, enervated, for long minutes, when, just like the day before, his Mamá's voice came. "Tinne? The Residence told me you were up. Are you coming to breakfast?" She'd always been the one to gently keep the Holly sons in line.

He grunted, groaned, but it was no good. He knew he couldn't escape a Family breakfast, Lady and Lord help him.

He had ducked his Family the night before, but it wouldn't be possible today.

"Ilexa?" he murmured, then the cat strolled in from the waterfall room. He didn't know what she'd done, but every hair on her looked sleekly groomed, even her whiskers.

"Your appointment with the Healers is in a septhour," his Mamá said, and her voice was so neutral, without its usual lilt, that he shut his eyes in hurt—for himself, for Genista, for his Family. "I'll be down in quarter septhour," he replied with his sleep-roughened voice.

"Yes, dear." She sounded relieved.

"Oh, and Ilexa is back. Please set her place in the corner of the dining room."

There was a hesitation. "Ilexa's back?" A lifting of his Mamá's voice and spirits.

"Yes."

"I'll make sure she's welcomed."

A delicious meal for his prodigal Fam then. Tinne was sure whatever he ate would taste like ashes.

Ilexa came over to stand at the bed and gave a discreet lick of his cheek. *You look like a scruff.*

Tinne grunted, the schedule of the day—all the testing—crowding into his brain and tightening his gut. He levered himself from the bed. He washed quickly, dressed in a plain linen shirt and brown trous. His shirtsleeves and trous legs were extravagantly bloused, gathered at wrist and ankle. The excessive material would serve several purposes. His clothes were bespelled to soak up sweat and transform it to regular water and send it into the air. He'd also set warming and cooling spells into the fabric so he wouldn't suffer as much from clamminess and cold chills or flushes of heat like he had the day before.

The only good part of the previous day was T'Heather's pronouncement after his physical examination that he was in fine shape, if a little too thin. Tinne anticipated losing more weight during these fliggering tests. No one would like that.

Even after the tests he was ambivalent about the future. He wanted to think—to hope—that somehow he and Genista could overcome their differences. And he wanted the pain he associated with Genista and the loss of their child gone. He didn't think he could have both options.

Most of all, he wanted this testing *over*.

The results were looking poor but there was nothing to do but finish.

Six

♥

At Lark's orders, breakfast talk had been trivial. Tinne ate fast and hoped to give his Family the slip, but they accompanied him to the front door. He'd be taking a glider to the tests today.

"Tinne, you look terrible," his Mamá said. She was holding hands with his father as usual.

Holm snorted.

"Of course you wouldn't sleep well. I'll work on a Flaired lullaby for you," his Mamá said.

Holm snickered.

"Holm, don't be rude." Their mother rounded on him.

Holm raised his eyebrows. "Someone has to keep his spirits up." Holm stared at Tinne. "Looks like you sank into the Great Washington Boghole then Ilexa dragged you all the way back here."

"Thank you," Tinne said. "You look . . . radiant." He bared his teeth, but got a little satisfaction, as Holm looked aside and Lark smiled.

"I have to go," Tinne said.

Lark curved her hand around Tinne's cheek. "If I may?" But she'd already sent him a surge of energy that refreshed him more than the waterfall and banished the lingering bad dreams.

"Thank you." He lifted her hand and kissed her fingers. "Thank you all." The energy Lark had sent him was not hers alone, but a mixture of the whole Family's, given to him through her link with them.

All with the hope that his and Genista's marriage could be mended and the Family wouldn't be the first of the greatest Nobles to have a divorce. The scandal would smear everyone. For generations. He looked at his brother who would have to work as the head of the Family under such a cloud.

Holm inclined his head infinitesimally and sent on their brothers-only line, *Be well, brother. Do whatever must be done.*

Tinne shuddered. Holm had said that same phrase when he was caught in the quicksand of the Great Washington Bog-hole and couldn't get out. Tinne had managed to save them both. It could have been worse, Tinne could be next T'Holly. As always, he was glad that wasn't his fate.

Yes, he'd make everything harder on his Family for generations, but he didn't know that there was anything he could do to stop the divorce.

His Mamá was humming. His new lullaby. Lord and Lady.

"Don't call it 'Tinne's Lullaby,'" he said.

"I won't." She smiled at him, and he noted she looked much older than she had a couple of days before.

"Call it 'SecondSon's Lullaby,'" Holm said.

Tinne opened his mouth for a return insult, expecting to see Holm's twinkling eyes. They were dead serious. Despite his light manner, Holm was suffering along with the rest of them, sorry for Tinne's hurt. Tinne had the horrible suspicion that if he gave in to his own feelings, everyone would weep. Awful.

Then his father said. "This whole mess is my fault. I apologize. I . . . I . . . You cannot know how deeply I regret my actions." He blinked rapidly, though his taut face held a stony expression. Then he straightened his shoulders. "I received word from the Healers that you need time in the HouseHeart." He waved a hand. "It is scheduled for the next two years."

Tinne wanted to wince at the decree that depressed both of them, but nodded. "Thank you, I'd like to sleep there tonight."

"Done," T'Holly said.

His Mamá looked at Tinne. "Why didn't I think of that! Your rooms must be redecorated immediately. And Gen—and the other suite. We should have done that last year. Perhaps that will help."

Keep them together? He didn't think so. But his Mamá continued, "I'll scry Mitchella D'Blackthorn for a decorating consult. We can do this today. We'll mine the storerooms and attics." She squeezed his father's hand. "We have work to do."

"We certainly do." T'Holly sounded a little more cheerful at the thought of moving furniture all day. A distraction both physical and Flaired. "We can bring back the rest of the hunting cats now that Ilexa has returned, resume training. It's good to have plans."

Lark opened her mouth.

Tinne figured he knew what she was going to say. The Healers had recommended pink.

"Nothing pink!" he called to his parents as they left. "Not one pink thing. And leave my drums alone!"

Lark sniffed.

"The glider awaits to take Tinne to T'Heather," the Residence said.

Ilexa ran toward him, food on her whiskers.

Lark said, "I'm sorry, Ilexa, it wouldn't help Tinne to have you during the tests. He must get through them on his own."

Holm said, "You look different, Ilexa. Perhaps it's time for a visit to T'Ash for a new collar. Tinne can afford it."

After hugs all around, they all walked away.

"You should meet our FamCats," Lark said.

Relief flooded Tinne, time with his Family was over. Now he only had the ordeal with the Healers. Four tests left.

Horrible.

Lahsin awoke and stretched with a singing heart. She was free. Shadowy dream threats had haunted her sleep, but they were nothing like the reality she'd lived through, so she brushed them aside. Only to be expected when she'd changed her life so and coped with so many new experiences the day before: the surge of her Flair that would soon be freed, her confrontation with the Hawthorn guard, that was scary, the miraculous luck finding this garden, and then the dog.

The dog that was laying next to her in the warmth she'd

generated with her spell. Staring at her. She groped for the pruners, and her foot touched them.

The dog rose, looking a little stiff. He limped heavily, dragging a back foot, to the door that was still open, letting in bright winter sunlight. He turned his head toward her and said, *I am not yours. I am my own.*

Lahsin's breath shuddered out of her. That was something she should have said to T'Yew. And gotten "punished" for it. But she could say it now. "I am my own. I am free."

She went out into the sunshine. The air was warmer than freezing. The snow hadn't collected the way she thought it would, and was now melting into the ground. It would be a good, mild day. She couldn't wait to explore the gardens.

*T*he *Healers had rearranged the tests again. Tinne* didn't know what order the examinations should have been in, but when he'd arrived at the pink room there was already tension in the air, as if D'Sea and T'Heather had disagreed.

The first examination—of his communication energy—like the previous ones, didn't seem to go well. D'Sea and T'Heather's muttering confirmed that he had problems in that area, too.

He hadn't wanted to teleport Genista to them, couldn't form a good image of her without blazing emotions around her. He hadn't wanted to talk to her. When they asked him what he might say to her, his voice had locked in his throat, because he wanted to rage and whimper and scream. When they'd asked him to consider the same tasks using his brother, Holm, he'd had no problems. All of which certainly indicated that his relationship with his wife was . . . not good.

He was allowed a little break in the cleansing room, said a prayer that the next tests would be less wrenching, and was glad that his clothes were indeed soaking up his sweat. Pitiful that he'd begun to cherish the small moments of privacy here.

Looking at himself in the mirror, he noted that he hadn't appeared so wretched since . . .

He squared his shoulders. Since he and Genista had lost the child a year and three months ago. The loss of the babe would always haunt him. As, it seemed, the loss of his wife would. He just couldn't seem to stop the crash of their relationship.

He'd given up trying to hide his true feelings from the tests. Any chance of manipulating them was far beyond his powers. The whole ordeal was such that only the most determined of people would continue through it and he grudgingly admired that Genista had endured the tests. It would have been so much easier for her to request separate living arrangements.

But the Hollys wouldn't have allowed that. Every single one of them would have tried to "fix" the problem. Forever. She'd known them well enough to understand that. She was an intelligent, sexy woman, and it didn't seem like she was his woman anymore.

"Tinne?" called D'Sea from the other room.

He wiped the cooling droplets he'd splashed on his face away with an incredibly soft towel, gave his reflection a half smile and salute, and opened the door to new suffering.

*L*ahsin spent a happy morning, exploring some of the wonderful, secret garden. There was no doubt that it was the lost FirstGrove. There was the Healing pool, hot and filled with efficacious minerals as well as the remnants of herbal water plants, still imbued with potent Healing spells. The unexpected dip in it yesterday had helped soothe her emotional ills and perhaps regulated and replenished her Flair. On one side of the pool was a stone terrace, and Lahsin got the impression that there had been outside "rooms" of canvas where the Healers had worked. She hadn't seen a permanent HealingHall, but there was a water conduit toward the northeast from the natural pool to someplace else.

On the other side of the pool, the side the garden shed was on, was a series of benches and a long arbor covered with grapevines.

She walked down stone paths nearly covered with moss, found a gazebo with two bathing pools nearby, almost as warm as the springs but not containing Healing spells. It was evident that other people and creatures had found this place from time to time.

The land dipped and mounded, and she found herself strolling north along the western wall that curved inward. The trees and plants fascinated her—old Earthan trees and plants mingled with Celtan ones—and hybrids. It gave credence to the supposition that the same ancient spacefaring people had colonized Earth and Celta millennia ago.

Then the wall stopped curving and became straight, hooking up to the gray stone north city wall half a block away. That gave her the clue that FirstGrove was actually nestled in the northeast corner of Druida City.

It was a large chunk of land, but still able to be hidden in the vastness of the city the colonists had measured and defined. The ancients had made the walls with their strange machines, expecting their descendants to fill the area of the city.

So two of the walls of FirstGrove would be city walls, the north and the east.

She hadn't found the sacred grove itself, though there were glades and natural copses. In the northwest area she discovered herb gardens gone to seed drying into stalks, set inside ragged hedges of boxwood. The scents nearly overwhelmed her, and the fragrance of cooking herbs like sage made her mouth water.

At that moment she saw the glint of glass in the distance to the east, and her spirits rose. A greenhouse or conservatory! It might be secure. It might hold food. It might even have a little no-time filled with snacks. She was beginning to daydream about food. Her breakfast had been a glass of hot herbed water from the pool.

She hurried toward the conservatory, now walking due east with the north wall of the city to her left. Since the only clear path wound between trees that seemed like a dense wood, when she stepped into an open glen, her breath caught.

Before her was a long, low building with a tower, a gilded ancient clock on one side, gleaming in the sunlight. The way the structure was situated and built meant "stillroom" to her—a place where herbs were dried and hung and stored. Where people made potions and pills, mixtures of everything from pretty scented potpourris to efficacious Healing infusions.

The door was solid, but there were no shields, perhaps because she sensed someone had been here more recently than the garden shed. In fact she got the oddest impression that a person had left with expectations that he would return.

She hurried inside, searched all three downstairs rooms,

and found some working no-times—with only fresh herbs in them. She explored the whole building. The stillroom had bags of herbal poultices that she recognized as being for deep wounds, appearing to be no more than a few years old. But she recognized nothing that might help during Passage. Not even a recipe book.

She ran up the tower stairs and found a door in the ceiling that opened with a creak, then walked around marveling at the machinery of the clock itself. There wasn't much dust, and again, the great gears appeared as if they'd been cared for not too long ago.

Looking out the large northeast window, she saw the northern city wall marching along even ground, though beyond the wall in the north, the land fell steeply. On this side of the wall was the garden, made interesting by several levels of landscaping. And angled just far enough away from the northeastern corner where the city walls met and it couldn't be seen from outside was a two-story, redbrick house with white pillars framing the entrance. The place was large enough and certainly old enough to be a Residence. From her vantage point it appeared to be in good repair. Attached to it was a large, domed conservatory.

Movement caught her eye, and she saw the dog pounce— and miss—a wild housefluff, the hybrid of Earthan rabbit and Celtan mocyn.

Lahsin bit her lip. Birds and other animals lived in the garden. She had no doubt that the dog would eat them if he caught one. But she couldn't imagine hunting and killing them and cleaning them and eating them herself. As for trapping them, *no*! She imagined the eyes of a trapped animal. She couldn't do it.

Her diet would become vegetarian, but she still hadn't seen any vegetables, and from the looks of the grapevines, the thriving skirl population would have eaten them all.

How was she going to manage? Nothing for it, she'd have to go out into the city.

Since the very thought scared her, and she intended to teach herself to be strong, she figured that it would be a test. Noon was coming up, and the warmest part of the day. From what she'd experienced, the city outside the garden would be colder than inside.

Best go now. When it was warmest. When more people would be on the streets.

Before she lost her nerve.

T'Heather handed Tinne a warm red bag of silkeen with herbs in it. The fragrance of summer roses came to his nose.

"Knead that."

Tinne did, and emotions exploded from him. Pain—that Genista hurt him so. That they'd loved and love had died and she realized it and wanted nothing more of him. Anger that she was putting him through this, had put herself through this. That she wouldn't stay with him. That the scandal would be atrocious. That his reputation would be besmirched for all of his life.

More anger, more bitterness, root bitterness, that his father had done this to them with his broken Vows of Honor. That his Mamá had supported his father, as she always had, to the detriment of her own health and her son's and her daughter-in-law's.

Grief. Grief so deep he had to fight to survive every moment. His babe had died in the womb.

Grief that his brother had been disinherited, torn from him, from the Residence, from the Family.

Grief that Tinne had been forced to break the link with his Family, too, and disinherit himself.

All the emotions that the past had worked on him, scored into his heart and body, tore from him, and he screamed and rocked and shouted.

Even more—back further—emotions he'd thought he'd dealt with. The horror of finding himself locked in a small sphere with his brother, the sensation of that orb being shot into space. Seeing Celta fall away below him and Holm, the starry sky engulf them, frightened to his core.

Circling the planet then falling, falling into it. More terror as he wondered if they'd die. Both of them. The sons of T'Holly, his only children, leaving their parents unknowing of their fate, grieving.

The rough landing, the bruises. Knowledge that they were in a wild and dangerous part of Celta. The trip with Holm, angry at each other for their actions in getting them into this mess, fear coming out in harsh words and feelings.

Following his brother into the boghole, seeing him sink to his death.

Desperation.

Relief when he saved his brother, and they made it back to their parents.

More horror with the firebombspell in the Council Chamber, watching people burn to death as he futilely tried to save them. He yelled, then thrashed.

More grief. A blow that nearly crippled him. His Heart-Mate wed to someone else. To GrandLord T'Yew, who'd never appreciate her, love her, cherish her, as Tinne would. His determination to save his brother from his parents' ire, his proposal and quick marriage to Genista. The blooming of his love for her as they both worked at their marriage.

So it circled.

And circled. Worse than any Passage, any of the fugues that freed his Flair, the deathduels.

Until he could stand it no longer, and he screamed and screamed and dropped the silkeen bag, and it was over.

And quiet.

The two Healers watched him with infinite sympathy as he set his head in his hands. His whole body shook for minutes that seemed like eons.

D'Sea glided toward him, crouched, put her hand on his knee. "It's all out now, all your negative emotions, you'll Heal now."

"I thought I had Healed," Tinne muttered from behind his hands. He was too raw to look at anyone. "Except for the child, and this new hurt." And his HeartMate. But he didn't think that the Healers had understood all the events and reasons behind his emotions. Thank the Lady and Lord for that.

D'Sea shoved a large softleaf into his hand, and he used it to mop his—sweaty—face. He heard T'Heather's footsteps as he paced the room, glanced toward the man to see the Healer rubbing the back of his neck. "I'd forgotten that little trip you'd taken around the world."

"Someday I hope to forget it, too," Tinne said lightly, again wiping his face, then murmuring a couplet to freshen his clothes. "Spacefaring is not for me. If I'd been my ancestor, I'd have stayed home."

"None of us will forget the firebombspell." The words seemed torn from D'Sea. Tinne wondered how many of the FirstFamily Lords and Ladies she'd treated for that emotional shock.

T'Heather stared at his hands, turning them over. "I couldn't Heal."

D'Sea pulled another softleaf from her sleeve and dabbed at her face, rose to stand. "It's the past, and over."

"Yes," Tinne said, shifting back to lounge into the chair he was beginning to loathe. "So I suppose you measured my—emotions?"

Grunting, T'Heather walked over. Both the Healers looked down at the red silkeen bag that was pulsing like a heart. D'Sea drew in a long, audible breath. Ignoring the pouch on the floor, she brought over another one. This one was pink. She offered it to Tinne. "We will consider your marriage now. Take this and think of Genista."

He didn't want to do this. It was the last thing he wanted to do in his life.

"Leave the boy be," T'Heather said. "This session has been bad enough. We can do this tomorrow."

Relief leapt inside Tinne but he gritted his teeth. "I want this over and done."

Reluctantly, Tinne took the bag.

Lahsin left the garden by a different door. The exit was more southerly and closer to city center. Pretending a confidence and independence that she hadn't quite mastered, she walked with a purposeful stride to the nearest market square. Keeping her face shadowed and her body draped shapelessly with her hooded cloak, she bought three meat pastries from a shop, then scuttled outside to eat them. One she actually kept for the dog.

Thinking she could use her burgeoning Flair to grow plants in the conservatory, or even in the garden shed, and counting her pitiful gilt, she decided to buy vegetable seed packets or small plants. She waited until she saw several people enter the greenery shop. She'd already tested the place with her Flair, knew where the seed packets and sprigs she wanted were kept, and which were the best suited for her purposes. Most Noble Residences had greenhouses for fruit and vegetable propagation during the winter. Yet she lingered in the warm and pretty store, enjoying watching people and how they interacted.

She couldn't remember how long it had been since she'd been on her own in town. More than three years ago, before her marriage? How depressing. No wonder her palms dampened as she exchanged a few bland words with the busy shopkeeper when she bought her items—seeds, a sprouter, and three small plants of wheatgrass and beans.

By the time she stepped back outside, the sky had darkened to gray. To her alarm, snow began to fall before she got a block away.

A few streets later, someone called her name. "Lahsin D'Yew. I've found you."

She whirled around, saw a tough, lean man, and knew exactly who he was. The tracker. "GrandLord T'Blackthorn."

Seven

*L*ahsin bolted into an alley. *Wrong move.* It was a dead end, and the tracker, T'Blackthorn, followed her in.

Clutching the cloth sack containing her purchases tight, she set her shoulders back, lifted her chin. "I am not D'Yew. The stirrings of my Second Passage have started. I'm an adult, and I repudiate the marriage. You can't make me go back!"

The man winced and glanced a few feet behind him at the street. A couple of passersby had hesitated and were watching them. "Do you think we can discuss this privately?"

"There is nothing to discuss. I will not return. I will never return. I'm an adult, I don't have to go back." Right then and there she decided that he'd be *perfect* to hear her repudiation of the marriage.

"I, Lahsin Burdock, repudiate this marriage to Ioho Yew, GrandLord T'Yew. I, Lahsin Burdock, repudiate this marriage to Ioho Yew, GrandLord T'Yew. I, Lahsin Burdock, repudiate this marriage to Ioho Yew, GrandLord T'Yew."

T'Blacktorn stilled, his face went expressionless. "I've tracked many people, GraceMistrys Burdock—"

"Don't call me that!" She darted a glance up and down the alley. She was sure she could run faster than him. Even with her sack.

"Don't you care that your Family is worried?"

"My Family? Did the Burdocks speak with you? Did *they* hire you? Do they want me to come home to them?" She snorted.

He hesitated, and she knew if he *had* spoken with her birth Family, they hadn't done anything except express an interest that she be returned to T'Yew. Her brother Clute wasn't home for the holidays from Gael City, then. He'd be the only one who'd care.

Anger and fear and the thought of returning to an unbearable place snapped something in her. She walked up to T'Blackthorn, grabbed his hand, and *sent* the last miserable day at T'Yew's before she'd escaped. The waking in his bed and feeling him stab inside her, uncaring of her pain. Breakfast with him and YewHeir where they belittled her, yet watched with careful eyes for any sign of Passage, of burgeoning Flair they could control.

How in the afternoon, T'Yew'd assigned her a task, then interfered so she couldn't complete it, then "punished" her. All her loathing of the man. All the fear. All the wild joy at her freedom now.

She yanked her hand from his grasp, jumped back, saw T'Blackthorn was still shaking his head at her memories, her emotions, and dashed past him to the alley entrance. She shot down another narrow passage. This one had side corridors along it that went in three different directions. He might follow her, but once she was inside the garden, she'd be safe.

Wouldn't she?

She took off.

Lady, I am an honorable man. I would not take you back to that. They'd linked enough that T'Blackthorn could send her the thought. She snapped any lingering connection and ran.

This time, because the snow was thick and people sparse as the winter day came to an early end, she *could* run.

She sensed when he turned his back and strode in the opposite direction.

So she ran faster because she was free and no one would take her back to a stifling Residence and horrible FirstFamily rules.

Was T'Blackthorn an honorable man? She vaguely recalled hearing his name, but no comments about him. She'd have to think about her impulsive action, what she'd done, later. Now she hurried with her treasures to her sanctuary.

She hoped he wouldn't betray her.

*F*inally, *finally all the tests were done.* *Tinne* leaned heavily on the wash cabinet in the refreshing room, avoiding the mirror over it. He had to look gray. He *felt* gray. His hair was probably gray, too, though that might not be seen since it was usually white blond. The lines now engraved deeply on his face must be visible, though. He felt as if he'd lived lifetimes. Seven dreadful lifetimes, as a matter of fact. The physical examination had been the only one that hadn't taken any toll.

Cave of the Dark Goddess, he was weary, but at least it was over.

Everything was over, his old life, his marriage. He had no doubt what the verdict would be on the status of his relationship with his wife.

A heavy silence from the pink room pressed against the closed door to the cleansing room. Eventually he'd have to go out. He was unsure whether he could cobble enough pieces of himself together to make a reasonable facsimile of the former Tinne Holly. The Healers seemed to have broken him down into components—communications, heart, Flair, sexuality . . . Puzzle pieces that had changed and no longer fit into the life he'd had before, the man he'd been.

It was only the travail. He'd be better after a night in the T'Holly Residence HouseHeart, and he was even looking forward to that! No one would bother him there as he reassembled himself. The Residence itself would help him make sense of the past and give him strength to continue with the future.

Meanwhile, outside the door, the Healers waited to give him the bad news. Say in formal words what they all already knew. How long would they wait for him to pull himself together? He thought the passing time was coming up on a good twenty minutes. A half septhour? A septhour?

Could he possibly put everything off for a full night? Sleep right here?

No. Soon someone would call his name, and he'd have to respond.

He ran cool water in the sink again, washed his face and the nape of his neck under his hair. He ran damp fingers over his scalp, giving it a quick rub. That tight scalp against his skull was a sign of stress. He snorted.

He stood, shifted his body—thinner by a few pounds—until all his parts seemed to settle into place, and breathed deeply. Putting on a calm mask, keeping his head up, he opened the door and walked into the horrible pink room.

He faced a semicircle of very serious people. His parents. The Healers. Saille T'Willow, the matchmaker. Ailim Elder, the SupremeJudge. His chest constricted.

D'Sea sighed, straightened even more. "It is the considered opinions of myself, FirstLevel Healer GrandLord T'Heather, and GreatLord T'Willow that the marriage between Genista Furze and Tinne Holly is irretrievably broken. Genista Furze Holly has requested a divorce, and I must agree that such an action would be best for both individuals."

T'Holly flinched, Tinne's Mamá sucked in a breath, "A FirstFamily divorce," she murmured. Her hand was already in his father's, and she squeezed his fingers.

"I reluctantly agree that this marriage can be ritually dissolved," Judge Elder said.

"When?" croaked T'Holly, Tinne's father.

Tinne found his voice. "As soon as possible. Now. Tonight." He ignored his Mamá's inarticulate protest. "With as few people as possible." He glanced at his father's lined face. "I don't want you, any of my Family there."

"We must support you—" his Mamá started.

"No!" He was breathing too quickly. With effort he steadied himself, managed a smile that had to be grotesque. "I know you support me, but I can't . . ." He couldn't go on.

"We need another FirstFamily Lord or Lady other than the Healers to agree to the divorce," Judge Elder said.

The Hollys remained silent.

"Summon Furze," Tinne grated. Genista's father.

"Not necessary," a young voice said.

Everyone turned to see a boy of about twelve. Young Great-Lord Muin T'Vine. He walked from the shadows, face somber, but radiating acceptance of the event like no other there. Somehow that eased Tinne's pain. The boy was a prophet, and this whole string of experiences now smacked of fate.

"Vinni." Tinne nodded to him.

Vinni nodded back, turned to the others. "I agree that the marriage of Genista Furze Holly and Tinne Holly be dissolved."

Tinne felt something inside him crumble, understood it was more of his connection to Genista.

Clearing his throat, Vinni said, "Genista and I have reserved the small round minor-temple near Southgate for the divorce ritual this evening. It is available immediately. She is already there." He grimaced. "She didn't want me to officiate as priest and Lord, requested that Saille T'Willow do that."

Saille inclined his torso stiffly. "I can do that."

To Tinne, another layer was adding to the nightmarish day.

Vinni said, "Genista would prefer SupremeJudge Ailim Elder officiate as priestess and Lady."

Another sigh, from everyone.

Ailim nodded. "I accede to Genista's wishes."

Tinne scrubbed his face, ignored everyone except Vinni. "The temple is ready now?"

"Yes," Vinni said. He gestured to a chest behind him. "I took the liberty of requesting robes for T'Willow and the SupremeJudge."

"We three can go then." Tinne's voice sounded too rough, but he couldn't modulate it.

"Yes," Vinni said.

Tinne looked at Saille, Ailim. "Please," he said.

Saille was the first to move. He went to the chest and picked up heavy scarlet and gold robes, laid them over his arm, held out a hand to Tinne. "I know the coordinates of the temple. We can 'port there."

Ailim went to the chest, took off her purple judge's vestment, drew a shimmering silver robe over her head, and smoothed it down. She rolled the judge's covering into a small ball and put it inside her large sleeve. She stepped onto the teleportation pad, then held out her hands, one to Saille and the other to Tinne. "Shall we go?"

A great breath shuddered from Tinne. Another ordeal, but it would be the last. Thank the Lady and Lord, this would soon be all over. He walked to Ailim, careful of his steps. His knees felt weak. Then he took Saille's hand as he joined them.

Tinne nodded to D'Sea and T'Heather. "Thank you for your expertise." He didn't look at his parents, couldn't afford to.

On the count of three, he teleported to the temple.

They did it as day vanished into night.

The temple was small and shabby, falling into disrepair. The tapestries on the wall were frayed at the edges, the wooden floor scuffed. It didn't appear to be a beloved neighborhood temple, perhaps discarded for something newer.

The darkness inside the main circular room was rich—and pulsing with emotion. A large white circular pillar of light encompassed the small pentacle that Ailim Elder and Saille Willow had cast.

Tinne had stripped and held his clothes. The ritual had demanded he be nude. Saille T'Willow had inserted the knowledge of the upcoming rite, the words and actions, into Tinne's mind.

Time to do this. He walked forward. There was no grit under his feet, so he knew the temple was clean, at least.

Entering the main space, he set his clothes on the floor outside the circle, then bowed to Saille, then Ailim. She gestured for him to stand within the western starpoint. He stepped just within its bounds.

Genista, also nude, entered from the other side, standing on the eastern point. She looked different. He scrutinized her, seeing *her*, and not the image of her he carried in his mind, for the first time in a long time. She was thinner, her body not the complete voluptuous delight he'd experienced when they'd joined after wedding. Her muscles looked more toned. Well, she had been—was—had been—a Holly, exercised and fought. He'd heard that, though he'd never trained her or with her.

Her face held a few lines.

Her eyes were sad, with a haunting that he'd avoided seeing because he could do nothing to banish it, and it only reminded him of his own grief.

His cock did not rise, and that was both slightly surprising and a relief. She was a beautiful woman, his wife.

His eyes stung as his heart wrenched. He wanted to stop

this. Wanted to turn back time to when they'd loved, when they'd been a couple.

It hurt to let go.

It would hurt to go on without her.

But the past was gone.

Love was gone.

It had died, and he had fought the understanding of that, even as emptiness had filled him where love had once been.

Low chants surrounded them as Saille T'Willow, officiating as God, and SupremeJudge Ailim Elder, acting as Goddess, closed the ritual circle. The divorce ceremony had begun.

"Take off your marriage wristbands and place them here," Saille T'Willow said sternly to Genista, offering a large wooden bowl. She did.

Ailim Elder spoke to Tinne, "Take off your marriage wristbands and place them here." Tinne did, putting them into her bowl. He and Genista had chosen the wristbands carefully from T'Ash. Jewels sparkled in gold. Lost treasure.

"Greet each other," Ailim said.

They hadn't. Now his bow matched Genista's, both more martial than formal courteous bows. Neither of them said a word.

A sigh drifted on the air, Saille Willow's. "You must meet, face-to-face, press your hands to each other's." He gestured before the altar.

Again Tinne and Genista matched steps, knowing the movements of each other even as their minds and hearts had diverged.

Their palms met. Her hands were smaller than his. Her touch both familiar, and not. The feeling, the link between them was gone.

"Genista, you say your spellwords now," Saille instructed.

"Tinne Holly, go forward with your life with my blessing and the blessing of the Lady and the Lord. We are no longer one, no longer together, no longer partners or mated. Blessings upon you." Her voice was steady, though her eyes filled.

Tinne opened and closed his mouth. He didn't want to say the words, wanted to deny, fight for her. A spurt of anger came. Would he always fight? Even when he could not hope to win? Even when losing was the better thing? Why did he feel this way, unable to let go?

He had to let go. There was nothing between them but sadness and grief and hurt.

That would stop when he stopped fighting. He coughed, met her eyes again. This time they were strong and level and clear.

"Genista Furze, go forward with your life"—he sucked in a deep, hard breath—"with my blessing and the blessing of the Lady and the Lord." His words sped up. Get it over. Get it over. "We are no longer one, no longer together, no longer partners or mated. Blessings upon you!"

There wasn't even a small "snick" as their link broke. Because there was no link. Gone, and he didn't know when.

"It is done," Saille said, voice deep with regret. He moved to Tinne's right, stretched out his hands to Ailim Elder, who stood opposite. They joined hands in the space between Genista and Tinne, under their pressed palms. The priestess and priest lifted their arms to push Tinne's and Genista's hands apart.

"The bond between these two is cut," Ailim said firmly. "Clean and never to be mended."

Tinne and Genista stepped back, Saille and Ailim stepped forward, between them. Linking hands again, they held them over the marriage bands in the bowl. "We take all energy and passion from these jewels and send them on their way," the two said.

The marriage bands disappeared. Probably to T'Ash. Tinne didn't ask.

"Go your separate ways, Genista Furze and Tinne Holly," Saille and Ailim intoned. "With blessings from the Lady and Lord."

Saille turned, blocking any sight of Genista from Tinne, and handed Tinne his clothes. He dressed, knowing from the rustle across the pentacle that Genista did the same.

Back-to-back, Saille and Ailim thanked the Lady and Lord and the Guardians of the Elemental Gateways and dismissed the ritual circle.

Tinne heard Genista leave.

He didn't know what to do.

"I'm sorry for your loss," Saille said, his arm coming around Tinne's shoulders to squeeze tightly.

"I'm sorry for your loss," Ailim Elder said, standing in

front of Tinne, eyes full of tears. She put warm hands on his face and kissed each of his cheeks. "It's a sad time."

Tinne swallowed. "Yes."

He didn't think he'd ever felt emptier—of words, emotions, needs. Pain was there, though. Loss, the loss of hope, of potential, loss of self-image, who Tinne Holly was—had been—was.

His gut churned, and he didn't want to stay in this place, didn't want to ever see it again, which was probably why such a small, out-of-the-way temple had been chosen. He turned and went out the door, stopped in the shadow of the small portico when he saw Genista, dressed in a new travel suit, walk steadily down the path.

A man came out of the shadows, joined her. She didn't acknowledge him, but he walked beside her. Just before they vanished from sight, he reached for her hand and cradled it in his own. She stiffened, but she didn't pull away.

She never looked back.

Pain. Anger. Anguish filled Tinne. He couldn't bear being here, couldn't possibly say anything to Saille or Ailim, couldn't even handle seeing them.

There was only one place where he could bear to be, only one place where he could safely release the anger and pain and expect comfort. Only one place that felt remotely like home.

The Green Knight Fencing and Fighting Salon. He didn't even have to form an image to teleport. He was just there on the teleportation pad.

When he walked into the main fighting salon, conversation died. Word must have gotten out. Gossip about the First-Families and the Hollys tended to spread fast. The newssheets had probably put out a special edition.

His gut tightened. This was going to be tough, people talking about him, his personal life, judging him a failure. He'd need all his courage. Maybe he should have gone home and drummed.

No one said anything to his face, but there were quick glances, murmured asides. Tinne used his G'Uncle Tab's private dressing room to change. The glimpse he'd caught of himself in the mirrors along one of the short walls of the salon had shown he was moving stiffly, letting tension affect him. Well, wasn't that why he was here?

His fighting wear—light loose trous and shirt, with wide short legs and sleeves, in Holly green, hung in a wardrobe with his G'Uncle's. When he opened one of the two doors, the scent of the man and himself and the salon wafted out. The smell brought more memories of his life, from childhood through the last few weeks. He set his head against the closed wooden door of the wardrobe and fought back the stinging in his eyes. The scent was the same. He was not and would never be the same.

His life had changed again. He didn't know how much more he could endure.

Though he *did* know that he would have the entire support of his Family. A distant thought, and more thought than heart-feeling, but it provided a sliver of comfort.

He gathered himself together and disrobed again. He'd never needed a workout so much, to release all the negative emotions after the divorce ritual. He threw his clothes away, the second set in two days—he kept a couple of changes here and upstairs in Tab's rooms—and let the heat of the waterfall start to work on his tense muscles.

Entering the main salon, he avoided everyone, went to a corner, and limbered up. Usually he joined a group and sparred with them from the first, helped his G'Uncle teach, since the Green Knight Fencing and Fighting Salon would be his some-day as Holly SecondSon. But he felt too vulnerable, his emotions rough.

So he practiced the basic fighting patterns by himself, not quite as automatic as they should be, until his muscles loosened and flexed as they should.

Finally he glanced at those in the salon. No enemies or unfriends. A good crowd. All men. The salon drew a predominantly masculine clientele, Noblemen serious about exercising, training, fighting. Or just enjoying the company of other men, or escaping their wives . . . no, stop that thought.

Tinne bowed to the room at large, saw a knot of his contemporaries in the corner opposite him, and strode toward them.

GraceLord Fescue, a blustery man beginning to go to fat, came up to Tinne and clapped him on the shoulder. "I am sorry you had such bad luck with the woman, but you're well rid of her. We all knew she was easy to bed."

Someone's sly laugh was the last slip of the knife under his skin.

He snapped.

Eight

$\mathcal{D}$istantly Tinne knew he'd made a mistake, coming here. He lunged at the small crowd of snickering men with Fescue. Were there five? Six? He ploughed into them, his body acting, his mind filled with a red haze. His fists and feet connected with flesh. Shocks zinged up his arms and legs. His pulse raced as he dodged blows.

Shouting. Tab calling his name? He didn't know. Words made no sense.

He didn't care.

Something hard cracked against his head, and he heard wood splintering. His eyes blurred, and he fell.

He hated falling, struggled against the grayness edging his vision.

He *hated* falling.

Bodies piled atop his.

A while later he regained his senses to find himself held in the iron grips of his G'Uncle, his brother, and his father.

His father had a wild light in his eyes, a thin line of blood ran from the corner of his mouth to his chin. "Haven't had that good of a fight in a long, long time."

Tab said in a disapproving tone, "Tinne went berserk."

Tinne winced. He'd lost control. Unacceptable for a Holly man, especially a child of GreatLord T'Holly.

His father let him go, rolled powerful shoulders. "It happens sometimes."

His brother's hands fell from Tinne. Holm stared at his father just like Tinne himself. They'd been given daily lectures on the importance of remaining in control during a fight. Then he realized his father was dealing with the pain of Tinne's divorce and the scandal as much as he.

He turned to look at Holm, saw an easiness in him that Tinne could only envy. Yes, Holm was sad, grieving for a lost sister-in-law, but his life was golden again. He had his woman, his position, knew himself and his station. He'd grown during his own adversities, when his identity had been shattered even more than Tinne's. Tinne looked aside. He could only hope to come through this as confident a man as his brother.

Holm said, "Are you all right? You know we would have been at the divorce ritual had you asked—"

"We wanted it private." His tone was too stiff. He pushed his fingers through his hair—his head *was* tender—and tried a smile. "Just as our wedding was," he said. "The fewer to witness our failure, the better. It was only us and the officiants."

With a nod Holm said, "I don't think either of you failed."

Everyone appeared uncomfortable at that. Tab scanned the empty room. "Just us. The last a'the spectators jus' slunk out the door." Tab shook his head.

Holm rubbed at a bruise forming on his forehead. "Must admit we gave a good show."

Tab grunted.

After a good shake of his limbs, Holm said, "I'm feeling the fight now and would prefer to soak away my stupidity in a tub with my HeartMate." He smiled. "Then she'll tenderly Heal all my ills." He walked over to the room holding the teleportation pad, opened the door. His last look at Tinne was serious. "I'll see you later. Your rooms have been redecorated—"

Tinne flinched.

"—at great expense, but I guess we've already taken the price of it out of your hide. And I don't forget you'll be sleeping in the HouseHeart tonight, so see you at breakfast."

"Holm has the right idea," T'Holly said, not meeting Tinne's gaze. Was the man feeling guilt at setting this whole chain of events in action? That might be good for him. Or was he embarrassed that he had a loving HeartMate and Tinne had no one?

Tinne watched his father leave.

Then Tab was behind Tinne, massaging his stiff shoulders. "Ya go home now. Ya took a good shot to the head, we all had to do a little mending Flair—better'n callin' in a Healer who'da been unhappy." Tinne blinked in surprise. Tab was the only one with a little Healing Flair, and he didn't use it often. But Tinne was glad he hadn't called T'Heather or Holm's wife, Lark. He'd had his fill of Healers.

"I'm sorry that this happened," Tab said. "An' no matter what anyone else says, we all know she is a good woman, was a good wife ta ya. You were right ta defend her."

"Thanks," Tinne forced out.

"She's a better woman than she was when she wed ya. On the road to ruin afore. You thinka that when you thinka her. You didn't fail."

"I did."

"No. Sometimes folk can't rise above certain experiences. The loss of a child. That's a hard 'un."

"Yes."

"An' sometimes destiny is at work, no matter how ya fight it." One last squeeze, and Tab was done. He didn't mention that Tinne had tensed again.

"Won't be no more talk about you and her 'round here." Tab lifted and lowered a shoulder. "Gotta face it. This scandal will last a long time." He looked around. "We'll lose clients."

Tinne thumped him on the shoulder. "We'll survive. The Green Knight Fencing and Fighting Salon's been going for three hundred years." As he scanned the place, he knew despite everything he'd been right to come and that he would survive, too. Since the day he was conceived, this place had been his if he wanted it, and he'd be a part of it the rest of his life, leave it to another Holly. It survived, and so would he. "But I'm sorry that we'll lose people."

Shrugging, Tab said. "Not your fault. It's Holm Senior's, an' he knows it." Tab shook his head. "Man leads a pretty flig-gerin' charmed life most of his years, but when he makes a mistake, it nearly ruins us all. Spoiled. Always was." Tab slung an arm around Tinne's shoulder. The older man stank of famil-iar heavy sweat. Tinne choked.

Tab went on. "Whatever spoilin' Holm Junior had got knocked outta him the last few years. And you, ya' done very

well. You're a good man. Coulda said no to Genista, couldn't
ya? Kept a cold 'n' civilized marriage goin'. That's how it's
always done. But she had the grit to cut herself loose from an
unhappy life, an' you let her start new. I'm prouda you, Tinne.
Proud of the man you are. Proud ta have ya as my Heir."

"Thank you." The adrenaline that had kept him going was
fading. Yes, he'd survive. Prosper maybe. Tomorrow.

"Waterfalls for us," Tab said.

"Yes."

"Then I'm up in my rooms. You do whatever ya need to ta
take care a' yourself. Dress warmly and take your long coat."

Tinne followed him to the men's dressing room. Tab
turned into his private shower, and Tinne went to the common
waterfall.

A quarter septhour later, Tinne left the salon, nearly stumbling down the stairs. He didn't have enough energy to teleport but he wanted to be alone to *feel* who he was. The tie
with Genista had been sexual, had grown strong into a good
marriage, then weakened. Now it was gone. She was gone.

Maybe he should accept D'Sea's offer of more emotional
shock and distancing Healing.

He crossed the street to a caff house, rubbing his head.
Cocoa with whitemousse topping and cinnamon sprinkles
sounded good. A small cup, because it was rich, and he was
unsure of his belly. He pushed the door open and a few conversations stopped, but not all of them.

Some voices with avidly laced tones continued rumor-
mongering with no mention of the Hollys or Furzes. Another
scandal had already surfaced then. A trickle of a sigh escaped
him. Good.

The line at the counter was small, and he smiled but didn't
flirt with the server woman as he usually did. She was just as
pleasant as always, perhaps with a touch of sympathy he refused to let rile him.

Taking his caff to an empty table, he glanced down and saw
the new edition of the evening newssheet. A three-dimensional
holo of a pretty, gentle face stared up at him. Arched brows
over big green, heavily lashed, slightly tilted eyes, small
straight nose, and a mouth pink against the skin he'd always
thought of as peachy. The headline spoke when he touched the

papyrus—a new technology—*GrandLady Lahsin Burdock D'Yew MISSING!*

Missing! Another jolt to the heart, the gut, all the other Goddess-bless points of his wracked body, spirit, soul. His HeartMate, disappeared.

His legs folded under him, and he lit hard in a chair, and his vision narrowed to a tiny spark of light in a world gone black.

No! He fought to keep conscious.

He'd thought the day couldn't get worse. He'd been wrong, but he'd fight. He'd always fight for what he needed.

Deep, even breaths. The dark lacing his vision receded.

His heart rate was too fast. He needed to slow it down and center.

And *think*.

More, feel. Search for that single hair-thick thread that lived deep inside him, the ignored link with his HeartMate. He'd connected with her during his Second Passage at seventeen and after his last deathduel. His emotions had spiraled out with exultation and touched her sleeping mind. The innocent sleep of a girl too young to be aware of the sexual and violent nature of his needy feelings. So he'd withdrawn, not wanting to besmirch her in any way. But he'd been man enough and curious enough to search and discover who she was. To watch over her.

Then the distractions of the feud with the Hawthorns and his mother's wounding had occurred, and he'd been totally focused on those wrenching events—only to learn *too late* that her Family had married her off to one of the FirstFamily Lords. In his hurt and to help his brother, he'd married Genista.

And had tucked the tiny HeartMate link deep inside him. There was no divorce in the FirstFamilies so the only thing he'd done with regard to his HeartMate was to make sure he was never at a social occasion where they'd interact. Not that she'd attended many social events. During the whole social season the year before, when his mother had been politicking for his father to become the Captain of the FirstFamilies Council, he'd attended many parties and hadn't met her. He'd heard she'd been at the annual Elder gathering to report the progress of the starship *Nuada's Sword*. But neither Tinne nor his brother ever went there.

Tinne stared into the dregs of cocoa at the bottom of his cup. He hadn't even been aware of drinking it, certainly hadn't savored it as he'd anticipated. He licked his lips, tasted a smudge of sweet whitemousse. The drink had still warmed him.

Staring at the words of the newssheet instead of the holo of his HeartMate, he wondered how T'Yew had lost Lahsin.

Lahsin. He hadn't said her name in his mind since he'd decided to marry Genista. His mouth turned down. Now Genista's name hurt the most, and Lahsin's seemed distantly soothing, when once it had been the other way around.

He read the article. It gave little information except that Lahsin was gone. He read it again. *When* had she gone missing?

The newssheet said two days ago. Tinne's breath expelled on a bitter laugh. Once again he'd been concentrating on circumstances in his own life and missed something vital concerning his HeartMate.

He leaned back in his chair, becoming aware of sidelong glances and whispers that would have bothered him a sept-hour ago, gossip circling back to him. Now it was easy to ignore.

Tinne wiped his mouth on a softleaf he'd gotten with his cocoa, spent Flair in cleansing the cup, and sent it to the rack to be used again. Sweeping his gaze around the room, he saw people flush and avoid his glance. Some met his eyes and nodded but made no indication to speak. Fine with him.

The windows of the caff house had darkened. It was full night and winter. The day hadn't been as snowy and cold as the one before, but it was no time for a girl of seventeen to be out on her own. Fear spurted through him. T'Yew had lost her.

When a FirstFamily Lord lost someone, they contacted Straif T'Blackthorn, the Flaired tracker, to find them. Straif was the son of Tinne's father's dead sister. Tinne's cuz. Tinne frowned. Hadn't Straif been out of town on another mission?

The need to find Lahsin tugged at Tinne. He sauntered to a private scry booth, shut the door behind him. Leaning against the wall he mentally called through his Family bond, *Straif?*

Surprise from his cuz. *Tinne?*

Yes.

The divorce ritual is over then? Do you want my help?

Yes, the divorce is done. I need to speak with you on another matter.

There was hesitation in Straif's thoughts. *The last few days have been hard on you. Shouldn't you return home? Doesn't your Family await?*

Tinne didn't want to think of facing his Family. They wouldn't treat him normally for a long time. Not that he knew what normally was. *I want to speak with you on another matter.*

There was a slight hesitation. *Come, then. I will meet you in the FamilySpace.*

Right, Tinne said.

Straif gave a mental snort, that was *his* favorite word.

Can you send me some energy? Tinne braced himself.

Of course, oh, beloved cuz. Teasing now, granting a favor.

Hey, I acted as your second in your duel! Don't pretend you don't owe me.

The energy zap, then the wave of strength behind it, had Tinne lifting to his toes. Damn, but Straif was good and his Flair potent. Obviously he had been living well, was carefree, and had plenty of rest. Lucky fligger.

Tinne cleared his throat, found the sound nearly a squeak, and winced. Then he left the booth and walked with tingling soles to the corner teleportation pad. He waited as people arrived, laughing, saw him, and hurried away. He flicked the light to show the pad was in use, then 'ported to Straif's home.

Envy curled in his gut at the welcoming and comfortable FamilySpace, done in earth shades to minimize childish messes. Straif and Mitchella had a teenager and a one-year-old. Both had toys strewn here and there. This place hurt a little, too. Tinne's feelings were too damn tender in every way. But he couldn't give up his quest.

Lahsin was young and alone in the cold winter night.

"Tinne, sit down," Mitchella, his cuz's wife, said in a throaty voice. She gestured with a tip of her chin toward a big furrabeast leather sofa. She held a black lacquered tray with a huge bowl of rich-smelling stew, a thick slice of bread, and a mug of caff. His stomach grumbled, and she chuckled. "Here's some dinner. Eat up."

He sat, and she set the tray to hover over his lap with a Word, handed him an elegant softleaf. "Thank you." He looked at her as the stew cooled. She was beautiful, with red hair, green eyes, and voluptuous curves. Much the same body type as Genista. They had been called the most beautiful women in the FirstFamilies. "Thank you," he said, and it came out more coolly than he'd intended.

Her smile dimmed, and she glided toward the door. "You're quite welcome."

"Forgive me," he said, brushing fingers through his hair. "I'm saying and doing things that I, that I . . ." His voice simply dried up. He turned to his stew and began eating, ripped off a hunk of bread. He didn't care that a big piece of furrabeast seared his tongue and down his throat as he swallowed.

Mitchella had come back, he could smell her perfume, luckily not at all like Genista's. He felt her hand touch his hair, a quick, smooth kiss on his temple. "Blessings, cuz."

He grunted. "Thanks, I need all I can get."

"I'll leave you to speak with Straif." She waved, and the wood laid in the stone fireplace lit into flames. The door shut behind her.

"Nearly insulted my wife, there," Straif said.

Tinne just grunted again. "The stew's good."

"Yes, we have a good cook."

Wiping his mouth with the softleaf, Tinne glanced at Straif, who'd taken a seat on the couch, had his body angled toward him, arm stretched out on the back of the sofa. Casual, easy. A carefree, well-rested, powerfully Flaired man.

Steady dark blue eyes met his. "So the ritual went we— is over."

"Yes. It's all over. Genista left Druida." He automatically tested his bond with her. Nothing. He chewed another piece of bread, which had seemed soft a minute before but was now dry. "I think."

Straif tilted his head, his eyes narrowed. "Yes, she's gone."

Tinne stared at his cuz.

With a half shrug, Straif said, "Her bond to the Family is gone, but I know her signature, and I'd know if she were still in the city." He continued gently, "You know your Family will always take care of her."

Tinne's shoulders hunched. "It's in the marriage contract."

"And you know better than that. T'Furze has stated he won't enforce the marriage contract payments. He's deeply humiliated."

"Must be if he's forgoing gilt, especially now that he'll have to pay out more in marriage settlements because of the scandal." Tinne shifted. "But it's Genista's gilt and T'Furze would punish her with it. I want . . . she should be comfortable."

"We'll see to it," Straif said. "I thought you'd prefer to have this conversation with me instead of your father."

Tinne hissed out a breath. "Yes. Your mission for the Council go well?"

Straif hesitated a second, "Yes. I delivered her NobleGilt to the mystic-who-lives-in-the-hills. As I do every year."

There was still half a bowl of stew, but Tinne was full. He hadn't had much of an appetite for a while.

"So when did you return?"

"Yesterday."

Tinne was familiar enough with T'Blackthorn Residence to send the tray to the kitchen. He looked at his cuz, but didn't copy his open body language.

"Time enough to track and find Lahsin D'Yew. Why haven't you?"

Straif's face went blank. "Any consultation I might have done with T'Yew would have been confidential."

"Lahsin Burdock D'Yew is my HeartMate."

Straif's head jerked back as if from a blow. "Fliggering Cave of the Dark Goddess."

"That's right. The Yews must want her back. Her Flair is strong. That's why he bought her from the Burdocks. That and because he wanted a son, more children."

"You seem to understand the situation more than is generally known." Straif scowled.

"She's my HeartMate, of course I knew the circumstances of her marriage." Tinne didn't look at his cuz. "When I wed, I put her out of my mind."

Straif stood and strode to a wall, said a password, and pressed a panel, and a bar revolved from the other side of the wall into the room. He poured stiff whiskeys for himself and Tinne, came back, and shoved the glass at Tinne.

Tinne knew he couldn't afford to drink it all. Not in his condition.

"I don't like being hired by a FirstFamily GrandLord who rapes and abuses a wife that is young enough to be his Child'sChild, then expects me to find and drag the girl back when she escapes."

Nine

❤

Tinne flinched, put a hand over his eyes. The food in his belly curdled. He'd abandoned his HeartMate to a monster. He rubbed his temples. He'd been twenty and the marriage had been several days old by the time he'd heard of it. He hadn't known what to do, had been coping with his own Family crises.

He hunched over, keeping his food down with an effort. "She was fourteen. I convinced myself he wouldn't hurt her. That he might cherish her." His laugh was ugly, and he regretted he'd said anything. "Later I thought he might build a good marriage with her, as I did with Genista." He straightened, gulped the whiskey down, turned to his cuz, unable to stop the flow of words. "I abandoned my HeartMate to a monster."

"No!" Straif's tone was sharp. "You did what you thought was right." He shook his head. "You have always done that, you're that kind of man, so don't second-guess yourself now." He did a quick pace of the room. "I saw her today. Went back and told T'Yew I refused his commission. Said she'd obviously known I'd be called in, had left me a Flair message outside of Southgate. Told him that she declared herself an adult, had repudiated their marriage."

Blow after blow. Tinne leaned back against the couch, let

the whisky dull his feelings, blur his vision. "Repudiated their marriage."

"She did so, to me. As she can when she is seventeen. I spoke to SupremeJudge Ailim Elder this afternoon. Confidentially. That's law."

"There are no divorces in the FirstFamilies," Tinne said. His tongue felt heavy now. "We just suffer through our marriages."

"Seems you've learned that differently. You look like you've been mangled by a grychomp."

Tinne inhaled, let his breath out slowly, steadied his pulse. Like he'd been doing interminably the last few days.

He heard Straif gulp his drink, then his cuz said, "Since you're going after her, you have to know."

"I won't say 'thank you' for that."

"You shouldn't have to deal with this mess with Lahsin, now. Just an unlucky life, I guess. How did you screw up in your last life to deserve this?" Straif paced some more. "I swore a truth statement before the judge as to what I learned had happened to Lahsin." There was the sound of spit hitting the hearth of the fireplace, hissing of the fire. "Fliggering Burdocks to let that go on. Didn't defend a daughter of the house."

"T'Yew's a rich and powerful FirstFamily GrandLord."

"Honor should not be bought."

"High-minded," Tinne muttered. "You saw her? She's in Druida? Well?"

Straif sat again, this time stiffly. "She's well enough. But I don't know that it's a good idea for you go after her. She can't be wanting a man around her right now. Certainly didn't want *me* near her."

"You're a FirstFamily GrandLord." Tinne found a smile. His energy was returning, with the food, with the whiskey, with the determination to *fix* something rather than break something. "I'm not."

Straif snorted. "Right. You're close enough."

"I'm not as old as you, certainly not as old as T'Yew. She's in Druida? Or did she really leave by Southgate?"

"I'm not telling you."

Then something Straif said finally penetrated. Tinne tipped his glass but the liquor was all gone. "You said she declared herself an adult." His gut was clenching again.

"Yes."

"That means only one thing. She's experiencing twinges of the freeing of her Flair, of her Second Passage."

But Straif said nothing.

"Alone, seventeen, a sheltered girl. Wintertime. With an oncoming Second Passage that could debilitate her!"

When Straif turned his head, he was smiling. He stood and offered his hand, and when Tinne took it, Straif hauled him up and led him to the teleportation pad. "The Blackthorns always track their mates."

"I'm not a bloody Blackthorn, I'm a Holly!"

"But you have a link to her." He clapped Tinne on the shoulder. "Port to Squawvine Square, you should pick up her scent there. Good luck."

"Straif—"

"I can't in good conscience tell you where she is. You'll find her, and the hunt will be good for you."

"Spare me."

His cuz sighed. "Sorry, you're spared nothing right now."

T*inne teleported to Squawvine Square. It was the last* real square just north of CityCenter and the beginning of a maze of little alleys. His ancestors had built the narrow lanes between the founders' broad, straight streets a couple of generations after colonization. Celta was harsh, and the population could not fill the already designed and mostly built grand city.

The cold air was sharp and filled his lungs and cleared his head. Maybe Straif was right. Maybe having a definite, short-term goal would be good for him. Maybe being outside in the crisp air would be good for him.

Or Straif could be crazy.

In any event, Tinne didn't think any rest was possible for him tonight. Too many new wounds as well as the new shock of the abuse of his HeartMate, his guilt at not attempting to save the girl-child she'd been, bled in him.

No one should have been in the square, but he saw shadows lurking around. More likely thieves and criminals than any law-abiding folk.

He shifted his shoulders, the long coat he wore easing

around him, the cold acting on spells in the fabric that sent more warmth to him. He began to overheat, so he stood and centered himself again, regulated his breathing again, and prayed to the Lady and Lord this would be the last time he consciously did both to relieve stress.

Surely he'd find her. He couldn't fail. Once again the image of her, young, frightened, helpless, and bruised, facing her Second Passage alone, drifted through his mind. As it did so, he unearthed the deeply hidden thread between them. Examined it. A pure and shining, throbbing silver. Something he hadn't ruined.

The mind Healer D'Sea wouldn't like that idea. She and T'Heather had emphasized that the marriage was over, was twisting and causing him and Genista pain. Injury had happened *to* them as a result of living in a place cursed with his parents' broken Vows of Honor. He still felt like a failure. If he'd acted differently or sooner, he would have been able to save his marriage.

Instead of standing here on a dark winter's night, watching Cymru moon rise.

Destiny?

He wasn't hot anymore. He shivered.

He was in no condition to interact with a HeartMate, especially as a man who would be lover and husband. He was tired of being a lover and husband.

She wouldn't want that, and neither did he, now. His hurts at the hands of a beautiful woman were so new and bloody. But she was young and naive and alone in Druida in the winter, expecting Second Passage. He could offer her friendship.

Though destiny might be at work here, his free will was equally strong. *He would not hurt Lahsin in any way.* Slowly he turned a circle, saw Eire moon, the same phase, waning to a sliver, on the opposite side of the star-sparkling sky with bright veils of galaxies.

He held the connection between himself and Lahsin gently, gently in his mind. Closed his eyes to the night. Thought of the holo on the newssheet of a girl on the brink of womanhood. Since he'd deliberately avoided her, he had no newer image to focus on. He closed his mind to everything else and sent his emotions, his *heart* to encompass the bond, to *feel* it.

The connection was warm and changing from silver to a sheening metallic rainbow. Of hope. Of the future. Something he dreaded but she anticipated. Warmth was heating inside him. Comfort.

What surprised him was that he felt no fear from her. He did sense a great anger—understandably so, and if she didn't work *that* out, her Passage could go badly. Fear, yes, inside him for her. Her last Passage would have been at seven years old. She wouldn't remember it much, wouldn't know that the Second Passage would be exponentially worse.

So he thought of the link, even whispered mentally to it. *Take me to her. To my Heart—to Lahsin.*

Trusting his Holly instinct, he followed the slight tug in the center of his chest.

He wound through passages so narrow they admitted only one person. Alleys twisting through buildings that blocked everything but a slice of night sky. He walked a long time, sensing he was going ever northward. But not west to the boundary of Druida City, where the six-kilometer-long starship *Nuada's Sword* sat on the cliffs above the Great Platte Ocean. Not due north to Northgate, the city exit to the Great Labyrinth and the fishing communities beyond it.

Northeast. He couldn't picture northeast Druida.

His feet tired, and he was glad he'd worn sensible boots to the testing, to the divorce ritual. Had that all happened on this day? The fullness of events of the day was stretching time, blurring the clarity of his memories. A blessing. His steps slowed as he came to a dead end at a tall wall of about six meters. Not the city wall raised by the founding colonists in large gray stone blocks but a brick wall, ruddy and stained, with a tangle of plant life climbing on it. Huge bare tree branches rose behind the wall, so that he had to tilt his head back. The wall was certainly not four centuries and nearly a decade old. But close . . . there was a sheen to the brick that spoke of ancient, strong Flair. Power that had been used so often and so long that it seeped into the walls and regenerated itself.

Squinting, he scrutinized the area. He didn't know this place. When he tried to think hard about it, his thoughts themselves became . . . slippery. He blinked and forced himself through the brush to touch the wall. It felt warm. Who lived behind the wall? All of the great Nobles he knew had estates in Noble Country, in the west of Druida. No one lived in the northeast.

Again he deliberately tested his link with Lahsin. Was it growing stronger with use? Probably, and he didn't know how he felt about that.

She was definitely behind the wall. Anticipation bloomed inside him. Success.

One action he'd taken lately that had harmed none, not even himself, that had resulted in success.

The feeling of accomplishment was a small treasure in itself. The tug was to the south. He went that way, and several meters along he stopped and pressed his hand to the wall. Significantly warmer. What would heat a wall? He didn't know.

The wall was curved. The city walls of Druida were straight, despite the landscape. North, east, and south stone walls marched in a line. To the west was the ocean.

Tinne followed the concave wall and touched it again several meters to the north of the alley he'd originally exited from. The wall was as cold as any regular brick wall in the winter would be.

He walked south, welcoming the pull on his bond with Lahsin, the warmth from the wall. Plant growth burgeoned because of that warmth, spreading a few centimeters from the wall, then stretching a full meter.

His breath came in huffs of steam. Plants grew lusher to his left. Ragged edges of buildings and the crevices between them were to his right, dark and cold and deserted.

He'd passed the last of her trail behind a thin tangle before he realized it. Easier just to walk backward a few paces than turn. He was losing energy.

The cold and the strain of tracking in the night were working on him. Nothing more.

He saw the small door, inset deep in the wall, went and touched the latch. The trace of her zinged to his toes. He pressed down. The door didn't open. He set his shoulder against the door and shoved. Again. Harder. Then stepped back, panting from emotional upset more than the physical effort, and stared.

He scented her. The faintest fragrance of fragile spring blossoms. She was in there, and he couldn't get in!

It was the last straw. The day crashed in on him, draining the last of his strength. He sagged against the door. As soon as he closed his eyes, images flashed before him, the room in T'Heather Residence. He shuddered.

D'Sea's and T'Heather's and T'Willow's faces as they confirmed his marriage was over. His parents' expressions. He groaned.

Genista, naked and beautiful, unreachable during the divorce ceremony. Not his. His lack of reaction to her. His breath sounded loud in his ears.

Feelings tumbled after the images, feelings he would never forget.

Guilt.

Relief.

Despair.

His heart wrenched, and the door opened to him. He smelled the rich scents of a garden estate, and it was warm. He could again feel Lahsin—and no distress or upset from her—but Lord and Lady help him, he had to concentrate on his unraveling self.

He staggered along a path. Despite the undergrowth no root or brush tripped him, which was good, because he thought once down, he would not be able to rise again.

A few minutes later he came to a clearing with a steaming hot spring confined in an elegant pool of curves before him. He saw the coat of arms on a pillar that was part of a grape arbor, that was gray in the twinmoonslight, probably gray in the daylight, too. *BalmHeal.*

That name explained everything.

There'd been much talk among the FirstFamilies when Ruis Elder finally told his whole story after becoming Captain of the starship *Nuada's Sword*. Since Tinne's and his brother's lives had been radically changed by touching Ruis Elder's life, they had been allowed to hear Ruis's tale, too.

This was the lost FirstGrove, the sanctuary of Druida and Celta.

The mist rising from the heat of the pool made the air too warm for his coat. He took it off. The place both soothed his heart and hurt it. A lost, untended garden, as lost as he was, as forsaken as he was.

Still no fear coming from Lahsin. He supposed it was enough to know she was here, safe.

He went to a bench, sat down, and put his head in his hands.

Ten

All the aches and pains of *Lahsin's* escape the previous morning and unaccustomed physical activity hurt even worse tonight. She stretched and actually heard some of her joints pop. Giggled.

Glancing around the room, she was pleased at its cleanliness and warmth. She'd made a temporary home in the largest of the three rooms of the clocktower-stillroom building. Permamoss had been available for a bed, and the walls still held housekeeping, warmth, and light spells. Luxury. She'd moved the drying trays to the edge of the room, bunched and hung herbs. Most were too old to be anything but faded decoration with a hint of scent. The little fuss of settling into her own space.

She'd never really had her own space.

Both this room—the middle one—and the smaller storage room had doors to the outside. The herbal preparation room, the stillroom, didn't. She had both doors closed.

Continuing with her crazy pity, she'd carved a large piece of bedsponge and put it in the storage room, along with the meat pie she'd bought for the dog. She left the outer door of that room open and announced mentally to the beast—the dog—that he could stay here. When she'd activated the spells, they'd swept through the whole building, even the clocktower.

She'd walked up to the conservatory and around the house, but hadn't gone in. Something about its brooding manner told her she'd have a Residence on her hands. An abandoned Residence. Who knew what that would have done to a sentient house?

But she was sure the conservatory would provide a good place for her to grow her fruits and vegetables. The glass structure had emanated both Growing and Healing Flair.

Now she had other needs. Like a long soak in a Healing spring. Her own Healing spring! As good as any HealingHall.

The clocktower and the stillroom were halfway across the garden from the Healing pool, so if she wanted to return to warmth and security at a reasonable time, she should leave now.

A few minutes later she saw a male figure sitting on the bench near the pool. Through some trick of the twinmoonslight he was clear. A man dressed in Noble fashion with his head in his hands. His posture spoke of despair.

What could a *Nobleman* be doing here? One who had enough gilt to make any problems go away?

Should she stay or run back to the stillroom? Was she going to be a coward for the rest of her life? Wasn't it time to face her fears and overcome them? She was on her own now and considered an adult. May as well act like one.

Daring, she walked around the end of the pool to the middle of the same side he was on, though he'd have to move fast to catch her. From the weary slump of his shoulders and the tiredness he radiated, she didn't think he could do that.

"Greetyou," she said, not adding her name.

He stood, and she saw he was young, no more than a handful of years older than she was. His lips formed her name, "Lahsin," but he didn't say it. Didn't say anything. Her heart sank. If this man knew her name, she was all over the newssheets.

He made a half bow, and the twinmoonslight caught on the thick silver of his hair. That intrigued her. What color was his hair in the daylight—prematurely gray or a bright blond? She could only tell that his eyes were a light color.

"Greetyou, GentleLady," he said. "Would you share—" He wobbled and collapsed more than sat onto the bench. "I was going to say you could share my bench if you wanted company." His half smile was rueful. "But I seem to be occupying most of it and, no offense, but I don't think I want to move for a while." His words were slightly slurred. Not drunk, she didn't think, but pure exhaustion or emotional trauma. Desperation.

He was being courteous. At what cost to himself, she didn't know, but it awed her a little.

His wave was more trembling fingers than sophisticated gesture. "But you can have the next bench."

She nodded.

He tilted his head, blinked, and she wondered if he was blinking fatigue away. Maybe he was as wary of her as she was of him. That was a novel notion, but before she had time to consider it, he said, "I see you'd planned to use the hot spring." He seemed to realize his pronunciation wasn't precise and his next words were slow but well formed. "The water is not simply a hot spring but a Healing pool?"

"Yes," she said.

"And I've interrupted you. My apologies." He moved his feet deliberately, setting them under his body in preparation for standing.

She put out a hand. "No, don't rise. The pool is large enough and the night dim enough for modesty."

"Modesty." He shook his head. "Not prized in our culture, or by our class. I'm used to nudity, but I see that a girl like you is not. I'll shut my eyes while you disrobe." He lowered his lashes, leaving Lahsin with a dilemma. She'd bathed often enough with both sexes of the Burdock Family, but that was years ago, before her body had developed. Since then only T'Yew, and occasionally Taxa, had seen her naked. And T'Yew had made her feel—not right, and very vulnerable.

But she'd decided to face her fears and do the opposite of T'Yew's expectations. So she stepped into a pillar's shadow and skimmed off her clothes, saying, "The pool's big and the light dim, and the best spot for Healing aches is this section."

"Truly?" He sniffed, but his eyes were still shut. "Smells bracing."

She dropped her clothes and the small stained but clean hand towels she'd found in the stillroom, then slipped into the water. Immediately the heat and the spells loosened her muscles, worked on her bruises.

He gave a low moan, and she shot into the deeper water of

the pool, but he'd only subsided into a horizontal heap on the bench. "I don't suppose you would let me share the Healing effects?"

Lahsin hesitated, but his dark, rumpled shadow didn't move. He didn't seem at all interested in getting his hands on her in any way. Or returning her to T'Yew or the Burdocks. He was preoccupied with his own problems.

The garden would let no one in who wasn't desperate, she reminded herself. It was the magic of the spellshields on the walls. She hadn't had time to study them, but she would—and she would reinforce them. They weren't like any spellshields she'd ever experienced. She thought they'd evolved themselves.

"You are welcome to share the pool," she said quietly. When his limbs twitched, she could tell he'd heard.

He heaved himself up and flung off his clothes as if they suddenly restricted him, or they'd been on a long time, and was nude. His back was to her and the twinmoonslight showed a fine, muscular man. A little too thin, she could see his ribs, then he shifted, and she gulped water. His body was very scarred.

Before she could react, he'd strode to the pool and dived in, gliding away to the far end. She heard tiny plashes of a head surfacing or an arm or leg cutting through the water. He swam well, and she sensed he was a natural athlete. She paddled to an indented curve of the pool near her clothes and activated churning bubbles by tapping a stone. The water was neck high and buoyant. She saw the flash of his body opposite her as he swam to the other end, looking as if he was circling it, exploring its dimensions. As she soaked, the sounds of his movement came less. The Healing spring was giving his muscles back their grace.

When he was a couple of lengths away from her, he veered into the center, then passed where she was and settled near his bench. Bubbles erupted from that area. They smelled differently, and she noted that for further investigation.

His voice carried easily over the water. "My thanks, GentleLady. This has been the best I've felt for days." The words still slurred but were laden with sincerity.

For the first time she wondered who he was, but since she hadn't given her own name, she couldn't request his. She didn't recognize him, though she had a hazy idea he looked like someone she'd met. She hadn't gone out much before her marriage, and since then, she'd rarely appeared in society and only with T'Yew and Taxa.

The water worked on Lahsin, made her curiosity a mild musing. She soaked until she felt fine. She lifted her arms from the water to grab the small lip of the pool and saw that the last of T'Yew's finger bruises were highlighted by the twinmoonslight.

A sharp breath from the visitor. His gaze fastened on her forearms and seemed to flash with fury, then he glanced aside. More silence, not uncomfortable. They had both found their way to this place, had that much in common.

Finally he turned and swam to the steps near his clothes and walked from the pool. Again she saw the shape of him. He was a beautiful man, excellently proportioned, with young, firm flesh. Not her FatherSire's age like T'Yew.

But her visitor was a *man*, fully an adult. A Nobleman, and if she let herself, she could *feel* his Flair. Her heart jumped a little in her chest. He could give her information on Second Passage! Was the fact that she might be suffering Second Passage in the newssheets? She rose from the pool, took her clothes, and stepped deeper into the shadows to dry off. She didn't know if he watched, but his matter-of-factness about his own nudity had made her feel less awkward. She had that to thank him for.

She pulled on her cape, ready to run if he came after her.

But he'd dressed and sat heavily on the bench, hair wet and slicked, apparently not noticing the cold. The soak in the pool might have eased his physical bruises, but it was evident that his spirit was the most damaged thing about him.

He glanced at her, and his stare went to her arms, so intent that she could almost feel her bruises burn.

"I could teach you self-defense."

She stared at him.

"Fighting," he said.

Her eyes widened. The thought had never occurred to her. Personal spellshields, yes, physical fighting, no. She'd never had the slightest chance against T'Yew. Not before, but now she was bigger. She flexed an arm.

"It can be all in leverage and using their weight against them," the man continued.

Using T'Yew's weight against him. Oh, she liked that
idea! But she scrutinized the Nobleman. She'd have to let him
get close to her to learn such a thing. She shook her head.

He smiled with lopsided charm. "Not tonight. I'm too blown
tonight." His smile turned wistful, and he looked into the distance, focusing on something only he could see.

She cleared her throat. "Who *are* you?"

Blinking, he met her eyes, and his gaze seemed to warm
her—she might be able to connect with this man, but didn't
want to.

Bowing with some grace, he said. "Beg pardon." He drew
in an audible breath. "You wouldn't have heard," he said,
stopped.

Lahsin's heart thumped hard. What hadn't she heard? Something about her father—his heart was weak. Or her brother?
Had he returned to Druida, was he looking for her? How had
her actions affected her Family? She hadn't thought much
about that, instead she had focused on escaping. She shoved
guilt aside. She'd done what she'd had to. She forced her cool
lips to say, "What?"

The man's shrug was from nearly hunched shoulders.
Probably undoing all the benefits of the pool. "I'm Tinne
Holly. My wife and I divorced today."

Her mouth fell open, until she was aware of cold air on
her tongue and closed her jaw. "There's no divorce in the
FirstFamilies," she said in a thin voice. Her repudiation of her
own marriage was unusual enough. The old book had cited
only five cases.

"There is now," he said. His voice was louder, rougher, but
didn't scare her. He wasn't looking at her. A grimace that was
supposed to be a smile. "All legal and on the law books and
everything. The seven tests—" He stopped again.

"Seven tests?"

"Of both of us to determine whether our marriage was
broken, whether we bonded well with each other on various
levels." He dropped the grim smile, frowned. "Be glad you
only need to repudiate your marriage." Then he shook his head
and looked around. "But you're here, too, so that couldn't
have been easy. FirstGrove lets in only the desperate." Something between a grunt and a sigh escaped him. "I'll leave
soon, though I'm sure I'll find my way back. Despite their

well-meaning love, my Family will pick at me, and the scandal is horrendous, no going out in public *this* Yule holiday season for any of us. Maybe host a party and see who comes, only our allies, I s'pose, an' I don't want to socialize with them, either." His voice slurred again, and he nodded in weary determination. "This place is a godsend."

"Goddess-send," Lahsin corrected.

"That, too." He linked his hands and stretched his arms. For the first time since she'd escaped, Lahsin was focused on someone other than herself, her curiosity piqued. It felt good, took her out of herself, reminded her that there was a whole world outside the walls full of people like her with problems.

A horrendous scandal. Divorce in the highest ranks of the land had to be. *Any* divorce was unusual and a scandal, would smear the Family for ages. She felt guilty for her own fascination.

His grimace still held a glint of the famous Holly charm. "My scandal's a little newer than yours. Or a little older, and overlapping. But fresh events will bring it to the headlines tomorrow." His smile became stiff. He rolled his shoulders. "I can bring a newssheet when I come tomorrow night."

That sounded far too much like a real plan of contact with another person.

"Bring newssheets," he mumbled and glanced up and down the pool. His eyes narrowed as he scanned the area around them. "BalmHeal FirstGrove Sanctuary. Good."

"You've heard about here?"

Again the flashing smile. "Yes."

She wanted to ask how widespread the knowledge was.

"Captain Ruis Elder lived here for a while, so did the boy Shade," Tinne said.

Lahsin trembled at the name of the most infamous murderer of their time. Shade had killed T'Yew's wife. If he hadn't . . . Lahsin shivered again.

Her visitor cocked his head, as if he saw her reaction. "Don't worry. The FirstFamily Lords and Ladies tried to find this place." Another unamused smile. "Cap'n Elder wouldn't tell 'em where it was. I don't think they got near it, and from what I know of the spellshields, it'll continue to keep 'em out. All but the desperate. Though occasionally there is a desperate FirstFamily Lord or Lady, I'd imagine."

Lahsin didn't know what to say. The longer she stood, the colder she got. She should return to the stillroom down the path she'd already cleared. She dipped a slight curtsy, knowing her cape would make her look graceful even if she bobbled the action.

"Merry meet," she said formally.

He inclined his head. "And merry part."

When she didn't add the last, he continued, "And merry meet again, Lahsin D'Yew." He'd have learned her name from the newssheets.

"I'm not D'Yew."

"Lahsin Burdock, then. Later." He vanished, teleporting home. T'Holly Residence? Lahsin shivered from more than the cold and hurried down the path. She knew more about the Hollys than she did about other Nobles. T'Yew and Taxa had resented the Family's preeminence and charm. The Yews had gone on and on about the Holly curse, which they believed was richly deserved because of the stupidity of T'Holly making an impulsive Vow of Honor, which he later broke.

Taxa had nearly gloated in satisfaction when the worst had happened—one of the Holly daughters-in-law had miscarried. With a jolt that had her stumbling, Lahsin realized it had been Tinne Holly's wife. His former wife.

They'd lost a baby. How hard. Now Tinne was here. Lahsin had heard that Genista Holly was a very beautiful woman, another bit of relief trickled through Lahsin. He wouldn't want her.

But he was a fighter, he *could* teach her to fight. If she dared let him get close.

Eleven

His ruse of being slow and weak had worked. It had been easy to let his tongue falter, his body hunch with muscles stiff from trauma. Lord and Lady knew his heart, mind, spirit, and soul had been pinched and prodded and measured enough in the last couple of days that they would affect his body.

Tinne leaned against the basement corridor wall of the T'Holly Residence's, a fortress's, secret teleportation pad. Even though it was known only to the Family, there were plenty of fortifications between the portal and the HouseHeart and Family suites. He'd recalled in his stupor that he didn't want to 'port to his rooms or to the main part of the house.

He pushed away from the wall, staggered down the hall on weak legs toward the HouseHeart. He tested his small link with Lahsin, she was safe and warm.

He had excellent night sight and had peeked when she'd gotten out of the pool. He hadn't seen any other bruises on her except those on her arms, and for that he was grateful. A flood of anger had deepened his vision to nothing but a red wave at a man who'd bruise a delicate lady. He was glad he was too tired to impulsively hunt down T'Yew.

All his emotions were raw, his nerve endings seeming on the surface of his skin. He could barely walk he was so exhausted, but he was reluctant to enter the HouseHeart. This, of all places of the Residence, should feel comfortable. Instead he wished he was back in FirstGrove. With Lahsin.

He flinched in alarm. He didn't want to forge ties with her. He was too tender now, as was she. But she'd looked well . . . except for those bruises that fliggering bastard T'Yew had put on her. Bruises on her body that he sensed matched wounds to her inner being.

His heart jolted as a shadow separated from the hall floor. He whipped out his blazer.

Greetyou, FamMan, Ilexa said.

The adrenaline surge jolted him from stupor. He managed a nod. "Greetyou, Fam." Then he lurched to the left, smacked the wall with his shoulder, and decided to lean against it.

Beloved Fam, she corrected.

Tinne suppressed a sigh. Those words were years old, but he wouldn't argue. "Greetyou, beloved Fam." His throat felt better than it had for the last couple of days. The steam from the pool, he supposed.

Ilexa sat in the middle of the narrow hall, to progress he'd have to jump over her. He wasn't quite sure he'd clear her. She tilted her head. *You do not look good.*

Could always trust a cat to be honest about a bad state.

I tracked you all over town tonight, she whined.

"I'm sure when you returned here, a prodigal Fam, you had an excellent dinner."

She brushed a paw over her whiskers and gave a small burp. *Went to small temple, then to CityCenter and the Green Knight, then to Noble Country and T'Blackthorn's, then all over northeast Druida, and finally to the Safe Place for the Wounded.*

Tinne winced as his route was listed. No wonder he was tired. Not only had he endured an eternal emotional journey, but he had been all over the city.

I waited long, then came here and only had a little nibble.

He knew better than to apologize to a cat. "Is that rare furrabeast on your breath?"

Her eyes shifted.

He moved forward with a solid, steady pace. At the last instant she jumped past him, high enough that he was impressed with her energy.

I will stay in the HouseHeart with you tonight, she offered.

"Good of you."

"Yesss," she vocalized.

It wasn't much of a duty for her. The HouseHeart was another sanctuary, one made specifically for those of Holly blood. And his Fam loved him. He could feel waves of affection coming from her, and beneath that, a deep tinge of concern.

So he walked to the HouseHeart door deep in the bowels of the Residence, lower even than the storage rooms. At the threshold, he disrobed as was custom, then bumbled through the small ritual to gain access to the chamber.

He barely made it inside and answered the soft greeting of the core of the Residence, the voice of his mother when young, before the sheer comfort of the place brought him to his knees on the sweet grass and he descended into sleep.

*H*e *woke in the HouseHeart and felt good. Oddly, the* first image that wafted to his mind was the black and silver silhouette of a slight young woman. Lahsin. A pretty girl. Not at all lushly beautiful like Genista. And when he probed the spot that would have held his wife he felt a . . . blankness.

Not pain that he'd loved her but guilt and confusion, an ache for the past and the lost babe, the good life they could have had. And for Genista . . . an odd relief. He would not see her hurting and be unable to help anymore.

He also recognized D'Sea's mind distancing Healing. No doubt she left some subliminal commands that would work on him, too, particularly when asleep or meditating. He shrugged, part of the price for the divorce.

His mouth twisted, the scandal was still to be weathered. Eventually shame would fade, but the smear would stick to him for the rest of his life. Be written up in history books. The first FirstFamily divorce.

Tinne Holly had not been able to please his wife and keep her.

Ilexa purred and butted against him and nearly knocked him off his feet. *Every day will be better. When I left I was sad, and I missed you, but every day got better, and I knew that someday the curse would be gone and I could come home.*

Philosophical bits from his FamCat first thing in the morning. Ugh. So he grunted and patted her head. "I missed you, too, I'm glad you're back."

He dreaded leaving the HouseHeart. Here, where generations of his Family had meditated or worshiped or taken a quiet moment, was a sense of peace nowhere else in the busy Residence.

He teleported up to his rooms, and his mouth dropped open. They were completely redecorated. He'd forgotten. No pink but bright enough colors that he winced. Whoever in their right mind would think he'd want deep red walls accented with gold? Did he see deep green, too? What? Was he living in a Yule treasure box for the rest of his life? And they'd hidden his drums!

All his life he'd liked the pale blue gray of his walls, the soft gray accents of chairs, the occasional black pillow. Staggering to the nearest chair—a burnished gold brocade with, Lord and Lady help him, a subtle orange tint in the weave, he wondered how he could possibly live here.

Without thinking he said, "Scry Mitchella D'Blackthorn. Immediately." He had to ask the Residence because he hadn't located the scrybowl in all the glittery gimcracks.

A holo of Mitchella formed over a red cloisonné bowl with a gold rim. "Here," she said.

"What did I ever do to you that you'd inflict this on me?"

She winced. "Your father insisted. He's very proud of the effect."

"Perhaps it was a good thing he never updated the Residence from his FatherSire's time," Tinne muttered. "I hadn't thought so before, but . . ." A movement caught his eye. "Ilexa, what are you doing?" He stared. She was fighting a cylindrical pillow as big as she, ripping at the thick strands of gold tassels. Too late to save the prey, he turned back to Mitchella and her pained expression. "A dark blue would have been nice," he said.

"I had in mind rich brown and cream," Mitchella said.

"I could have lived with that." But when he said the words, he doubted it. He'd lived in this Residence all of his life except for a few days at the Blackthorns'. The HouseHeart was good, it was too much of all generations, but the rest of the Residence reflected his father and Mamá. Could he live here?

Wasn't he loitering in this carnival of a room and talking to Mitchella because he didn't want to step out of the door?

"I can't stay here," he said abruptly. "Just can't."

Mitchella coughed. "Your Family's offering comfort."

"I can't stand their pity." Nor that in Mitchella's eyes, so he looked away.

"I'm sure what with the awful scandal, that your Family would prefer you show solidarity and stay."

"I can't live here." His teeth hurt. He was clenching his jaw too tightly. He met her eyes. "Find me someplace else."

Her gaze flickered past him, but he saw an idea spark.

"What?" he demanded.

"I hesitate to bring it up, since you don't seem to appreciate the garish—the bright, but the Turquoise House is still empty. You know, the house becoming a Residence. I've been using it as a show home. It's furnished and longs for inhabitants." There was silence as she watched him rake his hair with his hands. "It might be good for you both if you—"

"I'm not a damn project!" Fligger. "Beg pardon."

"Your feelings are tender," she said.

Womanspeak. Let her believe whatever she wanted, say whatever she wanted, as long as she did what he wanted. He thought of the Turquoise House. Bright, at least on the outside. In a part of Noble Country very close to upwardly mobile middle class, a shabby neighborhood. People might just let him alone.

Ha.

But they wouldn't be knocking on his door every two minutes.

"Tinne?" His Mamá called from beyond the door. "Breakfast is ready."

Another breakfast with his loving Family. He didn't know that he could survive the pity, or Holm's teasing to cheer him up, or his Mamá and father's political strategizing to minimize the scandal. He'd rather stay here and pound his drums, when he found them.

Ilexa trotted up, purring wildly, four golden tassels in her jaw. *Dead, dead, dead.*

He glanced around to see stuffing spread all over the room, the pillow shredded. Definitely dead. "I'll take the Turquoise

House," he said to Mitchella. "Send me a rental agreement at the Green Knight Fencing and Fighting Salon in a septhour." He'd break away from here as soon as possible.

Mitchella smiled, and it had no smugness, and especially no pity. He smiled back, bowed. "My thanks."

"You're welcome."

Breakfast was endurable. He took no part of the conversation and stood after he'd shoveled in eggs and toast and porcine strips. "Father, Mamá, I thank you for your heroic efforts in redecorating my suite." He ignored his brother's smirk. "But I have decided it would be better for us all if I lived separately for a time." He took in a big breath. "I will be moving to the Turquoise-House-Becoming-a-Residence owned by cuz Mitchella. Hopefully most of the scandal will follow me."

"Tinne, we need your support, and you need ours," his Mamá said. "We should stay together."

"I need to be alone for a while."

Lark frowned. "Your Healing program is dependent on weekly sessions in the HouseHeart."

Tinne waved a hand. "Fine, I'll return for that, for Family rituals, for a few meals, but right now I need to live alone."

"But you've never lived completely alone!" his Mamá protested, and her words hung in the silence.

Holm put a hand on Tinne's shoulder. "Let the man be."

T'Holly rubbed his face with his hands. "Go if you must." His voice was muffled.

Lark and Tinne's Mamá shared a look. "I'll scry D'Sea, the mind Healer, for her advice on this," Lark said.

His Mamá pleaded, "We only want the best for you."

"It's best I'm alone." He looked at the timer on the wall, and a corner of his mouth kicked up. "The Green Knight is starting a new beginning course today. Whether or not we get any students, Tab will expect me there." He went and kissed his Mamá's cheek, saw she held hands with his father. Met his father's sad eyes and kissed him, too, on the cheek, which brought a fleeting smile from the man.

Holm had followed him, kept in step as Tinne went to the teleporter. They embraced before Tinne stepped back.

"Do what you need to do," Holm said. An arrested expression came to his eyes. "You know, I've never lived alone."

Lark, his wife and HeartMate, glided up to him, linked arms with him. "Don't you think you ever will, either."

Holm grinned down at her. "Guess not."

But Lark's gaze was troubled as she looked at Tinne. "I'll call D'Sea for your Mamá's sake, but if you're sure—"

"I'm sure. Like I said, I'll be here for the HouseHeart sessions, rituals, some meals. I am not disinheriting my house."

"Right," Holm said.

"See you later," Tinne said and 'ported directly to his G'Uncle Tab's private pad. The minute he arrived he heard voices, which was surprising, since he'd been as sure as Tab that the salon would be shunned, especially for a beginning class. No one new would come.

Curiosity tickled him as he walked from the private space into the main salon itself and then to the outer waiting room. There he stopped and scanned the room where some teenaged boys lounged. The next generation of Nobles: Laev Hawthorn—son of Tinne's father's once enemy, was the oldest at nearly seventeen, he'd be having his Second Passage in a few months. Then there was Antenn Blackthorn and several Clover lads—an up-and-coming Commoner House—in their mid-teens. Muin "Vinni" T'Vine, the GreatLord boy prophet, was the youngest at twelve.

Tab said, "Let's get you sorted out. Laev Hawthorn, never thought I'd live to see the day a Hawthorn would grace my salon, welcome. You'da been havin' lessons at home."

"That's right," a man said, stepping from the shadows in the corner of the room. He bowed with not much style. "Cratag Maytree. I've been teaching him what I know, but it's rough and ready. We've had a fencing instructor from a lesser house teaching Laev, but I don't think it's stuck."

"It will stick from us," Tab said. He crossed to the man and offered his arm for a greeting clasp. Maytree seemed surprised, but complied, hand to elbow. The man was larger than Tab and much younger, about Holm's age.

Tab nodded. "We know who you are. Glad to meet here insteada over feuding blades. Tinne?"

So Tinne came forward and managed to meet the eyes of the man who'd been the Hollys' main target during the Hawthorn-Holly feud. Cratag's grip was strong and firm, but he applied no pressure to impress. "Greetyou," Tinne said, squeezing the man's rocklike forearm, then dropping his hand.

He turned to look at the boys. "So you all decided to be the Green Knight's newest class."

Antenn Blackthorn, adopted by Tinne's cuz Straif Blackthorn, stuck out his chin. "Vinni talked us into it. Said we should come. Said we will all be doin' business and such in the future so we'd better start learning about each other now."

Everyone looked to Vinni, the youngest, but Vinni was staring at Tinne. Tinne saw his eyes change colors from hazel to green, become intense, probe him. He even felt the wisp of a connection. Vinni had seen something in the future that had concerned Tinne, something that had prompted him to bring these boys to the Green Knight. Tinne wrenched his gaze away.

Hands on hips, Tab surveyed the new students, glanced at Vinni who had flushed. "Interestin' boy you are, Vinni." That's all he said about what Vinni might have seen in a prophecy.

Tab continued, "We have to sort you out. Laev, here, has had some trainin', and probably knows some good street fightin' but not much of the duello."

Laev straightened to his full height. "My MotherSire is a Grove. Groves don't feud."

Another snort from Tab. "The Green Knight will teach you to recognize when you should talk and when you must fight. We will teach you to fight when you have no choice, teach you to defend yourselves and your Families and your homes." Tab rolled into the opening lecture he'd given to hundreds of students in his forty years of teaching, after he'd retired from the sea.

Tinne said, "You're right, Tab." He bowed formally. "We must determine the skill levels of our new students." He gestured to the Clovers. "From what I hear, the Clover boys have rough-and-tumble fights often."

"We will teach them proper technique," Tab said, no hint of the sea in his voice, now. "Give them formal training. We already have three of your Family in the school. Two boys and a girl. No girls here today."

Vinni said, "I don't know many girls." He glanced at the others. "None of us have sisters."

"I do," Antenn said. "But she isn't close to my age."

"We have plenty of girls in the family," said one of the Clovers, sticking out his chest. They were one of the few prolific families on Celta. "But none of them wanted to come."

"A boys' class will do well enough," Tab said philosophically. He went over to stare at Antenn, and the boy straightened from his casual slump. "I've been askin' your dad to send ya to me for the last two years." He rubbed his hands. "But Mitchella wouldn't have it." He smiled. "Now you're mine."

Antenn paled.

"You recall anything from your days in the Downwind gang?" Tab asked bluntly.

Swallowing, turning even whiter, Antenn said, "No, sir, but I've been fighting with the Clovers for a while."

"No gang moves to unlearn, just boy stuff, should be fine," Tab said. He glanced at the others. "We all know everyone else's history here. But what determines status within these walls is nothin' but fightin' skill." He tapped his thumb against his chest. "I'm the Master, what ya would call FirstLevel in other professions." He swept a hand in Tinne's direction. "Tinne, here, is also FirstLevel."

He hadn't known. He swallowed surprise.

"T'Holly and Holm HollyHeir may drop by, too. Holm is second to me, T'Holly is third, Tinne is fourth. That's our standing."

Another surprise. Holm had overtaken their father. Tab's cool gaze met Tinne's. "Ya all can figure out why T'Holly slipped in the rankings. Think about it. Other life decisions affect *everything*." An oddly delicate way to refer to a broken Vow of Honor that led to a curse.

Tab continued, "While you're here there'll be no gossip about others' scandals. If any of you have a problem with anyone else, say so now. Tinne, you gotta a problem with Laev?"

Tinne blinked at the handsome boy with the Groves' height, the blue shading to purple eyes of the Hawthorns. The boy who had nearly killed Tinne's Mamá. But Laev had been a fearful, untrained child. "No," he said and bowed slightly to the boy who would be a FirstFamilies GreatLord. "I actually forgot." So many other extreme experiences had occurred since then. Though that one action on Laev's part had led to all the rest, the stupidity of Tinne's father. But T'Holly was a grown man.

"Laev," Tab said. "You got a problem with Tinne?"

Tinne flinched. He'd forgotten *that*, too. He'd killed the boy's father. Laev didn't look at him. "No, sir. It was a duel—"

"Both events were street melees," Tab said flatly. "In street melees anyone can live and anyone can die."

"That's right," Cratag rumbled. "The three of us were there, me, Tab, Tinne. Your father wounded Tinne near fatally, and Tinne killed your father. That's how it went. Could've been the other way around." He shrugged. "Anything can happen in a street fight. A child can wound a woman with a blade he didn't know was poisoned. A foot can slip and you're dead. That's the reason you're here, to make sure that if you ever have to duel, ever have a feud called on you, you're trained the best that you can be, and mistakes . . ." He shrugged again.

". . . are minimized," Tinne finished. The Clover boys were looking at the Nobles, fascinated. The mixture of Noble and Commoner would be all to the good.

"You have a problem with Tinne, Laev?" Tab repeated.

This time the boy set his shoulders and met Tinne's gaze. "No, I don't have a problem with Tinne."

Tinne's breath came out, and he realized he'd been holding it. He offered his arm to the young man. Laev grasped it, looked at Tinne straight. "You were twenty, only three years and a little older than me."

Raising his eyebrows, Tinne said, "I'm not that much older than you now, I'm only twenty-three." But he smiled. He recalled when anyone past the twenty mark seemed ancient.

Laev grasped his arm, squeezed and let loose at the same time as Tinne.

Tab said, "If any of you develop a problem with anyone else, you come to me or Tinne. If it can't be worked out, one of you will leave. The least skilled will leave, go to someone else to learn. But when you're all adults—after your Second Passage—you are welcome to join the Green Knight Fencing and Fighting Salon.

"Now, let's see what you can do. We will provide pale green robes for beginners. As you gain technique, you will proceed through fighters' robes, then, if you reach the proper level, you can wear your own house colors." Tab led the small procession from the entry area to the main salon. Tinne brought up the rear, shaking his head. Not a word had been said about the scandal the Hollys were embroiled in, his own divorce. But if it hadn't been for the precocious and strange Vinni T'Vine there would have been no beginners' class.

So he was grateful to the young prophet, more for Tab's sake than his own. But his mind still shied away from any contemplation of what future Vinni T'Vine had seen.

Twelve

❦

With *more enthusiasm and comradeship than* Tinne *ex-*pected, the youngsters donned sparring clothes. Tinne tested them with a basic pattern of attacks. None of the boys countered any move well, though a couple of Clovers tried rushing him with brute force and landed on their butts on the mats.

Tab demonstrated three attacks and defenses, set the boys to practice, and joined Tinne to watch. "I'm grateful for that Vinni T'Vine," Tab said. "We'll have more FirstFamily youngguns in this class tomorra."

"You think so?"

"I know this business, boy. The scandal coulda gone either way for us. Wildly popular or deadly empty. Figured most of our regulars who are serious about fightin' would stay. We *are* the best. An' those who treat this as a social club and fitness center, 'bout half of them woulda stayed, half found another place. But with this class"—he made a sweeping gesture—"we should do all right. *You* and the place should do all right. We'll still lose people, but if this bunch sticks, the Green Knight should be good for another century. These kids and their children. All a man can ask, to see his business continue." The Clover battling Laev Hawthorn jumped him, yelling all the time. "These Clovers." Tab shook his head. "Time to teach the duello to the middle class." He went to the pair, walking with a renewed spring in his step.

Tinne smiled. Tab and the older generations might think the Clovers Commoners, but Tinne was willing to bet that by the end of that century Tab spoke of the Clovers would have a title. Not just a "GraceLord or GraceLady," either. They'd move up the ranks to "GrandLord or GrandLady."

Cratag Maytree crossed to him, gave a little bow. "You and your G'Uncle do good work. Wish I had this training when I was young, but we don't run to such places on the Southern Continent." He glanced around.

With Cratag's and Tab's words on his mind, Tinne saw his inheritance with new eyes. Hard wooden floors with the occasional scar gleaming under miniature suns that washed the place in full spectrum light. The walls, also wood, of a lighter honey color. Weapons hung on one wall. Mats of deep green. The salon had a certain elegance, appeared as if it had been around for several centuries and would remain for more to come.

Cratag said, "It's good for Laev to know fighting. Think if his FatherSire had a better idea a few years ago, there wouldn't've been a feud."

"Hmm," Tinne said. The Hollys and the Hawthorns had been feuding since the current GreatLords were young.

Clearing his throat, Cratag said, "I address the salon."

"I am here," an older, raspier Holly voice, Tab's G'Uncle.

"A transfer of funds from T'Hawthorn to the Green Knight Fencing and Fighting Salon for the education of Hawthorn-Heir for the next year is approved."

"Done," the salon said.

Another little bow from Cratag. "This is a good place. I have no doubt that Laev will continue, but he'll be an adult soon and should be allowed to make his own choices. I'll leave him in your competent hands."

"Merry meet," Tinne said. The formal words seemed suitable.

Cratag appeared a little surprised, "And merry part."

"And merry meet again."

Nodding, Cratag left the salon, moving with a fighter's grace that Tinne recognized. He hadn't said anything about patronizing the Green Knight himself. Too bad.

The salon said, "T'Willow scries."

Tinne caught Tab's gaze, and his G'Uncle jerked his head for Tinne to answer. In the office, Tinne touched the rim of the large green enameled bowl. "Here."

Saille T'Willow smiled at him, three dimensional from the water droplets hanging over the bowl. "Greetyou. I'm sorry if I am interrupting your beginners' class."

Tinne was reminded that here was another man who was an ally with him and who would be sending his future children to the Green Knight. Tab was right. The place would survive. "Greetyou."

The GreatLord flushed. "It occurred to me when I saw the schedule that I have very little training in fencing and fighting. A GreatLord should not be delinquent in that."

Not when the most common way of settling differences was duels. "No," Tinne said.

"But I don't want to take a beginners' class. I'd like to arrange personal instruction from you, please."

"My G'Uncle Tab—"

"Would wipe the floor with me." A flashing smile. "He looks as hard as stone and intimidates me."

"Very well, let's schedule three times a week, two septhours. Twice for fencing and blazer work, one for fighting."

Saille grimaced. "All right." He was looking at his own calendarsphere, spinning silver near him. "MidAfternoonBell acceptable? Say on the days of Mor, Midweek, and Koad? I'm finished with my own work by then."

Tinne scanned his calendarsphere. "Fine, we'll use a private salon here."

Another brilliant smile from Saille. "My thanks, though I don't think I have any enemies except T'Yew."

The name jolted through Tinne, scattering his thoughts. He must have paled, because Saille said thoughtfully, "I shouldn't reveal my enemies, should I? But you're my ally, so you have a right to know. And I don't see T'Yew challenging me anyway. He wouldn't hire an assassin, he's too proud. He'd try to hurt me in other ways, manipulative bastard."

"We'll keep an eye out." Tinne kept his voice steady, but his skin had chilled.

"Couldn't hurt to know what I'm doing with a sword," Saille said.

"No." Tinne made a show of glancing at the door to the main salon.

"I'll let you get back to your class."

"Thank you." Though the day Tab Holly couldn't handle six rowdy boys would not come soon.

Tinne stared at the gently whirling water in the scrybowl, and instead of a bright office, saw a dark winter's garden. Saille T'Willow was enemies with T'Yew.

It was something they had in common.

*L*ahsin *walked confidently up to the conservatory door* and put her hand on the latch. She couldn't see much of the inside because the glass was tinted. She didn't know whether the plants had died away or grown into a non-fruit-producing tangle. Whatever had occurred, it was the best place for her to grow food throughout the winter, should she decide to stay that long.

She glanced at the glassed hallway between the conservatory and the main house. She would be entering a Residence. She set her shoulders. In the last confrontation with a Residence, she had won—through sheer underestimation on T'Yew Residence's part and with a wild upsurge of Flair— but she had escaped.

Staying and living in an angry Residence would be harder. Probably impossible. Good thing she had the clocktower stillroom for shelter.

For an instant she thought of making vegetable beds in the clocktower building but dismissed it. The storage room was the dog's, she might need the stillroom itself with the distilling equipment, and the drying room simply didn't have enough light. She'd spend septhours building plant beds that might not be deep enough.

So she kept her hand on the latch and quieted her mind to *feel* the spellshields of the place. She hadn't studied the protective spells in the walls of the estate yet, only knew they were unusual.

Here the glass was warm from the sun. A once proud place. A conservatory that had been well tended, welcomed people, held blooms and winter fruits and herbs from Earth itself. She caught the echoes of laughing people as they socialized during a party, doors wide open to the beauty of the gardens, sparkling and glowing light spells in different colors adding a festive air.

She breathed in deeply, whispered a little spell, and her Flair followed on the breath. The latch tongue depressed easily and silently and she was in.

The conservatory was warm enough to keep most of the standard native Celtan and the hardier Earthan-Celtan hybrids alive, but the more exotic plants had died. No heady steam or rich scents of tropical flowers—any flowers—greeted her. But those plants that had survived had grown abundantly, though she was disappointed that none bore fruit. Still, she was sure she could reclaim a bed or two and have vegetables ripening within days. Gardening was her creative Flair.

She closed the door behind her. Hands on her hips, she stood and turned, definitely time to trim here—rip out the weeds growing in a couple of the raised beds and snip off thrusting branches of shrubs and tendrils of vines. And prune the nut-bearing trees.

Around her she saw a forest of edibles, she only had to bring it back into fruition. Relief had her eyes stinging. She sniffed and rummaged for a tattered softleaf she'd put in her serviceable trous pocket. Living here all winter, until spring touched the land and she could go north, was possible. Luck had been on her side.

With that thought, she blew her nose and caught sight of a rough stone plinth—a solid symbol representing the stone-marker of fate itself—a garden accent.

For a moment she just stood and appreciated the place. She'd worked hard in the Burdocks' sunroom, making it a gem. None of the Yews nor T'Yew Residence would let her use her Flair in the GrandLord's conservatory. She'd had to sneak into an abandoned garden in order to cultivate a plot of her own. She'd only slightly regretted leaving that. Like the rest of the estate, it had not welcomed her, bloomed for her. But here! Her Flair was rising within her, becoming stronger.

Second Passage was to determine what her Flair was, and Third would be when her Flair would be completely free. Her fingertips tingled, and Lahsin thought that her gardening Flair would be confirmed. As for her main Flaired gift, judging from her experiences with T'Yew Residence and here, she was sure that her Flair would be crafting—or disarming—spellshields. It was a good Flair, and she was growing confident that she would be able to support herself and contribute to society with such Flair. If—no, *when*, she was free of the Yews.

Scanning the conservatory and knowing that she needed to get vegetables and salad greens in first, she picked out a couple of beds, went over and checked the soil, finding it rich, perfect. In one of the corners closest to the house was a stand and shelves for tools that looked well used but still good.

She stood still and absorbed the vibrations of the place. Then, for the first time in years, she performed a tiny ritual, speaking to the earth and the four directions and elements to ask blessings for her gardening work, requesting that the plants understand her needs and what she would be doing.

Straightening her spine and setting her shoulders, she got to work. After a few moments, she felt the air change and thought she could sense a rustling around her. The Residence had become aware of her.

She wouldn't speak first.

An oppression came, the odor of rotting vegetation. She breathed through her mouth. The smell hadn't been that strong a few minutes before, not even when she'd opened the door, though she had no doubt there was decaying plant life around her.

Snip. Snip. Snip. She continued her work, though her back tightened. Tension increased.

"Who are you, little girl?" the Residence said.

"Don't call me that!" The words ripped from her, the fury at all the denigrating remarks everyone had made while she was at T'Yew's. The slights her own parents and younger brother had made more and more often when they'd seen her. And that was rare.

A glass tinkling sound caught her attention. She stared down, appalled, as the small pruners in her hand rattled against the outside wall. Not only her hand shook. Her whole body trembled with fury.

It ate her inside. She hadn't known she could be this angry, and that frightened her. Hadn't she heard somewhere that strong negative emotions were bad during Passage? The low tones of a discussion between Taxa and T'Yew refreshed her memory.

*"The girl doesn't care for you, Father," A smirk from Taxa.
T'Yew shrugs. "No matter."*

*Taxa's little plucked and pointed brows rise. "We don't
want harm to come to her during Passage."*

*T'Yew's mouth curves in a cruel smile Lahsin dreads. "I'll
take care of that."*

*Lahsin shivers. She's looking through the crack in the
door from T'Yew's bedroom to his sitting room. He'll drug
her again.*

Sharp words from Taxa, including drugs. *Lahsin catches
the last of it. "—more she's drugged the less her Flair can
rise, and isn't this whole matter about using her Flair?"*

*Lahsin scuttles to the bathroom to be sick. Taxa knows,
they all know, that T'Yew also wants a son.*

Lahsin staggered a couple of steps to a workbench and
dropped down. Her pruners fell from limp fingers. She'd never
go back. She'd die before she went back. No. She'd *fight* and
die before she ever returned to the Yews.

But meanwhile the weight of her Second Passage lurked
in the back of her mind, sent initial sparks of warning through
her blood.

She was running from the Yews and the Burdocks and everyone outside now, but would eventually have to face them.

Her other battle, Second Passage, was here inside her,
would take place in this garden, Lady and Lord willing. She'd
have to survive that, too.

A voice like a cranky grandfather boomed. "What, you
rustle around in my places like a mouse and don't think I will
notice?"

Lahsin flinched. She sat up straight. "I thought FirstGrove
was for the desperate. I'm here. It's winter. So you should be
able to put those pieces together." She leaned down and picked
up the pruners. "I'm a good gardener. It's my creative Flair. I
can take care of this place and FirstGrove outside."

A grumble. The Residence was audibly talking to her.
Did that mean it had little power? Or that they weren't linked
enough that they could communicate mentally? Or what?

She felt so ignorant.

She looked around at the raised beds and the choked
once-pond. At the brush and trees that needed to be trimmed,

the weeds that must be pulled, the fruit-bearing plants that must be thinned so they would produce. She could do that.

"The grove outside has low standards," the Residence rumbled.

Had it said "no standards" or "low standards"?

"No one has come near *me* for long years. Yet here you are, stirring up my sleep. You'll clank around and fiddle and disturb me and then leave. Not worth powering up for. Not worth treating well." A snort.

But hadn't she also heard the loneliness of echoing halls?

The outside door creaked open. Lahsin leapt to her feet. The dog limped in. Beyond him fat snowflakes fell.

He saw her, slunk along the wall to the corner.

"BalmHeal Residence."

Creaky laughter. "No one has called me that in a long, long time. I do not let people in. Not many try to enter, but I do not let them in. I do not talk to them. Interloper."

"Do you have no-times with food?"

Silence for a few heartbeats. The dog appeared as skinny as ever, as hungry as ever.

"Wouldn't you like to know?" the Residence said.

"I can eat berries, fruits, vegetables, but there's a dog here—"

"What, you think I can't tell there's a FamDog?"

I am not a Fam.

"He's not a Fam," Lahsin said. "Not my Fam, either."

Another snort. "A dog. Dogs mess in the house."

The dog sat up stiffly, growled.

"He won't mess in the house."

"Let the dog talk for itself."

I WILL NOT MESS IN THE HOUSE. The dog's mental yell was so loud, it stunned Lahsin.

Rude beast, indeed. The grumpy old-man voice said, *You are not welcome within my walls.* Loud, echoing snicks, as if all windows and doors were being locked. Well, Lahsin could have told the ancient and mean one that locks wouldn't stop her. Antique spellshields wouldn't slow her down very much, either.

She shook her limbs out. *The dog needs food. If you have no-times, I will get meat for it.*

"And yourself." A cackle. "Don't pretend you're not selfish. There are plenty of beasties on my grounds, let the dog pay his way and eat at the same time." Dismissal.

"The dog—"

I can speak for myself, the dog said with dignity. *My right rear leg is bad. Catching game is difficult.*

"Too bad," said the Residence.

"What kind of being *are* you?" Lahsin demanded. "Weren't you the Primary HealingHall for centuries? How can this be BalmHeal and FirstGrove and a sanctuary for all who need one and you be so spiteful?"

"What has anyone done for *me*?" The Residence's voice had the power of anger behind it. "Abandoned me. Ignored me. I give nothing to no one. Not human, not dog."

The sliver of hope that had bloomed in the dog's despairing eyes vanished. He shifted a little and both his ribs and his ill-healed leg were obvious. Lahsin couldn't bear it. "I will work here in the conservatory and in the gardens of the estate for the food in your no-time storage."

The dog hung his head, slid a glance at Lahsin. *I will pay you back.* His mind voice was hollow.

We will work out terms, said Lahsin.

"Your 'work' does nothing for *me*. I have well-stocked, wonderful no-times, but I will not allow you inside. There is a small storage no-time in the Summer Pavilion in the east of the estate. You both should be able to survive on its contents this winter. If you are careful. Perhaps. Or perhaps only one of you will live." There was a carefully regulated "boom" that changed the atmosphere of the conservatory, which Lahsin took as its final word.

By the time she looked up, the dog had disappeared, though she sensed he was still in the glass house, rooting in old vegetation to make a nest for himself. She didn't know that the place was that much warmer than the stillroom building, but the thriving plants and the absence of obvious winter comforted her, so she thought it might do the same for the dog.

"I can live on grains and fruits and vegetables," she repeated, projecting her voice. "I'll check the no-time in the Summer Pavilion later and bring you the meat."

The dog didn't answer.

*   *   *

Tinne had put thoughts of *Lahsin* and *T'Yew* aside and was concentrating on pairing Antenn and Laev for sparring, when Vinni shouted, in a rising, shrill voice, "Stop!"

Everyone froze.

To Tinne's horror, a shadow flickered in the center of the fighting salon. A person trying to teleport. What was wrong with them, 'porting to a busy place where they could kill themselves or others?

Thirteen

❦

The figure materialized into a small girl, holding a fat housefluff under one arm and a fat cat under the other.

She looked around. "We wanted to see," she said, then, addressing the housefluff, "It's all boys." Laev and Antenn and Vinni shifted. She sniffed. "And it smells funny."

Tab stalked to her. "It smells like men's sweat. You come to take beginning classes in fencin' and fightin'?"

She blinked big blue eyes up at him, her gaze held a slight dreaminess that Tinne thought was typical. He also thought he should recognize her, but didn't. He certainly didn't circulate in her age group, or with folk who had children her age.

"Avellana." Vinni sighed. "Avellana, you aren't supposed to sneak away from your nanny."

"You taught me to, Muin," she said calmly.

Tab snorted. "He was wrong." His hand came down and enveloped Vinni's thin shoulder. "But as I recall, he 'ports real well. Don't seem as if you can. Who's teaching you to 'port, young lady?"

Avellana blinked, tilted her head, and looked at Tab. "I'm Avellana Hazel. I am six. I won't be starting fencing and fighting lessons until I am eight, after my First Passage. That's what Mommy said when I asked to come today. They don't think they'll ever give me a blazer to play with."

Good thing, too, Tinne thought.

Grunting, Tab said, "We'll see."

Everyone stared at him.

"Who are your friends?" Tab gestured to the housefluff and cat.

"Muin is my friend. That's why I am here." She lifted the housefluff. "This is his Fam, Flora."

Vinni closed his eyes and turned red.

Tab buffeted him on the ear. "You don't ever close your eyes in a fightin' situation, T'Vine."

Swallowing, Vinni said. "Yes, sir. I mean, no, I will never do so again."

"And this is my FamCat, Rhyz," Avellana said. The cat's purr filled the quiet room.

Tab went to the girl, took her chin in his big hand. "This is important, GreatMistrys—"

"I am Avellana Hazel. I am six."

"Listen to me, Avellana Hazel. It was wrong for you to teleport into a space you knew nothing about."

"There were no life signs in the space."

Tab's jaw tightened, then he spoke again. "There could have been. Someone coulda walked right into that space when you were 'porting."

She stared at him, finally said, "That would have been bad. Lives would have gotten tangled."

"Lives might have ended."

Avellana nodded. "I understand."

"That's why we only teleport to designated spaces, and teleportation pads always have signals."

"Light for stay. No light, go," Avellana repeated the simple rule.

"Correct. Now I want you to promise me that you won't teleport alone again until after your First Passage."

She stuck out her lower lip. Her gaze went to Vinni. He said nothing. She slid a glance around the room. Her eyes met Tinne's for an instant, and he knew he was looking at a powerfully Flaired young person who *could* teleport at eight instead of seventeen. He said, "Fams don't count. You promise GreatSir Holly that you will not teleport by yourself, without another *person* with you, until after your First Passage." A year from now, Lord and Lady willing.

"What if I don't promise?"

"Then you won't be coming here to learn fencing and fight-ing and maybe, just maybe, blazer work," Tab said, dropping his hand.

"That's mean!"

"That's the consequences of your own decision, your own actions." Tab stood up and crossed his arms.

She sniffed, talked to her cat, "A lot of boy smells."

The cat sniffed back. He was a tom.

"Maybe I and some other girls should add girl smells, too."

"You'll be allowed in only if you give me your solemn Vow of Honor now," Tab said.

"Solemn Vow of Honor," Avellana rolled it out, as if in-trigued, as if no one had asked such a thing of her before. "All right." She nodded decisively. "I solemnly vow by my very own honor that I will not teleport alone, without some other person, until after my First Passage." She looked up at Tab, put the cat down, and stuck her hand out. "Good?"

He took her tiny hand in his own, bowed elegantly over it, brushed a kiss over her fingers. "We're good. I'll see you in a few years, Avellana Hazel."

"We can't stay and watch? I might learn by watching. My parents let me learn by watching all the time."

Tinne believed that. Heavens knew what she'd tried to learn by doing.

"No," Tab said, "you can't stay. Classes are for students only. Paying students," he added when she'd opened her mouth again. The boys relaxed. "Tinne, escort GreatMistrys Avellana Hazel to the teleportation pad and back to her Residence."

Tinne bowed. "Yes, sir."

She turned those big eyes on him, studied him as he cov-ered the ground between them in a few paces. "He's good." She looked around. "Everyone's good here," she said, blinking her astonishing eyes at Tab. "I don't get to stay with these good people?" She sounded pitiful.

"No," Tab said. "And your folks are good people."

With a big sigh, she said, "Yes, but they are old and busy."

"I am old and busy."

"Your nanny will be looking for you, Avellana," Vinni said.

The little girl made a face. "Yes. But she is very old." She looked at Tab. "Even older than you. So old she has no teeth. She does not know what to do with me."

One of the Clovers spoke up. "Our family has placed a nanny at the Ashes, and I have a sister who has trained as a nanny and needs a good job. She's young and pretty." He smiled guilelessly. "She's taking teleportation lessons now, from an agency."

"Teleportation lessons from an agency." Avellana seemed to savor the words.

The Clover boy grinned. "My sister could keep up with you." He stuck his thumbs in the sash of his tunic, rocked back on his heels. "You tell your folks about Aralia Clover. Now go away, you're wasting our time and money here."

That seemed another new idea for her. Tinne scooped up the FamCat, set him in the crook of his arm, grasped Avellana's hand. She pulled away. "Muin must kiss Flora hello and good-bye first."

Someone snickered. Vinni turned red again. "Avellana . . ."

But she was marching up to him, housefluff outthrust. "You must always be kind to her, you know. She already almost died once." And that was said with such a strange inflection that the room quieted again.

Vinni bent and kissed his Fam, and Avellana returned to Tinne and slipped her fingers into his, then looked at the Clover boy again. "I will tell GreatLady Coll D'Hazel and Great-Lord Zabel Honeysuckle T'Hazel about Aralia Clover."

As Tinne walked Avellana to the entry lounge and the public teleportation pad there, he felt pulses of tingling electricity from the child. "You're very strong."

"Yes, I know, everyone says so. Then they all whisper that they do not expect me to survive my First Passage."

Tinne couldn't say something false, so he just grunted and squeezed her hand. "Most often we survive Passage." He didn't want to think of any hurt coming to this child or Lahsin during her Second Passage.

"Yes. But I got brain damage when I tried to fly."

They'd made it to the reception room teleportation pad. Tinne flipped on the light, pulled the child and the housefluff close, and checked on the cat. All were ready. "Better stick to teleportation," he finally said. "Faster anyway."

"Muin's working on the problem of me and Passages. He said so to Mommy and Daddy."

Tinne thought of how young Muin T'Vine, Vinni, had filled the beginners' class, helped them. "Vinni's a good boy."

"His name is Muin."

"Yes."

She looked up at Tinne with those blue eyes, showing bright intelligence behind wisps of dreaminess. "Names are important. You should call him by his proper name."

Before he could answer, the little girl teleported them to D'Hazel Residence, leaving Tinne gasping at the unexpected trip. The cat jumped from his arms and trotted away as if accustomed to strange events. Avellana hurried down a polished marble hall. He had the impression she hadn't been missed yet.

He returned to the salon, trying to forget about the dangers of Passage.

*L*ahsin didn't take the Residence's bait and go at once to the Summer Pavilion. The cunning in the Residence's voice had alerted her that it might be a futile trip. If she wanted food soon, the conservatory was her best option.

Straightening her spine and setting her shoulders, she got to work. When she was done, she pulled up a wrought iron seat and sank into it and simply stared. She'd worked long and hard to put the place in order; she wasn't even sure of the time of day. But the results were fabulous!

Wiping her sleeve across her forehead, she just gaped at the sight before her. She'd used Flair, of course, when it had come to her, in trickles or spurts or even a flood or two. But she'd also worked hard physically, she had a layer of dirt and sweat to show that.

More creative Flair had flowed through her fingers than she realized. The flagstones of the path were clean and showed thyme plants between them. Lower ground cover gave way to lush ferns and low trimmed bushes, then larger bushes and small fruit and nut trees, then, finally, to large trees whose branches brushed the glass. And the glass! Everywhere she could see a bit of the greenhouse itself, the glass was clean, nearly sparkling.

She turned her head to see the section she had planted with her vegetable seeds. Every time she'd walked by she'd sent them a little Flair, a little encouragement to grow, a little love. Green shoots were already poking through the earth.

She shook out her limbs and carefully put her tools away. She could use a walk in the brisk air. The snow had fallen for only a few moments before the sun had once again appeared, and there was no accumulation to slush through.

So she drew on her winter cape and left the conservatory with the satisfaction of a job well done.

Getting to the Summer Pavilion from the Residence was a struggle through overgrown paths and closed hedgerows. When she reached it, she noticed the place was clean and in better repair than the Residence itself, but had an odd smell. She found a tiny no-time, but it wasn't working. She searched the place and found one dusty, well-wrapped trail meal in a window seat.

Swearing under her breath, she left the place by a well-worn path to the square pools a short distance away. Definitely exercise pools and not Healing ones. Just the trace of steam rose from them instead of the thick mist that would be hanging over the main Healing pool. For a moment she thought she might stop and swim, but she wanted to return to the conservatory. Her work was not yet done.

The dog had seemed depressed, as if he might have finally stopped fighting. She didn't think she could endure it if he silently wasted away—as if she, too, might give in to despair. Somehow they'd developed a small bond.

So she trudged back to the Residence, determined to get in. She was taking care of herself, relying on herself to survive, and had a small string of victories now. She didn't want to lose momentum and fail. Too much depended on her confidence in herself—all of her future life, her successful weathering of her Second Passage, surviving the winter here, repudiating her marriage.

For an instant, Tinne Holly's image appeared in her mind, and before she brushed it away, she decided that she would let him teach her how to defend herself.

In the conservatory she stopped a few feet from the curled dog who looked at her with sad eyes.

"The Summer Pavilion's no-time is not working," she said.

Leaning over, she picked up a large set of pruners and clicked them together.

The dog's eyes fired. *Do not think you can kill me easily.*

She stepped back, sucked in a shocked breath, then shook her head. "I don't mean to kill you." Keeping her voice low, not knowing if the Residence could hear her but hoping not to warn it, she said, "I intend to get into the Residence."

The front door is stout, behind many rosebushes.

Lahsin looked ahead of her, through the glass pane at the portion of the Residence in view. She smiled, showing teeth, that felt good. Snicking the pruners again, she said, "I'll get in."

Settling an extendable ladder under her arm, she marched through the weak afternoon sunshine around to the front of the Residence. She was *not* going in any side or back door. No, she'd insist the entity deal with her as a person requesting entrance at the front door.

She stopped some meters from the front of the house. It had its back to the northeast corner of the city walls, facing inward to the estate. Behind it were tall trees that marked the line of the vine-covered walls. It had been a beautiful house, well proportioned of mellow red brick, with large windows now blank with the dirt of ages and trim that might have been tinted white.

There was a wide portico. The pillars were covered in thorny roses gone wild, which barricaded the front door. It appeared the whole porch was one huge mass of roses. The Residence no doubt had encouraged the growth. More daunting than she expected, even with the pruners she had, and she wasn't sure how long her Flair would hold out.

It would have been better if anger filled her. But she'd worked through that for today. It would come back. How many times she didn't know, but now she just wanted inside the Residence.

She started snipping the growth anyway, taking off long whips of thorny stalks. Some had bright rose hips, and she set them aside to use in potions or for decoration.

She thought of all that might be in the Residence that she could use—pay for with energy to clean and power the house—to keep her determination high, when a thorn caught her, sticking deep or sliding in a long scratch against her skin.

Her mouth watered as she thought of food from the no-time storage—premade meals she didn't have to try to cook herself. Meat. She could almost taste a good furrabeast steak.

Food for the dog, too. She was coming to like the dog. It was having a hard time hunting in the garden, and she couldn't imagine it surviving on the vegetables that she was growing in the greenhouse.

And she hoped for a library. Not just the ResidenceLibrary that would answer questions if she asked, with data, but also a roomful of books and scrolls and holospheres and maybe even memoryspheres of those who had lived here before. She thought she'd be blessed beyond her dreams if she found no-times and a library. And an inside bath.

So she wrung every iota of Flair from herself, all the strength from her fingers, hands, and body, to clear a path to the large front door. Beyond the thick outer layers of bushes were dead and brittle branches that were easier to pull away.

As evening fell, she reached the door, trimmed the last of the growth. Wiping an arm across her brow, she chanted a spell to send the deadfall to the compost pit she'd developed earlier near one end of the stillroom.

The door looked old and dry and cracked, desperately in need of reconditioning. Despite her aching body, Lahsin went back to the large conservatory walk-in storage area. There she checked on the dog, still curled tightly and sleeping, then pulled out some oil for wood, and even some stain. With a bit more Flair, one coat should be enough to reverse the damage of years and protect it for more. She thought she might have just enough power to do that. The Residence would appreciate a good door, wouldn't it?

She didn't know.

Another few ups and downs on the ladder, and she was ready to try the newly polished door latch. It was locked, more, it had spellshields upon it. They were somewhat like what she sensed cloaked the whole estate. It seemed to exude: "You don't see me, there is nothing here, you don't want to come in." Further, she could sense an additional backup spell that would be triggered if she tried to force the lock. Testing the strands of the spell one by one, she figured out that a wave of dread and fear would crash over a person who tried to enter by force. *Something dreadful awaits beyond the door. You don't want to proceed.*

She pressed the thumb latch down. Pushed. Nothing.

With a little sigh, she decided that she wanted to try diplomacy once more. She recalled the noise and fury of T'Yew Residence when she'd escaped and was sure she'd hurt it by breaking all those windows and doors. That being might have deserved her anger. This one didn't.

"Residence, you know that I'm here. Will you unlock the door for me and open the spellshields?"

"You'll raid my provisions!"

"Who are you saving them for? You can't eat them yourself, and I would promise to provide you with some of my energy"—if she knew how to give it Flair—"to give you strength. You've seen how I cared for the conservatory, have restored the front door." She waited in silence for a long minute, then shrugged and turned away. "Your no-times have probably failed and spoiled all the food anyway, the same as in the Summer Pavilion."

Instead of answering, the Residence slowly opened the door with a long *creeeaak* that had a slither of dread slipping down Lahsin's spine. Just the spell she'd sensed before. She took a shaky breath. The Residence wanted to intimidate her, would it, too, try to trap her?

But curiosity was overwhelming. There was only darkness ahead. "Lights?" she whispered, then, "Light!"

A flash erupted before her, blinding her for a few seconds, until she blinked the afterimages of white spots away. Then her mouth dropped open at the torches flickering in iron holders along the wall. They weren't really live flames, of course, but an affectation of some long-ago century.

"Come on in, little girl." The Residence chuckled, and for a moment Lahsin thought it sounded like T'Yew Residence, with all its malice. What could happen to her if she went in? It couldn't prevent her from leaving, not with spellshields, not if she bespelled this particular door to lock open.

But it might drop a chandelier or something on her head. Might let a board in a staircase break under her weight.

Was she being paranoid? Or sensible?

"I've changed my mind." She made sure her voice was firm.

"You obviously don't want me in there, and I won't go where I'm not welcome. I thought I'd shown you that I could only help, by reviving the conservatory. Not only the plants were tended, but the structure and the glass, too. I've restored your front door. Keep your food and your secrets." She turned her back on the gaping entrance.

"You're hungry! And the miserable hound, too."

Suppressing a groan, Lahsin picked up the ladder and her pruners. "I am, but you seem to think that I'm begging, or that I wouldn't return value for your provisions. That I'm a . . . a supplicant. I'd rather not deal with you on those terms. There's another who comes to FirstGrove and the Healing spring. I'll ask him to bring some meat. There's an empty no-time in the stillroom that I can program to store food."

"What do you give *him* in return for food?"

Good question. Lahsin lifted her chin. "Companionship, friendship . . . a listening ear. None of which you want from me. I trust you won't bar the conservatory from me. If you do, the dog and I will find some other place to stay. The man would probably help us get out of Druida secretly. Too bad, because I wanted to work on the gardens."

"Come back!"

Stepping into the cool winter twilight, Lahsin said, "No," and closed the door behind her.

When she opened the door to the conservatory to store the ladder and pruners, it swung easily in. She looked for the dog, but he wasn't inside and she didn't know if that was good or not, couldn't tell if he had heard her brief exchange with the Residence.

Still, it was a letdown that he wasn't where she expected him to be. She supposed she'd wanted some contact with someone else, even if it was just a clash of gazes.

The grime that coated her itched unbearably. Night had fallen, and her thoughts had gone back to Tinne Holly and the night before. Would he come back? Or was once in the sanctuary enough to soothe his soul?

She didn't know.

When she got to the pool, he wasn't there.

* * *

"*Welcome, welcome, welcome!*" the *Turquoise House* squealed in delight when Tinne wearily opened the door that evening.

It was Mitchella's voice.

"Thank you," Tinne said. Lights blazed on throughout the house. Mitchella had positioned small lights where they could accentuate art or furniture. The general decor was of simple, clean lines. The furniture seemed more square than what he was used to, and of a slightly lighter, redder wood.

"Clothes and personal belongings including three drums have been moved into the MasterSuite for you."

His favorite drums, then, but that wasn't what concerned him.

"Um," he said.

"Yes? How can I serve you, GreatSir Holly?" the House asked eagerly. It sounded close to becoming a fully sentient Residence.

"Call me Tinne—"

"Yes, Tinne! Thank you!"

"Could you not use that voice?" he muttered.

There was a long moment's silence as if the House was searching its memory.

"I have this voice, too." A sly, raspy feminine voice. The last owner's? He sighed. "Thank you, no."

"If you speak to me longer or read to me, I could use your's."

Two voices. Maybe it wasn't as close to being a Residence as he'd thought. Three choices. None of which he really liked. And wasn't he being picky all of a sudden about his environs? Maybe because he felt as if his skin had been peeled away, leaving him raw and sensitive to every little thing.

"Why don't we ask Mitchella—"

"Yes! I have scrybowls in almost every room, and I can initiate a call to GrandLady D'Blackthorn all by myself!" the House said proudly. "Turquoise House contacting D'Blackthorn Residence."

Tinne hadn't meant now. He shrugged, saw a large leather chair in oxblood red and sank into it.

"T'Blackthorn Residence." It sounded stiff. "D'Blackthorn is unavailable, Turquoise—"

"Contacting on behalf of my new resident, GreatSir Tinne Holly," the House caroled.

"Tinne Holly has immediate status. I will put you through," T'Blackthorn Residence said.

Tinne winced.

"Tinne?" a breathless Mitchella said. The large 3-D holo that the House projected showed her holding a female toddler.

"Greetyou, Mitchella." He stared at the baby. "I don't remember that one. A new addition to the Family?"

Mitchella bounced the young one in her arms. "Yes, we adopted her from the Saille House of Orphans. She has no Family except the explorer Helena D'Elecampane, who is on the Southern Continent and out of touch. The last time Straif tracked her to give her a message, he was gone for two years." Mitchella shrugged elegant shoulders draped in green and covered with baby spit. The baby gurgled and tangled her hands in Mitchella's red hair.

"You didn't inform my Family?" Tinne's voice was strained. His lost child would have been about the age of this one.

Fourteen

❤

$\mathcal{M}$itchella glanced away. "It's been too painful for Genista to tell her of our new children. Especially ones about the age—" Another shrug. "We just got her a week ago."

Genista would have heard. Tinne said, "The advent of a child into the Holly-Blackthorn Family is a blessing. We all welcome your children."

Mitchella's eyes danced. "It's the 'Blackthorn-Holly' Family."

"Like hell."

"You'll soon be telling *us* a new Holly is coming." She beamed.

"What?"

"Isn't Lark pregnant?"

Tinne's mouth dropped. Joy and pain speared through him. "Huh?"

Mitchella made a moue. "Uh-oh."

"I'm glad," Tinne croaked, keeping his face blank until he could banish the pain and embrace the joy of a new nephew or niece. Why hadn't Lark told him?

"I think she only knew a day or so ago. So why did you call?" The baby had subsided into sleep, still clutching her hair.

Tinne thought. "This House needs additional voices."

Mitchella's brows dipped, then she laughed again. "Don't want to live with my presence every moment? I'm devastated."

He said, "I don't care to hear myself all the time, either. Can you send some recording spheres"—he waved—"whatever, so the House can choose?"

"I haven't had this problem before. I suppose I could send over some Blackthorn memoryspheres—"

"No. Something new."

"Yes, yes, yes!" the House said.

"You could get recordingspheres from the public library—"

"No, no, no!" said the House.

Mitchella went on smoothly, "Or have some actors come over and read for the House."

"Yes!"

"Could you organize that?" Tinne asked.

"Yes." She smiled. "But you disappoint me." She wiggled her eyebrows. "Lovely, premier actresses . . ."

He put a smile on his face. He didn't even want a quick tumble. His libido was gone. "Actresses and actors," he said, paused, forced himself to be generous. "Let the House choose."

Picking up a writestick and papyrus, Mitchella made notes. "I'll supervise. Why don't we say three of each right now. For a septhour reading. Then the Turquoise House can choose one. I believe that would give enough range to communicate well—"

"Yes!"

"—but we will need material rich in emotions. A selection of popular genres—romance, mystery, thrillers, drama . . ." Her smile fluttered. "Coming-of-age stories . . ."

Tinne imagined the House trying out different tones on him. Why had he thought living here was a good idea again?

Another fake smile. "Sounds expensive. Good thing the salon is doing well and I have a cut of the profits."

Mitchella looked up, gaze intent. "You *are* all right?"

"Yes." He rubbed his growling stomach. "Need to eat."

"Oh, I'm sorry for keeping you so long. We eat early here."

"I have much wonderful food in my no-times," the House said.

Mitchella said, "I stocked it myself and checked today."

"Thank you."

"I'll take care of this voice matter for you."

"Thank you. Cut scry," Tinne said and watched with relief as Mitchella with her pitying expression faded.

"Food in the kitchen!" the Residence said. "What do you want?" It reeled off a list of large, fattening meals. He was thinking Mitchella wanted to fatten him up.

He chose a small furrabeast steak and green beans and bread, with rich ale, and could almost feel the calories pumping up his body. Then he put the dishes in their cleanser, and the House hummed as it made them sparkle.

Later, while he digested and stared at the crackling fire, the House whispered, "I forgot."

He prodded himself to stir from the half doze. "What?"

"There is a scry in the cache." The House sounded guilty.

"Is it marked urgent?"

"No."

"Then there's no problem. A man is entitled to come home and have a meal before attending to after-hours business."

"Oh. Thank you."

Tinne got the idea that the House was putting that down in its data library about human behavior.

"Play it," he said, tensed when Lark's face appeared. There *was* an additional aspect to her expression . . . a soft tenderness in the back of her eyes.

"Greetyou, Tinne." She paused, eyes shone with tears. "I love you, you know." His gut tightened until he thought he could feel every lump of furrabeast steak. Her mouth trembled. "No bad news, but I'd like you to scry me when you get this."

Tinne glanced at the timer. Before he could say anything, the House connected him with T'Holly Residence, and Lark's image rose again from the scrybowl. This time, her eyes were searching. "Greetyou."

He raised his brows. "Yes?"

"As you know, D'Sea has little experience with divorces, so she contacted other mind Healers who have." Those who'd work with Commoners or lower classes, Tinne deduced. Upper classes hid their problems, lived separately. "The consensus is that you should live apart if you want."

Tinne's brother, Holm, nudged her aside. "Lick your wounds in private." His face was sober.

Lark elbowed him back. Holm moved behind her and

wrapped his arms around her. "I'm afraid that's exactly what a couple of Healers said."

"So you're cleared to live in the Turquoise House, Lord and Lady bless you," Holm said. "But the parents and the rest of us expect to see you at least once a week."

"D'Sea believes that's essential," Lark said.

"Very close Family," Holm said. "Stressful events over the last few years."

Tinne heard some bitterness in his brother's voice. There'd been years when Holm had been out of touch with their parents, though Tinne had spoken with him every week. "Maybe *you* should have a little counseling?" he said, before he thought about it.

Lark frowned, glanced at her HeartMate. "That might be a good idea, especially under the circumstances." She looked back at Tinne. "Please come to dinner tomorrow." Her hands covered Holm's and squeezed. "We have an announcement. Tab and all of the Blackthorns are coming. Extended Family."

They were going to announce the upcoming advent of a new Holly child. Tinne felt resentment then let it go with a heavy breath. "I'll be there," he said.

"Good," Holm said, "thanks for throwing me to counseling with D'Sea." He didn't sound angry, just exasperated.

Tinne bowed, stretched his lips in a smile. "You're welcome. Later." Suddenly he wanted to be in FirstGrove. He didn't know why. Didn't want to analyze why.

Ilexa prowled in.

"I want you to accompany me tonight to FirstGrove."

She sat, lifted a front paw, licked it. "I am not a desperate animal."

"I think if you accompany me, you are allowed in."

She stared up at him with lambent amber eyes, a shade darker than her brown spotted gold fur.

Perhaps you are only sad. Does the garden let very sad people in?

He was too restless to have a damn philosophical conversation. "Turquoise House, where is the teleportation pad?" He should have explored the place, let it show off, but he hadn't, and that made him feel guilty. "I'll take a tour tomorrow."

"Thank you! The teleportation pad is in the far north room, exit the mainspace and turn left."

He walked around Ilexa, headed for the door. "Samba, the Ship Cat, went with Ruis Elder into FirstGrove, and she wasn't desperate."

Ilexa sniffed, rose gracefully to all four paws. *That Cat is fat. Has never been desperate for anything. All she thinks of is fun. "Let's go play."* Sniffed again.

Tinne looked down at her and wistfully contemplated "fun." He didn't know the last time he'd had any. He tried to recall the key to Ilexa. "I doubt she did much hunting in First-Grove. Place is probably overrun with critters."

Ilexa stilled, as if she'd already scented prey. Her tongue slid over her muzzle. *Good to chase, but I like civilized food.*

"I am stocked with excellent Fam meals, specially prepared by Danith D'Ash, the Fam mistress herself," the House said.

"House, you've bonded with Ilexa enough to speak to her telepathically. You're a strong entity," Tinne said. He scooped up newssheets before he left and threw a glance back over his shoulder. "I doubt Zanth"—the alpha male of all Fams—"has been in FirstGrove. He'd have boasted."

Eyes gleaming, Ilexa glided down the hall with him. She'd had a litter of three kittens with Zanth but the two of them were too competitive to settle into a relationship. Her purr was loud and smug. *I may hunt all I want there. I may tell Zanth of my many successes. But it will not be boasting, only truth.*

Tinne turned his chuckle into a cough. Ilexa stepped onto the teleportation pad.

Tinne sent a mental questing toward BalmHeal Estate. Nothing but black that faded to gray and a feeling "there is nothing here, you do not want to teleport here." He stood, amazed at the unusual spellshields of the place that limited teleportation. Incredible. Like those before him, he wanted to keep the place a secret and safe.

Are we going? Ilexa demanded, forming an image of the door closest to the Healing pool. *Shields let us teleport out but not in.*

He touched her head and they went, then was both pleased

and distressed when he had no trouble opening the door to FirstGrove. Obviously the secret garden still considered him a troubled soul.

Little wild porcine! Ilexa shot through the door and was off, running along a path that had been partially cleared since the night before. She jumped over a ragged hedge and was gone. Tinne distanced his mind from the cat's feral nature. She wasn't the same Fam she'd been before she'd left Holly Residence.

He wasn't the same man. He closed the door behind him. A few steps and the serene atmosphere wrapped around him. The distant winter city noise vanished completely, the feel of Lahsin's presence was like a soothing touch on his heart, and he didn't know that he liked that. Didn't want to need another woman. Definitely didn't want to have a HeartMate that would rip him into smaller shreds than he already was.

Grunting at the idea of another love going terribly wrong, he tossed the newssheets on the bench, strode to the pool, stripped to a swim loincloth, and sank into the water up to his nostrils. He nearly whimpered at the wonderful feel of the Healing pool. He didn't know what Lahsin felt when she was in the waters, but they seemed to reach inside him to ease heartache, soothe his spirit, and stroke his self-esteem until he believed he was a good man again. More, the water pulsed against old wounds as if breaking down the scar tissue and renewing muscle and skin to complete health. No wonder the FirstFamilies had kept this place for themselves! Served them right that it was lost to them and open to those with need.

After a few minutes, he scented Lahsin at the far end of the pool. Her skin held her own fragrance as well as the residue of the pool herbs. Casually turning his head in that direction, he narrowed his eyes to peer through the mist and saw her symmetrical shadow dark against foliage. He paddled to one side of the pool, found a curve with a bench, and sat.

She stood in the shadows, outside of reach, but lingered. Was she lonely? She'd have been surrounded by people since her birth. Both the Burdocks and the Yews were extended Families who all lived together like most Nobles. Was she missing people as he was? Glad of the time alone to reflect, but also yearning for undemanding human company? *Undemanding* was the key word.

Murmuring, knowing his voice would resound over the water, he said, "I've moved out of my Family Residence."

There was a jerky movement as if she'd started in surprise.

"Into an odd place. A House-Becoming-a-Residence." He looked directly at her, letting her know he was aware of her, keeping his body relaxed—hell, after the day he'd had, letting his weary body go limp was a luxury. "Have you heard of the Turquoise House? It's becoming an entity, developing its own Flair, just like you."

There was a moment of silence as if she was considering a new notion. She'd have lived in Residences, known the vagaries of sentient homes, their personalities.

She stepped into the twinmoonslight, a wraith of a girl, with slanting eyebrows, lovely tilted eyes, and a cap of dark thick hair, showing the elegant shape of her head.

"A House-Becoming-a-Residence?" Her voice carried well over the water, low and a little husky as if she hadn't spoken much during the day. He'd been surrounded by people, yet achingly alone inside. She'd been completely alone.

He told her about the Turquoise House, and she drew close enough to sit on a bench near the next curve. Then she shifted a little as she met his gaze, wary. But she seemed to believe she was safe from him there, fully clothed, on a winter night. He could have her in his arms in a few seconds. If she wanted to keep her distance, that was fine. He paddled over to her, keeping only his head out of water, though the pool got shallower.

He smiled.

She smiled back.

Progress for both of them.

"So," he said casually. "I forgot to ask you before. How do you know of this place?" He wouldn't have expected her to hear about it, or believe old legends. He knew of it because he'd made it a point to learn everything about Ruis Elder. That man had lived here for a while. Tinne frowned. If the First-Families knew that the place could harbor desperate criminals, they might try to find and destroy it again. He couldn't let that happen, had to protect it. The world needed a sanctuary for the wounded.

Lahsin stopped talking.

"I missed that." He smiled again. "Steam slowing my mind."

That seemed to reassure her even more that he was harmless. She glanced at the pool with yearning, her feet wiggled. Tinne got the idea her feet were sore and she wanted to soak them. So he retreated to the middle of the pool.

She eyed him, took off her shoes and liners, pulled up her trous legs, settled onto the rim of the pool, and dangled her feet. "Ahh," she sighed. Tinne's body twitched at the sound.

Lahsin said, "I met a guard when I left T'Yew's. He told me of this place."

"You command loyalty, Lady. Your absence was reported in all the newssheets, yet the man didn't come forward."

"He's a good man, he didn't come after me when he heard the alarm, though he must have thought I'd caused it."

"What alarm?"

She grimaced, looked aside. "I blew out all the windows and doors of T'Yew Residence. Destroyed all the spellshields."

Tinne stared. "I heard nothing of that. Fascinating." He laughed. "Truly? Everything? Like"—he waved a hand—"boom!"

Lahsin tilted her head as if gauging whether he was really amused.

"I don't lie, Lady," he said softly. "It *is* fascinating."

She withdrew her feet, considered him, put them back in. Another tentative smile. "I might have a Flair for spellshields."

"I'd say so! T'Yew will have to replace all his windows and shields. Good. And this guard didn't follow you, has kept quiet. Also good. Was he a city guard?"

"No, a Maytree. Hawthorn, I mean." Then her face stilled, brows drew down. "You won't hurt him or cause him trouble?"

"No. I wouldn't hurt him," Tinne said quietly. "So Cratag Maytree, a Hawthorn guard, told you of this place."

She nodded. "That was his name, Cratag. He said he found it when he first came to Druida."

"An excellent guard." If Tinne—or one of the other Hollys—had killed Cratag during the feud, the man wouldn't have been available to tell Lahsin of the lost garden. She would probably have been captured and . . . he didn't want to think what might have happened if she was returned to T'Yew. Tinne might have lost her completely. He shook his head.

"What?" she asked.

"Strange how destiny works."

She nodded.

"Now are you comfortable enough with me that I can get out of this pool? My toes are wrinkling."

Fifteen

♥

She eyed him. *She'd thought about him during odd mo-*
ments of the day, knew despite his appearance the night before, she'd underestimated him. He was young and strong
and trained in violence, he could have hurt her badly.

And no one would ever know.

He didn't look as weary as last night and wasn't menacing.
She thought he *wouldn't* leave the pool without her assent,
but was still wary. Yet when she'd sensed he'd arrived, she'd
come to see him. Not so much because she wanted to speak to
another person, but because he was so different than anyone
she'd known.

She pulled her feet from the water, dried her legs with a
small towel, and put on her liners and boots.

He didn't move, and when she looked at him again, his
mouth was grim.

"I'm sorry." The words came involuntarily from her, and
she hated that she'd reflexively apologized.

The water rippled with his shrug. "Don't be. I know
you've been hurt." Then he was swimming smoothly back to
his clothes.

He hadn't done anything to hurt her. Wasn't anything like
T'Yew. Her fear was irrational. She screwed up her courage.
"You can come out."

He levered himself from the water. He wore a swim loincloth, and somehow that reassured her and she sighed. A wind whisked around him as he muttered a dry spell.

"I think I'll be going. I was down here earlier," she said.

He glanced at her. "I wondered if you missed people. I've only been out of the Family Residence a day and worked with many students, but the quiet of the Turquoise House was unusual." Then he smiled. "When it wasn't talking to me."

She managed a small smile. "That was an interesting story."

He bowed. "I'm glad it amused you."

"T'Yew Residence was very formal. I don't miss it—or *them*—at all."

"Do you care to tell me of your day? It looks as if you worked on the gardens."

That he wanted to talk and made no move toward her helped. She walked closer, but remained out of reach. "I did. There's a conservatory attached to a Residence."

"A Residence? I didn't know that."

"I didn't go in," she said hastily.

He looked at her oddly. "Why shouldn't you?" His arm swept wide. "I think you and I are the only ones here, and I won't be coming during the day." He hesitated again, then said, "I was too tired last night, and we'd just met, but I need to know."

She stiffened.

"Where do you go? Is there anything I can do to help you?"

She hesitated, studying him, but he was here within the sanctuary. He could explore. "There's a stillroom, and I don't need help."

"Oh." His brows dipped. They were as pale as his hair, but thick. "You're warm enough? Safe?"

She managed not to step back, said firmly, "I'm fine."

"Good." Again there was a moment of silence. "You must tell me if you need anything I can provide."

"I can take care of myself."

A sharp nod. "I understand about pride."

"And payment for favors." Her voice was too harsh. T'Yew had never done anything from generosity or kindness.

Tinne's gaze met hers, eyes dark. He'd gone expressionless. "You think I'd demand payment for my help?" His laugh was equally dark. He flung out his arm. "We're the only two here. That gives us a common bond." His jaw flexed. "It's best for people in a desperate situation to bury any animosity and stick together. That I know from experience."

Before she could ask for details, a graceful form leapt out of the night.

Lahsin shrieked and jumped back, windmilling.

Tinne lunged forward, caught her flailing arms, steadied her, dropped his hands from her, and stepped back before she knew what had happened. She looked at the huge cat who sat, tail curled around her paws, muzzle shaped into a smug cat smile.

I am Ilexa, a Holly hunting cat, Tinne's Fam.

"You don't look desperate to me," Lahsin said, rubbing her arms. They seemed to tingle where Tinne had held her, not in a bad way, just in a new-person-touching-her way.

Cats go where they please.

Lahsin guessed so, though she didn't have any more experience with cats than she did dogs. The dog. *He* looked desperate, scrawny with matted fur, protruding ribs, and a crippled leg. Tinne's Fam was sleek and well cared for, as Tinne was himself on the outside. Lahsin still had fading bruises and the dog-who-was-not-a-Fam-or-companion was in worse shape than she. Ironic.

She shivered.

Tinne saw it, of course. She'd underestimated him all around, his speed, strength, vigor. Skill. She had second thoughts about the self-defense training. It was easy to think she could do it when she wasn't face-to-face with the man.

"Since I don't see that stillroom, it must not be close. You're cold and it's dark. Are you sure you don't want me to walk with you?"

"Yes."

"Still more afraid of me, or being in some sort of debt to me." He bowed stiffly, and she realized he was angry. It had taken a while to read T'Yew—his cool expression and colder eyes. She sidled away. "Why are you angry?" she asked, as if it mattered. T'Yew had always listed faults she'd never recognized.

Tinne flung up his hands. She flinched.

He scowled openly, that was a relief. "You insult my honor."

"I've found Noble 'honor' to be very flexible."

Staring at her, he finally sighed. "I'm sorry for that." His face altered subtly so it seemed less a mask, back to the mobile expressiveness she'd already realized was normal to him. He drew himself up. He understood pride, he'd said, and she saw that now. He looked as proud as his Fam.

"The Holly honor—" he stopped. "My honor has never been called into question." Then the mask dropped back over his features. "Genista, my former wife, asked that I respect her wishes and end our hollow marriage." The words tore from him, raw, and Lahsin regretted this whole conversation.

"To confine a woman against her will goes against everything I consider myself to be, my personal honor. I suffered through the divorce tests and the divorce itself. Let her go." His eyes sheened. "I think I can be trusted not to hurt you."

"I don't know you."

He rubbed his face. "No, and you've been taught to fear men." When he took his hands away his smile was sad and lopsided. "Your Family didn't protect you as they should have."

She shuddered. "I won't go back to them."

"Your decision, and I believe it's the right one. I'm not thinking clearly tonight, so I should go. But we *are* both here in this place, Lahsin. We are both . . . Healing. *I* consider that a bond. All my offers stand." He rolled his shoulders, met her eyes, and his own were back to a light gray. "It would make me feel better to know you knew how to take care of yourself wherever you decide to go in the future. You mentioned a stillroom, do you know how to use it?"

Lahsin nodded. "My MotherDam taught me."

"If you make me a few bruise-easing tinctures we'll trade."

She frowned, he must have massive resources.

"Tinctures I can use when I am here, before and after soaking in the Healing spring." He linked his hands together and stretched, let out a small groan.

"All right," Lahsin agreed. His openness prodded her. "My Second Passage is coming. I intend to ride it out here."

He nodded.

"And I think I'll spend the winter here."

"Good idea." His eyes held questions, but he said nothing. "I'll manage."

"Of course," he said, no doubt in his voice and that buoyed

her. He flashed her a tired smile. "Be off with you then, it's too cold for you to be standing out here."

She ducked her head. "Merry meet."

"And merry part."

"And—"

We are not alone here, Ilexa projected. She'd watched them with interest. *There is a wild dog. A wolfhound.*

Lahsin had forgotten the beast. But she didn't believe the dog would hurt her. She peered in the dark but didn't see it or sense it.

Tinne's face hardened. "I can follow you. Or go before. You must have cleared a path."

"It's crippled," she said.

His body relaxed. "Easier to defend against, though a wolfhound is a big dog."

"We've . . . talked. I don't think he'll attack me."

Tinne's brows drew down. "It's sentient?"

It is starving and can't catch good food. Ilexa sniffed, then she licked her paw. *I did not eat much of the wild porcine I killed.* Her shrug rippled down her back. *He eats slowly, as befits a starving thing. Perhaps intelligent for a dog.*

"Best take precautions," Tinne said. He went to the underbrush, pulled out a branch that looked torn from a tree. The length was about half a meter taller than Lahsin. With a few words and skilled fingers, he stripped the branch until he held a knotty staff.

"You knew that was there," she said.

"I'm always observant of weapons. There's plenty of makings for rough staffs around."

He held out the thick stick, end first. "Here, sturdy enough to fight off a wild dog. There's easier prey for him."

She hoped so.

"Also thick enough to bash me in the head and take me down."

She didn't think he'd yank her toward him, but hesitated.

Shaking his head, he laid the stick on the ground, turned, and walked to the bench and his cloak. "Take it."

She did. The staff felt good in her hands. Would make an excellent walking stick for the rises and hollows of the garden. She set one solid end down on the ground. Her fingers closed around it, perfect for her grip. Had he chosen it for that purpose? The man was much more dangerous than she'd thought.

"Merry meet again," he said abruptly and vanished.

Ilexa moved to four paws and stretched, keeping a bright amber gaze on Lahsin. *The dog is little threat to you. But I am. Do not hurt My FamMan, or I will rip out your throat.* She disappeared, too, as quietly as Tinne.

Lahsin was chilled. Stupid cat! Lahsin had no intention of hurting Tinne Holly. *She*, capable of hurting Tinne Holly. Ludicrous. But she'd stayed too long in the winter's night, she was cold, tired, and somehow more disheartened than she'd expected to be after visiting with him. She shuffled back to her sterile nest in the stillroom.

*T*inne had the Turquoise House wake him early the next morning for his tour. The House insisted that he and Ilexa eat first, then cleaned the fine china. With Ilexa trotting beside him, Tinne saw every room, praising the House's symmetrical beauty. Then Ilexa trotted off to the teleportation room and T'Holly Residence. There she'd be pampered and petted and fed another, less healthy, breakfast by Tinne's Mamá.

In the guest suite he looked at a wall mural depicting a bucolic view of Noble Country, with small images of the First-Families Residences that were modeled after ancient Earthan castles: T'Blackthorn's beautiful home, the long château of D'Elder, the island castle of D'SilverFir, T'Holly's tall, grim castle . . . all houses with intelligence and personalities.

"Turquoise House?"

"Yes, Tinne?"

"Do you have a HouseHeart? If you do, we might want to reinforce it. A Family will expect a HouseHeart."

The House didn't answer immediately, and Tinne didn't press it. Nor did he feel he had to declare his honor as he had to Lahsin. It had been vital that she know he wouldn't hurt her.

Finally, the House whispered, "Tinne, no one ever asked me that. But I do. I have a small hidden closet in the basement."

"Do you mind if I examine it?"

"No."

So he went down to the cold basement, goose bumps prickling his arms under his shirt.

"I can make the air warmer," the House said and did so, directing him to the closet. Tinne opened the door and stared. There were a few round pebbles in the corner. He peered at them closely, caught the glint of gold flecks. "These are your HeartStones?" He was incredulous. "Amazing you've developed so far with only these."

A pebble glowed. "Thank you," the House said.

Tinne swallowed. He hadn't meant it as a compliment. "Uh, greater Flair is developing in humans, probably in Residences, too." Narrowing his eyes, he studied the back of the closet. "We could make a hidden passage and chamber, move your peb—HouseStones." He shook his head. "I don't know how to do that. Better ask Mitchella D'Blackthorn." He waved a hand. "Tell her to consult me regarding the cost."

"Yes, Tinne."

He closed the door, set his hands on it, and crafted the best spellshield he could—mediocre—and walked back up to the teleportation pad.

"Wait, Tinne!"

"Yes?"

"I've spoken with D'Blackthorn!"

"Ah."

"She is going to ask the Councils for a research grant to pay for my needs! I will be famous!"

"You're already famous."

The walls took on additional color, and Tinne knew that outside, the place was bright turquoise.

"Thank you. You'll be reimbursed for the actors and moles."

"Moles?"

"D'Blackthorn thinks that moles will be best for tunneling." This was getting complicated. "Moles. Right. Good."

The House lowered its voice to a thrilling whisper. "There will be a secret tunnel and HouseHeart. I will trust you to move my HeartStones."

"An honor." He bowed. "Now I must go to work."

"I have much to do today, also. I will be busy!"

Tinne figured it had been bored. "Ilexa will probably return. You can entertain each other." Without waiting to hear what the House might say to that, he left.

The next morning *Lahsin* awoke in the stillroom. *She* thought the dog had spent the night in a corner of the conservatory.

She was warm—no, hot. The flush of incipient Passage was on her, and her body seemed to vibrate with Flair. She couldn't think of a better time to stretch herself in all ways and check the spellshields of the walls of the estate.

The north wall was closest, but she was most concerned about the curving wall, especially by the Healing pool. Those spells must be the best.

It would be fascinating to understand how the estate spellshields worked—letting in those desperate souls who needed sanctuary.

Her stomach growled, and she went to the counter and the bowl holding the few nuts that had escaped the wildlife and looked good to eat. She cracked them with a Word. Dry and hard.

Then sunlight slanted into the room, lighting it and illuminating the wooden counter. She stared at the rough tracing of a name on the wood. "Shade lived here." The murderer.

Sixteen

♥

*W*hirling, she mentally probed the estate. Surely she'd have felt lingering evil? She frowned. There was no terrible twisted darkness left behind by a murderer. She sniffed and smelled the same pleasantly clean, slightly astringent fragrance as ever.

Shade had killed the highest Nobles of the land, Ladies and Lords of the FirstFamilies Council. Everything she'd heard about him tinted him as an evil villain. He certainly had changed her own life when he'd killed Yew's first wife.

Lahsin touched the counter. No emotions remained. The garden let in only the desperate. Perhaps Shade's acts had been those of a man riddled with despair. Hadn't he been the one sole survivor of a psychically linked triad? That would warp anyone.

"Be at peace," she said as she traced his name. "May you rise above your tribulations in your next life." She felt a frisson along her spine. Whatever had spurred Shade's actions, his next life wasn't likely to be pleasant. It occurred to her that T'Yew might not like *his* next life, either. A man who'd abused great power. No, she didn't think he'd be pampered next time around.

Not that he was a very spiritual man. He probably didn't believe in the tenets of their faith regarding other lives, since he acted as if there would be no adverse consequences of his actions. When had he last been thwarted? Lahsin frowned. There had been a lot of stomping around and acid asides between T'Yew and Taxa last year about the new upstart T'Willow. Since Saille Willow seemed to have prospered, neither T'Yew nor his daughterHeir must have been able to do him harm.

But whatever they'd been angry about must not have been very important, if they were forced to let it go. Or they'd convinced themselves that the matter wasn't important.

The clock in the tower on the far side of the building clanged the hour, and she came back to the need to plan for her future. Food was going to be a problem. She had the old trail meal she'd found in the Summer Pavilion. Lahsin secretly hoped that Tinne Holly would come back, along with Ilexa, and the cat would hunt for the dog.

Now she was being ingenuous. The cat didn't like her or the dog. The dog would distrust and hate the cat, especially if it provided him with food because he was too crippled to hunt. The cat might do that just to gloat and act superior.

Even with only four beings occasionally on the estate, connections and relationships got tangled.

Not four, five.

There was the Residence.

She had to enter the Residence on her own terms, not by force or its grudging generosity. Most were formidable. T'Yew's could have killed her. She wasn't sure what, if any, spells constrained a Residence against harming its Family. She'd never been Family to T'Yew Residence and certainly wasn't here. But she was tired of being a victim.

That left negotiation. She was willing to clean and care for it . . . heat flushed through her, signaling that Passage would soon be coming. She needed a safe place to stay and would feel better inside a large Residence. If her Flair was for spellshields, she could offer the Residence a valuable service.

She took a step, then a hot tide had her grabbing for the counter, leaning against it, dizzy. When her mind stopped spinning, she was torn between getting into the Residence and being safer or satisfying her curiosity about the estate's spellshields. She pushed away from the counter and staggered. Her vision was off, showed wavy auras, as if her eyes looked *through* an atmosphere of Flair. She shook her head, breathed deeply, crossed to the door, and reached for the latch. Sparks rose from her fingers as she touched the metal.

How best to use this Flair?

She stepped outside and the fragrances of a winter garden—cold earth waiting, freezing air wrapping around bark—came to her, but more, too.

An odd, unusual scent. Flair. Strong and strange. Her nose twitched. *Spellshield scent.* Her feet made her decision, carrying her to the nearest wall, the north city wall. She couldn't make it to the wall beyond the Healing pool.

Hurrying now, she slipped through brush and trees. None of them scratched her, but seemed to slide off her skin. Interesting. Some sort of personal spellshield? She'd gone off without her cloak, yet she didn't feel the cold. Her blood pounded hot in her head and hands. Personal spellshield *including* a weathershield? She'd never heard of anything like that.

T'Yew had kept her in ignorance. She giggled as she lifted her fingers to push back a springy bare branch and sparks rose from them, singeing the wood. More nice smell. That wasn't right, hurting a plant that had done her no harm. She stopped, bobbled a curtsy. "Beg pardon," she sent to the small tree. Then had to grasp the small trunk to stay upright. She sent a rush of tenderness to the tree. *Thank you.*

Then she could see the gray stone wall beyond bushes, a small pocket between the towering trees planted close to it. She ran, fell against it. It wasn't as warm as the concave wall that stretched from northwest to southeast of the estate. The stone was rough against her face.

Grunting, she set both palms on the wall.

The spellshields rushed over her, flattening her against the stone. She could *sense* what lay beyond the wall, the gentle sloping ground to the fields along the road to the north and other towns. The north city gate was to the west, to the east was the northeast corner of this city wall. Maybe she'd look at that corner. Later, much later.

The wall was strong with ancient spellshields of the colonists themselves, a thin layer, to keep out the strange animals of Celta who would threaten humans, but with a welcome for their own kind. Was that welcome what made Druida City preeminent among the few cities of Celta? Or was it the strange, hulking starship that sat near the western cliffs of the sea? She vaguely sensed it as an alien being.

Coated onto that first layer of spellshield were many layers of protective spells created by Druida's Councils and the strongly Flaired FirstFamilies, during sacred holiday rituals throughout the centuries. Every quarter of the year people would gather in the GreatCircle Temple to protect their city and those spells would flow to the walls and along them. Strong. She'd never felt spellshields so strong as those inset into the city walls. They coated both surfaces, inside and out.

But there were more, odder spells, here in this wall and the one to the east. Spells that completely permeated the stones, the walls of BalmHeal Estate—FirstGrove. Illusion spells, Healing spells, spells drawing those who needed the place, a strange interweaving of them that merged with the city wall spells. Lahsin sank into them, realized that the very first of these were set by two—a HeartMate couple—BalmHeals. He a powerful Healer, she, like Lahsin, a spellshield Master.

The walls whispered. The surface that faced outer Celta, the north and east walls said: *We are strong city walls, but you do not look beyond us to what is inside this corner. Beyond this corner is a place that sleeps, nothing of interest.*

The inner surface said: *This is a sanctuary, a place of rest and Healing. Welcome and be Healed. Stay until you no longer need this place, beloved BalmHeal, FirstGrove.*

The curving wall inside the city spoke, too: *Come those who are in need, who are desperate, we will shelter, we will protect, we will Heal.* That whisper itself was a spell, audible only to certain ears, certain hearts, Lahsin knew. What was most often heard was: *There is nothing beyond us, but Celta itself. You are not interested in this piece of land. Nothing here to concern you.*

That was probably the reason that the warehouse area surrounding the estate was deserted, too.

Fabulous, amazing walls.

No BalmHeals had held rituals in a long time to reinforce the shields. The spells drew from outside but also worked with the warmth of the hot spring inside, the sacred grove that had been the first established in Druida by the colonists. They had graced it with all the love and gratitude they felt for their new home. They had lived *here* as they built their city, the walls with their fantastic machines, established their own estates. And FirstGrove remembered, still had some of that ancient energy.

She felt the grove itself, a powerful well of Flair far in the south of the estate. Someday she'd go there.

But now she *needed* to add her signature to the walls, ensure they were strong, that the whisperings would not falter, and give them energy and definition.

So she did, without knowing how.

She was hot, hot, hot. The spellshields themselves prodded her Flair, bringing it from inside her, igniting it into flames. She poured energy into the spells and walls. It lasted an eternity, as if she could sense every minute layer of every ritual throughout the centuries that had made the spells, until her legs couldn't hold her and she crumpled to the ground next to the wall, curled in on herself, and her consciousness faded away.

She awoke cold and wet, and with the dog nudging her with his nose.

*T*inne *watched the new beginner class of exuberant boys* head toward the male waterfall room. Some, like Antenn Blackthorn and the Clovers, were jauntier than others—they'd go to grovestudy group instead of private tutors like Vinni T'Vine.

Vinni's bodyguards had already arrived. Tinne didn't know the T'Vine guardsmen, and they weren't friendly. He thought they originally hailed from Gael City and trained privately in T'Vine Residence. Vinni must have done some fast talking to be allowed to train here. The bodyguards and Cratag Maytree—waiting for Laev Hawthorn—lounged in the entry waiting room.

Tinne caught Cratag's eye through the glass in the door and jerked his head. Eyebrows raised, Cratag glanced at the T'Vine guards then drifted through the door as if checking on the state of the sparring room.

Tab had gone to supervise the boys, and Tinne and Cratag were alone. Tinne hadn't thought of a way to be subtle, so he said, "I hear you know of FirstGrove, and I thank you for your recommendation and discretion."

Cratag's heavy black brows lowered as he scrutinized Tinne. "You have troubles of your own."

"That I do," Tinne said affably.

The guard glanced around, no one was paying attention to them. "Enough to find FirstGrove yourself." He hesitated, then continued, "You've spoken to the Lady."

"That I have. I want to give you her thanks."

Cratag nodded. "Done. Pretty little thing. Never liked T'Yew." He turned away.

Tinne cleared his throat. "Maytree, do you have a regular sparring salon?"

"Hawthorn has a fair enough room in the Residence."

"But Hawthorns are not known for their fighting. Good partners wouldn't be readily available."

"I'm a Commoner and have a gym membership."

Tinne nodded. "There will be a lifetime membership available for you at the Green Knight Fencing and Fighting Salon." He walked away but overheard Maytree mutter to himself.

"Entangled in Noble business again, FirstFamily business. Cave of the Dark Goddess."

Still, if the man took his profession and himself seriously, he'd accept the membership.

Then the boys swirled from the dressing room clothed brightly in their house colors, their chatter just as bright.

Lahsin yelled. The dog glared at her and hobbled a few feet away, stayed on all four paws, meeting her gaze.

Just checking.

"I'm not dead."

Stupid place to sleep.

She sat up shakily and brushed leaves and twigs from her clothes. Bracing one hand against the wall—which now felt warm—she rose, her joints stiff from the chill. She stopped a whimper, feeling she needed the upper hand with the dog. If this conversation went well, she'd proceed to the Residence.

The dog sat now, yellow gaze inscrutable, his tail hiding his malformed leg.

"Our agreement is still good."

He dipped his head. *Yes.*

"I don't hurt you, and you don't hurt me."

We do not attack or hurt each other.

"Right." She studied him. There was a slight perkiness to his ears that hadn't been there before. "The cat, Ilexa, said you ate a small wild porcine last night."

The dog's muzzle angled away as if he was embarrassed at feeding at something else's kill.

I ate the porcine last night. A mocyn this morning.

Lahsin really didn't want to think about that, and she noticed that he didn't say that he'd hunted the mocyn, deduced that, too, had been killed by the cat.

She glanced at the sun, saw it was nearing noon, felt empty of food herself. If she was lucky, some of her seeds in the greenhouse might have unfurled into tender salad greens. All day yesterday she'd sent them energy, had done so just before she fell asleep last night and when she awoke this morning. She couldn't harvest everything, of course, but something fresh along with the trail meal would be wonderful.

The dog was already limping away.

"If you come to the glasshouse, I'll share a trail meal."

Growling rumbled from its throat. *Tastes bad.*

"But it's filling!" She caught up and passed him.

A few minutes later they were both eating in the conservatory. Lahsin sat at a small fancy café table. The table and two chairs had been stored under a tarp, and she'd placed them in the center of the flagstones. The dog was near the place he'd made his den.

Some of her greens were ready to eat. She said prayers as she harvested them, dredged up a little more energy for them to grow lusher. Mixing the greens with watery clucker and noodles made the meal almost palatable. The dog ate steadily if unenthusiastically.

At least the ambiance was lovely. With just a little care, the plants appeared groomed and like an indoor garden instead of the tangle they were when she'd found them.

Midday meal was short, and she cleaned up everything quickly, set her shoulders, and said loudly, "I'm going to request a trade of services with the Residence again." She'd felt the occasional touch of the entity's mind.

The dog grunted and gave one last swipe of his tongue on the cracked dish, then stared at his empty plate.

"Do you wish to come with me?"

He switched his stare to her, incredulous. *No! I have told the Residence that I would not mess in it, that is enough.*

She would have liked his support. "Very well," she said stiffly. "I'll remind the Residence of that."

It knows.

"Is there anything else I can do for you?" she asked with a hint of sarcasm.

I did not ask you to feed me.

"We're both staying here for the moment. We have that in common—" She realized she was saying Tinne's words and stopped.

I am not a pet or a Fam.

"I know—" She flung up her hands. "What do I call you?'"

He growled. *What do you mean?*

"You don't like me to call you 'Beast' or 'Dog', or think of you that way," she said with exasperation. She could let her feelings out since they weren't near each other. "I've tried to treat you with courtesy. Do you have a name?"

Another growl, with a flash of sharp teeth. She was glad he was on the other side of the room. *I am me.*

"Well, of course, you're you."

Another snarl, this one not as threatening. *I am me to myself. No one has called me anything else.*

"No one gave you a name." Why not? He was an ugly dog, but he had the intelligence to be a Fam.

Didn't want no gift of a name. He glanced aside.

Lahsin shrugged. "Since we might be spending time together, I need to call you something. I can't call you 'me.'"

He got to his legs stiffly. *Don't need to spend time together.*

She huffed a breath. "It's winter. We both need a place to stay and food to eat."

I can hunt. He limped to the greenhouse door, looked out a window. From her seat on the ledge of a flower bed, she could see the trees being whipped by a winter wind.

He didn't appear to be doing a good enough job hunting. "FirstGrove has let us both in. I'm not going away soon. I don't expect you to be anything other than yourself, but when we're together I'd rather call you something, rather think of you as something other than 'Beast' or 'Dog.'" She waited, he didn't say anything. "I'll call you Strother," she finally said.

One of his ears rotated a little. *Strother.*

"It means dogweed." Daring, she turned her back on him and walked down the aisle to finish weeding a bed before she confronted the Residence.

Strother. It is a strong name.

"Stay or go." From what she knew of hurt joints, they would ache in this sort of weather.

I will stay. I can dig. I can move large rocks with Flair.

She hesitated, looked back over her shoulder, impressed. "Can you? I can make shields."

I know. The greenhouse shields are thicker now. The walls hummed when I found you. I am not bound to you, but I will answer to Strother.

"Thank you," she said with ironic courtesy. Just what she needed, two grumpy entities in her life, the dog and Balm-Heal Residence. She thought of Tinne Holly and his easy manner and wondered if he'd visit her that night.

The dog—Strother—retired back to his den under low-arching greenery and watched her.

As did the Residence.

Lahsin turned in place, scanning the greenhouse. She'd done very good work here, no one could deny that. Perhaps going to the front had been a mistake, as if she were a guest or Family.

She washed with water she'd brought from the pool and dumped it down a sink drain. The taps didn't work, but the drain did. She checked her Flair, but couldn't feel it at all; she had used what she usually had and more with the walls.

An image came of Tinne Holly teleporting. Must be nice to have such powerful Flair and the ability to use it. Until Second Passage came, she'd have to make do with what she'd developed since she was a child. Though now that she was free and less afraid, her Flair seemed greater. She didn't know whether it was because she was away from the Yews or because Passage was so near.

Determination infused her. She was tired of staying in the sterile surroundings of the stillroom, tired of reinforcing the shields around it and the conservatory to keep the weather out. If she was going to be casting weathershields, it should be a whole force field around the Residence, and based on the Residence's own spells.

She was tired of living like a beggar. She deserved better after all the work she'd done on the estate.

She was weary of lapsing into the manner of a child when her Second Passage was upon her and she was a woman, a legal adult.

She had made her own future. She might have run away from one Residence like a mouse creeping out of a house, but she would ensure that this Residence acknowledged her true worth as a strongly Flaired woman.

She marched up to the door between the conservatory and the main Residence and touched the wood she'd refinished. She could feel the old-fashioned spells, not nearly as strong as on the walls, and could unravel them easily. That was not the way. "BalmHeal Residence, I, Lahsin Rosemary, and Strother request entry. I have worked hard on the estate and here in the conservatory. I can restore some of your housekeeping spells."

"You are a child, you don't have much Flair. The dog has less yet. I am a Noble Residence, deserving of more."

"Yes, but I will give what I can for food in the no-time and a safe place to experience Second Passage."

"Will those others who walk the estate at night want in?"

"I don't know. You may negotiate with them separately. Tinne Holly is a powerful GreatSir, a SecondSon of a—"

"I know who the Hollys are! Enter, then, and when your Flair rises once more and you give me the energy for housekeeping spells, I will unlock the food no-times for you."

The door opened with a jerking creak, and Lahsin saw darkness ahead. She looked back and saw Strother's gleaming eyes.

Seventeen

❦

She stepped into the Residence and shuffled down the hall.
The door slammed behind her, and she jumped. There was a
crackle—a cackle—of creaking wood. She thought of Tinne
Holly and how he held himself when he was being casual.
Muscles with feigned looseness, hiding the fact that he could
act quickly, decisively. Her muscles were so tight they hurt.

She cocked a hip, put her hand on it, and adopted a bored
tone, even as her stomach squeezed. "Do you intend to scare
me, or do you plan to murder me?" Her voice might have
been breathless, but it wasn't a high squeak.

No answer.

Irritation swallowed her fear. "Discourteous." She let her
voice echo down the empty corridors, rattle around the house.
The hallway that ran the length of the house was coated with
dust. The only light came from a wide spot in the middle where
windows must be letting in the sun, probably the great hall.

The Residence slammed another door. "You are the one
who is rude! You poke and pry a body until they can't block
out your whining. You insist—" More emphatic creaking.

"Careful, you might splinter something of yourself, and
then where would you be? I can do housekeeping, but not re-
pairs." She kept her voice casual, discovered her hands were
fisted, and relaxed them.

"Housekeeping spells? Let's see you do some," it mocked.

Lahsin swallowed. She scuffed along, leaving long streaks of gray behind her, revealing a wooden floor, until she reached the grand hall. It was bigger than she'd anticipated, larger than T'Yew's, and that Residence was a castle. The space might also function as a ballroom. The tinted—papered?—walls were dingy. Groupings of furniture dotted the room, around the massive stone fireplace, in the front corners. The furnishings were so antique that Lahsin didn't recognize the style.

Nevertheless, she couldn't back down from the Residence's demand. May as well try the easiest first. In a loud voice and with the proper swooping gesture, she said, "Clean room!"

Little pops in the air surrounded her like laughter. "Did you actually think such a spell would work?" the Residence jeered. "I haven't had enough energy to clean a single room for centuries." More cackling. "Maybe once a decade I can pull strength from the land and do a 'whisk dust' spell." Then the voice became low. "I concentrate on surviving, just like everyone else who comes to the sanctuary."

Shrugging, Lahsin said, "I needed to find out for myself." She turned to the nearest wall, took a rag from her trous pocket, and wiped it. There *was* old-fashioned paper like in the corner room of Burdock Residence's attic. She might have liked this, a pale cream with sprigs of once-green leaves and spreading flowers that had been bright blue and deep red.

After sucking in a full breath, she put her hands on the wall. No interior shields, but faint traces of ancient human feelings—the joy of the dance, the wistfulness of the last dying Grand-Lord BalmHeal. The Residence itself had an enormous loneliness. An aching feeling of abandonment and betrayal. Her head swirled, and she was sinking, sinking, sinking.

Pain!

She gasped, saw blood welling from a puncture in her calf, and blinked at the dog—at Strother.

Focus. Housekeeping spell, or we don't eat.

True. Another deep breath. She wheezed, took her hands from the wall, and bent over.

"Puny," the Residence said.

She steadied her breath, ignored the throbbing of her injury. She could tend to it with herbs from the stillroom later if she had enough Flair for a minor Healing spell. She might have enough Flair to clean the room, but wasn't sure whether she could access her psi power. She was cold, and her Flair seemed to move like hidden fish under a thick slab of ice.

The dog slid his nose into her knee. *Work!*

She glared at him. He leaned a paw on her foot. Ouch!

Intelligent animals have Flair from birth. No stupid Passages.

Her eyes widened. He was offering her some of his Flair!

Food more important than Flair.

True again, but energy was energy. Flair might be the only thing keeping him alive.

He narrowed his eyes and growled.

"All right!" One. Last. Good. Breath. Hands on the wall. Grime underneath fingertips. Ignore all sensations.

Pull a small spark from Strother, spear it into the solid ice. Breathe! Dredge up that Flair. It's slippery. Don't lose it! *There.* Here it comes!

She gathered Flair, sent it into the wall and Residence. Through numb lips she cried, *"Clean room!"* then sagged.

Strother sat straight, cocked his head at her use of so little of his psi energy. Then his ears pricked, his nostrils widened. He pointed his muzzle toward the large door.

Lahsin squinted and saw the slightest whirl of air. She bit her lip, hoping it would grow. She'd become accustomed to being thought a failure, used to forcing herself to proceed with any task though she'd be scolded for it. But now, after several *successes*, the thought of failing stabbed through her.

It was agonizingly slow, but the spell built as a sigh of a breeze on a hot summer's day increased to a strong wind, then a whirlwind of a coming storm. Strother hobbled back into the main corridor, but Lahsin laughed as the spell pushed against her to clean every millimeter of the room and leave it smelling of tea tree.

Leaning against the threshold, she saw the wind die. The windows sparkled, the fancy patterned parquet floor gleamed dully, needing more refinishing. There was no hint of the heap of debris that had littered the fireplace.

"The housekeeping spell is done," she said weakly.

"For one room," the Residence grumbled.

"For your largest room."

The front door opened and closed—no squeaking. "Very well," the Residence said, then paused. "You may access the kitchen no-times and may use the small floral guest room upstairs. Dog—"

Strother! the dog mentally shouted.

"—may choose a closet."

Lahsin chuckled, stepped away from the wall, and nearly fell, weak from her exertions. She managed to put a hand on it and staggered, coughing, back down the hall toward the kitchen.

Strother had kicked the door wide. Murky light came from windows in the back and on the end of the house. The place was filthy. She should have cleaned this room first. Time enough to do so tomorrow, if she had the same amount of Flair as today.

The dog stood, drool stringing from his muzzle, in front of the wall with no-time food storage units. One would contain prepared meals, steaming or chilled, exactly the same temperature as when they were placed in storage. The other would have supplies. But how much of each?

Come ON! snapped Strother. His saliva pooled onto the floor, leaving a clean mark. Lahsin got the impression that he didn't want to sit on the dirty slate tiles.

Nearly panting herself, Lahsin went to the smaller unit that had a long chrome bar about chin-high. The panel that should have shown the list was blank.

"Residence, do you have furrabeast steak?" Just saying it made her mouth water.

No answer.

She put her hand on the bar. And couldn't open it. "Ooh!" She didn't have a smidgeon of Flair left to open the damn door.

Strother balanced awkwardly on his hind legs, scrabbled at the door, but couldn't get it open. His growls came deep and angry.

Damn!

Only one thing to do.

"I will lift you—"

I am too heavy for you.

"Not if it means food! And you can stretch tall, almost as tall as me. I'll put my hand around one of your forepaws and open the damn door."

Grunting, she lifted, dropped him as he wiggled. "Be still!"

He growled.

They tried again, Lahsin muttering, "Furrabeast steak," as she wrenched at the handle.

Failed.

The third time, breath ragged, shouting, they succeeded. Both of them moaned as the aroma of grilled meat wafted out. Lahsin swallowed spit. There were four plates of beautiful china, cuts showed the doneness. There were side dishes of potatoes and green beans on every plate. She nearly whimpered. Strother *did* whimper.

"Rare for you?" she asked.

Yes.

She took the warm plate and put it on the floor. He ripped at it, then took slow bites. She pulled out the well-done meat for herself and put it on the table. When she saw that the no-time had replaced both rare and well-done with additional portions, she moaned and closed the door.

Tears came to her eyes.

She carried the plate into the conservatory, leaving the door open to the main Residence.

It was the best meal she'd ever eaten.

*T*inne *finished his day with Saille T'Willow's first train-*ing session. The man was less of a tyro than he'd indicated, and said he'd had some instruction at a country manor.

After drawing up an aggressive program, they parted, and Tinne grinned at the hefty annual fee Saille had authorized. Whatever financial dip occurred because of the scandal—and there'd been a loss—the salon was safe for the year.

Tinne teleported to the pad in Turquoise House.

"Hewwo, Tinnie! Gweetingth!" it said in a girlish baby voice, complete with lisp. Tinne stopped, mouth open in surprise. Ilexa rolled on the floor with echoing cat laughter.

Tinne swallowed. "House, do you *like* that voice?"

"Two actorth came today!" it caroled. "Thith wath the beth voith."

Tinne suppressed a flinch, hurried to his bedroom. "Perhaps I can hear the other."

"Of course, Tinne." Dark, low, with a rasp that raised the hair on the back of his neck. Tinne recognized the voice from plays he'd seen. The actor specialized in villains, and the spin of horrific Flair gave Tinne the shudders. Apparently the actors weren't taking the request for a voice for the House seriously.

"You're right, the first voice is the best. Otherwise I'd think you an abandoned and haunted Earthan castle."

"Unless you want Mitchella's? I've heard that one the longest, have the greatest range," it said in Mitchella's tones.

He stopped stripping, held his clothes close. "No, let's go with the new female one. And speaking of Mitchella—"

"—you are due at an exthended Holly-Blackthorn Family gathering in half a thepthour."

"Yes. I'm changing now. Please request that T'Holly Residence send a glider for me." Teleporting took a great deal of energy. Even walking from the teleportation room to his own bedroom had been tiring. Or maybe his steps had dragged because he didn't want to have dinner with his Family.

Ilexa had passed him to stand in front of a mirror and was grooming herself. She turned her head and snorted.

"I'll be needing—wanting—to teleport to and from First-Grove tonight. To soak in the best Healing pool in Druida."

Her fur rippled in a shrug. *Perhaps I will go and kill more food for the dog.* She stood and pranced to him. *All cats are now talking about my exploits.*

"Uh, *secrecy*, Ilexa."

You told me I could boast.

He was afraid he had. "I made a mistake. The more who know, the easier it will be to find—"

No. The location blurs in my mind, on my tongue when I speak of it. And Zanth and other FamCats can't get in. They do not have a desperate FamMan. Ilexa smirked.

Tinne winced.

"The legendary FirthGrove?" asked the Turquoise House.

"Forget you heard that."

"You would have me wipe my memory?" the House said, appalled.

Tinne ran a hand through his hair. What happened to peace and quiet? He nearly shouted, "No! Please designate any references to FirstGrove as extremely private and personal, not to be disclosed to anyone without my authorization."

"My firth thecret! Done. I have a warm brithe brandy for you in your thitting room." There was the sound of a metallic drawer extending.

"Thank you."

"A new beverage-only no-time wath inthalled today."

"You had a busy day. House, could you try to make your esses a little harder, please?"

"Yethss."

"Excellent." Or about as good as it was going to get. He pulled on a new holly green shirt of silkeen with bloused sleeves, black trous gathered at the ankles, and low boots.

Brushing his hair, he wondered again whether he should visit FirstGrove tonight—recalled that the purpose of the dinner would be to announce a new baby. The clench of his gut told him that time in the FirstGrove might be wise.

Lahsin spent the rest of the day in the Residence. She'd swept out the room the Residence had assigned her, pulled off the bed linens, and gone, under protest from the Residence, into another room to hang them outside on its balcony. She'd tested the bedsponge and found it crumbly and soft, but acceptable.

Strother hadn't told her which closet he'd chosen, and she hadn't asked. He might prefer sleeping in his greenhouse den since the mild winter days kept the place warm. There was some heat in the Residence from ancient spells circulating hot springs water through the pipes, though the Residence had grumbled about spending more effort to heat the place.

There wasn't any plumbing, the Residence had admitted truculently. That system was different than the heating pipes. Lahsin had decided that item had to be the very next to activate when her Flair revived. She wasn't sure how much energy plumbing would demand, but didn't think it would be easy, and a lot less interesting than the estate spellshields. But no cleaning could be done without water.

Then she'd returned to the stillroom to make a salve for her puncture and a sore muscle balm for Tinne as payment for self-defense training. She hoped she could ask for the lessons tonight.

Though she said little Healing jingles as she made the ointments, she'd had no Flair to power them. So she said prayers to the Lady and Lord, too, and hoped blessings might work.

As she was fixing a hearty meal of stew and bread for herself, Strother strolled in, and she gave him a bowl of clucker bites. He hummed in pleasure as he ate.

Dark came early in the month of Rowan, the days getting shorter until Yule, the winter solstice. She'd wanted to retire in her not-too-clean-but-warm room and sleep on a real bedsponge. But Tinne always came late to the garden, after most people ate dinner. The more she thought on it, she believed it wasn't his work that wearied him. It was time with his Family and friends. Being the butt of a scandal couldn't be good.

She only hoped the Yews were suffering. Which reminded her that Tinne had brought newssheets that she'd ignored and left on the bench. They'd have disintegrated to garden mulch by now.

So she went late to the Healing pool, scraped the remains of the newssheet off Tinne's bench, and dropped them in the arbor. She couldn't distinguish whether the titillating first story was Tinne's divorce or her vanishing. The Hollys were always interesting to read about. The Yews and the Burdocks, less so.

As she slid into the steamy herbed water, she let out a quiet moan. She should do this every day, Tinne Holly or not! Secretly she wanted to see him. The dog was no company, and the Residence was a crotchety old man, needing and greedy for caring, and pushing friendly overtures away because of it.

Tinne Holly, despite his own problems, had still carried an air of stoic optimism about him. He'd weather this suffering because he was a survivor. More than that, a fighter. Lahsin admired him and wanted his courage to rub off on her.

He was nothing like T'Yew, or any of the older men she'd met since her marriage, which both comforted and frightened her. But Tinne was the best chance she had of learning how to protect herself in the future.

Perhaps tonight she'd be brave enough to let him teach her.

Eighteen

♥

Tinne stopped in the great hall of T'Holly Residence.
His brother, Holm, stood in the center of the chamber, arm
around his wife. Their parents were behind them, holding hands.
Beside them was GreatLord Vinni T'Vine, the young prophet.

All of the Family who worked in the Residence, on the
estate, or even hired out as guards for other Nobles in Druida,
had gathered. Tinne sidled over to Tab. The Blackthorns with
an actively fussing babe in arms and their other two children
stood off to the side. Everyone was beaming.

Tab, always astute, set his hand on Tinne's shoulder, and it
felt supportive, bracing.

Holm lifted his champagne glass and said, "I am pleased
to announce that Lark and I are having a child."

Joyful shouts came from everyone, reverberated against
Tinne's ears, reminding him that this had happened, too, when
he and Genista had announced their forthcoming baby. He
grunted, settled into his balance. Tab squeezed his shoulder,
sending Tinne some Flair. Which was good, because his knees
went weak and his gut roiled.

But he had to do his duty. Tinne forced a smile and with
careful steps, he walked to Holm and Lark. Silence fell.

Tinne met his brother's serious eyes. Tinne loved Holm,
but this was hard, hard. Stepping close he embraced his older

brother and hugged him tight. "Blessings," he choked out. The past was overwhelming him. His brother had not been in the gathering to wish him and Genista joy.

Holm held him close, sent Tinne more Flair. "Thank you."

Tinne turned to Lark, the Healer. Her violet eyes held a sheen of sorrow, though she smiled. He hugged her, too. And she gave him Flair. The Family bond expanded inside Tinne, and he felt the warmth of all for him, the acknowledgment by all of his loss, the rising gladness that a new child would be born.

His hurt was accepted, then it was eased by the love of his Family for him. He kissed Lark's temple. When he drew away his smile was genuine. "Blessings on you and the babe."

"Thank you, brother," she said. Her gaze searched his face. "You are looking better."

He summoned a chuckle. "The Turquoise House is endlessly amusing." And time in FirstGrove was Healing itself. And Lahsin was undemanding, had no expectations of him.

Lark smiled. "I'm glad."

Tinne's father avoided meeting his eyes. Tinne retreated, and the Blackthorns came to congratulate Holm and Lark, baby wailing. As soon as that was done, they muttered apologies and left.

Tinne returned to Tab, who said, "You did very well. I'm proud of you."

Holm put his hand on Vinni T'Vine's shoulder. "Vinni has agreed to be the oracle at the birth of our child, reading the character and strength of his or her Flair."

There were mutterings of approval.

"That won't be cheap," Tab said.

"Now let's celebrate together with good food and good ale." Holm gestured to the long tables at the side of the room, laden with a feast. Other, smaller tables were scattered throughout the large chamber. Holm led Lark to the food and took a plate, attentive to her choices. Voices rose as the Family discussed the news and headed toward the food.

Tab nudged Tinne. "Sorry, boy, but ya can't leave afore you eat with your folks."

"And you."

"And me. I'll be right with ya."

"Thanks."

"Ya done well," he repeated.

Tinne piled food almost absently on his plate, steeled himself, and took a seat at the table with his parents and brother and sister-in-law. Vinni T'Vine stood beside it.

"Vinni, will you stay for dinner?" asked Tinne's Mamá.

"I'd be honored, but I must go to the Reeds'." A smile too cynical for a child his age curved his lips. "I think they're angling for a free consultation without actually asking."

"Blessings, then," Lark said.

"And to you." He grinned. "This will be fun. You're the first folks to ask me to be an oracle, and I've been T'Vine six years. My thanks." He bowed smoothly and went to the door where a brand-new glider waited.

An awkward silence draped the table. All of them should have been asked to the T'Reed holiday party. They hadn't been, or Tinne would have had it on his calendarsphere.

Tab slashed a look at the others and leaned back in his chair. When he spoke the tang of the seaman was in his voice. "My invites haven't changed muchly." He shrugged. "The older, less Noble generation. We all know that scandal'll touch everyone sooner'a later." He inhaled and exhaled audibly. "The Green Knight has lost some patrons, but not 'nough to affect profits. Had some inquiries from middle-class folk, and we'll be makin' up the loss with 'em. New blood. Good business." He nodded.

Lark's shoulders hunched, and a wave of certainty washed over Tinne that she and his brother had plenty of holiday invitations.

The scandal revolved mostly around him and his parents then.

His Mamá straightened in her chair and lifted her chin. "Tinne, I believe you will find that your own message cache is full. We haven't been forwarding it to the Turquoise House." She reached over and took his father's hand. A flush came to her cheeks that he thought was embarrassment.

He said what he felt and what he knew might distract them. "I don't want to go out. Not even to the club."

His Mamá focused on him. "But you must!"

They weren't politicking this year but he kept that comment between his teeth. "I don't care to be social."

Lark said, "You are now an eligible bachelor again."

They all stared at her.

Tinne gave a crack of laughter. "Surely not. My marriage just ended in divorce. Not a good husband."

"You're wealthy, handsome, charming, Noble. The gossip in my women's club is that Genista was a fool to leave you."

"Why would I want to marry a woman who'd prefer a love-less marriage than to make a future for herself?" he asked softly. All the women in his life were strong enough to do that. He could only admire them even if he hurt.

"Good point." Tab nodded.

"What of your HeartMate?" T'Holly's voice grated out.

"No." He stood, knocking over his chair. As far as they all knew his HeartMate was still married. He'd choose when to tell them. If they knew she was Lahsin, they'd be after him to wed again, as soon as possible, perhaps smooth the scandal over.

No, he was too cynical. They'd want him to marry again to be happy, to find what they had. He didn't think such bliss was possible. He wasn't even sure when contentment might be within reach, or an absence of pain. "I don't intend to marry— to have a long-term woman—soon. I won't be bringing anyone here." That sounded as if he condemned them. "I don't want a lover." His words were deteriorating with his emotions, his control. He managed a courteous nod to his parents.

When he turned stiffly to his brother, Holm, and Lark, he softened. His love for them was untarnished. He found heart-felt and true words. "I'm very glad that you will be having a child. I'll welcome a niece or nephew. Blessings again." If he let it, the need to hold a babe in his arms might rip at him, so he smiled, nodded once more to Tab. "Merry meet and merry part and merry meet again." He left and only heard one last sentence from his Mamá's rising voice. "But what does he *do* in the evenings? Drum all night?"

He thought Lark murmured an answer, but it couldn't be the truth. He'd had no inclination to drum. He preferred to visit FirstGrove, take sanctuary, and meet his HeartMate, who had as many problems as he.

*L*ahsin was dozing on the underwater bench in the Heal-ing pool when the splash roused her. She blinked in the steam to see Tinne cutting fast through the water down the length of the pool.

He was hurting more tonight, then.

Squinting, she saw that he'd folded his clothes on his usual bench and had remembered to bring the daily news-sheets.

Since she'd had enough of the pool and he didn't want to talk, she slipped from the water and dressed, hesitating. He might not want her company, but she still wanted his. He was the only human she'd seen in days, so she'd linger. She walked around the pool and picked up the newssheet.

A hologram of her face projected from the front. She flinched. So *childish*. The image was only a few months old, taken on her Nameday. She hadn't looked in a mirror lately. She'd appear more like an adult now, wouldn't she? Or wouldn't her features get more definition until after her Second Passage?

She became aware of the murmuring of the newssheet. "*Burdocks Beg Lahsin to Come Home!*" There were smaller headlines in red. *Her Healer Is Standing By! Warns of Erratic Behavior!*

Suddenly she was cold, the steam of the pool clammy instead of comforting, the herbs astringent and stinging her nose. She couldn't seem to loosen her grip on the newssheet.

Her eyes tracked the print, and she got colder. The Burdocks and Yews believed she remained in Druida City. As she had, changing her plans from traveling north. They'd search for her.

Then she found her teeth grinding and welcomed the hot sting of anger. Healer indeed! *Which* Healer? She scanned the article. It didn't name the "Healer," though she could have used one after Taxa's pinching and Ioho's slaps and rutting. Did it mention her Second Passage? That she was an adult?

It did but with a slant. Her mother's face showed silver tear traces. "Lahsin is so delicate, she needs to be in a safe place." She was in a safe place, no thanks to her mother. "We worry so about her." Lahsin snorted. "Her husband is too distraught to speak . . ." With fury, Lahsin figured. As if he'd ever give a quote to a newssheet.

She threw the thing to the ground. Kicked it. Stomped on

it. Kicked it again into the arbor and ordered, "Disintegrate!"
With anger had come a tiny flick of Flair. She watched as the
newssheet became pulp held together by a spell, then turned
into mulch.

"Satisfying?" Tinne said.

He'd made no noise rising from the pool, droplets trailed
down his muscular body, caught here and there in his chest
hair and on his legs. He wasn't a very hairy man, though hair-
ier than T'Yew's sparse grayness. Lahsin liked that.

She realized she was staring and hurried away to her
travel sack, which she'd mended, brought out a large jar of
salve for him, strode back, two arms' lengths away from him.

He was dry, the air around him wavered with a weathershield. He wore only a swim cloth, and his hands were open at
his sides. He still looked like the most dangerous man she'd
ever met. He'd proven that he could move fast the night before.

The quiet stretched. Then he turned, went to his clothes,
and bent over to pick them up. His muscles appeared fine to
her, not needing anything. But she caught a glimpse of his
face in the shadows, and it showed grief.

"Wait." Without letting her mind—her fear—control her,
she scurried up to him, thrust out the jar.

He straightened and took the jar from her with grave courtesy. "Thank you." Opening it, he inhaled and his lips curved
in a slight smile. "*Thank you.* My G'Uncle Tab had an ointment that smelled like this when I was a child, made by his
MotherSire, but when it was gone, none of us knew the recipe." Tinne shrugged. "We're a Family of fighters." He scooped
some salve up on his fingers, held it to his nose, sighed. "Yes,
that's the right scent."

"It's a recipe passed down in the Burdocks. I didn't have
any Flair to mix in with it, but it has blessings." She stepped
back several paces.

"Blessings are always welcome." His smile fell away, his
hurt returned before he veiled it. He rubbed his arms and
legs, and his breath came out in another quiet sigh. "Nice."

"I can give you the recipe."

"Thank you, that would pay for anything I might teach you."

Since he'd brought it up, she said. "I *do* want to learn
self-defense."

He nodded, glanced at her with a steady gaze, and held out the jar. "Then why don't you rub this on my back?"

She opened her mouth, closed it, swallowed, stared at the jar.

He put it down. Turned his back to her. "Saille T'Willow got me a good hit near my kidneys."

The bruise was large and purpling. Lahsin winced. Set her mouth. She was *not* delicate. She was sturdy.

Tinne looked at her over his shoulder. "If you can't even touch my back, how do you think you'll be able to endure my touch for instruction?"

"I . . . I . . ."

A snort of exasperation. "Do you have your staff?"

"Yes."

"Go get it. You can hit me if you think I'll hurt you."

"I couldn't do that."

He turned to face her now, brows lowered, jaw grim. "Lahsin, I give you permission to fight, to hurt me if you think I'm going to hurt you. More. I give you permission to fight, to hurt *anyone* who tries to hurt you. Do you hear what I'm saying?"

"Yes!"

Nodding, he said, "Why don't you repeat after me, 'I am allowed to hurt anyone who is trying to hurt me.'"

"I am allowed to hurt anyone who's trying to hurt me."

"Good. I want you to say that three times a day. Now, can you put ointment on my back or not? This weathershield is tiring, and I need Flair to 'port home."

She lifted her chin. "I can rub the salve on your back." She didn't get her stick, but marched forward and scooped up the jar. He certainly hadn't hesitated to slather it on himself, it was a quarter gone already.

But she paused when her fingertips touched strong muscle under supple skin. He'd dropped the weathershield and though his body was warm, it would cool quickly.

"This is no time for hesitation," Tinne said.

So she rubbed his back, going easy on the bruised area. The salve *did* smell good. The consistency was excellent, just as her own MotherDam, Rosemary, had taught her, and it wouldn't stain the fancy shirt gleaming silkeen on the bench. He'd dressed formally. Maybe a Yule party.

Remembering how he'd swum in the pool, she didn't ask. He'd gone still under her hands, and his breathing was a little unsteady. She racked her mind for a good topic of conversation. "Tell me about the Turquoise House."

He did and began to relax, to sound amused. Then he stepped away from her, and keeping his back to her, he dressed. When he was clothed, he turned and ended the story with, "I can only hope the next actors are more competent. I don't know that I can live with that lisp very long."

Lahsin sniffed, wiped her hands on the towel she'd dropped on the bench, and sat down. "You're too picky."

He sat, too, leaving about twenty centimeters between them. Though she flinched in surprise, she didn't move. Instead, she told him about her own experiences with BalmHeal Residence, trying to make them sound funny, too. Crotchety old G'Uncle of a Residence. She said she thought Tinne had the better deal.

They lapsed into silence and as he stared into the steam, she wondered what visions he saw rising in the mist.

Softly, so he could pretend not to hear the question, she said, "Do you want to talk about anything else? You"—hurt more—"seem sadder tonight."

"My brother and sister-in-law announced they're having a child."

And he and his former wife had lost a babe in the womb. Terrible. "Oh." She hesitated then said, "It's a blessing."

"I know. Every Holly child is wanted." His smile was crooked. "Speaking of blessings, I gave them mine, of course."

She swallowed at how difficult that must have been, didn't know what else to say.

A minute later he roused himself and looked around. "You intend to stay here during the winter?"

"Yes." She smiled. "The food's good. I love gardening, I think it will be my creative Flair. My hands itch to put this place in order. I'd planned . . . " She stared at him, knew she could trust him, inhaled, let her breath out, and said, "I'd planned to go north to work in one of the fishing villages."

After another short silence he said, "You wouldn't have liked it." Then he shrugged and met her eyes. "Young, pretty girl. Bound to get into trouble if you can't defend yourself."

That fear had lurked in the back of her mind. Her throat closed, and she didn't speak until the lump went away. "You know I can't defend myself. I was never taught."

"Most people are, in their eighth year of grovestudy."

"I was married before that."

"Do you want to learn?"

"Yes!"

He inclined his head. "Very well, let's start." He stood.

"Right now?"

His smile was more like a grimace. "We can try a trust game. You'll note that I haven't hurt you." He paused, shrugged again. "Or I can teleport to the Turquoise House."

Another pause.

"Merry meet." He bowed as he started the formal farewell.

"Wait!"

Nineteen

Nervous, Lahsin licked her lips, which was a bad idea as the winter kissed them with cold. "I want you to teach me how to defend myself against T'Ye—against a man."

His half smile was replaced by an intent look. "I'll have to put my hands on you to do that."

She nodded. "Yes."

He shrugged and his coat settled differently, as if it became looser. A garment a man could fight in. He, all the Hollys, would always be prepared to fight, she realized.

"First, the trust game," he said. He peeled off his gloves and held out his hands. "Put your hands in mine."

She'd have to step forward, let him clasp his much bigger hands around hers, trap her. A trust game, indeed.

Staring at his hands, she noticed an infinitesimal trembling and glanced up at him. There were fine lines near his eyes that she hadn't noted before. He was in the garden, the same as she was. He was hurting, too, probably more than she was. She was more afraid and angry than hurt. Keeping her gaze locked on his reassuring one, she moved forward and laid her hands palms-down on his. They were warmer than she'd thought, rougher. She jerked them away, dropped her glance.

He continued to hold his hands out, but made no move to

grab her, jump her, or follow her. And she hadn't stepped back. Surely that was a sign that she was Healing. Of course Tinne Holly looked and acted *nothing* like T'Yew.

She laid her hands on his again, once more meeting his eyes. Utterly calm. They stayed like that until his thumbs brushed the back of her hands. She hopped back, more startled at the unexpectedness of the gesture than afraid of him.

His hands remained steady. She was breathing only slightly deeper than usual. No, she wasn't too afraid of this man if she could notice the tang of the herbs rising in the pool's steam.

She put her hands in his. This time he closed his fingers and anxiety came. She held it at bay a few seconds then pulled her hands away. Each time after that he held them longer, though still loosely. Finally he tightened his grip, but the minute she tugged, he let her go. She was panting, then.

He said no reassuring words. She liked that. Her eye was becoming keener, saw the easiness of his stance, not T'Yew's heavy prowl when he stalked her. She shut the memory off.

Each time she put her hands in Tinne's and he clamped his fingers around hers, she waited longer before she pulled away. Each time he released her as soon as she wanted him to.

She was breathing easier. She looked into his eyes. They were a silvery gray, still calm, as steady and warm as his hands. Reliable. Perhaps she could trust—

His hands clamped on hers. She struggled, but she was flung into heavy brush. Jerking around she saw his arm come up to fend off his Fam, fling *her* into the pool. The cat had leapt for Lahsin's back!

Ilexa's yowl screeched louder than Lahsin's surprised cry.

We were play fighting! Ilexa screamed as she zoomed from the pool to the warm garden shed walls. Her pale form shivered, shook water away.

"Lahsin didn't know you were play fighting," Tinne said. "Neither did I. Lahsin is too new to fighting to sense something coming from behind her."

True. T'Yew had always watched her run, enjoying her panic. No door would be locked to him. Nothing would stop him.

A snicker broke her memory. Twigs were poking into her. A meter from her—outside of reach—Strother sat and chuckled again. Since he was looking at the cat, Lahsin didn't think he was laughing at her.

Ilexa hissed, shimmered.

"Don't teleport away. You're my Fam, live with your mistake and embarrassment." Tinne winced as if his own words hurt.

Ilexa growled but wiped her sinuous body against an evergreen that was softer than it appeared. Not a stupid cat.

Tinne turned to Lahsin. Strother got up and lurched away as the man stepped toward them. Once again he held out his hand. She put hers in his, and he brought her to her feet with one smooth and easy pull, then let go. She was closer than ever before, only a few centimeters separated them. She could feel the heat of his body, smell the scent of his skin, herbs from the pool and ointment and man beneath. He smelled—fresher— than T'Yew. Heat rose to her cheeks at the intimate thought.

He was scanning her. "You're all right."

"Yes."

Nodding, he said, "Good." His lips curved. "Since I don't expect my Fam to apologize—"

Ilexa huffed.

"—I'll do so for her." He gave Lahsin a nod of approval. "You handled yourself very well."

She didn't understand. She'd just lain there in the bushes.

"You didn't scream, flinch, run away. You could have. Panic would have had you halfway to your clocktower now."

His words, the respect in his eyes, warmed her. She felt a surge of stunned pride. Someone thought *she'd* done *well*. She couldn't remember when she'd last been complimented on a task.

"I think that's enough for tonight," Tinne said. He glanced around and looked at the thick permamoss nearby. "We should do this earlier." He rolled his shoulders. "I have classes until WorkEndBell tomorrow, which is after night has fallen, and another obligation. But I'll be here soon after that." His gaze searched her face. "We'll start in earnest then."

He had faith in her, had given her more faith in herself. "Yes."

"I *will* have to put my hands on you, to correct your form, to pretend to attack—"

She matched his gaze with her own. "I can learn to accept it." Her smile wasn't as easy as his, but grim with determination. "I won't ever be a victim again."

He patted her on the shoulder. "Good." Then he stepped back, and Lahsin was jolted to realize she'd remained near him.

She looked at him, thought about repudiating her marriage to T'Yew to him. That was trust, too. But since he'd started teaching her, much of the unhappiness had faded from his face, even the mock attack from his FamCat had lightened his spirit. The evening's events outside this sanctuary had been hard on him. If she formally repudiated her marriage, she would remind him that he was here because of his divorce and the scandal around it. She'd rather he had some peace.

That was a step in her Healing, too. She was concerned more with Tinne's feelings than her own, had helped Strother and BalmHeal Residence. Doing for others eased her own hurt.

As teaching her would ease Tinne's.

She could wait.

He called for the cat, but she didn't come. With a half smile and a shrug, he teleported away.

The wave of power struck her before she was halfway to the Residence. She fell to her knees, throat closing. Flames engulfed her.

Not real. Not *real*! But they licked her skin.

She screamed. Nothing came from her mouth—or her mind.

She was isolated. Just as she'd been in T'Yew Residence. Just as there, she couldn't scream. Screaming, showing her upset, her fear, would make it worse. Would feed the cruelty in T'Yew's eyes, make him smile that lustful smile, and she'd be chased to his rooms. Family would avert their eyes—or laugh.

Hurt. Her mind swam, she didn't know where she was, what was happening, only knew that she must endure. If she survived, something better would happen. She clung to that thought even as T'Yew's laughter mocked.

Wetness on her hands. Snow? For an instant her vision cleared. She saw bright ice coating the frozen mud of a path.

Sanctuary. FirstGrove. The Residence was too far away.

Far too far. Lahsin shuddered with Passage, the real fugue, knew its tide was coming back to sweep her under. No, she couldn't make it to the Residence. Undergoing Passage outside in the cold winter night. That was bad. That could be fatal.

Tinne teleported—to T'Holly Residence, the corridor leading to the HouseHeart. Perhaps it was better to be here than the Turquoise House. The HouseHeart might ease him. He'd used up most of his Flair, and his mind hazed with exhaustion. He staggered to the door and heard laughter and murmuring beyond.

He stared, trying to comprehend.

His brother's laugh again.

Holm and Lark were in the HouseHeart! Celebrating the conception of the next generation of Hollys.

Tinne clamped down on the clawing pain. He had to get away. Instinctively, he 'ported.

Ilexa saved him. *No!* she screeched. *Stop!*

He did. Hung in nowhere for an instant.

Come here.

Reaching for the last of his psi power, he did.

Falling. Falling. He thought he screamed but heard nothing. Fell into Turquoise House's mainspace. His direction had been off. He'd have materialized in the wall. End of Tinne.

How had he managed to stop his 'port? Where had he been that split second out of reality?

He couldn't even whimper at the physical agony shooting through every nerve. Couldn't answer Ilexa's yowling scolds, could barely hear them. He crumpled half on the leather couch. It hurt his skin that felt scraped raw, then cradled him.

Again he fell. Into sleep, and dreamt of his Passages, the deathduels that Hollys experienced. Second Passage and that war with the gangs in old Downwind . . .

Lahsin smelled something. Something that might mean safety. Not FirstGrove . . . how she yearned for the fragrances of trees in the winter, a garden in winter. This smell was thick and feral and angry—as she was angry. Fire whipped through her again, and she screamed. And her screams were ignored, always.

Not angry! Can't afford to be angry. Uncontrolled emotion could kill during Passage. Stop it! Calm.

She heard ragged panting, saw puffs of air in the night as she crawled on hands and knees toward that smell, the bushes off to the left. She had to leave the trail and moaned when her raw and bleeding hand came down on a thorny twig.

Yet she continued. This time of clarity wouldn't last.

Ignoring the hurt, she scuttled faster, saw the dark hole.

Wavy lines of Flair obscured her vision.

She put on a burst of speed, found the hole and rolled into it.

Stink of dog. Of Strother. His old hidey-hole. But he slept in the Residence tonight. Her lips cracked when she laughed at the irony. The tears on her face steamed away when the flames of anger, the crackle of fear, of Passage, took her.

Tinne was not in good shape the next morning. Barely competent enough to handle the beginning class. Tab said nothing, but watched with a keen eye. When NoonBell came, after the last morning students left, the older man walked over, the roll of a seaman in his stride. He handed Tinne one of the mugs he carried. Tinne smelled the nasty Restore herbal drink but said nothing and drank half of it down.

"Didn't sleep well," Tab said.

Tinne reached for a towel and wiped his forehead. He'd been hot all morning. Hot all last night, too. Nightmare landscapes of deathduels had haunted him. "No."

Tab sipped his own drink. The scent of rich cocoa, whitemousse, and a sprinkle of cinnamon came to Tinne's nose.

"Got scries in the message cache for you." Tab scratched his chin. "Healers, T'Heather and D'Sea. Want a follow-up meetin'."

Tinne flinched. "Lord and Lady, no!"

"Nope," Tab agreed. "Don't want ya lookin' like somethin' Ilexa pounced and played with when ya' see those folks again. Told them ya'd see 'em tomorra."

"Thanks."

"So ya gotta look better tomorra."

Sinking into his balance, Tinne said, "I will."

"Good. Messages from the Turquoise House and Mitchella D'Blackthorn. Somethin' about actors." Tab sipped again, snorted a laugh. "Many messages from that young House. Take a long lunch an' see what's goin' on."

"All right." Tinne flung his head back and poured the last of his drink down his gullet, hoping to avoid the bitter dregs. They stuck to the back of his tongue. Tab offered his mug and with a wry smile, Tinne took it, let the rich flavor banish the Restore herbs. Someone should be able to make a better-tasting energy drink than that. Maybe Lahsin . . .

Everything clicked into place. He'd had surges of Flair last night that had thrown his teleportation off. Felt the heat of Passage like the fever during his Passage deathduels.

Experienced his deathduels again.

Passage! Lahsin's first true fugue had come.

Blood drained from his head. He *reached* for the bond between them. The strand pulsed sluggishly. She was alive. He couldn't tell more.

Tab plucked his mug from Tinne's hand and eyed him sharply.

He couldn't speak of this, not even to Tab. "I need to go."

Jerking a head at the door, Tab said, "Go."

Tinne headed for the office teleportation pad. Tab grabbed his arm in an iron grip. "No. Ordered a glider for ya' from T'Holly. Belated New Year's gift, your father said."

"Huh. Don't want a glider."

Tab's eyebrows rose. "You will use the glider. I don't want you expending your Flair so much that you can't work well."

More heat—embarrassment—flooded him. "Yes, sir."

Releasing him, Tab drank the rest of his cocoa, waved to the door. "Go. Be back by MidAfternoonBell, lookin' better."

"Yes, sir." Walking fast, but trying to look casual, Tinne went to the closet where his coat hung, put it on, nodded again at Tab, and strode out the door.

Winced again.

Outside there was a flashy two-seated glider in Holly green with silver trim. It had gathered a small crowd.

Furthermore, one of his distant cuzes who worked in T'Holly Residence grinned at him. T'Holly had provided a driver. Tinne could *not* take this vehicle to FirstGrove. He tried a smile at his cuz, and the man didn't seem to see anything wrong. Tinne lifted the door and climbed in. "The Turquoise House."

"Sure, Tinne."

"I have some business there, and"—he swallowed and lied—"want a rest."

"Can see that," his cuz said cheerfully.

Tinne didn't grind his teeth, but wanted to. "You can play with the glider until half septhour before MidAfternoonBell." The force of the acceleration slammed him back into the cushiony seat.

"Huzzah!"

*T*he whoosh of the glider hadn't faded before Tinne ran into the Turquoise House to the teleportation room. Adrenaline had washed away some of the weariness.

"Tinne, I have been scwying all morning!"

"House, in the future you are only allowed one scry in the morning and one scry in the afternoon to my business unless a person tells you it's an emergency."

Subdued, the House said, "Yeth, Tinne."

He knew that tone. "Sorry to hurt your feelings." He envisioned the overgrown door nearest to the Healing pool. The image broke up. He was too distracted. "What do you need?"

"Authorization for more actors to read. Scheduling advice—" the House used Mitchella's clipped, irritated voice.

"Done. Schedule as you please."

"Yes, Tinne."

One breath in, visualize the door to the estate. The stalks around the door were brown and brittle. Second breath in. The doorway itself was deep enough to have shadows, cold in the winter, light slanted *so* at this time of day.

And three, and he was there. No problems this time.

He pressed the latch and the door swung open easily. *Lahsin!* he yelled mentally.

Twenty

Tinne? Lahsin's mental voice sounded startled, as tired as he felt. But it had a quality he couldn't name, a comfort that he noticed but brushed aside for more important matters.

Loping through the bare hedgerows that were still dense enough to block sight, he ran to the Healing pool. She was there, soaking in her favorite spot, a paleness under her peachy skin that he didn't like seeing.

"What's wrong?" she asked.

He stopped short. What to say? It was illegal to tell her they were HeartMates, and he didn't want to, anyway.

Would she have called for him? For her HeartMate? Or for Tinne himself? Could he have missed such a call?

She hadn't *touched* him as a HeartMate. He'd have felt that. There had been no erotic dreams. He'd never had erotic dreams of Lahsin. Had feathered against her mind, her *self*, during his own Passages, but had never experienced those legendary dreams.

He wanted her to tell him about her Passage without prompting and was surprised at how much he wanted her confidences.

He looked at her, pretty face turning from child to woman, pretty body with high round breasts lifted by the water, hips curving from a small waist. Beautiful eyes, dark, dark green.

No wonder he'd been aroused by her hands the night before. Best shove those thoughts away right *now* so he wouldn't be in the same state when he undressed.

Meeting her eyes, he grimaced. How much to tell her? "Bad night. Still haven't recovered. G'Uncle Tab who runs the Green Knight told me to take a coupla septhours off." Was that statement vulnerable enough for her? He'd spilled his guts last night and didn't want to do so again. He shucked his clothes, and the cold stone under his feet curling his toes was enough to stop any incipient arousal. Then he dove into the pool.

The water, as always, glided over his skin like silkeen, both soothing his aches and stimulating the blood flow. The other HealingHall pools of Celta had *nothing* on this one. Maybe he'd tell his sister-in-law, Lark, of it. He trusted her, and she was a FirstLevel Healer. Not that she could enter, but some Healer probably should know. Then he surrendered to the movement of his arms and legs, the water around him, breathing.

When the rough edges inside him had eased, snicking into a good whole, he moved to a warmer part of the pool to soak. It was just a meter along the curve from Lahsin's preferred spot, on the same underwater bench. "Do you mind?" he asked.

"No," she said, matching his gaze, a good sign. Her eyes were clear. She didn't look at his body, but he'd seen her peek when he stripped. He'd be physically attractive to her, Heart-Mates were.

"Heat is great here, no wonder you like this spot," he murmured as he tilted his head back and closed his eyes. A thought occurred to him, and he sat straighter and stared at her. "Have you been warm enough at night? Do the places you've stayed have heat?"

"Warm enough," she muttered. "Yes." She glanced away, then back at him. Her shoulders shifted. Ah! She *would* reveal a confidence. Good. Good because she needed to let him get closer. Because it was sad that she was afraid of men. No, because she needed to learn how to defend herself, and he couldn't teach her if he couldn't touch her to correct her stance, her form.

Her smile was a slight curve of the lips. "Did you read any of the stories in the newssheets about me?"

He frowned. He knew a lot about her. Most instinctively from the link strengthening between them. He sensed she was nervous, not from his proximity, but because she worried about his image of her. Also good. "I read a little." He shrugged.

"Then you know that I'm going through my Second Passage."

"You mentioned that yesterday. Yes." His heart gave a hard thump in his chest. "Going through. Present tense."

She gave a short nod, didn't look away. "I've had surges before, but last night was the first real fever dream . . ." Now she lowered her gaze, sank down into the water.

"Cave of the Dark Goddess. I shouldn't have left you."

Her head swung back, surprise in her eyes. She stared. "Maybe some Nobles *do* follow their precious code of honor."

The statement wasn't exactly an unqualified endorsement of him. He flicked away momentary hurt. Any progress she made trusting men was good. "So you had a dreamquest last night?"

"Yes." A line knit between her brows. "But I need to know more about Passage." She looked away. "The Yews didn't prepare me." Bitterness laced her voice. "I asked BalmHeal Residence to access its ResidenceLibrary for me this morning, but it's not speaking to me, only creaking and slamming doors."

She turned to look in the shadows, and Tinne followed her gaze. The dog was lying there, watching them both warily. "Dogs, of course, do not have Passages."

There was a loud sniff, and the dog rose to his feet and pointed his nose toward some thick bushes. Ilexa jumped a hedge. *Cats do not have Passages, either.* Lip lifted in a sneer, she ran around the end of the pool to settle herself on Tinne's clothes on the bench. *But Fams can experience Passages with Our Person.* Slanting her gaze at Tinne, she said, *I was with Tinne.*

Tinne grimaced a smile. "I'll tell you what I can, but Passage is different for the Hollys than other Families." He studied her again. She was young, innocent in many ways. This next little bit wouldn't reassure her. Fligger.

He focused his gaze beyond her to the bare grape arbor across the way. "Hollys have deathduels during Passage."

Her delicate arching brows dipped. "Deathduels." Her dark green gaze steadied on his again. "Is that like it sounds?"

"Pretty much." He shifted. "The heat of Passage overcomes us, and we don't think. We go looking for trouble."

"And the death part . . ."

One of the old scars he'd gotten during his Second Passage at seventeen suddenly ached. He rubbed his shoulder. "That's real. Downwind taverns and the gang wars was my Second Passage. Ilexa nearly died."

"That's how you got your scars!" Her gaze flew away. "Sorry, that was rude."

"No, it was true," he corrected. "We Hollys don't worry much about scars. A lot of them came from Second Passage and the war with gangs Downwind." But some didn't. He touched his side where he'd lost a kidney, his chest where he'd nearly lost his life. "But later we feuded with the Hawthorns. Street duels."

Her mouth hung open a little.

The spot over his left middle rib throbbed, and he ignored it. He didn't want to think of those particular scars. Falling, falling, falling through space. The rough landing, cracked ribs, blood, bruises. The trek from the north to home in Druida.

He glanced at her again and realized his silence had been too long, she was studying him. Dammit, he *was* rubbing his ribs.

"What about Third Passage? You *have* had that, right?"

"Yes, recently." His laugh was half amused. "I can access my full Flair. Not many wanted to fight with me during Third Passage." He'd keep this short. During Third Passage he'd touched her once, maybe long enough for her to recollect if he nudged her memory. "One small incident with thieves inside the city."

He pushed off the wall to zoom to the other side of the pool, pulled himself out.

"I didn't bring new ointment. I need to make more," she said.

He didn't tell her that Tab's favorite herbalist had recognized the recipe and already delivered jars of the stuff. Tinne knew about pride and favors, everyone born of the FirstFamilies learned about pride and favors before grovestudy. "That's all right. Just as well, I have classes to teach this afternoon. All of them, probably." With a Word he dried himself, and a couplet took care of clothing himself.

He turned and thought he caught her staring at his butt. "Have you been repeating that phrase I gave you?"

She nodded.

"You think you can handle my touch?"

Mouth set, she nodded again.

"Good. I'll be back later this evening for *your* first lesson in self-defense. Which attack do you want to learn to handle the most—from the front, side, or back?"

She went pale, swallowed, and said, "Back."

He quieted his tones, sending Flair in them to reach her across the water. "Can you deal with that position?"

"Yes." It was sharp, firm. She got out and dressed.

"Good. I'll bring the latest information there is on Second Passage for you. Do you need anything else?"

"Thank you for the information." She set her chin. "Otherwise I'm perfectly fine." She watched him put on his foot liners and boots. Ilexa sat straight up on the bench, having grumbled when his clothes had been whisked out from under her.

The cat sent her a not-quite-nice smile across the pool. Behind Lahsin, the dog growled, apparently taking the baring of fangs as an insult to him. He looked up at her, yellow eyes glowing slightly, and moved away. Lahsin gritted her teeth, but continued, "I want to do this," she muttered.

Tinne heard her. "What?"

She projected her voice. "Upon coming of age, I, Lahsin Rosemary Burdock, repudiate my underage marriage with Ioho T'Yew. Upon coming of age, I, Lahsin Rosemary Burdock, repudiate my underage marriage with Ioho T'Yew. Upon coming of age, I, Lahsin Rosemary Burdock, repudiate my underage marriage with Ioho T'Yew."

To her surprise Tinne jerked like a puppet whose strings were pulled. Ilexa hissed and jumped away, tail whipping.

"You can't tell me that," he said, his voice rough.

She stared in amazement, hurt. The dog's rumble became louder, longer, more threatening.

The cat lifted her muzzle. Her nose twitched as if smelling something bad. *We will go now.* She disappeared, and Tinne shook his head like she'd given him a head blow. He raised both hands palms-out in a helpless gesture.

Tears started behind Lahsin's eyes, she whirled and bolted down a cleared path toward the Residence.

She'd thought he was her friend. Her only friend. *Fligger* it. The whole situation. He was just a man who was using contact with her to ease his own pain.

Like she was?

She didn't want to be reasonable so she shoved the thought aside, set her jaw, and quickly regretted it as she stumbled over a root and her teeth jarred. But it got her brain working. Maybe she'd read the rules wrong. Maybe like other laws she had to make the announcement to a Lady or Lord with Great or Grand or Grace before their name. Tinne was only a SecondSon, a GreatSir by courtesy, Noble in his birth, but without a real title of his own and she didn't see him testing for his own title. He valued his Family even though they were maddening him. He loved them, and they loved him. They were maddening because they loved him.

Once Lahsin would have said her Family loved her, but now she sincerely doubted it.

Another strange idea buzzed. Could *she* test and take a new title? Become a GraceLady in her own right? How lovely. She chuckled, then stopped. Her emotions were swinging again. She checked her inner health. No, Passage was not roiling up. She should be safe today. That was one question she could have asked Tinne, how often Passage surged. She might have gotten some sort of idea how often they occurred once they started.

Tinne's hurt of her still felt sharp, but, again, the man he was wouldn't hurt her on purpose. Perhaps she had misremembered the rules or they'd changed.

She'd better go back and ask.

But of course when she reached the pool he was gone.

All were gone.

Loneliness struck.

*H*e'd hurt her. *Tinne walked the twisty passages be*tween the abandoned warehouses outside FirstGrove. Ilexa had prowled ahead to hunt rats, and Tinne was grateful. He wanted time alone. He'd wend his way to CityCenter, do a small 'port from a public building's teleportation pad to the Turquoise House. Then he'd assign it the task of discreetly compiling information on Second Passage. That should keep the House busy and happy.

But he'd seen tears in Lahsin's eyes. He ground his teeth. She had surprised him, and he hadn't thought quickly enough. Not that he could have said much. He couldn't reveal he was her HeartMate. Maybe she'd think he believed he was an intimate friend?

No.

He hoped she didn't puzzle out that he was her Heart-Mate. It would be awkward all around, and he wouldn't feel right about returning to FirstGrove. And he wanted to. She *needed* to learn self-defense.

He didn't want anyone to put bruises on her ever again. *This* he could give her. If she showed up for their lesson tonight.

*T*aking the long way back to the Residence, Lahsin put her conversation into perspective. There was time enough to repudiate her marriage after her Passage. That must be endured first.

She *had* progressed in solving a problem. She'd asked Tinne about Passages. She hadn't learned much that applied to herself, but she trusted him to bring more information that evening.

Now if her body could only instinctively trust him not to hurt her, but that wouldn't happen anytime soon. Her mind would have to be in control there. So she said the phrase he'd given her. "I am allowed to hurt anyone trying to hurt me."

Tinne hadn't meant to hurt her, had gone out of his way to reassure her. He could have already done a lot of things, the least of which was turning her over to T'Yew, the Burdocks, or a guardhouse. Instead it seemed like he'd help her.

He'd looked as rough as she'd felt. Bad night, he'd said, and she worried a little over him. He hadn't said anything about how his former wife might have hurt *him*. Hadn't breathed a word about the loss of a child in the womb. Lahsin nibbled her lip. Maybe he was talking to others about those griefs, but she didn't think so. He was probably squeezing them down into a corner of himself where he could ignore them, like a man would do.

She shrugged, she couldn't force him to talk about his hurts, just listen if he wanted to do so. If he bottled those hurts up inside, they wouldn't explode on him. Unlike her own emotions that could shatter her during Passage. She must figure out a way through her own hurt.

The soak had been her second of the day. She hadn't made it to BalmHeal Residence until after a good plunge in the Healing pool. She'd used some of her Flair to wash her clothes in the corner of the pool near one of the drainage holes.

The Residence hadn't forgiven her for staying out all night, or for coming in after she'd obviously been to the pool. Strother had awkwardly risen from a corner of the kitchen and that *had* speared guilt through her. He couldn't open the no-times by himself. Though she had some distant dreams the night before that he was ranging the estate following the Holly cat. A cat who hunted and left him newly killed prey and boasted and laughed. That might have been part of the Passage dream, but she didn't think so. She sniffed, remembering their scents.

So she'd given the dog a meal of furrabeast steak and had scrambled eggs for herself, had studied the antique storage cache and managed to program it to open twice a day for Strother . . . just in case. He hadn't said anything to her, either.

The chill on her face as she turned northeast warned of a new heavy snow. They'd been lucky in the garden with no snow sticking to the ground.

She still hadn't fully explored the estate, particularly the south. If more than a few inches of snow fell, she wouldn't want to. Her current path was rough and overgrown, and she was tempted to use some more of her new well of Flair to clear it. Her Flair was developing, becoming stronger; it was a pond instead of a puddle. When she'd mastered Third Passage she could access a lake.

The path and the rest of the estate would have to wait. The Residence needed a lot—plumbing and housekeeping spells, security spellshields, weathershields. No doubt it would tell her in great detail. She squared her shoulders when it came into view. "I am allowed to fight. I am allowed to hurt anyone who tries to hurt me." Breathe and modify the phrase. "I'm allowed to be rude to those who are rude to me." If she wanted a chandelier dropped on her head, or tooth marks on her person.

Adult or not, some things had to be worked up to, and dealing with the Residence was one of those. Her step didn't hesitate. If snow was coming, best make the place as livable as possible. But even before she entered the side door she imagined the grumpy, whining tone of the house battering her ears.

*T*he rest of the day went well for Tinne. After the swim, soak, and conversation with Lahsin, his mind and body cooperated. Tab gave him a grunt of praise at the end of the afternoon and dismissed him. His G'Uncle would take the weekly club night. He was looking forward to sparring with the members. Tinne had chuckled and shaken his head and left his mentor grinning. As the scandal faded slightly, some of the men who'd dropped their memberships had rejoined—for a greater fee. This was the first evening for new members of the lower nobility and middle class. As Tinne walked from the back private rooms through the main salon, he saw Cratag Maytree limbering up, eyeing Tab.

Tab was eyeing him back.

Tinne thought that particular new member would give Tab something to be busy and happy about.

Tinne stepped outside. Afternoon, and it was already dark. Yule and the lengthening of the days was still a couple of weeks away. This time of year weighed on his spirits.

His driver was waiting, whistling. Tinne had slid in next to him before his cuz noticed. "Turquoise House, then if you want the glider for the evening, you can have it."

The man glanced at him. "Aren't you sleeping in the HouseHeart?"

"No." Not until he could forget that he'd nearly surprised Holm and Lark last night.

He'd never taken Genista to T'Holly HouseHeart, never made love to her there. Hadn't even considered it, and guilt gnawed at him. How long was he going to feel this failure? Probably the rest of his life. It would fade, but now and again it would jump out from the shadows and bite him, like all deep regrets. He could only hope the sharp teeth would dull.

With a dance of fingertips on the controls, his driver sent music lilting through the glider. More music written by his Mamá to soothe him. He gritted his teeth. Thankfully the man didn't say a word or resume his whistling. As they approached the Turquoise House, the greeniron gates opened. Tinne hopped out, snapped down the door, gave the roof a thump.

His cuz grinned, waved, then the music changed to a hard, charging beat. Tinne had no doubt that the man was going to take a woman for a ride.

*T*inne and Ilexa ate dinner, she boasting about how well she'd hunted the night before, what a chase she'd led the dog on. He grunted but didn't comment.

Then the Turquoise House spoke of its research into Second Passage. How it had mined information from the PublicLibrary, had requested data under the seal of a secret password through the library from HealingHalls' Archives and even FirstFamily Residences. Tinne complimented it as he picked up three holospheres of information from the den's cache, put them in his coat pocket, and took the newssheet from the delivery box.

"Do you come back here tonight? T'Holly scwied to thay that you sshould th-sstay in the HouseHeart of your Family Residence." The Turquoise House sounded as if disobeying T'Holly or the Family Residence would be a terrible sin.

Tinne rolled his shoulders, tried to loosen up as he walked to the teleportation pad with Ilexa. "I'll be back." *Couldn't* go to the HouseHeart tonight.

Then he 'ported away and was gone from Family expectations and responsibilities. He stood before the door to FirstGrove, spirits rising. He was following *his* wishes, *his* expectations and responsibilities, and that made all the difference.

*L*ahsin saw him as soon as he exited the hedgerow tunnel. Relief filtered through her. He'd come. He moved with fluid grace—Tinne Holly getting back into his stride.

She still only had two changes of clothing, and she'd dressed in the loosest, as if it were grovestudy exercise time. In fact, as she'd changed, she recalled that midafternoon grovestudy exercises were some sort of defense moves, and she'd practiced them. Should have practiced them all along, she supposed, though they wouldn't have done any good against T'Yew. He had had her in his power. She banished the thought and the past.

Tinne set the newssheets and some memoryspheres on the bench, then took off his outer garments, and she saw the thin aura of his weathershield. A good weathershield. Better than hers . . . and she was nervous.

He glanced at her, his gaze lingered. "Still interested in training?"

Twenty-one

❤

"Yes." She shifted from foot to foot. She didn't want to talk about that afternoon. His tight face eased, as if he didn't want to bring up the subject, either.

He looked away and said, "I haven't studied this area for the best place to train. We don't want to fight on stone. That mossy place looks good." He narrowed his eyes. "But there's a decline toward the pool." Hands on hips, he surveyed the place.

"There's permamoss beds in the far northwest of the garden," she said, her voice only a little shaky.

"I'll look around, I'd like to stay near the pool, but we need clear space for physical exercise and for twinmoonslight."

She hadn't thought of any of this! Hadn't been prepared.

His mouth quirked. "I should have thought of this earlier. I'll have to cut some of that permamoss for matts, but not tonight. Tonight will be very gentle." He loped off.

She called, "The southeast pool area is mostly moss, too."

He nodded and headed in that direction.

She was definitely less prepared than she'd anticipated. More anxious. Too bad. She'd just have to scrape up her courage. She *was* determined. She would learn how to defend herself. No one would make her a victim again.

She tugged at the hem of her tunic, glanced at Tinne. He was stamping on the moss, then he did a fighting pattern, nodded again, and tumbled. Since she didn't want to look away from him, wanted to watch his body move longer, she tore her gaze from him.

The newssheet caught her eye, and she walked over to the bench. Tinne's scent of man and recent soap rose from his clothes. Why was she so sensitive to him?

Because he was the only person she'd spoken with for days. Because she would soon let him touch her.

She glanced at the newssheet. *Reward for the Return of Lahsin Yew to T'Yew*, it screamed. Her nerves jittered when she saw the six-figure amount.

Tinne put his hands on her shoulders, she jumped. "Easy."

But she twisted away, panting, and thought her eyes wheeled in fear. "They'll catch me." Her fists curled, but she kept them tight to her chest, didn't strike out. "They know I haven't left Druida, and if I go out, anyone who sees me will give me up for that amount of gilt."

"Breathe, Lahsin." Tinne's voice was calm. "If you look, you'll see it's the regional copy."

She was shaking her head. "That goes out in Druida, too."

"Balance, Lahsin!" His voice was sharper. "Ground yourself."

An old grovestudy command. She sank into her balance. Her hands fell to her sides, and she gulped in big, even breaths.

"Good, you haven't forgotten everything. If you have fear when you fight and direct it at yourself, you will freeze. If you direct it at your attacker, you will fight. Fight, Lahsin."

He was right about the freezing bit, she could barely think, only feel. Her fingers curled into fists. "I can't."

"Yes. You. Can. What's your phrase?"

"I am allowed to hurt—"

"Yes."

"I can't."

"Why not?"

Her insides twisted with fear. "He'll hurt me more if I fight."

"When you fight, you will get hurt. Accept that."

"He hurt me more if I fought and screamed. He likes it. It excited him, and he'd hurt me more."

Tinne's face set in grim lines, but he said, "You will *not* freeze. You will fight and strike and put him down and run away. That's what I'll teach you."

She wanted to believe him. Her terror was receding. She lifted her gaze to stare him in the eyes. They were fierce and determined. How she wished she could feel fierce and determined!

"I can't run. There was no place I could run." She heard her fears and her reality spilling out of her mouth.

Tinne swept an arm around them. "You ran. You're here, and he can't get you here."

She was cold, inside and out, she rubbed her arms. "If I fight, he hurts me worse. He likes to see me run, because there's no place I can run to in the Residence that will hide me."

"You will fight, and you *will* hurt him. You will knock him down and run. You will scream. There is no door that can stop you, no window that will not open to you. You broke them, remember? Broke the full spellshield of a FirstFamily Residence, *before* your Passage. You won't be leaving here until after your Passage when you have more Flair. Are you listening to me?"

Her breath hitched with the hurt in her chest. "Yes." She wrapped her arms around herself, sank to the bench, and rocked. Cried. Let the harsh sobs tear from her chest.

For a moment Tinne looked wounded, too, as if he remembered his own hurt. He sidled to her, sat next to her, lifted his arm slowly, and put it around her shoulders. With his touch, she felt his emotions. Not nearly as calm as they seemed. He wasn't tentative solely for her sake but for his own, too. He'd tried to comfort a woman in the depths of despair before and been rejected. And had taken those hurtful blows into himself.

Lahsin leaned against him and wept, the night deepening around them, the steam rising from the Healing pool thickening until they were lost in a place of their own. As she cried, she sensed his own deep pain. Her hand came up to his chest, and it seemed as if she made a connection with him, cried for them both.

When she went into a hiccuping aftermath, he handed her a large, clean softleaf from his pocket, then moved away.

She scrubbed at her face and blew her nose. His back

was to her. He looked toward the south, where they should have been training. "Do you still want your first lesson in self-defense?"

His voice was expressionless, but his shoulders showed tension. She straightened her spine, cleared her throat. "Yes."

When he swung around there was approval in his eyes. "Good." He sighed, and Lahsin heard relief.

"Fighting, like everything else, is a matter of energy and balance. Most times when you are attacked, your assailant will be moving. The first thing you must do is keep him or her off balance, go in the direction he or she is moving. Then break his or her grip, strike, and scream, or scream as you strike, put him or her down and run away." He walked to the mossy area, gesturing her to follow as he went into lecture mode.

"We will practice moving attacks first." He slid his gaze to her and took up a stance in the middle of the space. Lahsin had always thought of this as a resting area for patients. Its purpose had certainly changed!

Tinne continued. "You'll also learn how to defend against a strong stationary attack where your arms are trapped. First, warm-up and motion. Let's do primary grovestudy exercises of breathing and stretching. Energy work."

They did. After that he came at her slowly and gently from behind. He was an interesting, efficient teacher. This aspect of him was easy on his emotions—a retreat for them both.

The screaming part of the lesson brought the cat to watch with hard eyes, and Strother, who stayed in the shadows. Finally, when Lahsin had broken away from Tinne for the third time and he hadn't eased his grip, they soaked. And after that, he got out, threw the paper away, and indicated three holospheres. "Use your anger when we fight. You have enough of it, and you must drain or master it before Passage, otherwise you'll be in danger. Passage can amplify emotions, and if they're too large, your Flair can break you as a vessel too flawed to hold it."

Even in the hot pool, Lahsin shuddered. He hadn't sounded so severe when he'd been teaching her. So she rose and dressed, dried herself with Flair, using Words she'd heard as a child.

When she turned back to him, she said, "I'll have more salve for you tomorrow evening."

He smiled, nodded. "Make some for yourself, too."

"Yes."

Then he bowed. "Merry meet."

"And merry part," she said.

"And merry meet again." He gave her one last look, studying her. Her face was flushed, and she looked satisfied. He let out a little breath. This would work. She'd learn.

He'd praised her at every step, and she'd done well, especially since every time he touched her in the beginning, she'd trembled.

He put a dark knit cap over his hair, wrapped a scarf around his face, and lifted his hand in farewell. Then he headed at a jog to the nearest door. Outside the walls of the estate, all was quiet, as usual. He teleported to a public pad in a caff place near the Turquoise House. He wanted cinnamon caff before he returned to the Turquoise House, wanted the bustle of people. He'd discovered the shabby caff place earlier, but now he'd stop and try it.

When he walked into the room, talk hitched, then continued. The server, a tall boy with carroty hair, nodded and made his drink perfectly. Tinne tapped a pattern on the nearby scrybowl, authorizing a good tip. By the time he left, his body had relaxed and he strolled with loose muscles, feeling the coolness of the winter surround, but not touch, his weathershield.

He opened the greeniron gates and turned into the short glider drive to the Turquoise House.

Walking toward him was Genista.

The jolt went through him to his toes. He stopped, stunned, and settled into his balance.

"Hello, Tinne."

No, *not* Genista. The actress had his former wife's voice wrong. At her most seductive Genista never had a subtone of slyness. A few more steps toward him and he saw the walk was wrong, too. Too calculated a rolling hip movement. Probably looked better from behind.

His hot caff slopped over his cup, and he accepted the burn.

"It's a pleasure to meet you." Her voice was low and throaty, now more Mitchella D'Blackthorn than Genista Hol—Furze. She stopped less than a handspace from him. Her scent was very close to Genista's—right soap, perfume, dusting of cosmetic Flair. He swallowed hard to keep his gorge down.

She saw it, misinterpreted it, set her hand on his forearm. Her hands were all wrong, too, and it helped the buzzing in his brain. Genista's fingers were more spatulate, not as pointed.

"I'm Morning Glory."

He nearly gagged at the too-cute name. He liked morning glories. He pondered how to play this game. She obviously had deliberately set out to make herself as much like Genista as possible. Gossip must have him pining for his lost wife.

Stepping away so her arm would drop, he raised his eyebrows, sipped his caff, and settled his hand on his blazer. Her eyes followed the last motion, and she licked her lips.

Worse and worse, violence excited her. Too damn bad he was wealthy and still seen as a good match for bedding or marrying by a dishonorable adventuress. A woman who made herself attractive in the manner of his ex-wife repulsed him.

Another sip of caff, and he let the sweet cream sit on his tongue to take the nasty taste from his mouth, welcoming the trickle of hot beverage down his dry throat. He kept his face impassive. She shifted, set her hand on her hip, tilted her head.

"You've been auditioning for the voice for the Turquoise House?"

Emotion flickered in her eyes—nearly the same shade of blue as Genista's, then vanished. He didn't have time to understand it, but something made him wary.

"That's right." Her lips curved slowly in a smile like Genista's, also too practiced. "I think I can say with certainty that my voice will be the best for the House. It prefers me."

If it did, the House was not as smart as Tinne believed.

She reached out, and her fingers penetrated his weathershield. She made a purring noise at the warmth, then her hand insinuated itself through the gap in his cloak to touch his chest. Horrible.

He took a long pace back, kept his voice as cool as the air. "I'll let you know if the Turquoise House wants more readings."

She pouted, followed him with mincing steps. "But I thought you made the decisions."

"No."

"What if I want you . . . to let me have the job."

"I'm not the one you need to convince. As for . . . wanting . . . I'm perfectly capable of determining what I want, when I want it. That's not you. That will never be you."

Her hand flashed out, fingers ready to rake his face. He countered it with negligent, precise force. She glared. "I heard you were charming. All the Hollys were charming. As much a lie as all the rest."

He inclined his head. "You listen to too many rumors."

She hissed.

Ilexa slid from the shadows, hissing, too.

Morning Glory jumped backward, her cape slipped down. She wasn't wearing much, a shoulderless tight dress. Something no Noblewoman would wear in public. He studied her critically, sipped his caff. "If you want to be taken as Genista Furze, you're going to have to tone up that overblown body better."

An outraged female sound.

Another hiss from Ilexa.

"Ilexa, please show the actress to the gate." He'd close and lock it from now on.

His Fam circled the woman lithely, swishing her tail.

Morning Glory huffed to the gate and left with a clang.

Instead of returning, Ilexa used Flair to jump the greeniron gate and follow the woman. Tinne heard a muffled shriek. *Don't kill her*, he offered mildly. This drink was better than what was served at the expensive place across from the Green Knight.

I will just play with her a little. I do not like her mocking our former Lady.

Rapid footfalls followed by silence.

Tinne's offhand manner fell away. His stomach knotted.

Genista. Morning Glory.

The raw wound opened again. He'd loved Genista, now she was gone. Morning Glory was a terrible caricature of Genista, but managed to shock him back into painful awareness. Good emotional jabs, excellent game playing. She'd never know how much she'd scored.

He blinked and focused on the front door of the Turquoise House. It wasn't glowing tonight, that was unusual. In the dark its color seemed to be slightly off. He shrugged, opened the door, and walked carefully to the mainspace and the huge furrabeast leather sofa. Sinking into it, he put his cup carefully on the side table and propped his face in his hands.

Lahsin. He wanted Lahsin. Not for sex but for simple companionship. Her complete honesty. Her innate goodness. Just her.

His HeartMate, the only woman he could ever imagine living with. He could acknowledge that much at least. Her presence helped him as much as the renowned FirstGrove Healing pool. He liked her company, liked her. She was undemanding at a time when he needed no demands. He didn't doubt she'd find herself. She'd grow and learn what she wanted, and she would obtain it. That was in the slowly unfolding future. Her potential amazed him. Watching her discover her own power was fascinating.

Even more fascinating than the amusement of the Turquoise House.

Who hadn't spoken a word. He liked the silence. If he wanted, he could listen to one of his Mamá's new compositions. The rooms would fill with beautiful music.

But something was wrong with this new charge of his, too. "Turquoise House?" he called.

No answer.

"House?" A little louder.

Nothing.

"House, I am worried for you. Please respond."

"I am here." It was a whisper. In his voice.

"What's wrong?"

"There was an actress here."

"I know," Tinne snapped.

A longer pause. Tinne sensed he'd hurt the House's feelings again. He picked up his cup and swallowed a mouthful. The drink was even better as it cooled, there was an additional spice . . . and he was trying to ignore the effects of lingering shock and a sensitive House. He took another drink and rubbed his chest.

"I'm sorry I was short."

"You apologize? To me? As if I were a person?"

Cave of the Dark Goddess, he didn't want to go through this tonight. Too bad. "Of course. You are a person."

"You're sure?"

Tinne rolled his eyes. "Yes."

"That actress didn't think so."

The House didn't sound like a petulant child, but more like a bewildered child who'd taken an unexpected blow. He'd heard that note in Lahsin's voice, too. He shifted tense shoulders. "House, do you have a recording of the actress's time here?"

"Yes."

"Perhaps you should play it for me."

A cold draft trickled along the floor from the open fireplace, as if the House whimpered.

"I don't sound good," the House confessed.

"You've always sounded fine to me," Tinne fibbed. "Go ahead, play your memory recording of what happened."

"You won't laugh at me?"

"Have I ever laughed at you?"

"I don't know." It sounded pitiful.

Tinne finished the drink, the last rich swallow of syrup had settled to the bottom. Then he got up to prowl some tension off as he threw the cup in the cycler. "I haven't laughed at you. You've amused me." He added fast, "Like my Family does."

"Really?"

"Yes. Go on," he coaxed.

"Sit."

"I'll stretch out on the couch." He went to the long couch and settled in, head on the softly sloping padded arm.

"Good."

Echoey coughing came, then before his amazed eyes, a swirl of motes glittered and gathered into a misty picture. Tinne's eyes widened. "You have viz."

The picture vanished, and uncertainly the House said, "I was told that Residences have viz."

"Yes, above scrybowls or on wall screens for communication or data retrieval." He thought about it. "Or, perhaps in specially made crystals to hold and view such memories, I've seen that in a newly rebuilt Residence, but not the ability to . . . to show a real scene in midair. You have a great talent here!"

The weathershields over the large back windows vibrated— with the House's returning enthusiasm, Tinne hoped.

"Really?"

"Yes. Show me."

As Tinne watched, his anger turned from a simmer to barely contained fury. The woman had belittled the House about everything from its immaturity to its lack of Yule decorations. She'd made her own goal of snagging Tinne clear and had declaimed her latest part, not bothering to read anything.

After it ended, there was a pause, then the House said tentatively, "She made me feel bad. And stupid. And . . . young."

"I'm sorry for that." He sighed. "I like this mainspace. Very much. Enough that I haven't wanted any holiday decorations. I like you very much, you're an excellent companion." His jaw flexed. The woman must have thought both of them stupid not to recognize what she'd done. But figuring out the consequences of her mean-spiritedness was less important than the injury to the Turquoise House's emerging feelings.

Tinne put the right amount of exasperation in his voice. "Turquoise House, you *are* a youngling, just coming into your identity and Flair. What is wrong with that? Everyone is young once, so accept it and move on."

"I make mistakes."

Tinne snorted. "That isn't entirely a factor of youth. We all make mistakes. We hope we make *fewer* mistakes as we grow older, but that's not always true. Take my father, for example." The bitterness in his voice stopped him, but he felt the Turquoise House's sharpened attention.

"That is true," it said, with just the same inflection that Tinne had had. This would drive him mad.

"Turquoise House, *think*. You will be a very long-lived entity, perhaps even forget you were young—"

"I would like to forget this night," the House rasped. Tinne was all too aware that he'd rasped quite a bit lately. Cave of the Dark Goddess.

"You should enjoy your youth." He stopped and chose his words. "You've been tormented by bullies. That happens to many child—young people, an unfortunate fact of life."

"This is true."

Tinne sighed, thought of the few voices the Turquoise House had. Not enough. "Why don't we use Mitchella's voice for now."

"I don't want a woman's voice." Sulky but determined. How often had Tinne sounded sulky? Not at all, he hoped.

"All right." What would work? "How about deepening my voice by half an octave."

"Like this?" Very deep voice.

"Thank you, that's less eerie for me. Now, when people have—uh—emotion—hurt feelings, we consult a mind specialist."

"The mind Healer D'Sea. You'd call her to talk with me? Ooh, thank you!" The bass rumble of his voice squealing was something he could have done without. Tinne tapped his head lightly on the wall and left it there. Dealing with an infant house. Calling D'Sea to consult, just the person he didn't want to meet for the next few decades. "She's scheduled to meet with me tomorrow. We'll move the appointment here." Maybe the Turquoise House would distract her.

"Thank you, thank you!" said the House, sounding slightly less subdued. "New thanks is not for making an appointment with D'Sea," the House said. "But for touching me."

Tinne grunted, he hadn't thought of that. Feeling stupid, he ran a hand up and down the smooth door molding. The House gave a grateful sigh. He lifted his fingers. "I'm going to bed. It's been a long day." He didn't even want to drum.

He walked down the pale blue hallway to the MasterSuite, recently changed to a more masculine style. The tinting was shades of green, the furniture a deep burgundy furrabeast leather, the bedsponge on a platform just the right height for Tinne to flop down upon. His drums were in the corner.

After skinning off his clothes, he fell on the bed, rolled to his back, and watched gentle, Flair-made misty clouds drift across the high ceiling in ever-changing patterns. He thought of the women in his life.

His Mamá, charming and talented and effervescent. So devoted to his father that she'd never admitted he'd made a mistake. They had HeartMate love for many years. Tinne began to see that their way of marriage wasn't the only way.

His brother and sister-in-law had struggled to be together. Though they, too, were HeartMates, they were complete individuals melding lives.

His *ex-wife*. That was the word the press was using, gotten from outside Druida and less-stratified classes than the First-Families. An unpleasant-sounding word, with horrific meaning. The flame of passion built into love now exploded and gone, dead and in ashes blown away with the wind.

He had loved Genista. He mourned that love, that life, but it was fading into the past. The shock of the divorce still made him twitch. Genista, lovely, voluptuous, generous. Playful, laughing, exciting. Sad, wretched, grieving. He could finally admit that he was relieved that the marriage was over. Dissolving it was the right thing to do.

His love had died before their marriage had. Their love had died. Both people had to work to keep marriage meaningful and fulfilling. Even HeartMate marriages.

His mind wandered to the actress bitch who'd put on a shoddy outer wrapping to appear like Genista, but had no notion of her true inner worth and beauty, and used his past and pain for her own grasping ends. Could there be any creature lower than that?

"Turquoise House?" Tinne asked.

"I'm here!"

"Please scry T'Furze and tell him there's an actress called Morning Glory impersonating his daughter, Genista."

"T'Furze would not be pleased?"

"No, he's an older FirstFamily GrandLord. He won't be pleased someone continues to stir up scandal. His Family is affected, too. We can leave it to him to deal with the actress."

There was a few seconds of silence. "I have reported the information to T'Furze Residence. It is informing T'Furze immediately." The House sounded satisfied. "You don't mind that I want a male voice?"

"It's usual for a Lord to have a female voice for his Residence, a Lady to have a male for hers. But you are your own person. You have several female voices. If you want a male voice, you should have it."

"Because you are not going to stay with me," it said matter-of-factly.

"No. You're a good companion, but someday I'll return to T'Holly Residence."

"You are honest. Mitchella says it may take time for the right permanent Family to find and value me." The House sounded proud.

"True." He wriggled under the bed linens. The knots in his

muscles from the latest emotional crises had finally loosened, and his mind drifted like the clouds.

"Tinne, does a consultation by D'Sea cost a great deal?"

"Probably." He yawned. "My Family is taking care of Healing bills."

"I don't think I need her. I am maturing. I can solve my own problems. I have been scanning in psychology texts for my ResidenceLibrary."

"Good." He rolled over, and his mind turned to Lahsin. Sweet, troubled, his HeartMate. Also maturing, solving her own problems. Just being close to her was enough for now.

*Lahsin had taken care of the plumbing. Now she fin*ished housekeeping spells on every floor and went back to the small guest room the Residence had grudgingly offered her. Hands on hips, she stared at it. A large bedsponge in the antique style, set on a tall platform with wooden posts going up to a top frame of carved wood. She didn't like the bed curtains. She'd had to clean them several times, since the Residence insisted they be kept. During each cleaning spell, she'd expected them to disintegrate. But they now showed summer blue with fat pink roses. Not her favorite color scheme. Someday she'd be the one to furnish her own bedroom and sitting room, but not yet.

She'd tried the door handle to the Master/MistrysSuite, but it was locked. She hadn't been able to peek into the Heir-Suite, either. She'd have liked a sitting room but was stuck with this chamber with faded brownish walls that had once been a pale, drab pink.

The bedsponge and frame were positioned oddly, crammed against a short wall opposite the back windows that faced northeast. They would look better on a side wall.

Rolling her shoulders, she dug deep for her Flair. Oddly enough, sparring with Tinne had given her more access to it. Being with him stirred it up.

"You are moving my furniture around."

"The better to clean the rooms. You could use a new look."

"I like my furniture where it is." Several doors slammed. Lahsin rubbed her head.

She was blessed to have found this place. It would be too much to expect perfection. Dealing with BalmHeal Residence was teaching her lessons, too. Patience.

She wondered how long it would be until she lost that patience and what would happen when she did.

Twenty-two

❤

$\mathcal{T}$inne *dreamt of Genista—and falling. He was stuck in* a dark and barren landscape and his once-wife was walking away from him. He called her name, and she didn't answer, didn't hear. Much like those months he'd tried to comfort her after her miscarriage, their loss.

So he ran after her and didn't see a break in the white snow and fell into a pit. Blackness of space and streaking smears of stars surrounded him, whirled around him as he fell and he knew he would land and die painfully and alone.

He woke with a suddenness that took his breath, panting. His mouth was dry when he spoke, "House, what time is it?"

"It is TransitionBell."

Figured, the time when souls slipped on to their next lives. "Thank you."

Ilexa, sleeping on a pillow in the corner, snuffled, lifted her head, and squinted at him. *You woke me.*

"Sorry." He rose.

His Fam muttered at him, *I know that look. Now you will drum. All night long you will drum.*

"Maybe."

Cat sigh. *Maybe I will not stay.*

He shrugged. "Don't then, *Fam*. The House will keep me

company. It doesn't care if I drum all night long, do you, Turquoise House?"

"No, but perhaps you should have some Sleep Well drink."

A good idea.

"Huh. I've never heard of this Sleep Well drink. Did Mitchella D'Blackthorn stock this drink?"

No answer.

"Who provided this potion?"

Ilexa glanced away, then back, and answered, *Your brother's wife, Lark, sent it.* Ilexa's smile got toothier. *It will soothe bad dreams, give good dreams.*

Tinne scowled. "I'd rather drum."

"I like the drum," said Turquoise House.

Snorting, Ilexa said, *House does not need to sleep.*

"Feel free to leave," Tinne told Ilexa, knowing her pride would keep her here. He *needed* to drum, his hands itched.

His Fam lifted her muzzle. *I will stay.*

Nodding, he dressed in loose-knit trous and shirt, went to the corner chair in his bedroom, and pulled up his drum. He started slowly, long seconds between each thump of his fingers. A processional march—formal, sad. Genista leaving him and not looking back. He gritted his teeth and let grief move through him. He had loved her once.

A rapid pattern as he ran toward her. He played of the yearning and regret and anguish that he couldn't reach her, hadn't been able to reach her for a long time. The vibration of the drum skin through his fingers sent signals throughout his body of the emotions he hadn't acknowledged.

Tottering on the knife edge of the hole. The horror of falling. The drum seemed to shriek under his fast hands.

Abrupt loud stop.

His breath was ragged, he made it even.

Another sound came, not of his making, but he recognized it. The opening of the beverage no-time in his sitting room. No doubt the Sleep Well tisane. Would it taste nasty? But he was weary. Might as well surrender to his Fam's nagging. With a last reverberating pat, he set his drum aside. Walking into the sitting room, he took the steaming bold red earthenware mug, sniffed. With a hint of cinnamon, the liquid was milky, maybe it wouldn't be too bad. He swallowed it in a few gulps, as Ilexa sat in front of him, encouraging him with her purr.

Before he put the mug in the cleanser, he could feel the potion working, slowing his thoughts, calming his nerves. "Good night, Turquoise House. Good night, Ilexa." He went back to bed.

He awoke in the morning aroused and with a fading erotic dream of Lahsin. Surprised, he puffed out a breath. He'd thought it would take longer for his sexuality to return from the deep freeze it had been in for months. Obviously not. He shouldn't have been surprised. After all, his body *had* stirred the last time she'd stroked her salve on his back.

Closing his eyes, he recalled the soft touch of her hands. Shouldn't do that, it was not the way to let his erection subside.

He stretched and groaned as his muscles pulled. Yesterday had been full of sparring from the moment he'd walked into the Green Knight to the time he'd 'ported to the Turquoise House. The time he'd spent in the Healing pool had helped, but not as much as if he'd had the ointment, too. So the question was, did he want to continue to have Lahsin apply the salve?

He snorted as he rolled from bed. Of course he did. His body liked her touch. She was his HeartMate, and everything in him recognized that. But he welcomed the fact that he seemed to be Healing emotionally. The horrible dream in the night and the drumming had helped. He felt better than he had yesterday, a good thing, too, since D'Sea was checking on him. He was glad that he'd changed the venue of the appointment from her home office to the Turquoise House, sure the emerging entity of the House would pique her curiosity.

He dressed. He did want Lahsin's hands on him. It would be good for her to know a man could be vulnerable, too. That touching a man wasn't wrong or wouldn't lead to terrible experiences. He'd have to be careful. But knowing that his sex drive was back in full force was good.

He greeted Ilexa and the Turquoise House cheerily and ate a big breakfast, inserting comments periodically as the House chattered. A glider horn sounded. Tinne flung the front door open to bright sunlight and crossed to the glider with a spring in his step. Lifting the glider door open he slid in next to his driver, who appeared tired and groggy. With a smile on his face, Tinne slammed the door shut.

* * *

As the week wore on Tinne felt more like himself—or a new self. Each day was better than the last. He was emerging from the shock of the divorce and the fog of depression that followed. The testing was blessedly dimming in his memory. When he entered new gathering places talk would quiet then rise again, but he was becoming accustomed to that. He ignored social invitations and spent the evenings with Lahsin.

She progressed well with her training, was intelligent, determined, flexible. She might actually be able to break free from an attacker and put him on the ground with a blow or two. Lord and Lady knew that her shriek was good enough to impress Ilexa, and the woman ran fast.

He watched her closely but saw no signs that she'd endured another Passage fugue. This gave him mixed emotions. She seemed to be Healing, but still held a great underlying anger that showed when they trained. He encouraged her to use it in her fighting as long as she remained in control and suffered the bruises when she didn't. Since she didn't bring up the topic of Passage again, he kept his warnings to himself.

She was outwardly happy and spoke of tending the gardens and working in the stillroom. She matched his stories of the Turquoise House with those of the "grumpy old man" Balm-Heal Residence. She seemed satisfied to pass the winter in FirstGrove. While Tinne didn't say anything against that, either, he did gently hint that she should foray into Druida now and again to see what was happening. Lahsin had retorted that the newssheets were informative enough.

Snow held off, and the holiday spirit increased as Yule approached. This kept Tinne cheerful, and it rubbed off on Ilexa. His Fam had told him that since she hadn't returned for New Year's a month and a half before, Tinne should gift her a jeweled collar from T'Ash on Yule. He'd been noncommittal to the cat, but pondered what he might give Lahsin that she would cherish.

Not a HeartGift. He'd created one but it was secure in the T'Holly HouseHeart cache. Lahsin wasn't the young girl whom he'd first connected with during his own Second Passage. Yet she wasn't a full adult woman, despite how his body reacted when she stroked salve into his back. She touched him with innocence. She'd only known rape and nothing of clean lust, hearty sex, or love. Not that he wanted anything of love, either. Not for some time yet, years maybe.

As for his touching her, he'd had female students before and never had problems with lusty thoughts during training. He labeled Lahsin "student," and focused on teaching her what she needed to know to protect herself. It worked for now.

But afterward . . . when he rubbed salve on her back or soaked in the pool with her . . . then he could free his natural instincts. The Healing pool was hot enough, and the herbal mixture such that he wasn't aroused when in it.

So the days passed and every night he visited Lahsin. The door to the sanctuary opened easily to him, and he knew that though he felt better, he was still Healing.

*O*ne *morning at the beginning of the next week, something* bothered Tinne. An itching between the shoulder blades, a warning nibbling at his mind's edges. He'd been aware of the feeling when he'd awakened, but couldn't pinpoint the cause.

Time and again, he sought his evolving link with Lahsin, checked on her well-being. She'd delighted in the light skiff of snow, the pristine whiteness of it as she'd walked from the Residence to the clocktower. As he was finishing his first advanced class, she was humming, distilling something fragrant.

She was well. As he took a blow on the shoulder, he yanked his mind back to teaching. His body had reacted, pivoting, blocking, evading. Tab called, "Time!" Everyone stopped fighting, bowed. Tinne's student was grinning, the first time she'd gotten a punch under his guard. He smiled and praised her.

After the students filed out, Tab gave him a hard look and once more dismissed him for the morning. Tinne wanted to protest, but couldn't. He wasn't doing himself, students, or the salon any good.

So he showered and dressed, bundled up against the cold—colder and snowier than in FirstGrove—and slogged onto the slushy street. At least the sun was shining, white in a sky bluer than usual, wisps of ice crystal clouds contrasting brightly. Winter in Druida, with Yule later in the week. That thought almost made Tinne smile, but the tingling between his shoulders turned into something cold along his spine. He checked on Lahsin who was now in the greenhouse. A pretty place to be on a day like this.

Like Saille T'Willow's lovely conservatory. Tinne frowned. Something about Saille T'Willow and Lahsin . . . it clicked in his mind. If T'Willow had an enemy, it was T'Yew. Something was going on with T'Yew. Tinne didn't have a link with T'Yew, but somehow he knew the man was plotting. The Yews hadn't been allies with the Hollys for centuries—Tinne'd researched them after Lahsin had married T'Yew. Again guilt cycled through Tinne. He hadn't protected her.

Then. He was doing his best, now. She was protecting herself well, too, twining extraordinary spellshields around First-Grove. Shaking off the guilt, he grabbed a cup of hot caff, then teleported home.

"Greetyou, Tinne!" After D'Sea's successful visit, the House was experimenting with "age-appropriate" voices and was stuck in the warbling, cracking tones of a boy becoming a man.

"Greetyou, House," Tinne said.

A scent of bayberry wafted through the room. "Viz my cuz for me, please." Straif T'Blackthorn would know how else Yew would try to find Lahsin. Tinne strolled to the scrybowl.

"T'Blackthorn Residence," answered that stately house.

"Tinne Holly for my cuz Straif." He shouldn't have had to announce himself, T'Blackthorn Residence was being pompous.

"T'Blackthorn is not in," T'Blackthorn Residence said. "Do you wish to speak with my Lady?"

"No, thank you. When will Straif be available?"

"He'll be back for Yule. He's in Gael City."

"Thank you." Tinne cut the connection. He wandered through the House, thinking and sipping his caff. "Viz T'Willow for me."

"At once! Viz in the relaxation room initiated."

Two doors down. Apparently the House thought Tinne was a bit tense. This conversation with Saille wouldn't calm him, either. He strolled into the room to see Saille T'Willow looking at him from the wall, wearing an embroidered scarlet dressing robe. The background behind him showed a sunny room but not the conservatory. There was a gently steaming pool and verdant plants mocking the winter outside the glass windows.

Tinne's heart squeezed. He'd like to be in the Healing pool with Lahsin.

"Greetyou, Tinne. What can I do for you?" asked Saille.

Tinne swallowed the caff, which suddenly tasted bitter. He shifted his shoulders, didn't take a seat. In a neutral voice, he said casually, "I was wondering if you knew what T'Yew was up to." The Hollys kept an eye on their enemies, but Tinne didn't know whether Saille did.

Saille's eyes sharpened. "One moment, I need to go to my study." The screen darkened.

"I'm sorry to interrupt you," Tinne said.

Saille grunted in reply, the screen flicked on again, Saille stood behind an ornate desk, staring at a piece of papyrus. "I got a note from the Sallows, a distant offshoot of my Family. GrandLord Caprea Sallow received a visit from T'Yew, who requested a tracking team of a trainer and dog."

Tinne's chill intensified, permeating his bones. "There are such things? Dog trackers?" That didn't sound good for Lahsin.

Saille's expression turned grim. "Apparently so." He glanced down at the papyrus. "Caprea wasn't enthusiastic, but didn't feel like he could refuse a FirstFamily GrandLord. He assigned his weakest team to the job." Saille met his eyes again, hesitated. "Have you heard the rumors circling 'round regarding GrandLady T'Yew?" Now his voice was expressionless.

Taking another sip of his drink, Tinne shrugged. "No. Social conversations tend to stop as soon as I enter a room." No one at the Green Knight talked to him about anything but fighting. He was still avoiding holiday parties. "I hope the rumors are crucifying him as much as those are regarding me."

Saille winced. "The Yews have put out that young Lahsin is mentally unstable, made worse by her upcoming Passage."

Tinne's teeth hurt. He was clenching his jaw, he relaxed the muscles. "Not surprising." He snorted. "At least he can lie." His own situation was all too clear—clearly divorced.

"I don't know how many people believe him. He doesn't have much goodwill, even among the FirstFamilies, let alone the rest of Druida. Naturally other whispers are running rampant, that he was cruel to Lahsin, and she left."

The muscle in Tinne's jaw flexed. Clamped teeth again. "I'd imagine that's closer to the truth."

"People are willing to believe the worst of T'Yew."

"Rumor's like that. When did this tracking team start?"

Tapping a forefinger on the report, Saille said, "They went out late yesterday afternoon."

"Late afternoon means in the dark. It snowed. How well do dogs track in the snow? It's been more than a week."

Saille spread his hands. "I don't know. Should I ask Caprea?"

"No. Thank you."

With an inclination of his head, Saille said, "Very well." He smiled. "I'm on good terms with him. An honorable man." Meeting Tinne's gaze, he said, "The rumors about you are that your divorce was an unfortunate result of the effects of your parents breaking their Vows of Honor. Your reputation is good."

"Thank you," Tinne said.

"We'll stand with you, the younger generation," Saille said.

That wrung a chuckle from Tinne. "Speaking of the younger generation, we've got a lot of them at the Green Knight."

"They'll support you, too. The disapproval isn't about you," Saille said. "It's about divorce. No one wants divorce to become popular. We humans are still too few on Celta to be easy with breaking strong Family ties that will help us thrive."

"Spoken like a true matchmaker, a proponent of marriage and Family," Tinne said. There had been no good options for his situation, but better a divorce than an empty marriage.

"May you find your HeartMate and HeartBond," Saille said softly, in the tone of a blessing.

Tinne flinched, didn't meet Saille's gaze, didn't want the man to see that he had already found her. And to see that Tinne had as little wish to bond with Lahsin as she did him.

But that shouldn't concern him now. He had to make sure that he was the *only* one who found her. "Thank you again," he said, and bowed to Saille as he waved the viz to end. He set his cup down and rubbed his hands together, sensing danger.

Twenty-three

*S*ince *the old BalmHeal Residence wasn't speaking to* her again, Lahsin left the greenhouse as soon as daily upkeep was done and walked west. The land was smoother in this direction, without the slopes and terraces and occasional dramatic drop-offs of the south and east. The snow was lighter, too, and she wanted to examine the fruit groves better.

She was running her hand over the gnarled trunk of a crabapple tree when she heard vicious growls and snapping teeth.

Strother was ripping something apart.

Right outside the west wall's door. She ran, not knowing what to do. It was madness to take prey from his wide, wicked jaws.

Yelps. Cries. She put her hand on the door latch.

Then she heard human curses. The sizzling whine of a blazer.

Lady and Lord!

More cursing, then crooning, then the slight sound of someone teleporting. Away, she hoped. She found her hands over her lips, pressing her own cries back into her throat.

A low moaning whimper came.

Strother?

She had to help. She glanced at the sky. It was bright and

sunny. There would be no hiding from anyone outside in the small cobbled yard between the door of the estate and the back of a deserted warehouse.

Another groan, this time fainter. It *was* Strother, and he wasn't coming through the animal door. Wasn't teleporting. Wasn't even scratching at the human door.

His mind touched hers, full of pain, then the mental link dropped away.

Her heart thumped hard. The dog knew she was close, behind only a wall and spellshields. Safe in the garden. The whimpering stopped. He didn't ask for help. Didn't beg.

They hadn't been together much since they'd entered the Residence. He'd avoided her.

She couldn't leave him. Foolish or not, she'd come to care for him, and he was hurt. Her mind flew to her stillroom medicines, those she'd found in the old no-time there, the Healing pools themselves. She could take care of him.

Yanking the door open, she rushed into the courtyard— into emptiness and quiet and the sun glittering on crystal rime coating empty windows. She swept the courtyard with a glance and saw the depression of footprints and paw prints in a trail in the middle of the narrow street to her right. Saw heaps of disturbed snow. Saw bright red blood on white.

"Strother?"

Nothing.

"Strother!"

Arms hugging herself, she looked around. In the shadows there was a darker gray heap. She ran over. His yellow eyes watched her. There was blood on his muzzle and claw marks along his flanks and near his thin underbelly.

She whimpered, knelt in the snow by him. He lifted his upper lip, displaying white fangs with flecks of blood, and growled deep in his throat. She pressed her lips together, met his eyes. Not touching him, she studied him, swallowed hard when she saw that the other animal—another dog?—had gone for Strother's bad leg and mangled it. Raw red muscle and white tendons were visible.

Could she mend him together somehow—encourage the muscles to knit together as she encouraged plants to grow?

She had to try.

She looked him in the eyes again and formulated her

thoughts clearly. *I am going to take you back into FirstGrove. It's a Healing place. We will see how we can fix you.*

He made a sound between a snort and a snarl.

His mind had roiled with pain, so she spoke aloud. "I'm going to carry you in."

You. Can't.

That stiffened her backbone. She narrowed her eyes. "Yes, I can. If I use Flair." He was a big dog, almost as tall as she was when he was stretched out. Definitely too heavy for her to carry without hurting them both.

Sliding her arms under him, she prayed that her Flair would come to her summoning. After her first Passage fugue it had turned sluggish again. Today she'd used a little of it while distilling her potions, working in the conservatory, nothing major. This would be major.

Probing her memory of grovestudy and spells, she found a simple rhyme that should make Strother lighter. It worked, but she still grunted as she rose from her squat. She staggered a step, and he growled again. She wanted to snap at him, but didn't have the breath for words. She was already trembling from the effort of holding him and knew she'd be counting the steps to the Healing pool, envisioned the path. Smooth. Tinne had smoothed it as some of his own grateful work to the garden. Good.

With slow precision she turned toward the entrance.

She'd left the door open!

Stupid.

But she sensed no one was near or watched from the shadows. The door being open would help her. She should have thought of opening it *before* she picked Strother up.

Live and learn.

Strother's pants came shallow, laced with whimpers. Would he live?

*I*lexa!" *Tinne strode through the House. His Fam liked* to sleep in different rooms, but she was here. *Ilexa!*

What? It was said on a yawn. *You disrupted my near noon nap.*

I need you to hunt.

Hunting! She trotted toward him, sat, and slicked a paw over her whiskers.

"You know the Sallows, the animal trainers."

Caprea Sallow is a good man. T'Holly boarded some of the other hunting cats there.

"Yes." Tinne shook past memories off, present circumstances were more urgent. "He has dog and human tracking teams."

Of course.

"I didn't know."

Dogs have been used for centuries to track. They have good noses and are amenable to training.

"Can you track the trackers? Now? Find out where they've been and follow their path?"

"Yess," she hissed, sprang to her feet, and shot out of the animal flap in the entryway.

If they get too near FirstGrove, lead them away!

She didn't answer.

Once again, Tinne checked the bond between himself and Lahsin. She was sobbing. He 'ported to the door nearest the Healing pool, opened it, and ran through the hedges.

She was in the pool, supporting Strother, who kept up a low growl. Blood swirled in the water.

He ran to her, into the pool. Looked at the dog and winced.

"*T*inne!" Lahsin's teeth chattered as she mangled his name. She was cold, frightened for Strother. She'd raided her own medicines and those in the ancient no-time, 'ported them near the pool, and slathered them on the dog in spite of his protests. She'd carried him to the Healing pool and let the water bathe him. He seemed soothed, but wasn't Healing. She'd tried the little mending chant on one of his minor slices, and it brought the flesh together, but blood still oozed from the wound. All she could really do was put a force field—a shield—over his wounds to keep them sterile and let Heal on their own.

She didn't want to do that.

Now Tinne was here, taking the dog's weight from her. "Go to the garden shed and warm up. I'll handle this."

"He isn't Healing." Tears left cold trails on her cheeks.

"What happened?"

"He got into a fight with another dog near the northwest wall entrance."

Tinne nodded shortly. "I see. Probably the Sallow dog tracking team that T'Yew hired to find you."

"There was a man, but I didn't see him or the fight. He and the other dog were gone by the time I got out there. I was checking the fruit trees when I heard . . ." She stopped babbling.

Tinne was eyeing Strother's wounds, and the dog had lifted his head to glare at him, increased the threat of his growl, but Tinne ignored that. "Only one thing to do. Take him to D'Ash, the animal Healer."

She stood straight, but her insides quivered. "We can't go out. Can't go to a *GreatLady* of all people."

He raised his eyebrows. "I'll take Strother myself, make up a story." He said it easily, but she could tell he was disappointed in her, and shame welled. Was she going through life afraid?

Resentfully she felt that he was never afraid. Never had been afraid.

She looked at the suffering Strother. His eyes were narrowed, distrustful of Tinne. *Man stinks of cat. Always.*

Lahsin glanced around. "Where's Ilexa?"

"Tracking the dog and man. We'll find out their route, see if they can report anything that can lead to you."

"Oh." She stared at him and shivered again. "You want me to trust D'Ash."

"She's a good woman. Once a Commoner, you know. Loves animals. The Ashes are allied with my Family. They can be trusted to keep matters confidential."

Tears prickled behind Lahsin's eyes. Tears of fear and shame at that fear. "The more people who know . . ."

"Having a GreatLady on our side can't be bad."

But would she be on Lahsin's side?

"We can trust them," Tinne said.

"Them?"

"Both of the Ashes."

Now he wanted her to trust a FirstFamilies *GreatLord*, the highest of the high, one of the most powerful in the land. Like T'Yew. She could never trust a GreatLord.

"Not like T'Yew." Tinne met her eyes, his own a light gray.

D'Ash, whispered Strother.

Lahsin glanced down at him, saw a yearning in the dog's gaze, licked her lips. "You'd trust her?"

D'Ash, he said reverently, then stiffened, his gaze going beyond them. He snarled.

Every Fam or animal would trust D'Ash, said Ilexa.

Lahsin glanced over her shoulder to see the cat sitting in a cleared space near the pool. The hunting cat lifted her nose. *You are all in water. Can't be good for you.* Then she tilted her head. *I suppose the dog likes water. Strange creature.*

Strother's growl echoed from the marble sides of the pool.

Ilexa slid her eyes toward Tinne. *I deserve a treat from D'Ash for my work this morning.*

Lahsin looked helplessly at Strother, who was not getting better. At Tinne, who was expecting her to overcome her fears and act like a woman who cared more for a friend than herself. At Ilexa who knew Lahsin's secrets. She didn't trust the cat.

Blood trickled down onto Lahsin's hand from one of Strother's wounds. That made up her mind. She was growing stronger. She was learning self-defense. Not ready to leave FirstGrove altogether, but she should be able to go outside now and then, not hide away like a frightened child. "Let's go."

"Clasp my hands under Strother. On three, I'll 'port us. I have a good visualization of D'Ash's office teleportation pad."

I can 'port myself, Ilexa said. *Don't need to go into that nasty water.*

"Of course you can," Lahsin said, teeth chattering.

"I think I can dry us all off on the way." Tinne smiled crookedly at her.

That would be a fine spell indeed. She shrugged. She still didn't know all the man's capabilities. "Thank you."

"One Strother-dog, Two Strother-dog, *Three.*"

There was a whoosh, more air movement than Lahsin was used to when someone 'ported her. But they landed on a large teleportation pad that smelled of stridebeast.

"Emergency here!" Tinne called through an open door. The room beyond, an office with several doors, was empty.

A small brown-haired woman shot into the room as Tinne

and Lahsin moved carefully off the pad. The woman bustled up to them, frowning. "Dogfight wounds. I just treated Vimin Sallow's dog and sent them home," D'Ash said. "Who is this?"

"Strother," Lahsin said.

"Hmmm, bring him into my surgery."

Tinne scanned the pad, the room, and lowered his voice. "Holly business, confidential. I claim secrecy on behalf of an ally."

D'Ash looked up from Strother, glanced at Tinne, rolled her eyes, and said, "Residence, lock down my offices and initiate all privacy spells. Inform all callers and visitors that I am unavailable for a septhour or so."

Incredible that she could Heal Strother in a septhour.

"Done," said the Residence in a female voice.

"Follow me," D'Ash said.

They took Strother into a dim blue room and put him on the thick permamoss examining table. Tinne went to shut the door, got hissed at by Ilexa, who trotted in and took a corner chair as far from the table as possible. D'Ash spared her a look. "You didn't inflict these wounds."

I am with my FamMan. We are working together.

D'Ash stroked Strother, shook her head. "Dogfights. Not enough dogs to have them fighting." Shook her head again. "Vimin Sallow's bloodhound, now this guy. Not good at all."

"Males fight to protect their territory," Tinne said.

"Sallow's dog got too close to Strother's den?" D'Ash asked.

"That's right," Tinne said. "Can you Heal him?"

"Of course."

"I'll pay the bill from my personal funds."

"No," Lahsin said. "I'll pay." She could somehow, even a large bill. Give D'Ash her necklace? No. Definitely not. Her HeartMate had *made* the necklace, would know who it was for. Lahsin would pay somehow. Now the decision had been made and her immediate fears were gone, she was focused on Strother—as she should have been all along.

She swallowed as D'Ash checked his eyes, tsked, and shook her head over his leg. Lahsin found herself holding Tinne's hand.

Strother thumped his tail once, something Lahsin had

never seen him do. He'd been quiet the instant they'd arrived. *It's D'Ash*, he said in awe, as if meeting a legend.

But his gaze didn't go to her, instead he looked at Lahsin. *You brought me to D'Ash.* For the first time she saw approval, gratitude . . . love? Then he closed his eyes and went limp.

"D'Ash!" Lahsin cried, fingers tightening around Tinne's.

"Busy here," D'Ash said absently, running her hands down Strother's skinny body, stroking the coarse coat.

Tinne murmured in Lahsin's ear, "Strother's just resting. He feels safe." Tinne lifted her fingers to his mouth, kissed them gently with warm lips. "He trusts you to protect him."

*B*y the time they all returned to BalmHeal Residence, Lahsin was exhausted. She'd insisted on paying for Strother's care by setting new shields around T'Ash's workroom walk-in safe. She'd been nervous that her Flair wouldn't come or wouldn't be sufficient for the task, and T'Ash increased her unease by watching her with an inscrutable stare, arms crossed over his chest. She didn't think he—or D'Ash—believed her when she said she was a visiting relative of a minor Grace-House. She was sure they recognized her from the newssheets, but she continued to lie. Despite everything, she couldn't force herself to trust them. They were too powerful.

Still, she'd *felt* the shields of T'Ash's vault and known they were very good, placed by old Alder who'd left his mark.

But when she finished, hers were better.

Now, as she stared down at Strother bedded on soft permamoss in the closet he'd chosen, she couldn't stop the fine trembling of her muscles. She had the lowering feeling that the only thing that kept her upright was Tinne's steady arm around her waist.

And she didn't mind that arm. It was incredibly strong and muscular, but not constraining. All she had to do was move a step away, and it would drop. Nor was Tinne projecting anything but mild friendship. Definitely no dark lust.

She didn't want lust from him, though she enjoyed rubbing salve on him and took her time. She frowned. Tinne wasn't capable of *dark* lust like T'Yew. That conclusion itself was a relief.

D'Ash had sent Strother into a deep sleep. Lahsin hadn't watched when the GreatLady had rebroken Strother's bad leg and reset it. It looked straight under Lahsin's own protective shields. New red mended flesh that would become scars showed the recent wounds, fur wouldn't grow there. Tooth punctures were on his muzzle. Strother had not been a handsome dog; now he was ugly. Also as part of her payment, D'Ash had taken DNA from Strother to trace his heritage. There were very few feral dogs.

Suddenly the small room, the smell of astringent herbs used on Strother, even Tinne's musky masculine scent caused Lahsin to go dizzy, go hot, then cold. She shuddered hard.

Tinne looked at her with lowered brows, concerned. "What?"

Lahsin wrapped her arms around herself, couldn't prevent a moan or manage a smile. She was afraid she knew what this was. "Passage." The next psychic storm was on her in earnest.

Twenty-four

❤

"*Fligger,*" *Tinne said roughly, and swung her into his* arms.

"Wha—?"

His intense face filled her vision. "I'm staying with you. No one should experience Passage alone. Give me leave to stay."

A mist seemed to veil his face, all except his eyes, which had turned a brilliant, shining silver. How was that possible? Maybe it wasn't his eyes. Maybe it was her own. What color were her eyes turning?

He jiggled her, and her bones ached, and she whimpered. She was so cold! She needed a shield against the chill. She could build a shield to block it, couldn't she?

Loud jumbled words assaulted her ears. She winced, then sorted them out. "Give me leave to stay and help you."

Help? That sounded wonderful. Help. But a price was always paid for help, except for her brother Clute. He was the only one who had ever helped without counting cost. Because he loved her, and when you loved there were no balance sheets, no counting of cost. She loved Strother, now.

"*Lahsin!*" The demanding word blew through her head. She moved and was caught by his silver gaze again. Not Clute, Tinne.

"Help," she said, and didn't know whether she was asking

his price or accepting him without it. Then she knew the cold would kill her if she didn't start building her shields, and she reached for her Flair, and it came so lava hot she thought she'd incinerate, and then she didn't think at all.

Passage was different for every person, Tinne reminded himself as he carried Lahsin down the halls of BalmHeal Residence to her room. The Residence had snapped directions to him and now appeared to seethe in silence.

On the second story at the far end of the other wing. He snorted. Of course Strother had chosen his own closet to be well away from Lahsin. Tinne had a feeling that when Strother awoke from Healing, he'd expect a place in Lahsin's room, if not her bed.

For a fleeting instant Tinne thought of being in bed with Lahsin, then the notion was gone, to his relief. He only wanted her safe. Maybe a few years in the future when they had both Healed from their emotional ills, they might consider a closer relationship. Right now, he was fine with just being her friend.

And helping her through Passage.

She wasn't shivering anymore. The texture of her skin had changed under his hands, she felt nearly . . . slick. A shield? Her personal Flair was for shields, no doubt about that. He'd experienced her change in the shields around FirstGrove and seen it when she'd layered protection over T'Ash's safe.

That GreatLord knew she was Tinne's HeartMate, of course. Tinne hadn't said a word, but T'Ash had been Tinne's brother's best friend for years, knew most of the Holly secrets, and would have guessed. With a look, Tinne had asked him to keep his mouth shut, even from the Hollys.

"What's wrong with the girl?" asked the harsh voice of BalmHeal Residence. "Is she going to die? No dying within my walls! Stupid to have let her inside in the first place."

From what Tinne had seen, Lahsin would be able to breach any walls, any shields, at any time. "For a Residence who housed a Healing Family and other great Healers for centuries, your bedside manner isn't very nice," Tinne said. "She's undergoing Second Passage, as you well know."

"She can stay," the Residence grumbled. "As long as she doesn't die during Passage. Is her line strong?"

"Strong enough," Tinne said. She'd surprised him by going to T'Ash's with him. Granted, he'd prodded her a little, but she hadn't given into her fears, though she'd had bloody evidence that her husband continued to search for her.

Ilexa joined him, purring. She'd eyed Strother and her manner had taken on an awareness that when Strother Healed, he might be a match for her. *Do you want my report, now? The T'Ash cats told me the Sallow dog was hurt worse. Smaller dog and not as mean.* She said it almost with admiration.

"The Sallow dog was just doing a job. Strother was defending his territory, the only place that has accepted him."

The only person who has accepted him?

"Maybe. No surprise Strother won with so much at stake. Questions do remain. Did the Sallow hound know that Lahsin was behind the walls? Does he or the man know this is First-Grove?"

Sallow dog-nose is good. He'd picked up a trace of Lahsin's scent, was casting up and down the narrow path between buildings. He did not find the animal path between the bushes and the wall, did not go there. Ilexa sniffed. *Full of thorns. Don't know how Lahsin made it through. Strother has thick matted hair, thorns catch on it.* Ilexa paused to lick a patch of sleek hair.

"Shields," Tinne said. "Lahsin has a Flair for all sorts of wonderful shields. She had a need to go along the path, probably unconsciously put shields around her as she went."

I will go and check with Sallows and learn what their Fams have to say about this event.

"Good idea," Tinne said. He refrained from saying she'd get another meal from them. She'd picked up bad habits during her time on her own. With a slight pop, she teleported away.

He reached Lahsin's room, used Flair to open the door, and kicked it shut. He laid Lahsin gently on the bed, wondered if he should pull the window curtains, whether dark or light would be better. Wondered whether he should put a blanket over her. What did he know of "normal" Passages? Hollys always fought duels.

Sniffing, he said, "Residence, what's that smell?"

"A mixture efficacious for Passage. The girl is not the first one to go through it here."

Tinne didn't doubt that. Surely Passage was as tough or tougher on their ancestors. Worried parents would bring their children here, especially during First Passage at seven.

"Thank you," Tinne said.

"I have only lost twelve."

Tinne gulped and tried to remember the last time he heard of someone dying during Passage. That didn't happen as much with the FirstFamilies as it did with the lower Nobles and middle-class Commoners. Because the FirstFamilies had had Flair longer, valued it, sometimes bred for it.

Dying during Passage wasn't news Families circulated. He stared at the slim figure of Lahsin. She was a Burdock, of lower Noble GraceHouse rank. She'd demonstrated great Flair during her first Passage and had been tested for Flair. Those results, too, had placed her at the top of her group.

If he squinted, he could see a hazy aura around her. Shield or Flair?

It would probably be best if he held her, curled himself around her but he couldn't bring himself to lie in bed with her. He had not slept with any other woman than his wife in years.

Yet he could not leave Lahsin, either. He was aware of the bonds they'd already made between them. Just looking at her tugged his emotions. So young . . . Even if she hadn't been his HeartMate, he couldn't leave a person who was becoming a friend alone to her Passage.

She shuddered, flung out her arms, thrashed. That confirmed his decision. He couldn't leave her, couldn't join her in bed. So he drew a chair close to the bedsponge and linked fingers with her. Her hand squeezed his tightly.

Then he let himself sink into a trance—more like falling, which he hated, but which he was willing to endure for her.

Suddenly he was *there* with her, not quite in the real world, but not totally in a world that her mind constructed, either. Heat blazed through her, through him, as if he touched a star. He knew she'd been cold, but now she was burning up, screaming in her mind, in his. Flames licked at him, and he tried to erect a small shield, and that spurred her.

"No," she cried and showed him, dream hands dancing quickly, spellwords that made no sense speeding from her brain to his. The power of her Flair whirled around him.

Then they were in a translucent cage together, a cylinder that the storm could not penetrate. Elemental fears and bad memories and nightmares battered against the tube but produced no sound. Pellets of icy sleet that should have thundered, fiery rain that should have hissed. Eerie silence. He saw hideous faces in the steaming mist.

She turned to him with a sudden, sweet smile. "I can do this. I can shield myself. I can shield you, too."

"Yes," he said.

Her smile widened, triumph lit her eyes. "I can master my Flair."

Tinne didn't tell her that she'd have to embrace and control those shrieking, heated emotions to truly master her Flair.

He woke septhours later, the day was fading into evening. His fingers were still wrapped around Lahsin's. He glanced at her and saw that she'd sweated through her clothes, but didn't think he should awaken her. He certainly wasn't going to undress her.

He didn't remember the full Passage and was glad of it, but knew it was over for now. He had no idea when it might hit again, but thought it wouldn't be tonight. His deathduel Second and Third Passages had occurred every night for five nights.

But he didn't know Lahsin's cycle. Passage could come upon her the next day, or night, or in an eightday. She could have one or many more fugues. She could have flashbacks. He wished he knew more about Passage. "Residence," he said in a low tone.

"What do you want?"

BalmHeal Residence was definitely not the eager-to-please Turquoise House.

"Do you have a ResidenceLibrary?"

"Of course," the voice grated.

"Tell me about Passages." Lahsin's grip had relaxed, but her fingers still curled in his own. Soft. He kept hold so they wouldn't slip away.

"Why don't you ask the girl? She's read everything in my physical library. I'll wake her."

"No, let her sleep." Flattery might help. "You have housed

many powerfully Flaired and renowned Healers and must have observed and recorded their methods." He glanced at the timer. "This Passage lasted about four septhours. Based on that—"

"I modulated the room temperature according to the girl's body temperature."

"Well done." He cleared his throat. "Based on the many cases you must have witnessed, can you give me any idea of when her next wave of Passage will be?"

"Passage is individual to the person," the Residence said pompously.

"Thank you for confirming that." Tinne stayed casual.

There was a couple of minutes of silence. Lahsin gave a little sigh and rolled over, her fingers slipping from his. She curled into a ball. Tinne stood and put a light blanket over her. Then he stretched and shook his limbs out. His body was stiff.

The Residence still didn't answer, playing a waiting game. "Perhaps it would be best if I asked Primary Healing-Hall." Now the premier Healing grove on Celta.

"Upstart." A hesitation. "My best estimate is that the girl won't have her next experience with Passage before tomorrow afternoon."

Tinne bowed. "Thank you."

An itching came at the back of his mind, someone probing for him. He had to leave. G'Uncle Tab would be concerned, and it was nearly time for Saille T'Willow's training. Tonight was also one of the nights that he was supposed to spend in T'Holly HouseHeart. He'd looked forward to the serenity of that, but now he didn't know.

He wanted to stay with Lahsin.

Just being in her presence eased some soreness within him.

That might be a dangerous sign that they were becoming too close. Close enough that he was in danger of more than caring.

He looked around for a memo sphere and didn't see one, but there was a writestick and papyrus on the bed stand table. Lahsin's pretty penmanship showed notes on Passage. Tinne didn't read them, but turned the papyrus over and wrote: "No self-defense training tonight. Rest. See you tomorrow evening." He hesitated long over the closing, then scrawled his first name.

When he opened the bedroom door, Strother rose from the place he'd been lying across the hall. He inclined his head gravely at Tinne and trotted in gracefully. The bad leg was Healed, moving as strongly as his other three.

He was tall enough to look over the bed. His nose wrinkled. *Smells not like herself. Scared sweat.*

"Passage," Tinne said, thinking the emotional upheaval over Strother might have sparked it.

Strother gazed at Tinne. *This is a good person.*

"I think so."

The dog nodded, studied Tinne from wary eyes. *You are a good person, too, despite you have a FamCat.*

Tinne bowed. "Thank you."

A half smile formed on Strother's muzzle. *FamCat did not stay with you when times were hard. Came back afterward. I tell her that. Not loyal like a dog.*

With a chuckle, Tinne shook his head. Strother was more intelligent than he appeared.

Strother studied Lahsin. *She might be a good FamWoman.* Tinne heard loneliness in the sentence. Strother continued, *I could help her. I am big and strong and tough and mean to bad ones.* He lifted and rotated his once-crippled leg. *My leg is good now. I could leave, but that would not be loyal.* His gaze slid to Tinne. *She helped me. She fed me. She took me to D'Ash.*

"She paid for your Healing with her skill."

The dog snorted. *Pay, pay, pay. Humans obsessed with pay. Doing what feelings say to do is more important.*

Tinne stared.

Cats think of this "pay" stuff, too. Strother's lip curled.

That was true.

My feelings say to stay and become Fam to Lahsin. I like her very much. He hopped onto the chair Tinne had vacated, curled up, and watched Lahsin. *She will love me. That is best.*

*L*ahsin woke, her body aching as if she'd been beaten. Her mouth tasted horrible, and there was an unpleasant odor. As she came fully awake she realized with a wrinkling of her nose that the odor was her. Hurriedly she glanced down at herself. She was atop the bedsponge. Dirt and sweat showed on her, along with old blood—Strother's blood—but it didn't look like she'd lost control of any other bodily functions. Except . . . she put a hand to her face, which seemed tight in spots. Tears.

Her sigh was more a groan as she propped herself on her elbow. "Definitely going to soak in the Healing pool."

I will go with you. There is a shallow pool that I like. But first we should eat dinner.

She whipped her head to the direction of the mental comment and groaned as her neck cricked. Strother lay in a large chair pulled near the bed. She narrowed her eyes, a hazy memory of Tinne sitting there. He'd been here, right?

Yes, he'd carried her to her room. He said he would stay, so of course he must have. The room itself was unusually warm.

She met Strother's big eyes and couldn't quite make out the expression, but it wasn't something she'd seen before. "Are you all right?"

He stood in the chair, took a step, and was on the bedsponge, muzzle close to her face. *I would be your Fam.*

Her heart gave one hard thump, and tears welled again so that she had to swallow. A companion! A real animal companion, a friend for life. She stared at him. "Are you sure?"

He looked away, walked easily on the bedsponge to the end of it, and hopped down. *I am sure. You fed me. You took me to D'Ash. You cared for me. Care for me.*

She got the idea that it was easier for him to say that when he was a shadow among shadows. Only a small glowspell light hovering near the bedside table lit the chamber.

Swallowing, she rubbed her face. "I guess that's true. I *do* care for you. I like you."

A movement and he was resting his muzzle on the bedsponge, staring at her. *I like you, too, and we are much alike.*

She stood on wobbly legs, stiffened her knees and spine, and did a half bow. "I would be honored to be your Fam."

Strother lifted his head and nodded, turned, and nails clicking on the wood floor, he walked to the door. It was open a little, and he slipped out into the hallway. *We can go on much like we have been*, he said.

No incredible emotional links, then. She didn't know

whether to be glad or not. *All right.* With a yearning glance at the waterfall room, she decided her dirt would be best soaked off. She left the overwarm room, too.

Strother turned his head, and she saw the gleam of his eyes. *But we will stay together from now on. We will travel together.*

She sniffed, her feelings were still rocky from Passage. *That suits me fine.*

He grinned, and his big, sharp teeth gleamed, but she didn't notice them as much as the tender expression in his eyes or the little hop he gave in pleasure.

She followed him down the cool halls and the stairs at the far end of the corridor that came out on one side of the kitchen. *Thank you for waiting to eat dinner with me.* She waved the kitchen lights on. Flair welled within her. She had more now; it came to her faster and felt more polished—easier to work with.

Strother grunted, took a stance beside the no-time. *I would like wild turkbird tonight.*

Lahsin raised her brows. *A feast meal.* Wild turkbird from the old no-time of BalmHeal Residence would be different than wild turkbird now. Tempting.

We have had a full day.

Understatement. *Yes, you had your leg reset and are no longer crippled, and I have undergone Passage.* Suddenly she was ravenous. She chose wild turkbird and rice, requested a plate of dark turkbird meat for Strother. The no-time opened and showed steaming plates. Her mouth watered at the aroma.

Using a hot pad, she lowered the plate to the floor for Strother, then went to a small one-person table and chair that she'd found in storage. The table was topped in large, old tile squares showing herbs. One had a piece missing and the chair was battered and had a short leg.

She got water for them both and sat, then said a blessing. Strother murmured a half growl that she thought was his contribution to the prayer. *One more thing before you eat.*

Yes?

The man, Tinne Holly, watched over you during Passage.

I know.

Strother nodded. *You will thank him. But the Residence also helped you. It made the room nice with good smells and made it warm when you were cold and cool when you were warm.*

Thank you for telling me. She cleared her throat. "Residence?"

"I am here." And still cranky.

"Thank you for helping me during Passage," she said.

"The doors to the MasterSuite and the HeirSuite need refinishing," it said.

Lahsin suppressed a sigh. "I'll do that tomorrow." But she didn't let the Residence's manner taint her appetite. The meal was fabulous. She'd have liked to ask the Residence for the recipe, but figured it was considered a Family secret.

When she returned to her room to get her cloak and roll up some towels for herself and Strother, she saw the message from Tinne. No lessons tonight.

This time she let a long sigh escape. Truthfully she wasn't ready for self-defense training. Her body hurt even when she walked slowly. But she would miss talking to him.

She would miss peeking at his body.

She would miss putting her hands on his firm back, stroking ointment into his supple skin.

Twenty-five

❤

The next morning a cold nose sliding down Lahsin's arm and a little, high-pitched whine woke her with a jolt.

Strother stepped out of reach. *Past time for breakfast.*

"Wha—?" She sat up and glanced out the windows. The day was gray, no sun, it was later than she thought. She usually woke at sunrise. A look at the timer told her it was an hour past WorkBell. Late.

It has snowed all night, is still snowing, Strother said.

"Huh." Not very smart this morning. "Thank you. Give me a minute while I use the waterfall room."

Strother sighed. *You never come out of the waterfall room in less than a half septhour. I will go down to the conservatory. When I hear you in the kitchen I will meet you there. I would like scrambled eggs for breakfast.*

"I didn't know dogs ate eggs."

I do. Raw and cooked.

She didn't want to contemplate eating raw eggs. Shell and all? "Fine. Be down soon." She took care of her bladder and her morning breath. She was still pretty clean from soaking in the Healing pool the night before, but stood a couple of minutes under the waterfall anyway. She loved that she could spend so much time in the waterfall without punishment.

A few minutes later, she was eating at the café table in the greenhouse, her chair set to see outside and the soft, thick flakes of snow swirling down too fast with no sign of stopping. By the time she finished, a good twelve centimeters had fallen. That wouldn't melt away quickly as previous snows had. Winter had come for good and all in FirstGrove.

She thought of Tinne. She wanted to see him tonight—every night. Wanted to talk to him. That was not surprising, since he was her only solid contact with the outside world, but it was more. She liked him, cared for him. Thinking about *not* seeing him made her as irritable as BalmHeal Residence.

One option would to be to go to the Turquoise House, but she hadn't mastered teleportation. That skill usually came after Second Passage. Taking inward stock of herself, she thought she might have enough Flair, but no practical experience. That was something she could remedy. She'd listened closely to her brother Clute when he'd explained it to her and had teleported *with* people many times. The experience yesterday hadn't surprised or confused her. No time like the present to safely experiment.

She memorized the atmosphere, the light, the area of the conservatory and told Strother what she was going to do and told him not to wander onto the flagstones. Then she walked to the kitchen and visualized the greenhouse. *Yearned* to be there. With a loud pop, she arrived.

She'd done it, all by herself! Shrieking with glee she danced around, then visualized the kitchen and checked to see that Strother was in the conservatory with her. She teleported to the kitchen successfully. The rest of the morning she practiced and refinished the door to the MasterSuite.

She couldn't wait to tell Tinne that evening.

Maybe, now that she could teleport, she might venture into the city.

Maybe.

Tinne felt great. The night before had gone well. He'd been focused on all his lessons and had been able to face sleeping in T'Holly HouseHeart with equanimity. He'd drummed there, with its approval, then had settled down on the soft moss and slept.

This morning his teaching was going equally well, and he checked on Lahsin several times through their stronger link. The increasing bond was a concern, but he tucked it away. He sensed when she awoke and narrowed their connection.

Between morning classes, Ilexa appeared and waited until Tab was in the main salon before she spoke. *I am ready to tell you about the Sallow household.* She burped discreetly.

Tinne had completely forgotten that, so much else had happened. His muscles tightened. Damn. "So?"

Nasty Lord went there with nasty daughter. Sniffed at them. Ilexa demonstrated a disdainful sniff. Even though this was not good news, Tinne's lips twitched at his Fam. He liked having her back. "And?"

Treated Caprea bad. Like a stup, unFlaired Commoner. Sallows didn't like. Dogs didn't like. Housefluffs didn't like—.

"—I get the picture."

Nasty Lord and daughter go away mad. They do not listen to Sallows, don't ask questions about what Sallows learned or know.

His shoulders had tensed again, he rolled them. "What do they suspect about FirstGrove?"

Sallow man tracker not know anything, worried for dog. Dog-nose smelled FirstGrove, strangeness in walls, but big pain came after, and big mean dog lives beyond walls, and dog-nose doesn't want more pain for self or Sallows, so tells self to forget. She groomed her whiskers. *Not hard for a dog to forget bad stuff, expect humans to take care of it. Little minds.*

"Ahem, yes." His relief made Ilexa all the more amusing.

I did very well. I have been wonderful Fam. Going to FirstGrove with you. Hunting for crippled dog. Helping with self-defense lessons, she said virtuously.

Tinne figured she'd enjoyed herself doing all of that. "I've already bought you a Yule gift from T'Ash."

A flick of her tail. *Time to check on T'Holly Residence, then. I should get gifts from your Family, too.*

He laughed.

Tab came in and watched, hands on his hips, as Ilexa vanished. His lips curved in a genuine smile when he met Tinne's eyes. "You did well this morning. Have been doing well since the divorce. I'm proud of you." Though Tab made sure to say those words often, it was still balm on recovering wounds. Tinne didn't feel like such a failure.

"I've had to leave a couple of mornings," Tinne said.

Scowling, Tab said, "Who wouldn't? But you come to work. You give it your best shot. That's courage in itself."

"Thank you."

*L*ahsin chivied BalmHeal Residence into letting her have a place to train. Yesterday she'd linked with Tinne and given him teleportation visualizations naturally, trusted him to bring them back to the Residence. So she trusted him that much, and since she hadn't heard a long list of complaints from the Residence all morning, she thought the house trusted him.

After restoring the HeirSuite door, she went to the indoor exercise room and cleaned it. It wasn't overly large for an exercise room, but one whole wall was mirrors, and she flinched at the slight figure she made, still looking frail and girl-like.

She was a woman, soon to have adult Flair. She squared her shoulders and turned from the mirrors, then goggled at what she saw. On the opposite wall were racks of weapons—short and long sticks, swords, even shelves of blazers within easy reach.

Two permamoss pads, thinner than those used for beds, were set at angles on a scarred wide-planked, honey-colored floor. It looked fine to her. She hoped Tinne would find it acceptable.

*T*hat afternoon, Tinne was slightly distracted, thinking of the Yews, the bounty they'd put on Lahsin's head, the lies they'd spread about her. Plenty of people would return her to the Burdocks or Yews for the huge reward. Perhaps he'd been wrong in nudging her to leave FirstGrove, especially before she was finished with Second Passage. The Ashes would keep their mouths shut, but one little slip . . . she was safe inside the FirstGrove walls. She should stay there.

The moment he entered the Turquoise House, it said, "I had

a viz from BalmHeal Residence. You told me to keep secrets about it and FirstGrove, so I told no one else, but I think I am the first other Residence it has spoken to in over a century!"

"What did it say?"

Hesitation. "It was not too courteous, but it sent you images of the teleportation pad at this time of evening at this time of year. After a heavy snow. It said that the *estate spellshields will be open for teleportation to this pad only*."

"Ah." Interesting that could be done. He wondered if it was because of Lahsin's Passage last night. She was probably tinkering with the spellshields.

"You will be going there tonight, as always?"

"Yes. But I will be sleeping here."

"Thank you."

"Ilexa will probably be here for the night, soon."

"Ooh. FamCat. More information for my Residence-Library. It has taken longer to gather data on FamCats than expected. I do not altogether understand FamCats."

"You aren't alone in that." Tinne scrutinized the viz images, formed one in his mind, held it, and teleported.

Lahsin was waiting for him.

*S*he had second thoughts when she saw Tinne examining the room. When they trained outside she could run away. He might be faster and catch her but she knew the land better and could escape. That thought had lurked in the back of her mind.

Hands on his hips, turning in place, he studied the room, nodded. "It's a good space."

"Thank you," the Residence said snidely.

Tinne bowed. "Thank *you*." Obviously he understood how to treat a sour old man Residence, too. He went and tested the mats. "Acceptable, but after snowmelt I'll cut more permamoss pads. Usually it would be far too late in the season, but Balm-Heal Estate, the legendary FirstGrove, is warmer than all of Druida."

"Humph," said the Residence, but there was a pleased note in the sound.

He and the Residence were getting along fine, and that

made Lahsin a little nervous. She didn't want the Residence to prefer Tinne to her, just as previous Residences had preferred others to her. It was a matter of safety.

It was a matter of trust.

She didn't trust the Residence, despite the things she'd done for it.

She looked at Tinne, who was walking around the room, getting a feel for it, as a person who worked in such a place would explore new surroundings. This was a matter of trust of him, too. How much did she trust him?

She'd sensed he had no sexual interest in her. Knew he still hurt from his wife, his marriage, his divorce. Would that stop him from wanting her as a woman? Probably. Even T'Yew had waited for several years after his wife's death before he bought Lahsin.

At the far corner of the room, Tinne stopped and sent her a level gaze. His hands were open at his sides, but new tension infused his body. "Lahsin, rape is not about lust, it's about power and control."

She shuddered. "How did you know I was thinking—"

"Your expression. I will not rape you."

The suppressed fury in his voice had her sidling to the door. She was facing an angry man. Angry men were dangerous.

"Yes, I'm angry," he said. "I'm insulted that you would think such a thing of me. My pride and honor are hurt."

The door was open. He hadn't closed it behind him when he'd followed her in. Thinking through the mist of fear in her brain, she understood that he had left it open for her. Fighting rooms probably had their doors shut when people were training.

"I am standing here in the corner. Not coming after you or threatening you in any way. I can control my anger, and I wish no power over you."

He stood like he was rooted, hadn't moved a millimeter toward her. Her breathing steadied from short, ragged gasps.

"I'm angry, too, that anyone would hurt a woman." He swallowed. "Rape a girl. That is wrong. Your Family was dishonorable to let that happen."

"He paid them a lot of gilt, because I had great potential for Flair. He promised them he'd wait to take me to bed. He *lied*. To them. To me. He's a FirstFamily GrandLord, and he can do whatever he pleases." Her voice was high and thin, and then she wasn't even speaking, but sobbing. She folded in on herself, wrapped her arms around her legs. Her vision was blurry with tears, but she saw that Tinne still hadn't moved.

Silence. His feet shifted, but he didn't take a step.

"Ah, Lahsin." His voice sounded sad and thick. "What happened to you hurts my heart."

There was grumbling from the Residence but no words.

"The Holly Family runs mostly to men," Tinne said. "But I have a Mamá and a sister-in-law." A heavy silence. "I had a wife. I know how to comfort a woman, Lahsin. If you'll let me."

She made a mewling noise, clapped her hand over her mouth, and wept some more.

"If you can't reach me mentally, tell the Residence yes or no. I can help." He paused. "It eases my own pain to help."

"Ye—eh—ehsss." She gulped. Her chin quivered, and her mouth pulled down. "I am weeping *again*."

"Emotions don't just go away and stay away. You lapse," he muttered almost to himself. "Grief. Guilt. Hurt."

Then he was there, lifting her into his arms, crooning wordlessly, cradling her. Somehow that was what she needed most, to be treated like a hurt child, the girl who had been confused and scared and wounded. Who had been in the power of a man with no honor. A man who had lied and paid to get what he wanted and was uncaring of any others' feelings but his own.

She clung to Tinne as he carried her, moving down the hall. The Residence was muttering something about a nearby sitting room, grumbling because it was using precious energy to clean it.

The tears came and came. She didn't know she still had so many in her. He found a huge rocking chair—or the Residence or he 'ported one—and they sat and rocked. He continued with the soft flow of murmured words, how she was good and strong and a survivor, and she should release all her grief.

A long time later he set her on her feet and handed her a large, clean softleaf.

She wiped her face and blew her nose, feeling better. A little embarrassed that he knew of her troubles, but not much, because they were equal. She'd seen how his own problems plagued him. Her insides were washy, but lighter. Tears *had* been a release. She hadn't shed all she needed to, and behind the tears there was a waiting tide of anger, but she was fine for now. She mopped her face while he went to the door. "Do you need to go?"

She was glad that she neither whined about him going nor had any eagerness for him to leave. A fine next step in trusting him.

He turned. "No, not right now." His mouth quirked. "But the Turquoise House worries."

An easy topic that piqued her curiosity. "Tell me."

"Silly upstart," said the Residence.

"The Turquoise House was honored to be speaking to such a renowned Residence."

No comment from the Residence, so Tinne continued, "The House hums with the energy of a young entity, always learning, always growing." He hesitated. "Not like this place who is like an ill-tempered oldster." He raised his voice. "But I believe this Residence isn't happy at being disturbed from its sleep and fears being left and neglected again."

Lahsin swallowed. "I'll want to do something for Balm-Heal Residence, so it isn't always abandoned."

"We'll think on it," Tinne said. "Ready for your lesson?"

After blowing her nose one more time, she stood, tall and straight. "Yes."

$\mathcal{T}$*his was the best moment of the day for Tinne. The an*ticipatory minute before Lahsin put her hands on him, rubbed salve into his very tight back. She hadn't seemed to notice that his back had gotten tighter since they'd first started this nightly ritual.

Her fingers skimmed his shoulder blades and, as always, his shaft hardened. He closed his eyes, enjoying the touch of her hands, the scent of the fragrant salve, their link. The connection between them was growing. He was helpless to stop it. He needed her in his life.

"You have a bruise here," she said, and he knew she frowned.

She needed him in *her* life. He'd helped the night before during Passage, would probably help through the remaining fugues. He swallowed hard. Passages were scary things.

"Tinne? This bruise . . . "

He shrugged, felt it. "Just a bruise."

"But how did you get it?"

Looking over his shoulder at her, he smiled. She was using Flair, little surges that sparked the minor Healing components in the ointment and sank deep and warm into his muscles. "Lahsin, I fight all day long, training all levels of students. In the advanced classes we often have free-for-all melees, rough-and-tumble. I don't notice every bruise."

"Oh."

They were surrounded by drifts of pristine snow, wrapped in the thick steam rising from the pool that isolated them. He didn't think she'd be able to see his erection if she peeked around his body. Not that she ever did, though she stared openly at his backside now. It was a step in the right direction.

No! This was friendship. He didn't want anything more. He sucked in a breath, and she took that as a signal to massage him deeper, and it felt great. He groaned.

"Tinne?"

"Just feels good." Understatement. "The Healing pool and this rubdown always feel good." He didn't want to talk about it, searched for another subject. "It's wonderful that you're learning to teleport." He hadn't known anyone who was self-taught in that—well, perhaps young Avellana Hazel. Precocious child. Perhaps under all her anger and fear was a precocious Lahsin. That made him smile.

"I took the image for here from your mind. I didn't even need you to hold on to me. I did it all by myself." She grinned.

"You did. Actually, I think we shared our visualizations of the pool from previous observations. You know it better, of course, but you're teleporting as well as anyone who studied with a mentor."

The warmth of pride tingled from her to him through her palms. She'd rested them on his shoulders as she usually did just before she ended the massage. He leaned into her, and they lingered in the moment, then he let the cold touch the front of his body, and his natural passion faded. He turned, kept his eyes on her face. "Want me to smooth the salve into your back?"

She pinkened, he saw a flash of yearning. What sort? To be touched by him or by anyone?

Her long stretch bobbed her pretty breasts into view. "No, thank you. I should return to the Residence."

In record time he said a now-familiar couplet, and he was fully dressed, a new skill he'd learned. He felt better with his clothes on. "I'm glad I persuaded you to soak tonight."

She nodded, narrowing her eyes to see beyond the steam. "Yes, it was lovely. Hot springs and cold air, the pure white snowbanks. Yule's coming, I'm looking forward to it. I'll decorate a little."

He couldn't stop himself. He lifted her hand to his lips, met her eyes. "You are a special woman, Lahsin."

Her eyes widened, her smile flashed, and then she was gone without even a hint of a pop of displaced air.

Precocious. He wondered whether he'd be able to handle her once she was completely mature and her inner demons were gone.

A smile still on his face, hands in his coat pockets, Tinne walked from the caff shop to the Turquoise House. He'd wanted a little company and had greeted other regular customers. People had come out in the cold, snowy night to hear a local band. There had been smiles for him, he was being accepted into the neighborhood. As himself and not because of his Family.

He stopped at the gate of the Turquoise House. It was glowing again. All the ground-floor windows were lit, bright squares of yellow making an intense pastel effect.

As he walked up the path, in the back of his mind he heard the distant burbling of the House. It was talking to someone.

Twenty-six

❤

The door opened, revealing a tall man in excellent physical condition dressed in the full-sleeved shirt and modified narrow-legged work trous that were currently the height of casual fashion. Both garments were black. He held a book, finger inserted to keep his place.

The last actor. Tinne had been notified that a final person had requested an audition. Tinne held out his hand, searching his memory for a name. "Merry meet," he started, the man's style demanded a formal greeting. "GrandSir Cerasus Cherry?"

The actor chuckled, shook his head, offered his own well-kept hand. "Raz, merrily met indeed, GreatSir Holly."

Now *that* name Tinne knew, an up-and-coming actor acclaimed by theater critics. "Raz." Tinne smiled, shook the man's hand. Good, strong grip. "I saw you in the production of *The Silver Hand*. Great job."

"Thanks." He stepped back so Tinne could enter, then followed him back to the mainspace.

"Greetyou, Tinne!" said the Turquoise House in a ringing tone that sounded like Raz.

Tinne raised his eyebrows. "Greetyou, Turquoise House." He turned to the actor. "I thought you'd be gone by now."

Raz shrugged. "Time got away from me." He smiled, and it

was fully as charming as anything a Holly could produce. Gesturing to a stack of books, he continued, "The Turquoise House and I kept finding passages we wanted to test. We bored the ears off your FamCat, and she left. Interesting Fam."

"That she is. Looks like thirsty work," Tinne said. "Do you want anything to drink?"

"Not necessary. I was just about to go."

The House spoke, "I want this man's voice."

"Sounds like you have the basis of it," Tinne said. He considered the man. Refined, Noble features that fit an actor— deep-set eyes of sky crystal blue, good cheekbones, strong jaw. He wore his auburn hair straight back and long, to his shoulders. He carried himself and moved well. Ambition was in his gaze.

Tinne figured he'd go a long way in his career. "Bill me for any time after the initial consultation. I don't know how long it will take for the House to get a full and expressive voice, but you're hired. Make appointments at your convenience."

"Thank you. I anticipate only another couple of septhours. The Turquoise House is a quick study." Definitely a resonant voice, another of the man's good tools.

Raz picked up his coat. "With your, and the Turquoise House's, permission, I can finish this job tomorrow morning."

"Fine with me," Tinne said.

"Fine with me," the Turquoise House said.

Raz grinned, showing perfect, white teeth. "The Turquoise House might have chosen my voice, but I believe it will continue to use your phrasing."

Something Tinne hadn't thought about. "I suppose so."

Setting a bookmark in the volume he'd been holding, Raz placed it on the stack and swirled on his coat with a flourish.

"You weren't one of the original six," Tinne said.

"No. I heard about the project through the grapevine."

"So you were particularly interested in the job, and I thank you on behalf of myself and the Turquoise House, but why?"

"The project sounded fascinating." Another quick, genuine smile that lit his blue eyes. Raz glanced around. "An actor is always interested in immortality." He spread his hands, grasped at air. "And it often eludes us. To have our name remembered, some vizes and holos of our performances." Again he shrugged. "But this," his voice deepened. "To be the voice of a House, a Residence. That will last for ages."

"Yeth!" cried the House, delighted, in the old baby voice.

Tinne's wince was matched by Raz's.

"She is an excellent actress," Raz said, obviously recognizing the voice. "But will be better when her roles as ingenues are finished."

"Ah," Tinne said, coughing to hide his laughter, then sobered. "What of Morning Glory?"

"She knows her techniques," Raz said, as if ready for the question. He eyed Tinne. "Odd thing about Morning Glory. She quit her current play mid-run this morning. Said the part was stale and actually left Druida for a break."

"Good!" the Turquoise House said.

"She didn't impress us," Tinne said.

Raz nodded, looked toward the large viz screen, and bowed as if that were the eyes of the House. That notion caused Tinne a qualm. How much could Residences *see*?

"Thank you for this opportunity and the acceptance of my voice. I'll return tomorrow morning at WorkBell." He pivoted toward Tinne and bowed again. "My thanks to you, too. Merry meet."

"And merry part," Tinne said.

"And merry meet again," Raz finished, then vanished, leaving a slight dark blue swirl of sparkling air behind him.

The man was an actor of talent all right.

$\mathcal{T}$*inne struggled awake from a dream of falling.* $\mathcal{H}$*e* gasped and thrashed until he was tangled in the linens. Then he just lay until he thought his limbs would take orders from his brain.

Another dream-remembrance of falling, and they were getting worse. He'd had such dreams ever since that horrible time in the starship lifeboat, circling Celta then falling, falling, falling. Had endured the nightmare when his Mamá had been wounded, when his HeartMate had wed, when his brother had been disinherited, and Tinne himself named HollyHeir. When he'd disinherited himself.

He'd had them every time his life had changed for the worse.

That's what it meant, the falling. That his life had changed, and he'd have to adapt and adjust and change, too.

He didn't want to change. Never wanted to change.

But, like other times, like the trip into space and the falling back to Celta, he'd have no choice.

So he breathed evenly and thought of *good* changes. His mother had Healed, he'd married Genista, his brother and his brother's wife had returned to the Holly Family.

Tinne was rubbing his chest again, over his heart. He must face facts. He was a survivor and he'd been coping, or pretending to cope.

His marriage had ended. No matter how often he thought himself over the shock, the falling dream sucked him back into it.

Or it might mean something else, something equally threatening.

His HeartMate was available to marry.

A groan tore from him.

Ilexa sighed sibilantly, hopped on his bed, and stared at him. *First you dream bad. Then you groan a lot. Then you drum. How is a cat supposed to sleep?*

His life had changed when she'd left it, too, and when she'd returned.

"A little sympathy here. Life's changing too much."

She sniffed. *Life is new every day. Stupid to think next day will be the same as day before.*

He couldn't wrap his mind around that cat philosophy.

You go to food bowls and hope they are full. You hunt. You play. You do things for Family . . . She glanced at him slyly as she curled up near his feet. *You buy presents for Fam.*

He grunted.

You live each day. Only way to live.

"Yeah."

And you don't dream, and tonight you don't need to drum, do you? A cat smile.

"Guess not."

Yesterday gone. Tomorrow not here.

A good philosophy. He just didn't think he could follow it. Too much had happened to him to not be wary of the next sucker punch from life.

Like falling in love with his HeartMate.

He cared too much for her already. He'd entwined himself too much into her life.

This time when a woman walked away, he'd be torn to pieces.

*I*t had taken Lahsin days before she'd decided she'd celebrate Yule with more than a simple ritual. She bustled around the Residence, prodding the stuffy old-man persona into providing her with decorations and lighting, cleaned them all with her Flair. She now had a stable pool she could call on at any time. She didn't know how it compared with anyone else's, and it wasn't quite as deep as she wanted, but it was there. Even more would come after the next fugues of Second Passage. The psi power would funnel primarily into spellshields, then gardening. The rest would have to do for general spells such as housekeeping and teleportation.

The pool she'd have after Second Passage would not be the rich sea of Flair that she would have after her Third Passage in a few years. She longed for that and sighed.

She made cider with an edge to it, garnished with a tiny cinnamon stick preserved in the no-time that was so pungent, she knew it came from the Ship *Nuada's Sword*, ages ago. A bit of nutmeg and a hint of mace, and the cider was right.

She gathered boughs of evergreens that fell to her feet when she asked for bounty. With a little flush, she brought in holly showing red berries. Yule was the end of the old Lord, the Holly Lord, and the beginning of the new, the Oak Lord.

How long would Tinne Holly come to the garden? Sometimes she sensed he was lighter in spirit, sometimes darker. She couldn't tell if or how he was Healing. Somewhere inside, he was grieving for a lost marriage, a love who'd slipped from his hands. For a few instants she envied him having such a love.

Then she recalled that Passage was the time when one connected with a HeartMate, and she trembled, had to step away from the still so she didn't spoil her salve recipe.

She didn't want a HeartMate, couldn't think when she *would* want one. Her parents weren't HeartMates, but her

MotherDam and MotherSire had been. Like all HeartMates, they'd died within a year of each other when she was twelve. She missed them.

Sniffing in the pleasantly spicy air of the stillroom, she swallowed. They and Clute were the only people she missed, and here she was preparing for Yule, a holiday most often celebrated with Family. She put the thought from her mind, finished her task, and went back to the echoing, empty, grouchy Residence. But she'd made a difference with it already. It smelled better, was cleaner, and its truly nasty moments were decreasing.

She consulted her list in the blue green parlor on the first floor. The solstice candle needed to be set in the great hall, on the Yule candlestick. She wouldn't bother with a Yule log. But she didn't know where the massive candles were kept, hadn't pushed the Residence. To light a candle that she might only use through Ostara, the spring equinox, seemed wrong.

She shifted her shoulders. Tinne had promised to help her ensure that the Residence wasn't abandoned after she left. She didn't know how they, she, would manage, but she would. A vow.

A sense of lightness filled her. It was good to have a goal outside of her own self, good to help someone else.

She continued to hum and decorate. Everything was going well until Passage struck.

Lahsin's Passage hit near the end of his afternoon class. It was free melee, and Tinne was holding his own against all comers. Then the bond between himself and Lahsin tugged hard, and the world faded away into the sensation of drowning in grief. He took one hit, then two, then people piled atop him. A distant bell rang, WorkEnd, class was over. Then triumphant crowing by his intermediate students at beating him. Weight came off him, and he heard feet heading to the waterfalls as the room emptied. He stayed where he was, aching in body. Aching in his heart from trying to deal with Lahsin's bleak mood, trying to send her hope.

Only when strong hands lifted him, shook him, and his G'Uncle Tab's outraged face came into view could Tinne grasp a corner of reality and stay there.

"What's wrong with you, boy?" Another shake from a frowning Tab. "You were doin' well, don' go slippin' on me now. An' don' get distracted during melee, Lady and Lord!"

Tinne would have snorted if he'd had the air. "Passage," he gasped, and was thumped so hard to his feet his soles stung.

"You've had all your deathduel Passages. Didn't I sweat out every one of them, watched from the shadows?"

Tinne blinked at him, trying to keep his vision clear, ignore Lahsin's wild sobbing and how it twisted his heart. "You did?" Couldn't catch his breath, must have taken an elbow to the gut. He leaned over, hands on his knees, panted, still staring up at the heavy downward brows of his G'Uncle.

"Yes. So don't give me fliggering seaspray about Passage."

"HeartMate," Tinne managed.

Tab went still. He had iron notions about HeartMates. Then Tinne was gently picked up and carried to the inner office and placed in the big, soft client chair.

Tinne had kept Lahsin's secret, hadn't spoken of his HeartMate. Most FirstFamilies knew he had one, but not even his Family knew her identity. His fingers were curved around a short glass of whiskey. "Drink it down," Tab said.

Fire touched his lips, burned down to his belly. This was the strong, aged stuff. Tinne coughed. Tab pounded his back.

Somewhere else Lahsin had collapsed into black despair. She wasn't erecting shields against these emotions as she should have been. The urge to go to her strengthened. He didn't have much time. His breathing shortened, and he steadied it. Waves of blackness rolled to him from her.

Of everyone in his Family, Tab deserved to know about Lahsin, and, finally, Tinne wanted to tell him.

"This one'a the reasons Genista left when she did?" Tab asked.

Tinne winced, Genista's name still striking too hard. "I've kept the bond between me and my HeartMate as thin as a mouse hair, even during my own Third Passage last summer." The link was open now, and her emotional hurt pained him.

Tab grunted, went to the window, and looked out. "Holm Junior told the rest of us that she'd been married young to another." Anger laced Tab's voice, but Tinne figured it was for fate, not him.

"Her name is Lahsin Burdock Yew."

Pivoting on his heel, Tab stared. "The missing girl."

"Young woman, yes. She made it to FirstGrove sanctuary."

"Thought that was a myth."

Tinne set the glass down and rubbed his eyes. "No."

"An' you've been goin' there at night."

Tinne looked up.

Tab said, "I've scried a coupla times." His lips twitched. "Talked with the Turquoise House. Funny youngster."

"Yes." Blackness encroached on Tinne's vision, Lahsin was sinking deeper into depression. His throat was closing with fear. Tinne pushed himself to his feet. "I have to go."

Tab nodded shortly. "You do that." He hesitated. "Met the girl last year at the party on *Nuada's Sword*." Again a corner of his mouth lifted. "The timing party." The events at that party would go by that name for as long as it was remembered. "Pretty girl. Not a good marriage with T'Yew, didn't treat her well, anyone could see that. You go to her. Help her. It'll be good for both of you." Tab turned back to the window. "You spend as much time with her as ya need." He rolled large shoulders. "I'll take the classes, mebbe upgrade cuz Nitida to an apprentice, was thinkin' about that lately, wanted to run it by ya . . ."

"Fine," Tinne said, he had to leave *now*. Darkness crept around the edges of his vision. He walked carefully to where the teleportation pad was, stepped up onto it, and set the indicator.

"People will miss ya, gossip, think you're a wimp about the divorce."

"Fine," Tinne parroted, searched the link between himself and Lahsin to find her. Crumpled on the stillroom floor, not even in the main Residence!

He 'ported to outside the northwestern door. The area was deserted as usual, so he flung open the door, heard his own breath coming fast and hard.

Once inside the walls he strove to recall the layout of the stillroom. He prayed and 'ported again, using up a lot of Flair.

The place was dark, only her moaning breath told him she lived. It was his turn to take care of her. Now he visualized her bedroom in the Residence, hoped he got the light right. Tinne had been looking out on a gray day dissolving into night.

He stumbled as he landed with Lahsin. Clouds had covered the last remnants of the sunset, and the room was dark.

"Passage!" BalmHeal Residence screeched. "Where have you been? She was out of my reach, no one to help, not even that mongrel beast."

"I should have sent my Fam to watch her," Tinne mumbled, just now thinking of it.

"Yes," the Residence agreed. Suddenly the air in the room grew drier, warmer. The Residence was manipulating the atmosphere for Lahsin's comfort.

Tinne set her on the bedsponge, shuffled off his exercise shoes, and crawled onto the bed with her, pulled the cover over them. No hesitation in holding her. She was fading—he sensed it. Drowning in the depths of an ocean of negative emotions.

He tried, but he couldn't follow. Her memories were too different than his. He hadn't been close enough to see them flash in his own mind, to understand exactly what she was experiencing, and to try to mirror her memories with his and pull her back.

He'd never been close to her.

He'd felt grief and despair, but she was beyond him, sucked into terror. His worst terror had been the spine-slicking, body-shaking orbit of the planet in a spaceship escape pod, and how could he ever link that to whatever her worst terror was?

Gently he tugged on their bond. It responded in a sluggish fashion. He was losing her. No! He simply couldn't lose another person, another woman, he cared for.

Twenty-seven

❤

Tinne did the only thing he could to reach Lahsin in the throes of her Passage. He recalled his own last Passage and the time they'd connected. He'd been slumped against a wall, sword bloody from killing robbers who'd set upon a Noblewoman returning to Druida. He'd been heartsick that he hadn't been able to stay his hand and change a fatal blow to a disabling one. But he'd had no choice, the man had been trying to kill him.

The touch of her had come to him, like a soft hand smoothing over his brow. His sweet HeartMate. Young, innocent in many ways. He'd accepted her soothing, eased under it, then realized she wasn't his wife and squeezed the link to a tiny filament, sent her mind spiraling back where it belonged. He never knew if she'd been aware of that moment, or their link.

Now he set the memory in the front of his mind, tightened his hold, and *called* her mentally. *Lahsin. Lahsin!*

A very faint word rose to his mind. "Who?"

HeartMate. HEARTMATE! Only that would bring her back. Surprise her enough to push the other emotions aside.

HeartMate? A tiny echo.

Yes. Come back. Don't leave me alone. The plea rang with sincerity. He might not want an intensely intimate tie, but he didn't want to lose her.

He couldn't send love to her, how could he when he didn't love her? So he sent hope. Simply hope. It flew from him as a shining golden glow like the sun rising over the horizon.

She cried out again. Seeing a landscape of terrors?

Build shields!

Another flash of surprise. Comprehension. She snapped shields around herself, included the link between them. Then a distorted image of a naked T'Yew came, face heavy with unwholesome lust. Tinne cringed. He did *not* want to experience her wedding night. Even recalling his own wedding night with a laughing, voluptuous Genista was better. He sent that *feeling*, how it should be between a couple during their wedding night.

Lahsin rejected it—with anger, bitterness.

Use your anger to negotiate the seas of Passage.

That was the image, white-capped towering waves, dark, salty as the ocean of tears she'd cried. Cold, frightening waves that tore into slashing slices of water.

Rage came from her, hatred . . .

No, control your fury, your hate! He screamed into the hurricane wind. *They will open you—*

It was already happening. Her shields had cracked, the riptide tumbled him over and over, sucked him under, cold as a watery grave. He saw a jumble of red anger, then black terror—Lahsin—snagged her and held her close.

She struggled, screaming, screaming, screaming.

Build your shield!

Clang! A capsule surrounded them. He smelled brine and his sweat and her tears and terror. Blood.

From the wedding night—she said.

No! He let her go, faced away from her.

Who are you?

Do you want me to claim you?

No!

Then let my identity be.

A few seconds of silence. *I can't see you clearly.* She sounded subdued. *Thank you for saving me.*

You're welcome. He was stilted.

You are a man of violent passions. She shivered.

No. I am a man of strong passions. He'd clamped a lid on his own emotions just to survive each day. And he'd make sure he'd show none of them to her in reality.

If they made it back.

She angled herself away from him, the brightly glowing ball of her true self—her soul?—dimming a bit in a sulk.

Then rocks hit the capsule. It tumbled. Light strobed in hideous sheets of blinding white.

Tinne fell into terror. This was *his* worst nightmare, falling through space.

Lahsin's orb touched his own, steadied him, moved away.

He thought he heard a sigh.

Now we ride this out?

Yes. But you will have to embrace the storms and your Flair if you want to be a whole person. Understand. Accept. Master. The words had been rote for him during his own Passages.

Understood, she said with irony, the last thing she said.

They endured together, linked by a thread, but staying apart. They survived the sea, the landslide avalanche, the whirlwind, and the fire, and when they were back on a tossing green sea again, she opened her shields and floated.

Tinne returned to reality. A low light surrounded the bed-sponge, left the rest of the room in shadow. He rose to his elbow and cut off a groan at the aches of his body. Staring at Lahsin, he saw she was deep in a natural sleep.

Muttering a word to clean the imprint of his body on the linens, he swung his legs over the side of the bed, stood, and collapsed when his knees gave way.

He was shuddering. Didn't know what to do. The Passage had affected him, too. All he could think of was getting away. If he faced her, everything would change. They'd be awkward with each other and were too new of friends. If he was here when she awoke and she realized he was her HeartMate, they might never bridge the discomfort of that understanding, the experience.

It was better that he go.

If he'd spoken his name during Passage their emotions would have clashed and they could have died. As it was, their emotions were far too tender and disturbed to make a relationship.

After coughing, he said to the Residence, "Don't—" He stopped words that might irritate the Residence. "Please don't tell Lahsin that I stayed with her. I came to check on her, found her in the stillroom, brought her here where you'd take care of her, and left."

"Just what you did do," BalmHeal Residence said.

"Right." Tinne was bone weary. Grime coated more than his body; it was like a layer over his mind. "What time is it?"

"TransitionBell."

Deep in the night's dark, very early in the morning. Tinne glanced at Lahsin again, her cheeks showed the slightest rosy blush on her golden skin. Beautiful. He arranged the blanket over her, cleared his throat, and said, "Can you estimate—"

"I estimate one more fugue no sooner than a week."

Air escaped Tinne in a quiet sigh. He bowed. "Thank you, Residence."

The Residence opened the bedroom door. Tinne shook his head and teleported outside T'Holly HouseHeart. He needed the place tonight. His own emotional shields had eroded to soap-bubble thinness. Ilexa joined him, purring for him.

He'd no sooner closed and bespelled the door behind him than he fell to his knees on the sweet grass floor. His clothes vanished at a Word, and he lay panting and gave in to his own storm of grief and despair for all that had happened. The shudders of emotion left him as weak as a child. He rolled along the floor to the sacred fountain and allowed it to cleanse him outwardly as he hoped his inward self was cleansed.

How long would grief shroud him? Years, probably.

But when it diminished he would be barred from First-Grove.

He didn't know which was worse.

*Lahsin woke but didn't open her eyes. She stretched in*side and checked her Flair. She had more than ever. Passage lurked like the line of a storm squall on the horizon. She'd have to suffer through it again and master her emotions, but she was optimistic that she could.

By herself. Without the aid of her HeartMate. A tingle ran down her spine.

It had been strange connecting with him, almost familiar. Like she knew his touch . . . or the touch of his mind brushing hers.

Not sexual. In her studies of Passage there had been references to sexual dreams with one's HeartMate. She was glad she was spared that.

She didn't want to think of her HeartMate. Only admitted that his sharp words and strength had saved her. He was strong and powerfully Flaired. Strong physically, mentally, emotionally. Far too strong for her to fight if he'd wanted to capture her in the HeartBond.

But he hadn't, and that was fine with her.

She let out a long breath.

Strother licked her face. She shrieked as she jerked to sit.

He stared at her with sad yellow eyes. *I am sorry that I wasn't here.* He looked away. *I was outside. It's good to hunt outside. I went to my Family's house, where I was crippled.*

She grabbed a pillow, needing to squeeze something tight as anger spurted through her. "Did you attack your Family?" She wanted to attack T'Yew, even Taxa would do. She put the pillow down and thumped fists into it.

Strother leapt off the bed and stood watching her. *My Family is dead. They died the night I was crippled in the accident.*

The red mist coalescing before her vision disappeared. She felt tired. "Oh."

I was not Fam. There were only three men.

"What kind of accident?"

There was bad wind and snow. The roof collapsed.

Lahsin squeaked. She couldn't imagine a thing. "Was the house a Residence?" Suddenly she was grateful for even the irascible BalmHeal Residence.

The shaggy hair over his eyes lowered in consideration. *It was not a house. One of the small warehouses near here.*

She stared at his ugly face, his large form. "Tinne said you were a wolfhound." She reached out and rubbed his head, he rumbled approval. "I've never seen a dog like you. Not that I've seen many." She moved her hand to stroke his floppy ears.

I do not know where I come from, Strother said. *I only remember the three men. I think they found me south of Druida.* He nudged her with his nose, and she rubbed his head again.

"You are awake. It's about time," the Residence said. "I've moved some additional breakfasts from the long-term-storage no-time to the kitchen no-time. Can we get back onto a schedule? It is three days before Yule, and I want my holiday lights bespelled and more decoration on my banisters."

Lahsin wrinkled her nose. "I smell bad again." She didn't want to remember the fading details of her Passage, only recalled that it was scary. That was warning enough.

You smell like Lahsin after an ordeal. That is only right. Strother sighed and rubbed the underside of his muzzle on the bed, closed his eyes. Pleasure welled in Lahsin. He trusted her. *I am sorry that I was not here for your dreamquest.* He hesitated. *I felt some of it. Felt odd. Didn't know what happened until I was back inside. We are Fam companions.*

"Yes, we are." She wet her lips. "I wasn't alone."

Tinne Holly brought you to your room, Strother said.

Lahsin blinked, lifted her hand to rub her temples. It smelled doggy. "I remember I was in the stillroom." She grimaced. "The decoction is spoiled by now. At least there is a fail-safe spell on the still." More work to redo, and the Residence hadn't given another snide prompting, though she thought the atmosphere seethed with impatience.

"I'll have to thank Tinne again."

All that Holly cat talks about is Yule gift from her Fam-Man. Strother lifted his head in a proud gesture. *I do not need a Yule gift from my FamWoman. Caring is enough.*

Lahsin's eyes stung, she swallowed. Once again her emotions were more on the surface after Passage. She petted him. "Thank you, but I can manage a gift for you, and I *do* care for you."

I know, I can feel it. As she swung her legs over the bed, he moved aside for her. She wobbled to the window, lifted a curtain, and peeked out. "Sunny."

Cold, but not bitter. Go to Healing pool?

"No, that can wait until this evening after my lessons." That perked her up. She was learning to control her body better physically, surely that would be a good basis for harnessing her emotions during her last Passage fugue. She grinned. "It looks like Yule. I want a wreath for the door."

"About time," the Residence said.

Lahsin ignored it and headed for the waterfall, singing a holiday tune.

* * *

In the last couple of days before Yule, Tinne kept his relations
with Lahsin casual and easy, making sure she didn't associate
him with her HeartMate. He'd been surly during Passage, and
now he increased his charm. Only one small situation occurred
that had to be handled delicately.

On the night before Yule, he "attacked" her from behind, pulling her roughly to him. Instead of falling back and
making him lose his balance, then following with the counter
they'd practiced many times before, she froze.

She'd felt his arousal.

He'd known it would be only a matter of time before his
body reacted to her during their sessions. Spending the night
surviving Passage with her had brought them closer than before,
physically as well as emotionally. He was aware of her. His
body wanted her urgently, also expected after a long celibacy.

But it was awkward.

He dropped his arms and sighed. "You froze, you internal-
ized your fear instead of using it to fight and escape."

She remained silent.

He came to face her. Her eyes widened, and her gaze
dropped as she stared at the front of his trous. He clenched his
jaw as his arousal became more intense. She looked back up,
and he saw fear in her eyes. She tensed, shifted for flight.

"Don't run."

Keeping her gaze on him, she inhaled, scowled as she
fought her own fearful reactions.

"You're younger and faster than T'Yew," she said.

"I should hope so."

"Harder."

That pulled a laugh from him.

She frowned, her cheeks flushed to the color of a ripe
peach. "Your sex is bigger than T'Yew's—"

"I should hope so."

"—and though you aren't as tall or as bulky, your muscles
are harder." She looked away and began to quiver.

His humor vanished. "I could hurt you more, you mean."

She nodded.

"Lahsin." He kept his voice gentle. When he touched
her chin, she flinched. "Look into my eyes, Lahsin. Yes, I'm

aroused. I'm a young man, and you're an attractive young woman. My body reacts naturally around you. But, Lahsin, a man isn't only a cock. And a smart man doesn't let his cock rule him."

Her mouth dropped open.

"I control my body, it does not master me."

She met his gaze, her stance eased a little. "Of course not." Her voice was too high.

He raised both hands, palms out. "I will never force myself on you, Lahsin. *Never*."

"Of course you wouldn't." More deep breaths. "You can have any woman you want."

His turn to flinch. "I'd rather you believe in my honor and my word and my self-control."

"I do." She sighed long, and her muscles loosed with it. Tinne knew that she'd overcome her fear and wouldn't run. "You'd never want an unwilling partner."

"No." He hesitated, but the words had to be said. "T'Yew is a powerful FirstFamily GrandLord, accustomed to getting what he wants." Like Tinne's father, but so much worse, and Lord and Lady knew, Tinne had paid dearly for T'Holly's arrogance. Tinne hoped the fates would call payment due on T'Yew. "And T'Yew's sexual proclivities are not that of any normal man." Deep breaths. Her gaze was steady, and that was good. "He's twisted, Lahsin, to want a wife so much younger than he."

The sadness in her eyes hurt Tinne's heart.

"He married me on my fourteenth Nameday. The youngest legal age." Her lips firmed, then she said, "He wanted a son."

"Well, he didn't get one, did he?" Tinne tried to be brisk but failed.

"No."

He looked away, he should reveal a vulnerability, her fingers still trembled. "I haven't had sex in . . . months." His voice was rougher than anticipated. "My reaction's natural." That was much more difficult to say than he'd thought, and he regretted it.

Her eyes turned curious, but all she said was, "What do you do when teaching women at your salon?"

"I usually wear a groin-guard. No one can tell whether I'm hard or not. Since we'll be progressing to strikes against the groin in the next lesson, I'll bring one."

She nodded. "All right." She straightened. "Let's try an attack again. I *will* unbalance you. I *will* follow through."

"Yes," Tinne said. "I'm proud of you, Lahsin. You overcame your fear and stood your ground, were calm enough to listen. I respect you." He bowed twice. First a formal bow of Nobleman to Noblewoman, then he changed his stance and bowed as they both did before a training session.

She bowed back, watching him. "I want to learn more than self-defense," she said. "I want to learn fighting."

A lump formed in his throat. He nodded, then he walked behind her to attack her again.

A half septhour later, Lahsin was smiling, appearing pleased with herself. She'd solidly mastered the defense for a grab from behind. She wasn't vulnerable to that attack any longer. Satisfaction filled Tinne, more than he'd had since he'd begun teaching. Usually other members of the Holly Family taught grovestudy groups self-defense, but maybe he could work a class into his schedule. Maybe bring the group into the Green Knight to train as some might want to continue, like Lahsin. It never hurt to have more business.

Tinne soaked opposite her in the Healing pool. They'd 'ported to the pool after the lesson, and Tinne noted she'd become proficient in that skill, too. The pool itself was warm, and the snow around it was white with no tracks.

He watched her from under lowered lids. They didn't speak. There'd be no more shared rubbing of salve, not when he was so aware of her sexually and she knew of his desire. He wouldn't embarrass either of them but he'd miss the tending.

When he'd gotten the maximum benefit from the pool, he rose, dried, and dressed, keeping his movements unhurried.

Once again he bowed to her, keeping his eyes on her face. "Merry meet." He hesitated. "I don't know if I'll be here tomorrow night . . ." He realized he wanted to be, very badly.

She nodded. "Yule with the Family is important."

". . . but if I can come, I will."

"I'm not celebrating the ritual at sunset but at midnight, if that makes a difference," she said. He sensed she was crafting her own ways different than the Yews and the Burdocks.

"Thank you," he replied gravely. "I will come then."

Hunching a shoulder, she said, "If you want. Blessings of the holiday." She was having trouble keeping her own gaze on his face, had peeked at more than his ass when he'd gotten out of the pool. He lifted a hand and teleported to the Turquoise House, considering her expression. It appeared to be a yearning—for Family to celebrate the Yule with?

For him? He'd like that. Too much. Shouldn't think of that.

Twenty-eight

❤

The Green Knight closed at noon the next day for the winter solstice, Yule. Classes had been light, especially thin of women, who continued to be those who managed holidays. Tinne hadn't seen his Mamá or his sister-in-law, Lark, for days.

He had held a small Yule ritual in the Turquoise House and anticipated two more with his Family and Lahsin.

Dressed in his most flamboyant clothes of red and green silkeen with gold trim, Tinne arrived at T'Holly Residence a full septhour before the early sunset. Ilexa was already there, showing off the emerald collar he'd given her to the other Fams.

He went to his rooms in T'Holly Residence only for as long as it took him to snag his best ceremonial drum. The body was deep reddwood, the skin excellent, accented with gold tassels. He'd stenciled holly leaves and berries along with mistletoe around the top and bottom.

His rooms looked appropriate for the season, but he still didn't want to live in them, wanted to remain in the Turquoise House with little pressure. He had begun to like living alone. It was improving his temper and maybe his character. A good experience, being away a while from his overprotective Family.

He set his drum in the large gathering room that would host the Family after the ritual. To his surprise, his father had decided the ritual should take place outside in the sacred grove. T'Holly had gone to great lengths to clear the snow and erect a weathershield—a minimal weathershield so the Family would experience the touch of winter. Tinne got the impression that his father had used his own great Flair for these arrangements, but Tinne was glad he'd brought his heavy llamawool cape.

He let himself be absorbed into the bustle of preparations by his Mamá after her absent kiss. He dressed long tables and sideboards in holiday linens ready for great platters of food.

Then it was time, and they trooped to the grove. Tinne stood between his brother and Tab, linked hands with them as the whole circle was doing and felt the sweet surge of Family Flair. They stood and let the winter silence envelop them as the sun died.

He thought he'd suffer through the Yule ritual with his Family, but it went well. The pervasive love was there as always, but his father showed more humility as he officiated as priest, more of a willingness to allow the spirit of the Lord to move through him. T'Holly was more clear-eyed regarding fate, looking to a future that would never hold what he'd wanted all his life—years of the Captaincy of the FirstFamilies Council and thus all the Celtan Councils. Tinne was impressed. And touched even more when his mother went through the ceremony as the Lady with a bright gaze and soft expression.

His father had changed, and in doing so, the relationship between his parents had changed, and his Mamá welcomed that, too.

Everyone *felt* the change when the energy from T'Holly and D'Holly cycled through them. There was less fierce determination in obtaining his own goals from T'Holly and more openness.

Instead of asking the Lady and Lord to fulfill his wishes, T'Holly asked to be led to the right destiny.

The Flair that flowed through the circle was finally free of any taint. The party afterward was as loud and raucous and joyous as those Tinne recalled from his childhood.

When most of the Family had retired to their bedchambers to celebrate privately or to rest, Tinne went upstairs to his old rooms. There he stashed his drum and got a sturdy bag and put his gifts into it. He sauntered to the teleportation room and 'ported to BalmHeal Residence, glad Lahsin continued to keep this opening in the house's spellshields for him.

It was a septhour before midnight, and when he arrived, he sent his mind questing through the too-silent Residence. Surely she wasn't holding the ritual outside in the grove! But she might have sufficient Flair for shields . . .

No, she was in the stillroom, probably getting apple cider for the ceremony. He sniffed and smelled freshly baked bread, but didn't know if she'd baked it herself, imbuing it with good household spells as most Ladies did, or whether she'd pulled it from a no-time. She wouldn't have had any true grain from the last summer. Did BalmHeal Residence have a special no-time for ritual foods? Would it share with them?

He carried his contributions to the ritual, drink in a new fancy carafe he'd bought the day before from a glass artist. The carafe was for the Residence. Tinne had two gifts for Lahsin. Gifts were usually given on New Year's Day, right after Samhain, a month and a half earlier, but he hadn't known Lahsin then.

That stopped him. It seemed like he'd known her forever. But he hadn't known her at Samhain.

He didn't like to remember before the divorce. Just a couple of eightdays ago, but the catastrophic event was like a jagged tear in his life. Before and after. Always would be. When his tender mind skittered to memories of Samhain, there was misery. They'd—he'd—lost his unborn child just before Samhain last year.

Switch mind and emotions back to Lahsin!

He hadn't known her. That seemed odd since she graced his thoughts with her presence. He'd never acknowledged their link, never let it grow from a microfilament. Perhaps she had been like a shy bloom in the very back of his mind, as quiet as she'd been with the Yews. To think of her, to want her when he was married to another, would have been dishonorable.

"You just going to march through my halls with no greeting, son of the Hollys?" demanded BalmHeal Residence.

Tinne winced. Bowed. "Happy Yule, oh, great Residence."

It grunted. "Come to do a ritual here? Got a gift for me?"

Tinne said a spell for his sack to hover, he reached in and revealed the carafe. He held up the elegant teardrop-shaped glass of deep ruby with gold accents. "For you."

That caused a few seconds of silence.

"Good manners. You are welcome to stay this longest night."

"Thank you." He noticed candles burning along the hallway, there'd been one in the teleportation room. "Did Lahsin light every candle?"

"She lit the great ritual candle in the great hall before sunset and said the prayers. I took some energy and light from that one to set the rest afire."

Tinne bowed again. "Blessings." He hadn't needed to bring any gift to T'Holly Residence, but had given the Turquoise House something. It was another being he hadn't known at New Year's but which had become important to him. He'd given the House all of his Mamá's compositions and listened to effusive thanks. He'd lit the great candle—one that would last through the night and be lit on each of the major holidays for the rest of the year and burn out on this night next year—in the well of a fountain. He and the House had said prayers together, and he'd summoned energy and Flair to charge the most important House spells for the year. Mitchella had only funded the spells on a need-to-use basis.

The Turquoise House had played a triumphant fanfare, and Tinne had left the House smiling, sure that music would play all day and night. It had taken so little to please the House. Tinne didn't think it had even occurred to the House to ask him to stay. It was accustomed to being alone on holidays.

As this Residence was. He repeated, "Blessings for you over the next year."

"And for you," BalmHeal Residence said stiffly.

Then the air changed, and Tinne knew Lahsin had arrived. He felt a wisp of hope from the place and winced again. She wouldn't stay, would move when she felt safe, or in the spring. He wouldn't stay, either. Not here nor in the Turquoise House. Sometime he'd move back to T'Holly Residence, and in the far future perhaps to the rooms over the fencing salon.

"Merry Yule, Residence!" Lahsin's voice caroled through the house. She sounded happy, and that warmed Tinne, much as he thought it warmed the Residence itself.

"Greetyou, Lahsin Rosemary," the Residence replied.

Tinne blinked. He hadn't known that she'd taken a surname, her MotherDam's Family name. A MotherDam who was dead, had been dead before Lahsin was sold to T'Yew.

A name as pretty as the girl . . . woman.

"Holly SecondSon is here," the Residence said.

"Oh."

He strode down the corridor to meet her and found her putting away her cloak and humming a little spell to dry and clean wet splatters.

"It's snowing?" He hadn't glanced outside for septhours.

"Yes. I wanted to walk in it." She smiled, and he was relieved to see it was genuine. He hadn't known if she'd wanted his presence. "Thick, beautiful snowflakes. I don't think it will last. I've become more weather savvy. The snow is a simple blessing on this longest night." She shivered.

"Passage?" he asked too sharply.

She chuckled. "No, just cold. I don't want the Residence to use all its energy on heat, especially on this room."

Tinne glanced at the elaborate candlestick, gleaming bronze in the light from the single, huge, multi-wicked candle it held. Around the bottom were fresh pine branches, giving a nice scent.

"You've done a lovely job."

Her smile widened. "You should see the ritual room. I'm using an old corner room, not the HouseHeart."

The Residence wouldn't let her into the HouseHeart. She could probably sense its thick shields and force it, but Lahsin would never force anything, even in desperate straits. He was afraid she was still too soft.

But no defensive training tonight. He held up the bottle. "I have an offering for the ritual and a gift for the Residence." The carafe gleamed richly.

"So beautiful." She reached out but brought her fingers back, like a child told too often not to touch.

"You should carry it, as priestess and Lady tonight."

As she took it, her fingers brushed against his, sending a sweet surge of energy through him, something he refused to savor when they were training. Tonight was different. The longest night, the celebration started so long ago on ancient Earth, but brought here and modified to this planet's revolution. Picking up a bulging sack, she went to the hall.

With a sideways glance at him, she said, "Do you intend to be priest and Lord tonight?"

"Just a participant," he said. "If you want me to—"

Her shoulders relaxed. "I only crafted the ritual for the Lady's part." She turned, left, and went down the corridor.

"Spent septhours in the library," grumbled the Residence.

He smiled. "I don't have any experience in being priest or Lord, haven't crafted a ritual. Though there are some that I could do by memory, I suppose." He shrugged. "Don't know that I'll ever be a Lord in a ritual as I'm not the Heir. My father officiates Family rituals, and when he passes on, my brother will be the head of the Family, and he and his wife will lead."

Lahsin stopped. "But surely you will have intimate Family—"

Tinne stared at a flickering flame in a sconce down the hall. "I have no plans for another marriage or children for now." He glanced at her. "Just like you."

She shivered. "No, I don't want to be married anytime soon, either." She started walking again, and Tinne kept pace.

"Most people would expect the both of us to wed again soon."

"I don't want to," she said.

"Me, either."

"Does your Family pester you?"

His smile was ironic. "Not yet."

"That's good. But you're a man, they won't be able to force you into doing what *they* want."

"Family pressure is Family pressure, so that's not as easy as it sounds. You're an adult, no one can force you to do anything, either. It was wrong for your Family to force you as a child. Lahsin, you should file a suit against T'Yew for abuse."

"I'm free from him. That's enough." She grimaced as she gestured to a door at the end of the hall. "Now I am not in a fit state for the ritual."

"I'm sorry."

"I was the one who brought up the topic."

"Is the room ready for the ritual? Putting it in order . . ."

"It's prepared."

"Then let's enter with good intentions and meditate."

She inhaled deeply, let the breath go slowly. "Yes."

He opened the door and held it. She placed the carafe on the decorated altar, between a loaf of bread and plump berries, took out a pretty ceramic jug of cider and put it by a plate of sweet cakes. The altar was low, with fat pillows on the floor, another ancient custom from the first days of the colonists.

Four large ritual cauldrons stood in the exact cardinal directions, off-center of the walls of the room. Small branches, dropped from storms, not cut, along with colored incense were at each cauldron. When they were lit during circle casting, they'd provide heat and light for the ritual. Tinne liked the setup.

"I've used some old ideas," she muttered.

He smiled. She sat down on a corner pillow of fiery red velvet fringed with long strands of red beaded crystals.

Making a show of glancing around the place—at once simple and exotic—he returned his gaze to her. "Wonderful. It reminds me of a HouseHeart."

"I've never been in a HouseHeart," she said wistfully.

He opened his mouth to comment, realized it would be negative, and stopped. Sinking onto a huge light blue velvet pillow, the seams beaded with skycrystal, he said, "The Turquoise House and I have started constructing a HouseHeart for it."

"Can you build a HouseHeart? Don't they just evolve?"

Tinne shrugged. "I don't know. The FirstFamily Residences all have keystones, HouseStones, that were infused with Flair. The Turquoise House has stones but no secure place."

"Midnight is coming, you'd best be starting the ritual," the Residence said with a window rattle. "Stinking up my walls and my tapestries and pillows with incense."

"They will be all the more cherished and spellbound that way," Lahsin said softly.

"Don't know when someone will do another ritual. Might mold in the meantime from what you're doing tonight."

"We won't let you be completely abandoned again," Tinne said. "That's a blessing you should consider on this holiday. Tonight should be a night of light, not grumblings."

A frigid wind swept the room, the door banged open and

shut, and Tinne knew the Residence had subsided into another sulk.

"I think you offended it." Lahsin tilted her head and smiled, and Tinne felt the warmth of it. Feelings stirred inside him. He liked being with her. Too much. Her smile faded, and she looked away. Her long, pretty fingers played with the fringe. "Tinne, why are you here?"

"No one should be alone on Yule, do a ritual alone."

She looked baffled. "Some people like being alone."

He couldn't tell if she was one of those. Introverts. Maybe she wanted him to go, but he was determined to stay. He lounged back on his pillow, stretched out his legs. Behind him, even through the tapestry, the stone wall was cold. "Perhaps I came to celebrate Yule with a friend."

Uncertainty appeared in her eyes, "We're friends?"

"I hope so." Point made, he came away from the cold wall.

She flushed. "Let's meditate on how that even in the longest night, the dark of winter, there is always the spark of light and hope." She glanced at him from the corner of her eye then closed her lashes and shifted on her pillow.

Tinne swallowed at the sight of her, beautiful and young and touched by sorrow, but still with the burning brightness of hope.

Hope he wasn't sure he had. But he closed his eyes and settled into his inner balance.

A few minutes later she rose without speaking. Without thought, he stood, too. She went to the altar, lit a white taper, then crossed to the cauldron in the east, and he joined her. She held out the candle and said, "Call the Eastern Guardians of the Circle." So, he did. When she gestured he lit the incense, then handed her the candle to light the cauldron.

They cast the circle together, and it seemed like the most natural thing in the world. With the Turquoise House, his intent and focus had been on the young House itself, grateful that he'd had such a place to stay and wanting to give back to the House.

With his Family, he'd been one of many, a beloved son, but still held a supporting role.

Here, now, with Lahsin, he finally felt the ritual was for himself—and her. Concern flickered through him when he realized they were creating memories, bonds, between them, and that probably wasn't wise, but it was too late. He set the disturbing notion aside and focused on the ceremony, took his place on his pillow, and let her draw and weave the energies.

Her ceremony was beautiful. She was slow and careful in her simple phrasing, her gestures graceful. Tinne subsided into a semi-trance, like he did during the best rituals. Half hearing her prompts, he responded correctly, gave and accepted blessings.

"Our Yule meditation," she said. "In this time of dark, we reflect upon old habits that have not served us well and release them. They are dead and gone and will fade away, letting new ways come. This dark is fertile, holding the seeds of our new hopes and dreams and lives, nourishing them like rich soil. Let us focus on the new aspects of ourselves to be revealed."

Her voice was so fervent, her determination so strong, Tinne thought he felt a spark of hope flash to him through their bond and burn inside. It felt good.

"As the dark needs the light, the light needs the dark. We have experienced dark times this year, times of"—her voice wobbled a little, Tinne's breath shortened—"pain and fear and despair. But we let the roots of those negative emotions shrivel and die in this longest night, to be replaced by joy and the wonders coming into our lives with the lengthening days and brightening light."

Hurt came. He didn't fight it. The more he fought, the less he'd heal. So he let it come, recognized the pain of divorce. But it was *past*. He'd put it behind him and embrace the future.

"We accept the blessings we receive every day and thank the Lady and Lord. We are grateful for the seeds lying dormant in winter, the buds and blossoms of spring, the bounty and food of summer and harvest."

Time to eat food and drink of the summer. Tinne's vision turned from inward to outward. Lahsin poured from the carafe into small ritual mugs. Her eyes widened at the thick, orange liquid. "Orange juice." Only those with conservatories or willing to pay a good amount of gilt could have fresh orange juice in the middle of winter. She scooped berries into the mugs, offered one to Tinne, and lifted her own. "Blessings of the Lady and Lord as we move into the light."

He took the mug. "Blessings of the Lady and Lord as we move into the light." They drank, and she smiled. "So sweet!"

She looked into her cup, beamed at him. "Like sipping sunshine!"

So he drank with her, and the atmosphere of the room became more joyful.

Soon they ended the ritual and took the food and drink from the altar and put the victuals between them as they leaned back on the pillows.

A scritching came at the door. *All saying words is done?* asked Strother. *Flair came and went. Feel better. You done?*

Lahsin stood. "Yes, we are, time for a sharing of gifts."

I do not need any gifts, he said with anticipation.

Twenty-nine

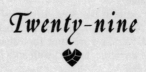

$\mathcal{L}$ahsin opened the door, and Strother trotted in. For reasons known only to them, a big, red ribbon was tied in a bow around his neck. He looked ridiculous, but Tinne kept his mouth shut. He also realized that he didn't have a gift for the dog. He *reached* to the Turquoise House for a bag of cat treats he had hidden from Ilexa. Since she was still loafing at T'Holly Residence, engorged on Yule feast, she'd never know that he'd given her treats to Strother. He'd replace them before she found out. With effort, he 'ported them to a spot behind the pillows.

The dog sneezed, blinked watery eyes. *Too much smoke smell in here.*

With a wave and a little regret, Tinne banished the fragrant spirals of incense, another bit of the ritual atmosphere that had blanketed him and Lahsin together, gone.

"I have gifts," Lahsin said, looking at him and Strother.

The dog sat, his tongue lolled out.

"I do, too," Tinne said. "Gifts between Fam and person, then mine to Strother, then Lahsin."

Strother wagged his tail and gave an approving look to Tinne. *My first gift.* He sat straight and watched as Lahsin brought out something wrapped in softleaves. She put it in front of Strother, and he pawed at it until a string of beads fell out.

A Fam collar! Strother sounded thrilled.

Tinne studied it. The necklace was composed of bright dried berries and larger rose hips of orange and red, accented with dark seeds and a nut or two, all strung on thread.

Lahsin untied the bow and fastened the collar around the dog's neck. "It looks good against your gray fur."

Sure wasn't emeralds.

But Lahsin had made it with her own hands, and that was more important than emeralds, though Ilexa might not think so.

"I've spellshielded the string. It will only break if you get caught and can't get free."

The dog's brows lowered.

"I'll make you a new one if that happens," Lahsin said.

Strother grinned. He trotted to the door and brought a large mass of gray brown something gently held between his jaws. He dropped it at Lahsin's feet and sat with a doggie grin.

"Mushrooms! Prized truffles! Ooh."

Wagging his tail, Strother said, *I have heard that people consider these tasty.*

"We do," Lahsin assured him. "I haven't seen these in the estate, where did you find them?"

Strother's chest puffed out with pride. *Saw little ones near my den in the glasshouse. Sent them Flair, and they grew. For you.*

"Thank you!" Lahsin hugged him.

The dog rumbled satisfaction, then turned his head to Tinne. Tinne brought out the packet of treats. Strother's nose twitched. *Good morsels.*

"Treats."

Lahsin raised her eyebrows at the wording on the envelope: *Special bits for your FamCat from D'Ash.*

Tinne shoved the packet to Strother, who gave it a strong sniff. "Good." He decorated the wrapping with drool.

Lahsin opened the package. "You want just one or all of them?"

Strother appeared torn. *Some now. Most for later.*

"Excellent," Lahsin said, and fed him about a third.

Strother crunched and slurped. *Human gifts*, he said.

After washing her hands in a bowl of water on the altar, Lahsin reached under the cloth and brought out a small potted plant. "I didn't know if you'd really come," she said to Tinne. "But I made you a gift anyway." She handed him the pot.

It was a delicate evergreen tree he'd never seen before. He touched one soft, flexible branch. "Nice. What is it?"

"A Norfolk pine. They only grow here and in the great greensward of *Nuada's Sword*, the Residence told me. When I found it, I did some research. Norfolk was a place on old Earth."

He met her eyes. "I'll cherish it."

She handed him a note. "The tending instructions."

Tinne slipped the page into his bag and turned the pot around to admire the small tree from all sides, until Strother nudged him. Tinne turned to his bag and lifted out his presents.

He had brought her two gifts. One was pale green training robes trimmed in dark green.

Her eyes lit up. "Real robes!"

"Yes. The trim shows you're a second-level beginner."

She clutched the robes to her breasts. "Really? Am I?"

He smiled. "You have a few holes in your training and need to learn the first basic pattern, but you could probably win any match with my beginning students."

She did a little hopping dance at that and put the tunic on. Only then did Tinne realize she was wearing old clothes, though the aura of the Goddess had cloaked her during the ritual.

Strother was nosing Tinne's bag. *Something else, here, something that smells of stridebeast.*

"I have another gift, one made with my creative Flair."

Lahsin looked up with curiosity in her eyes.

Tinne pulled out a small drum he'd made . . . *not* his HeartGift. She grinned and eagerly took it from him, settled back on her pillow, and began to thump with enthusiasm but little technique. He laughed, pulled out his own drum, equally small, and poured his feelings through his hands in cheerful, rapid beats.

"Now we can follow the ancient ways and drum the night away and to the dawn!" Lahsin raised her voice over the sound.

Strother's muzzle gaped. *You will pound on those all night?*

"Yes!" Lahsin threw back her head and laughed.

Her laugh reached inside Tinne, stirred him near painfully, touching places that had been wounded by another woman.

Strother went to his portion of the food and ate and drank politely, then burped and turned to Lahsin. He cast a yearning eye toward the cat treats, but then lifted his muzzle in pride. *You will put my treats in the no-time?* he asked.

"Yes, the Fam no-time in the kitchen that the BalmHeal Residence has so graciously opened to us now."

Tinne figured it hadn't been gracious at all. She glanced at him. "May I keep the orange juice?"

"By all means. The juice was for the ritual, the decanter is my gift to the Residence."

I will be able to get my crunchies when I want. Good. Then I will go out and show my new collar to other Fams.

Perhaps he was not so very different than Ilexa after all.

Lahsin's hands fumbled the beat. Tinne stopped. She looked at the dog. "What other Fams? Do they know about me, us, here?"

Tinne didn't like hearing her anxiety. The mood of the night was deteriorating.

We are secrets. All Fams have secrets. Strother slid a look at Tinne. *That cat has secret places, where she stayed when she wasn't loyal to you.*

Hurt pinched him. He stood and moved to the altar, filled the Lord's goblet with cider. The scent of it rose, hard cider, well spiced. Cinnamon tantalized his nostrils. "I'm sure my Fam has secrets," he replied. "I don't press her for them." The smooth bite of the cider went down nicely and warmed his belly.

Strother looked at Lahsin. *I go to meet foxes. Foxes are clever and never tell secrets.*

Tinne eased. "The FamFox are led by Vertic. I know him."

The dog nodded. *They are good to run with, faster than me. I couldn't keep up. But now they wait for me, because I am big and hunt well.*

"Ah." Tinne bowed, and the cider fumes went to his head. Potent. "Good hunting, Strother."

The dog yipped cheerfully.

Lahsin stroked Strother's head, and Tinne envied the touch.

"Go enjoy the night and be careful," Lahsin said.

Strother yipped again and waited for Lahsin to open the door. When she did, he ran, claws clicking on the hall floor.

Glancing at Lahsin, Tinne saw sadness come back into her

expression. He wanted the special feeling of the ritual, the giving of gifts, to linger. Splashing some cider into the Lady's chalice, he handed it to her, gave her his most charming smile.

She smiled back, drank deeply, and licked her lips.

His insides tightened. He stooped, picked up her drum, and handed it to her. "Shall we?"

"I'm a complete novice," she said, but it didn't seem to bother her. That was progress.

"Doesn't matter. Only the giving of a joyful sound to the sun and the universe matters on this longest night," he said.

Before she took the drum, she poured more cider into her chalice, then went back to sit on her pillow and grab her drum. Tinne followed.

They didn't drum the dark away and to the dawn. They drummed for two septhours, taking frequent breaks and drinking the cider. Then Lahsin started flagging. Holding her gaze, Tinne finished his spell pattern to draw luck through the winter and let his hands fall from his drum to his knees. His palms tingled. Lahsin finished her uneven beat seconds later.

He hadn't expected Lahsin to go as long as she had. She fell back against the pillows, flushed and giggling.

Beautiful.

Desirable.

His head was muzzy, too. He knew that pushing strands of her fine silk hair away from her face was dangerous, but the dim warning of his brain was overcome by the need of his body. The need of his emotions to see her happy, to treasure this moment. To share more pleasure with her.

As he'd played, his blood had heated, had pulsed to the rhythm set by his hands, until all was vibration.

She smelled so good.

He drew closer and closer, watching her eyes widen, but there was no fear in them, and now he couldn't draw back until he kissed her, tested the softness of her lips with his own. He put his mouth on hers, and a shock of desire whipped through him. Too strong. She must have felt it, too.

Her lips against his in a simple kiss was wondrous. Her mouth was so soft, her scent so sweet, Lahsin and incense, and Yule and Lahsin.

Then she opened her mouth, and her tongue touched his, and feeling exploded through him. He clamped his arms around her, brought her to him, felt the softness of her breasts against his chest, the insistent throbbing of his shaft as her stomach slid against him. He groaned.

He plunged his tongue into her mouth. She tasted of oranges and apples and cloves and cinnamon, and he was lost. All thought vanished so only need remained, the need of a man for his true woman. *HeartMate*—the word echoed in the back reaches of his mind, and he ignored it. He only wanted to be with Lahsin. Be in Lahsin. Only hoped she wanted him, too.

With a murmured word, their clothes vanished. She trembled, and he held himself still, throbbing, wondering if she would stop him or push him away. She didn't.

Light flickered from the fire in the cauldrons.

"Let me show you," he murmured. "Let me show you how it should be. How much pleasure a man and woman can share together." He *sent* the feeling behind the words, the caring, the yearning, the joy of Lady and Lord moving within each other.

He touched her breasts. They fit in his hands, her nipples beading in the center of his palms, drawing another groan from him. Marvelous. Such soft skin. How he had missed this dance of passion—but it had never been like this.

Because their bond was wide open and full of rushing emotions. Her wonder at pleasure she'd never felt, spiking desire. Yearning for something she sensed but hadn't tasted.

He should slow down, should savor this, but couldn't. He was panting, ready, and thought his whole body would explode. He slid his hand down her smooth skin over her subtle curves and touched the core of her. Damp. She gasped and arched to him, his fingers slid into her, and he felt the connection rip through them.

He had to be in her, now, now, now.

Slow down. The one thought rose to his mind. He didn't want to heed it, but even as he set his hands around her hips he knew she was young, not filled out yet, with delicate bones.

Her nails nipped his back. "Yes!" she cried, and he surged into her.

The world vanished. There was only the rich dark of need, the sensual fragrance and warmth of Lahsin, her body wrapped around his. Her emotions flowing with his.

Delight.

Perfection.

Desire.

He lingered until she rocked her hips, and his followed. They moved together.

They shattered together.

She went limp beneath him, and he rolled to their sides, she opened sleepy, blurred eyes to him. *Now I know*, she sent.

A little frown crossed her face, then there was a slight whoosh, and a bedsponge was under them, linens settling around them. Tinne's throat closed. It took powerful Flair to teleport them to her bed like that. "Lahsin?" His low voice trembled.

But she'd dropped into sleep, holding him tight. His own arms were wrapped around her, and he didn't think he could leave without waking her. He wanted to hold her. He *didn't* want to think about what he'd—they'd—done. He felt too good. For the first time in a long time . . . he felt complete. He'd just close his eyes for a little while until she loosened her grip . . .

They awoke in the dark and loved again and again.

Just before dawn, Tinne drifted to the surface of consciousness, savoring the delightful, languorous aftermath of excellent sex. He'd heard that HeartMates could share dreaming sex, but had thought it would be less than satisfying.

He stretched, his foot and hand brushed another. His eyelashes swept open, and he struggled to recall where he was. Not his suite in T'Holly Residence. Not the Turquoise House? Jacknifing up, he saw the rumpled silk of Lahsin's hair in the dim light of predawn.

Fligger!

What should he do? Stay or go?

He wanted to escape.

What would be the best for her?

His breathing was too loud. His *heart* was too loud, rushing in his ears.

How could he have . . .

But it had been so natural, as natural as his hand now instinctively reaching out to brush Lahsin's hair away from her face so he could see her.

His trembling hand. He snatched it back to rub his temples. Tried to recall her words in the jumble of erotic memories. Endeavored to separate her feelings mixing in their bond during the lovemaking from his own. They were too tangled, he couldn't.

He glanced at her. She was still here, hadn't run away, 'ported to anywhere else, or locked him out.

Narrowing his eyes, he checked her Flair. No spellshields surrounded her. That was good, he supposed. He didn't see any bruises on her from him, thank the Lady and Lord.

He'd been urgent, but he hadn't been rough.

Not any of the three times they'd made love. Cave of the Dark Goddess. Sometime during the night he should have come to his senses. But he hadn't.

He tested the bond between them, narrow on both sides. But stronger than ever. He couldn't remember the loving in detail but knew neither of them had offered the HeartBond to the other.

Maybe this would be all right.

Since the sun hadn't risen, Yule was still being celebrated. The Green Knight wouldn't open until late that evening for general sparring. No work forced him to leave.

Every woman he'd ever known would have wanted him to stay until she woke. It had taken him only one furious argument as a youngster to learn that lesson.

But Lahsin wasn't any other woman. Would she be afraid that he was there? Embarrassed? Would her feelings be hurt? He couldn't bear to hurt her feelings.

Couldn't bear to see her hurt in any way. The room was cool. He pulled the covers over her bare golden shoulder and slid down beneath them to cradle her against him.

Thirty

❤

She woke to hard arms around her.

It wasn't scary, and that almost alarmed her. The thought of liking T'Yew's touch was hideous.

Fog cleared from her brain before she raised her lashes. This wasn't T'Yew, old and harsh and triumphant.

This was Tinne, young and vibrant and virile. She could tell he was virile, because he was aroused. He wasn't harsh because he did nothing to seduce her or claim her. So she opened her eyes and saw the concern in his.

She smiled, and he sighed, smiled himself, and she noticed his lips as never before. Good lips, not too thin and not too full. Slowly bending toward her, he put his mouth on her temple and kissed her gently, tenderly. All his movements were deliberate, as if he didn't want to scare her. She heard him inhale and thought he was smelling her, or their, fragrance. Sniffing herself, she scented healthy sweat and the herbs from the sheets and the pretty floral smell of the candles.

A chuckle caught in her throat, but he must have heard it because he pulled back and his white blond brows lifted. His smile widened. "Blessings upon us, the sun's returned."

The standard greeting for the morning after Yule, the winter solstice, when the longest night had passed and daylight would grow longer until the summer and the month of Holly itself. She liked that notion, liked all the little whimseys passing through her mind. Liked his arm around her even more.

Putting her hand against his chest, she pushed gently, and he let her go, his brows went down. His chest expanded as he drew in air. "Last night was very special, Lahsin." His gray gaze deepened from the edge of silver to dark clouds.

Under his scrutiny she swallowed, stopped herself from pulling up the linens that were around her waist. Her breasts were bared to his view. She ignored her feelings of inadequacy and met his eyes. "Last night was wonderful." She had a hasty flashback of them rolling over the bed, both moaning, and blushed. "I didn't know that sex could be like that." She looked aside. "I thought I'd never like sex. Thank you."

His brows went up and down. "Neither of us were thinking." She giggled.

"And I'd like not to think again," he said. He touched her shoulder, traced her collarbone and down between her breasts. Keeping his eyes on her, his hand delved beneath the covers, traced her stomach, which clenched in anticipation.

If she thought . . . she shouldn't think. She should let her body rule. He stroked her between her legs . . . just . . . right. Her body dampened.

She reached for him, set her hand behind his neck, and brought his lips to hers. She thrust her tongue inside his mouth as his finger entered her and all thought wisped away.

His sex was hard, she felt it against her, thick and strong, and the thought of him inside her sent tingles from her breasts to her core. Her hips arched against the probing of his fingers, the maddening circle of his thumb on her most sensitive flesh.

Physical delight. Her body and mind recalled how wonderful sexual climax was, and she was eager to find it again.

She kicked off the linens and drew him down so she could feel his smooth, supple skin against hers. Let a yearning sound escape. Again she arched, twisting to caress his sex to show him that she wanted him. In her. Now!

He chuckled, then gasped. His hands slid over her hips, held her still, and he plunged inside her.

Pure bliss. She wrapped her legs around him, rocked with him, panting now, enjoying each slide of him in and out of her. Her hands clamped around his back, and the feel of his muscles bunching against her sensitized palms added another layer to the sheer pleasure inundating her.

He slowed, and she whimpered in frustration.

"Look . . . at . . . me," he said.

Her eyelids flew open, she hadn't known she'd closed them, only felt the tension gripping her body, winding tight.

She could only see the sharp contours of his face, his eyes, that were huge pupils with a rim of the darkest storm clouds.

He stopped and though she writhed under him, she couldn't make him move the way she wanted him to, needed him to. "Tinne," his name came strangled from her throat.

His grin was fierce, showing white teeth. "My name."

"Tinne."

"Yes, again."

"Tinne!"

He withdrew to her very entrance, and his eyes went distant. He held himself, and her, on the brink of completion, their breaths coming to the same beat, their pulses matching. Pleasure built and built and built.

He thrust inside her, and before he was completely hilted, she screamed in release and exploded with delight so great she thought she'd die.

A while later she became aware that their breaths came ragged, and his weight on her was a muscled heaviness that should have scared her, but didn't.

The only comparison to T'Yew that she made was that there was no comparison. Tinne was her only lover.

His eyes were closed now, but he rolled, and she was atop him. The movement nudged his sex deeper within her, and another orgasm rippled through her. She moaned and saw his lips curve in smug satisfaction that made her smile, too. She didn't begrudge him any triumph. He'd done what she thought no man could ever do and taught her body to enjoy sex.

She collapsed against him, her nose in his chest hair, and inhaled his scent.

They lay there, together, and it was wonderful.

"Blessings upon us, the sun's returned," the Residence said, voice bouncing around the room.

Lahsin jerked, rolled off Tinne, grabbed the covers, and pulled them up to her neck, as if the Residence could see her.

"It is past time for the Yule candle to be snuffed," Balm-Heal Residence said disapprovingly. "If you do not rise within a few minutes, the candle will not last until next year."

Tinne's eyes met hers. Neither of them would be here next year.

She struggled with huge emotions—having a new lover, the shadow of the past and of future Passage, leaving here. She shook her head, not able to sort through them.

Tinne's calendarsphere pinged into existence. "Breakfast with the Family in quarter septhour!" He winced.

Lahsin studied him. "Does that expression mean you dread leaving or dread staying?"

He caught her fingers, brought them to his mouth for a kiss. "I could never dread staying."

That sounded like something he'd said all too often to other women. The Holly charm was certainly strong and effective today. She drew her hand from his grip. "Don't tell me lies, Tinne. You never have in the past, please don't now." To her horror, her throat had clogged with tears. Too emotional!

"Do you want me to stay or go?"

She was all mixed up. Didn't want to think at all. "Will there be problems if you don't show up for breakfast?"

Another frown. "Yes."

Her breath left her in a sigh that even she couldn't figure out. "Then, go." It was easy to smile, to touch his handsome face, brush away a strand of silver white hair from his eyes.

He got out of bed and looked around the room until he saw the door to the waterfall room. "I'll be right out." He ran a hand through his hair and cast her a glance. "You think on what you want to do." Then he smiled at her with tenderness. "Whatever you want, Lahsin, I'm agreeable." He picked up his colorful clothes.

She stared at his fabulous body until he shut the door. Then she shifted, and her own body sent her signals from the sensual night, the slide of the sheets against her bare skin, the remembrance of shattering pleasure. She was still in a muddle when Tinne walked out. His hair was slightly damp, his clothes had changed colors from red and green to a shiny gold silkeen with silver trim. The color of the sun.

He chuckled. "You haven't moved."

She shook her head.

"Let's try a few questions." His face sobered. "Answer with the first thing that comes to mind."

She nodded.

"Do you want to continue your training?"

"Yes!" No question.

"Do you want to learn fighting?"

"Yes." This was a lot easier than thinking.

"Do you want me to come tonight for training?"

"Yes."

"Do you want me to stay tonight for loving?"

She didn't know. Her grip around the linens tightened.

"I'll continue to train you, Lahsin, never think I won't."

She licked her lips, his gaze fell to them, and a slight flush came to his cheeks. She knew that look, now. It brought a response from her body, a tightening inside, an anticipatory pleasure. She answered without thought, "Yes, stay for sex."

A flicker of wariness showed in his eyes, then he nodded. "I'll do that."

She smiled. "I'd like to drum tonight, too."

His stance eased. She had begun to notice things like that. "Training, then soaking, then drumming." His grin flashed and took her breath, when had he ever looked so carefree? "Sex anytime after the training." He strode to the bed, took her hands, and kissed them. "Later, Lahsin, sweet." Then he 'ported away.

Her mind was still considering soaking and sex.

Lahsin smiled for a whole week. Each day she did more for the Residence and the estate, paying special attention to the landscape surrounding the Healing pool. The snow had melted, and no more had fallen.

She'd passed her beginning fighting test and was solidly in the second level, deserving of her robes. She was learning drumming, too, through watching and listening to Tinne. He'd refused to formally teach her, saying everyone must develop their own talent. Hers was commonplace beside his, but it gave her an outlet for her emotions. For her anger. That was rising from the depths of her more often now that she felt secure.

She was afraid of her anger, of how it might affect her in her looming last Passage, which hovered near like lightning ready to strike. So she released it in her training and drumming.

She and Strother had developed habits—eating together, telling each other about their days. He'd been scouting Druida, and she'd asked him to keep an eye out for solitary places she might be able to teleport to and from. He'd been to the Turquoise House. When reporting that trip and his conversation with the House, his tongue had lolled in amusement.

She wasn't quite ready to leave FirstGrove, even to examine teleportation places. Not until after her last Passage when she'd be strong enough in Flair and truly an adult. But she read more of the newssheets every day, flipping quickly past the entire page that posted a reward for her.

Tinne was wonderful. He spent most nights with her, but somehow he knew when she would prefer privacy after their soaking and left. Once he had to sleep in T'Holly HouseHeart.

She gave thanks to the Lady and Lord who'd given her this sex partner. With him she began to experience and enjoy her own sexuality, though she hadn't quite gotten up the nerve to explore his body as much as she wanted. And though he was open in bed, she hadn't seen him as lighthearted as that first morning. He seemed to have withdrawn slightly from her as their relationship changed. Sometimes she caught him studying her and didn't know what it meant. Did he think she might hurt him? Such a casual affair wouldn't do that, and she was sure they could maintain their friendship after . . .

After one of them Healed enough to be denied FirstGrove.

*T*inne felt like he was tottering on the edge of a crumbling cliff. He enjoyed being with Lahsin but knew it was unwise, the tenderness and caring he felt for her was too strong, too close to real love. He didn't want a love that would rip him apart.

He didn't think that Lahsin knew her own emotions. She was physically open during sex, but kept their emotional link narrow. Furthermore, she didn't seem to realize that she was having bad dreams. More than once, he'd found her thrashing beside him, whimpering, tears on her face. When he touched her to soothe, she pulled him into insistent lovemaking.

The estimated time of her next Passage had come and

gone. Tinne worried that meant her next fugue would be bad.
That she was somehow not allowing it to come, that some
secret inner shields kept it away. He wondered what might
ignite it.

The bond between them increased in power and intimacy.
When they made love, the HeartBond unfurled between
them. He was her HeartMate, but he guarded his heart and so
did she.

That night Tinne showed Lahsin a new fighting pattern,
worked with her on defenses to side grabs, soaked, and had
fabulous sex. He was still awake when she began to tremble
and gasp. Ordering on a glowlight, he turned toward her,
stroked her. Pretty Lahsin. Then he touched a blush rose nip-
ple and watched it harden and smiled.

Her eyes opened.

He raised his hand from her body immediately, and when
he saw her eyes widen in incipient fear, he put his hand behind his back.

"Don't," she whispered.

"Don't what."

She wet her lips but met his eyes, her own big and green.
"Don't stop. It feels so good."

"Lahsin—"

Her gaze met his and clouded. "I have a HeartMate."

Everything in him stilled. "You had a bad dream, of him?"

"No." She pushed tumbled hair back from her face.
"But . . . a HeartMate . . ." Her eyes were vulnerable, as if she
was asking him to tell her what to do. He couldn't. He wasn't
ready for this discussion, felt like he was on the brink, ready
to fall.

He bit back, "So do I." Instead he ground out, "Do you
want him?"

"No!"

He grabbed the bed linens, anchored himself. "Do you
want me?"

"Yes!"

His gut unknotted with relief.

"But shouldn't I want him instead of you?"

He lifted his brows. "Do you know him?"

She frowned. "No. Not much, and he's been as grumpy as
BalmHeal Residence. I'm afraid he's older."

He laugh-coughed at that, slid his hand into her hair, relishing the silkeen slide of it, gave it a little tug. "That's usually how HeartMates work. The one who is older experiences Passage first and knows first. You're young. He's bound to be older. I'm older than you."

Her eyes screwed shut. "It would be horrible if he is as old as T'Yew. Horrible."

Tinne wanted off this subject as quickly as possible. He would let passion distract them both. He brushed her lips with his. He didn't want to talk about this, was treading as carefully as he had when he'd been in quicksand. That led to a falling sensation, and he closed his eyes, concentrating on Lahsin's lips, on her taste. Berries. She always tasted of ripe raspberries to him. He swept his tongue over her lips, and they parted. Taking the invitation, he forayed inside, and the depths of her mouth revealed more taste. Lingering orange juice—liquid sunshine—woman becoming aroused—his own body stirred, fast and hard—berries, berries, berries.

She pushed at him, and he obligingly rolled away, onto his back, then she was the one leaning over him. Her hair brushed his chest, and he trembled.

Her expression was still troubled. "Should we be doing this?"

He allowed himself a snort. "You don't want to?" Her little nipples were already tight, there was a slight sheen to her body, and he scented her arousal.

"Yes. I do. I didn't think I'd ever want sex, but you've been so wonderful."

His stomach twisted again. At least she hadn't said what they had together was "just" sex.

She pressed her lips to his, feather light, and he groaned. He hadn't seen her coming. He'd closed his eyes without even knowing. When she withdrew he opened his eyes. She met his stare, her pupils wide, her lips red, then looked away. "It's more than just sex," she whispered.

He reached up and curved his palm around her face, turned her head back so he could see those eyes he could drown in—fall endlessly in. "It's not just sex. It's caring."

She smiled, slowly, beautifully, set her hand on his shoulder, and tugged. But he had other ideas. He framed her waist with his hands, lifted and set her on his lower abdomen, a little above where he really wanted her. He felt her butt wriggle against him, and he let out a groan.

She giggled.

So he flung his arms out. "I am at your command."

Her eyes widened even more. She pursed her lips. *"Really?"*

That one word told him how she had grown. It wasn't a light, girlish question, but a low statement, rich in implication. He swallowed. "Yes."

"I get to explore you?" Her eyes gleamed.

"Yes."

She rubbed his chest with her hands, scraped her nails over his nipples. He arched as the sensation went straight to his cock, thickening it. All his blood swept to his groin. But he didn't need to think. Not with Lahsin.

HeartMate.

He didn't need to listen to the whisperings of his mind, either. The wariness of his heart. All he had to do was feel, let his body enjoy.

So he did. Her hair teased him. Her lips teased him. Her hands stroked and caressed until he was begging between ragged breaths.

Then she licked him. All over. His control broke, and he set her where he wanted her, and she moved onto him, took him into her, and there was nothing but need and sex and climbing to the top of the mountain and falling exquisitely until he exploded into a thousand stars. He hoped when he landed it wouldn't be fatal.

Thirty-one

❦

The next day Lahsin did her regular chores in the morning, spent some time in the early afternoon in the stillroom, then decided to finally visit FirstGrove itself. It was near the southwest bit of the estate, close to the south door. As she approached she *felt* the atmosphere change. The air wavered before her eyes.

She'd passed through another spellshield, one she'd never sensed, couldn't sense now as she turned back to try. Then she understood it wasn't *quite* a shield. It was a spell that enveloped the grove, made from ancient traditions, emotions, rituals. A spell that came from the ground and the trees themselves.

It was warmer here, the light brighter. She thought she saw a wayward sparkle of Flair. She breathed deeply, and the air was different, as if she drew in the essence of the trees. With another full inhalation she tried to identify the fragrance that tickled her nose, separate the scents of the various trees. She couldn't.

FirstGrove.

Tall, beautiful trees of Earthan and Celtan origin. Trees that shouldn't quite grow together. They formed a deep semi-circle with a grassy area in the middle, one that must be dotted with wildflowers in every other season. In the center was an altar that radiated age and Flair.

As if in a dream she walked up to it, touched the rough top.

Passage swamped her, spiking her temperature, sending her nauseated to her knees. Bad. This was bad. This was the *worst*.

This was the *last*. She knew it. If she survived this, she would survive Second Passage.

Immediately she erected spellshields, felt herself surrounded by an impenetrable bubble. She strove to ground herself in the real world, tried to see the trees of FirstGrove. Failed.

She didn't know the place well enough. Had there been a stand of birch ahead, or was it some other white-barked trees?

Again and again she tried to grasp reality, but it was futile.

So she took a moment to regulate her breathing inside the altered reality and looked out on a rough dark green sea that spiraled to a whirlpool.

With effort, she levitated her capsule, sent it slowly floating over the funnel. The vortex got darker and darker as it narrowed deep into the ocean, but at the bottom was a ravishing, glowing pearl.

Dread slithered through her. The pearl was her Flair, and the only way to get it was to let the awful water suck her down.

Explore the depths of her own emotions so she could grasp the prize.

If she didn't drown.

She hovered for a while, gathering her courage, preparing herself.

She wanted that Flair. It was part of her she needed to claim.

She wanted to live.

She *could* do this.

She *would* do this.

She stationed herself above the center of the funnel. With luck she'd plummet straight down, would survive the fall and the last few whirlings around to the pearl.

Keeping her eyes open, she disintegrated the spellshield around her. A whistling wind made up of the voices of all the people she'd ever known slapped her hard. She hadn't realized there was a wind, as she tumbled through the air. She fought it, wrenched her arms, which were flattened to her body, out and up and put her hands over her ears. Still she heard the cacophony. The gale pushed her back, back, and dropped her to the edge of the whirlpool.

Fear ate at her, tears blew from her eyes to be lost in the wind, though the water was a gentle, wide circle here.

She would have to experience everything, accept her emotions, her anger, shame, guilt.

Terror.

All right, terror first. She was afraid. Of Passage, of life. But fear was part of life. She felt it soak into her, lodge inside her. There would always be fear, and sometimes it would escape and beat frantic wings of panic at her mind.

She could live with fear. She could squeeze it into a little ball inside herself and let it come when useful. And if she was frightened, she could push through the fear and do what needed to be done. Fear made her heart pound, it coated the back of her throat, but she ignored the taste, breathed through it. Mastered it with determination to survive.

She *could* do this.

She *had* done that.

Terror would not swallow her.

The ocean, which had been tinged black with fear, changed.

Whitecaps turned bloodred. She spun faster and faster, well caught now.

No turning back.

People still yelled in her ears. No!

There was an instant's quiet. Then the voices rose again, the most important to her first. Tinne's! She gasped, sucked in water, plunged under the waves, struggled above them, thought of her lover. Heard his voice. Strong. "You are allowed to hurt those trying to hurt you."

And then he was there. Not Tinne, T'Yew.

Here. Standing motionless, a man of patterned darkness, this patch here the wrongness in him that liked to hurt others. This shiny design, pure selfishness. There was pride in the figure's stance, the lift of his head. He was larger than life, engorged with the essence of his character—the acceptance of entitlement, that he was better than any other who walked Celta.

Her pulse thudded hard in her head, racing now, louder than any of the voices. The only other sound was her own whimpering.

All else was blurring by them at a speed she couldn't comprehend, but he and she were here, in this moment.

He was real.

She'd thought all ties were broken to him, but he raised a hand, and she felt the tiniest of threads, no more than a few molecules thick. Connected to her.

His teeth gleamed, and they were huge and sharp and white.

Terror rose again.

But she had mastered it and pushed it away.

You undergo Second Passage, wife, and I am here with you.

Go away!

No. You cannot escape me.

He'd said that often enough, in just that gloating tone. She waited for his ugly laugh. He always laughed after that.

He laughed.

Fear bubbled through her blood.

She fisted her hands but did not run. The world was moving fast enough as it was, down and down and down. Would despair be next?

She couldn't think of that because her second's inattention had brought T'Yew closer. All his fingers grasping. Swallowing, she stood her ground and lifted her chin.

He reached for her—to slide his nails gently down her cheek in the nasty caress he liked? To slap her?

But he could not touch her.

She stared.

He frowned.

The terror diminished enough that she heard voices—a chorus—her own, the masculine tones she associated with her HeartMate. They all said the same thing. *The thread he holds is of your own making. You can sever it. He has no bond with you that you do not allow.*

T'Yew's face contorted with disdain, contempt. He, too, heard the voices, she realized.

They lie, he said, tugging on his thread, and she squealed at the sharp, vicious pain. *You did not repudiate me before three true witnesses.*

He laughed again.

Shouts, her voice not in the mix this time. *The link is from you to him. He has nothing to bind you with.*

She didn't understand. She hesitated, felt herself sinking again, whirling, sick. She could not escape.

Cut the tie. The sharp command came from her Heart-Mate.

She followed instinctively and snapped the link.

Before her amazed eyes T'Yew flew into the spinning world, shouting.

She gasped and got a mouthful of water. Salty water and knew they were her own tears. She was curled up, and the voices had faded to a background behind her sobbing.

Despair and failure this time. Not black like fear but soaking waves in shades of gray. She'd almost drowned in these before and didn't understand how to fight them.

Or accept them.

There would be grief in her life. She knew that. There would be lows, but maybe she could avoid any more despair. Grief was like fear, something no one could avoid.

Somehow she thought despair was less. If she had a kernel of hope inside her, despair might be avoided. If she kept that kernel of hope with the other seeds that would sometimes flower—fear and grief—she could rise above the waves.

She grieved for the young child and girl she had been, the person she might have been if T'Yew had not bought her. It was an ache, this grief, a hurt that had not Healed. But it could Heal, if she accepted the past. Hard, hard, hard to do.

Failure. Guilt. Failure at not being able to save herself before this, guilt at failing that young girl.

Demanding more of yourself than is possible. Perfection, Lahsin? Her HeartMate's voice again.

She hadn't realized that was the basis for so much hurt, the need to be perfect.

Put away your past, your feelings of failure and guilt. A crack of laughter from her HeartMate, not as unpleasant as T'Yew's, but humorless. *I guarantee you will feel failure and guilt in the future, so learn how to deal with them now. Accept that you are human, that you err and will err again. Then put it in the past.*

She didn't like his astringent tone. *Forget about it?*

A sigh that sounded almost familiar. *Don't forget your past. Learn from it. Don't repeat your mistakes.* A short pause. *Or try not to repeat your mistakes.*

Like you've done? She was aggravated.

But he was gone.

She shivered in water that had turned cold. With despair, with failure, with guilt. Again she saw her younger self, grieved for the innocence lost. She'd been a good girl, a little precocious, but good. Had had "be a good girl" drummed into her. Enough so that she went along and married T'Yew, and had striven to be good for him.

Put it away in the past. Accept what happened, move on. She snorted. Nothing to do *but* move on when caught in a whirlpool like this, cold and salty.

She warmed herself by building a little shield, aware of the downward plunge again, her stomach falling with the rest of her. She looked down. She was three-quarters of the way down, the pearl glowed huge and beautiful, a creamy pink.

Lahsin didn't delude herself. The last part would be the worst. The most negative emotions would hit her then. The tight, fast, hard emotions that gripped her more than anything else. Anger.

Or fear and anger mixed together.

And now the fear of her anger.

One rotation.

Two.

Dizziness.

Her HeartMate was gone. The voices were gone—or the good ones. Now she only heard hissing whispers that she thought belonged to T'Yew, Taxa, her parents. She shuddered.

She could reach for her HeartMate, she knew that inside her. But she was afraid of the cost.

Afraid of him.

Afraid of herself.

Another negative emotion. This wasn't true fear, real terror, but it was a stepping back—from life, from love.

From pain.

Fear of pain. There should be a one-word emotion for that, too. Maybe because there wasn't, it was easier to beat, to rise above. To accept and go on.

No one liked pain, physical or emotional. But like fear

and grief and failure, pain was part of life. No way to live life without it.

Get used to it, or used to dealing with it. Accept pain.

It lanced through her.

And think of joy. She tried, couldn't, and was caught in the pain. The pain of being taken forcibly by a big, selfish, arrogant man.

That was past. It was *over*.

She was down in the ocean again, couldn't breathe. Could drown.

Could, could, could.

What happened to "*could* do this"?

Think of joy.

That morning the dawn had been beautiful. As pink as the pearl she strove for now. A sparkle flickered in the water around her, a little bubble that lifted her spirits and lifted her . . . more joy. Think of Yule, the soft glow of the room, the comfort of Strother and the Residence and Tinne, the beauty of the holiday ritual. The taste of cider and liquid sunshine.

She rose and panted above the ocean and smiled when she saw the pearl.

Then the sea turned red again with threatened pain, and joy vanished like a popped bubble. She struck out and batted the fear of pain aside. It slapped back, hurting her, feeling like T'Yew's slap. She raised her arms in defense, and her side was pinched, hard. Taxa's pinch.

Lahsin spun and spun again, but couldn't evade the hurt, the pain, the knowledge that it could get worse. No!

Anger seized her, dragged her under. Scenes from the past played in her mind. Her parents were visiting her at T'Yew's. He was there, so was Taxa. Lahsin's mother was all simpering compliments and praise for the stately Residence and furnishings. She dodged Lahsin when Lahsin had followed her to try to talk. Her mother didn't listen, *wouldn't* listen to anything that might sound sad or bad or make her think.

Lahsin's father was genial and greedy, tucking a few gold coins T'Yew gave him into his trous pocket, not seeing Lahsin as anything but a commodity. Lady and Lord. He'd never loved her.

Instead of slinking away to the small white box of a bedroom, waiting in trembling fear for T'Yew to stalk in with a smirk on his face, Lahsin stood in the middle of the sitting room and looked at her parents and screamed. Watched their faces change. Then her younger brother was there, too. Everyone but Clute.

She stormed at her Family, waved flailing arms, and screamed and screamed and screamed. Like she'd screamed during training. The thought steadied her a little, and she surfaced from the anger, could gulp in a few breaths.

Then T'Yew was back, naked, sparse gray hair on his chest, red throbbing erect penis, a glitter of unholy pleasure in his eyes.

She fought him, but her blows passed through him, and his eyes gleamed brighter and brighter with the glee of chasing her.

Anger overcame her, and she screamed more, fought like Tinne had taught her, but nothing seemed to work. He still grabbed her, bore her down. She struggled. Fright finally cleared the red rage from her vision. Her hands went through him!

He could touch her, but she couldn't him! Why not? Gasping, she felt his hideous weight on her, her legs being forced apart. No! But it didn't stop him. Horror rose again, then fury.

Too much emotion to think.

She should be able to reason this out . . . felt his hairy leg slide between hers.

She *had* to think. Through the fear and the anger. Shut down the emotion.

He wasn't really here, that's why her blows did nothing.

But she felt his hard shaft against her thigh.

No.

She *remembered* his hard shaft against her thigh. That's why she couldn't fight him. Her memories and her emotions still controlled her.

What to do?

Remember something different.

Joy had banished grief and despair.

What would vanquish anger?

Peace. She went limp, not in wretched acceptance as had happened in real life.

This wasn't real life.

This was Passage.

She visualized serenity—the rose of dawn on the pure snow of FirstGrove. Even as his hands came up to hurt her breasts, she thought of the beloved Healing pools, the lap of the water against her skin, the scent of them, which would ever and always be remembered. The image of T'Yew vanished.

She hung for a moment in silence. Then realization thrilled her. She'd done it! She'd mastered her anger. Here, at least. This time, at least. She didn't doubt it would return, but for now, she'd done it!

She fell into pale pinkness.

Flair enveloped her.

This wasn't the whirlpool anymore.

She was *inside* the pink pearl of her Flair. It pulsed around her, but she didn't know what to do.

As she calmed, other positive memories crowded her. Tinne smiling in pride as she finished her beginners' test, applauding her. Strother's big yellow eyes, his tongue lolling. The brightness of the Yule candle fighting back the dark in the Residence's great hall.

More personal feelings came, of Flair. How she felt when she teleported. How she'd put her hands against the walls and learned the shields, accepted them, then added her own strength and energy and twisty pattern to them to secure FirstGrove.

Pop!

The bubble burst around her, drenched her with pink sparks flowing in every blood cell, pumping through her heart, skittering down every nerve, embedding in every tensile strand of muscle.

Flair!

It was hers.

The strange otherworld vanished. Lahsin found herself on all fours, panting, head down, body running with sweat. Her hands and knees were cold on the dampness of the snowmelt ground.

The freezing ground. Night had come, bright and brittle with cold, the sweep of stars so bright that they hurt her eyes. She could have frozen! Could still freeze.

She whimpered. The atmosphere of FirstGrove was oppressive to her too-sensitive nerves, too rich, too powerful, too old.

With a ragged couplet she was back in her bedroom of the Residence. She toppled and grabbed the bedpost.

Heat coated her again.

She staggered from the bedroom. In a daze, she half shuffled, half ran to the conservatory. Flair filled her until she swelled with it. Her skin itched. She had to get her hands in rich soil, fill a pot with soil and plants. Make her HeartGift. Understanding made her stumble. She was going to make her HeartGift!

Thirty-two

❦

 T *here were cool spots on her cheeks, tears trickling from* her eyes. She wanted her HeartMate, was forced by her Flair to create something especially for him. But her inner self rebelled, didn't want to want him. Didn't want to do this.

She stopped outside the door to the glasshouse, lost in a struggle. Another thought swam through the murk in her mind. What would happen if she *didn't* make a HeartGift? Would she lose him forever? She didn't like that notion, either. She didn't want him now, but the long years of the future were another matter. Forever was a long time.

A chuckle came to her mind. Him! She propped herself against the wall. Their link was too strong, too intimate.

I made you a HeartGift in the last hours of my Second Passage. Haven't given it to you yet, have I? Free your Flair and let it take you where you must go. Do not put limits on it now. Don't agonize over this. Then he was gone, as if he had shut the door on their link. Anger ignited, and she doused it. No more allowing anger to master her. Better that she let herself tap and master her Flair. Much better.

She blinked and blinked again, saw that she was in the hall, the door to the conservatory closed ahead of her. With slippery palms she opened it, breathed in the scent of verdant plants and left the door open as she stepped through into the brightness of the glasshouse.

Then she let her Flair guide her hands, her actions, barely noticing what she was doing . . . filling a large pot with soil. She'd barely be able to carry it when it was planted. That didn't stop her. Finding sprigs of the plants she wanted, setting them around the rim, like some sort of miniature garden. Something inside her fretted that this wasn't a plot of land. A plot and a special garden would be better. She ignored that. *This is what I have to work with.* She directed her Flair.

She formed a thin three-dimensional heart-shaped frame, put little plants around that. She blinked again, but couldn't quite focus. This time she knew it was because her mind and emotions were shielding her from knowledge. Fine with her.

Interesting, said Strother.

She didn't know when he'd joined her, but he lay near the potting table, head on his paws.

"You . . . aren't . . . sharing . . . this . . . Passage . . . with . . . me?" she gasped.

We are not that close yet. He cocked his head. *Perhaps your Third Passage.*

She shuddered, couldn't stand thinking of enduring this again.

When he said nothing more, she slipped back into the trance daze and finished her gift. She didn't pause to examine it but wearily grunted with each step as she moved it to a spot where she wouldn't have to look at it. A place where it would receive the proper amount of light and water from the watering spell.

She panted, the green of the flora seemed to reach and twine, blocking her vision, and her sex grew heavy, needy. She was sending sexual energy to these plants! They were growing because of it. Too strange. She reeled back, nearly ran backward all the way to the door, and plunged back into the hallway.

Strother followed, kicked the door shut with a hind leg . . . the leg that had been injured. He liked using it.

The plants felt some of your mating energy, he said matter-of-factly. *But most of the sex-feel is in the planter markings.*

She hadn't even realized she'd marked the planter. She

looked down at her hands where dark slashes of ink ran across her fingers, her palms. Vaguely she recalled chanting when she'd decorated the pot but didn't want to remember more.

She made it to the couch in the great hall and collapsed.

A while later she surfaced to see a shadow near her. Her stomach jumped.

"Who?" Before he answered she knew it was Tinne. For some reason she'd thought it was her HeartMate. Muddled.

"It's Tinne, with a gift," he said softly, and his shadow solidified into his familiar muscular form. She rubbed her eyes. "Wha are ya doin'?" Her voice was as blurry as her vision.

She rubbed her eyes, smelled the fragrance. He'd brought a huge bouquet of cut summer flowers.

"Congratulations on weathering your Second Passage."

Her lips stretched in a grin, and she felt them crack. She would need salve on them later. "Thank you," she croaked.

"They're pretty. But not as pretty as you." His head tilted. "Why don't I take you up to bed where you'll—we'll?—be more comfortable?"

Holding out her arms, she said, "*We'll*, yes, please. I'd like to sleep with you." He swung her up into his arms, and she cuddled against him. "You smell so good."

He snorted. "That's the flowers."

"No," she mumbled as she tucked a hand close to his heart and fell asleep again.

*T*inne spooned around *L*ahsin but didn't sleep.

Her Passage had hit him during his private lesson with Saille T'Willow. The matchmaker, of course, deduced what was happening before Tab ran to them both.

"I'll take care'a him." Tab hauled Tinne over one shoulder.

Tinne groaned as his stomach hit his G'Uncle's bone. Tinne thought he was drowning. "Private . . ."

"Yes." That was Saille's voice. "From my experience you'll have to help her. And there may be a link for the HeartGift."

"I'm puttin' you in my bedroom!" Tab shouted, and Tinne was dumped onto the bedsponge, and he knew he'd lost some moments and this wasn't the first time Tab had said that.

He weakly flapped a hand in agreement.

"Right," Tab said. "See ya later. I'll stay at T'Holly's." His eyes gleamed in the dark, expression intense. "*Help* her."

Tinne tried.

Now and again he thought she heard him. He'd reached out and steadied her while she whirled into the depths of her own being.

He waited, suffered, endured.

Triumph! He felt her joy, rubbed his face on Tab's pillow, which he'd pummeled and squashed. Then became hot. He shot from the bedsponge when he realized the bond between them had gone fiery with sexual energy. Got to the waterfall before he felt the stroke of her hands on his cock, and he arched in release.

He huddled in the tiled corner of the waterfall and thought about her Passage. He thought he'd kept his anonymity. She didn't know who he was. When would he dare to reveal himself?

Later he took her flowers cut from T'Holly conservatory. He'd told himself that she'd expect him, Tinne. Had heard his voice as well as the "HeartMate" one. And he needed to see her.

Now, lying against her, painfully aroused, he knew that their moments together like this were numbered. Her Flair was hot, dazzling. She'd soon feel the bond between them better and deduce who he was.

He closed his eyes, and the falling sensation came back. He tightened his arms, and she anchored him. He didn't fall, instead he swirled down and down and wondered what to feel, what to do.

But in sleep the falling nightmare came back—based on far too much reality. He was in the lifepod shot from the starship in Druida, circling Celta. His brother wasn't with him. Of course not, Holm had already fought and mastered his own demons.

It was a relief that Holm wasn't here. Holm couldn't die with him, and it gave him more room. The pod had been damnably cramped for a person who'd lived all his life in the spaciousness of Celta.

The top half of the pod had been clear to see blinding stars and the black darkness between them. Tinne swallowed mouth-watering fear again and again, tried to think.

Soon the pod would begin the long fall to the planet. Or would it? Before Holm and he had become accustomed to the lifeboat and space and the control board, the starship below had commanded the pod to land.

Who knew what would happen in a dream? Would he circle forever until he dried up as a husk? Worse, would he fall onto the other side of Celta, have to make his way home from there? Would the fragile lifeboat be speared by a mountain, be sucked into a boghole, drop into the ocean where he could drown?

He found himself shuddering like a scared child and stiffened his spine. This was his dream, he would control it.

But the dream . . . all the falling dreams . . . were all about the lack of control, especially of his own life.

Huge sweeping changes had happened *to* him that blindsided him. Events he had no control over that left him emotionally reeling through life, barely able to get his balance before the next tragedy.

Just like this uncontrolled lifeboat. He was tumbling now, end over end in a freefall through space, stars smearing into white flashing blurs, the pod plunging to the planet.

And he knew this test was as vital as any Passage.

Changes might continue to happen to him, but he had to take control, be flexible, accept them more quickly so he could plot his life. Being his own man would do that.

He may not be able to control change, but he could control his self-judgmental reactions to change. Like he could control the flight of this boat.

He wrestled the steerstick of the pod down, forcing it to go where he wished. With his mind, he stopped it from tumbling.

Breathing hard between the rictus of his gritted teeth, he *controlled* its flight. Set it down, gently, gently.

In FirstGrove, where he knew Lahsin awaited him.

*T*inne *jerked awake, his brain still echoing with the si-*lence of space. He welcomed the drumming of his heart and his aroused cock with sheer relief. Lahsin was there, so he woke her and loved her fiercely. Her Passage, his dream, and the crafting of the HeartGift had worked on both of them.

When she bounded up, eyes gleaming and ready to start her day, they stood under the waterfall together and made love there.

She had all the energy he lacked, and he smiled and shook his head at it. The decisions he'd made in his dream prodded him. So he kissed her and repeated his congratulations and pride, then teleported to the Turquoise House to clean up before work.

He greeted the House and listened to its chatter, stroked Ilexa for long minutes to soothe them both. Their Fam bond would never be as strong as before, but he loved her and told her so.

He had to call his brother. Holm would be up. Lark had Transition Shift at Primary HealingHall so they kept early hours.

Tinne couldn't deal with his parents and their expectations of him now. He didn't know their emotional states, how they were coping with the scandal and the loss of T'Holly's long-held dream forever. They'd always been a unit before everyone, including their sons. He certainly had never known what they discussed privately unless they'd told him. Those exchanges were usually prefaced by T'Holly saying, "Your mother and I have been talking . . ."

Tinne knew they loved him, they made that clear, but he'd always wondered how much they understood him—or Holm.

Too much pondering for a man of action, a Holly. Tinne set his shoulders. He was putting off his own plan of action. Pulling up a chair to the scrytable in the mainspace, he sat and ran his finger around the rim. "Holm Holly at T'Holly Residence."

"Here." Holm looked up from his desk. He had an ink smear on his cheek and a brush in his hand.

"What are you doing?" Tinne asked.

Holm grimaced. "Lark thinks the baby's room should have a banner of my calligraphy." Holm's creative Flair. "Ancient symbols of good luck, fortune, happiness, whatever." Holm shrugged. "Gotta practice."

Tinne found himself smiling. "You have months before the birth, you'll get it right." He turned in his chair to look at the creamy walls of the Turquoise House mainspace. "In fact, I think this place could use a short banner. You can give one of your efforts to me. Adds a little more personalization to the room, and I'm sure the Turquoise House would like it."

"I would *love* it!" the Turquoise House said. "I would like the glyphs for 'happy home' and 'long life' and 'large Family.'"

Holm grumbled, "Thanks, just what I need, more pressure," but his lips twitched, and his eyes were amused. "What era do you want it from, TQ? Ancient Earthan, first colonists, modern?"

"TQ," the House gave the initials an extra resonance. "That is a nickname. TQ. I like it."

Holm winked at Tinne. "Thought you would. Might irritate Mitchella D'Blackthorn, a change of name she didn't approve."

"I like TQ," the House said stubbornly.

"Right, TQ," Holm said. "I'll send you a banner within the week, if you tell me which style. Consider it a Yule gift."

"Thank you! I will research the styles and let you know. I will send a message to T'Holly Residence," TQ faltered. Obviously T'Holly Residence intimidated the young House.

"I'll inform the Residence that I'm expecting a scry."

"Styles," the House muttered, and Tinne knew its attention had been drawn elsewhere.

"So, bro, what do you want?" Holm leaned back in his chair.

"It's the scandal," Tinne said bluntly. Holm's face went carefully blank.

"I've been reflecting on the Family." Tinne cleared his throat. "It occurred to me that you will have to deal with the scandal as T'Holly for the rest of your life."

Holm's eyes darkened. Tinne thought he saw a flash of pain as his brother rolled down his bloused shirtsleeves.

"I am with the popular opinion that believes our parents brought this upon us all," Holm said. His intense gaze met Tinne's. "I don't know that I told you how bad I felt, how sad, when you and Genista lost your baby." He blinked rapidly, stared away from the bowl, then looked back at Tinne, grim lines around his mouth. Holm touched his heart with fingertips. "I *can* tell you that if something happened to Lark's and my child . . ." He shook his head. His gaze bored into Tinne, his lips flattened. "You know that I think you're the better man of us, I think you have handled everything that has occurred to you with grace."

Tinne's mouth had dried, his heart picked up its beat. He didn't want to talk of this, didn't want to remember the long pain that could still pierce him unawares, so he focused on his brother's last statement, tried to speak lightly. "And I think you are the best of us all . . ." He managed a lopsided smile. "Well, Lark, maybe." Back to the topic. "The divorce scandal—"

Holm shrugged. "I have good friends and allies."

"The mud of scandal smears and sticks."

Raising his brows, Holm said, "It's done, nothing we can correct. You're behaving honorably, the rest of us are, too. We can only weather this latest situation together, as always."

"*Not* as always. The parents didn't—"

"—You always stood by me. I'm standing by you. That's not going to change in the future, is it?"

"No—"

"Then we understand each other. We live our lives. That's all we can do, is live our lives as well as we can."

Tinne heard a door creak, and Holm's face lit. Lark must have walked into the room. Holm brought the front legs of his chair down and rose, towered over the scry, and held out his hand. Then he smiled down at Tinne. "Lark is on a shortened schedule at the HealingHall." He lifted his HeartMate's hand to his lips and kissed it. "We *live*, Tinne. Let the others gossip about the Hollys. They've been doing that since before we were born."

"If the gossip affects the next generation?" Tinne raised a hand to Lark as she came into view. She smiled at him, too.

"We will deal with that as it comes. Our children will *not* suffer because of their FatherSire's and MotherSire's actions." Holm's jaw flexed. There was the steel Tinne needed to see, what he'd scried to see and reassure himself that he wasn't alone in this fight. That Holm didn't consider him a failure.

"Blessings, Tinne," Lark said.

Tinne could barely find his voice. "Blessings, beloved sister-in-law." He smiled. "You, too, brother."

"Sure," Holm said. "Later." With a wave, the scry ended.

Tinne put his face in his hands, glad he was sitting down.

His timer dinged, and he straightened. He was due at the Green Knight, and it was time to get on with his life.

"Lady and Lord, no more great changes, please," he prayed.

Thirty-three

❤

After she and Tinne had hot, crazy sex and he'd left for the day, Lahsin felt energized. Almost *too* energized.

Her Second Passage was over.

She'd survived.

So much Flair!

For a septhour she practiced teleporting around the estate. From the sacred grove to the summer pavilion, from the summer house to the garden shed, from the garden shed to the stillroom. She overshot, every time, only a step or two, but that could be fatal. She didn't understand why and blamed it on the fact that the sun hadn't totally risen and the shadows were odd.

At breakfast she ate with Strother, who slurped up his food, then sat on her feet and rumbled approval of her Flair. *Feels good. You could Heal me now, if I had tooth wounds or a bad leg.*

"I don't think so, I'm not an animal Healer."

Little Heal spells and ointment and Healing pool and your Flair would be enough after such a fight now, he insisted.

Lahsin didn't want to remember that time. She shifted in her chair and picked up the newssheet.

I have watched dog-nose from a distance. He remembers nothing. Man never knew anything.

"Thank you." She scanned the news, a rehashing of the Mugwort scandal, a lower Nobleclass Family who were members of the Christian religion, which was generally called Cross Folk. The Lord and the Lady of the Family had been experimenting with pylor. That smoke-drug was now forbidden, since many believed it had contributed to the black magic cult murder spree the previous year.

The next page had Lahsin's own childish face staring up at her under a huge "Reward." She turned it quickly and noticed a small red-bordered item. Another ad, this one read: "Happy Lapp, I'm back. I've missed you. I'm worried. Please meet me at our old place afore grovestudy, Artyclu."

The piece of toast she was holding fell from her hand, missed the plate and the table, and landed jam-side up in front of Strother's nose. He licked it. *Berry sweet. Good.*

Happy Lapp. She winced. That was her brother's nickname for her. Clute was back in town. He should have been here a week ago, for Yule. Lahsin turned to the weather page. Ah, Ambroz Pass had just been opened, that would have delayed him.

Finally her brother had arrived from Gael City. Excitement fizzed through her. She had so much she wanted to tell him!

Just when she didn't need him anymore. She grinned. She'd found sanctuary, survived Second Passage on her own!

She wasn't as thrilled as she would have been if she'd seen the small note two eightdays ago. Then she'd been a fearful child.

Looking back, she couldn't have imagined the person she was now. She knew how to take care of herself. There wasn't any reason for Clute to worry, like he said in his ad. But he loved her, had never approved of her marriage, though he'd left for Gael City soon after that and hadn't been back.

Of course she hadn't survived Passage without help—the estate, the Residence, Strother, Tinne, even her HeartMate had supported her. How rich she was now.

Glancing at the timer, she saw that if she was going to meet him this morning, she'd have to hurry.

She couldn't teleport to their old meeting place, a park. It had been too many years since Clute walked her to grovestudy. The small teleportation area might have changed, the park might have been spruced up, and her skill was shaky this morning.

Clearing her throat, she said to Strother, "My brother is in town, he's a good man. I'd like to go and meet him."

Strother's ears lifted a little, he got to his feet, ignoring the damp bread now bare of jam. *I am your Fam. I will go.*

"How well do you teleport?"

I am alive.

Good point. "Well enough, then."

Yes.

"He wants to meet at Horsetail Park."

Strother's gray black brows beetled. *That park is on Root Boulevard near CityCenter.*

"Yes. Lower Nobleclass. It was close to our grovestudy park and library. We can teleport to the library." It was a small branch, but those teleportation areas never changed.

Libraries don't like animals, even Fams.

"That's true, but I can't linger in the library. I can't afford for anyone to notice me much. Yet."

You are adult and strong with Flair. No one can hurt you.

She smiled and wished it were true. "The library teleportation pad is near the back entrance." Hesitating, she said, "Why don't I meet you at the park?"

Yes. I know the park and can hop there.

"Good." Again she looked at the timer. "I'll grab my hooded cloak and teleport from my bedroom. Don't come into it."

Strother nodded. *I will hop from my den in the glasshouse.*

"Good." She bent down and rubbed him. "I love you."

He licked her face. *I love you, too.*

*H*orsetail Park was a long, marshy strip curving at the end. It was pretty in a severe kind of way, since it had few trees, but during warm weather it was rich with grass and flowers.

Lahsin had 'ported to the very edge of the pad in the library. The fact that libraries kept shields around their pads had stabilized her. She must not have become accustomed to all her new Flair. She'd hurried from the place before anyone besides the librarian had noticed her, and since her hood kept her face in shadow, she thought she was safe. The street was busy, but it was cold, and she kept a weathershield around her with an additional factor to blur her features.

Once in the park, her heart twisted. There were so many memories here of playing with her brothers, of Clute with her hand in his. She'd walked the length of the park before he arrived.

He stepped off the teleportation pad, stared at her, then jogged to her. He wasn't a tall man, and was stocky, but his face was beloved, the green Burdock eyes and heavy jaw. When he was only a pace away from her, he said, "Lahsin, is that you?"

Sighing, she pushed her hood back and let her weather-shield clearly show her face, then she flung herself into his arms. So solid and dependable. He felt great and smelled like Clute.

He drew back, holding her hands and scrutinizing her, then he touched her face. "You're thinner."

Probably just toned more from all her training. "It's so good to see you." The feelings rushing through her were unexpected . . . good childhood memories. They seemed to weave her life together from then to now. She couldn't speak.

"Oh, Lahsin." He sounded sorrowful. His eyes were anxious.

She managed a trembling smile. "I'm good."

He shook his head. "Not my Happy Lapp anymore."

"No," she croaked through a tight throat. "But I'm content." She wished she could take him to FirstGrove, but knew through their link that he enjoyed his life.

The wind whistled around them.

Clute frowned. "So thin, more delicate than I recalled."

Her turn to shake her head. "No—"

"And Second Passage coming for you."

"I already—"

His gaze went past her. "I did the right thing," he said.

Fear clutched her belly. She whirled and saw T'Yew tele-port into the area across the park, followed by Taxa. He scanned the landscape with scorn, saw her, smiled the smile that looked nice until you saw his eyes. The depressFlair cuffs attached to his belt glinted. If he got those on her, it didn't matter how much Flair she had or how many personal shields. She was doomed.

"What have you done!" She spun to face Clute.

He still held one hand and with the other, he took her arm.

"Lahsin, I'm so worried about you." His tone rang true. "You're so delicate, gentle. Second Passage must be a nightmare for you. Let us help."

She tried to jerk her arm away and couldn't. She knew how to hurt him, to put him down and strike, and run, but this was her *brother*, Clute, who loved her.

"Let me go!"

"Oh, Lahsin," he repeated, shaking his head.

She hesitated too long. T'Yew strode across the yellowed grass.

Opening her mouth, she let out a fighting scream, knew there was too much fear and anger in it.

Clute stumbled back. She reacted as she had been taught and went with him, overbalanced him. They fell.

*T*inne heard *L*ahsin scream, had a vision of her outside FirstGrove, in the city. He'd get her direction from their bond, go to her. "Stop!" he ordered his beginning class.

Everyone froze, as trained.

"What?" demanded Tab.

"HeartMate. *Danger!* 'Porting." He felt her fear now, more than was reasonable. Some unknown factor.

Tab linked arms with him, face granite. "I'll go with you. Class dismissed! Cuz Nitida, mind the salon."

In a wink they were there, across a length of ground from her. Not quick enough. T'Yew had her.

*S*he'd jumped to her feet, but as always when he was chasing her, T'Yew had been too fast. "I will never return to you, *never*," Lahsin forced a whisper through chill lips.

"Always the dramatic child," T'Yew sneered. He unsnapped the depressFlair bracelets from his belt with one hand, kept the fingers of his other bruisingly clamped on her arm.

Lahsin screamed in his ear, yanked her arm away, and pivoted.

"Don't turn your back on me, *wife*." He grabbed her from behind.

Her Flair sizzled through her, putting power into her elbow jab. He gasped and let her go. She didn't run but turned.

He lunged for her. She kicked at him, hit his groin. He mew-led, grabbed his sex, toppled toward her. She struck out, one hand, not fisted. Hit him in the temple and watched, appalled, as the life fled from his eyes.

His body fell to the ground.

There was the smell of death.

Taxa was screeching. The woman had been sauntering, was still meters from Lahsin. Clute was swearing somewhere near her.

Tinne and Tab Holly had appeared. Tinne was running to-ward her, stopped.

The whole thing had taken only a couple of minutes. Her hands came to her mouth to stop her own scream—of horror.

More people were teleporting into the park. She watched, un-believing, as young Vinni T'Vine came along with T'Blackthorn and T'Holly and D'Holly, then T'Ash.

SupremeJudge Ailim Elder appeared.

Lahsin's heartbeat in her ears drowned out all other sound. She had doomed herself.

Tinne walked to her, followed by Tab and all the others.

Tab looked down at the body, shook his head. "Excellent defensive moves. Terrible form in the offense. Terrible."

"I only taught her defense." Tinne's voice was strained.

"I killed him." Her voice was far too high. "How could I kill him?" She stared at her hand. She'd hit T'Yew with the flat of it.

Clute looked pale, eyes wide, mouth open. "Oh, Lahsin, I didn't know he'd attack you. Had those filthy cuffs." He swal-lowed, stepped forward. "It was the Flair. Had to be. I saw it crackle around you." His mouth grimmed. "He shouldn't have laid hands on you."

Tinne said, "Pity you didn't decide that sooner."

"I didn't know!" Clute rubbed his hand across his eyes. "The Family always told me she was happy with him."

"Lahsin endured her last Passage fugue only a few sept-hours ago," Tinne said. "Her new Flair has not quite settled."

Tab snorted, eyed the body, shrugged. "This whole thing was the consequences of his own actions. Destiny."

Taxa's screams held a new, horrible note. Circling the men, she flung herself at Lahsin, hands curved in claws.

Lahsin summoned a personal spellshield and Taxa's fin-gers bounced off of it.

"Handy Flair," Tab said.

"Why didn't you—" Clute started.

"Her body reacted as it was taught to," Tinne said.

Taxa stood panting before them, expression edging toward madness. "I will make you pay," Taxa said, fury mottling her face. "The murder of a husband is a despicable thing, bringing down the full punishment of the law. Banishment. Death, even." Her words were evil and gloating. "You made my life, my father's life a hell, and now you kill him. Oh, you will pay."

"He wasn't my husband! I repudiated the marriage to three neutral witnesses." Lahsin forced stuttering words through her lips. She was so cold, even under her shields.

"You lie. You have no witnesses. Who would support *you*?" Taxa slapped at Lahsin, hard. Again her hand bounced off of the shield. She snarled. Lahsin took a pace back. Two men grasped Taxa's arms, one to each side. She struggled then subsided, raising her chin and looking every inch GrandLady D'Yew, a FirstFamily GrandLady, rich in gilt and status and Flair.

"I . . . I repudiated it to T'Yew Residence." Lahsin shivered, took a breath, tried not to watch as a newly arrived T'Heather examined T'Yew's body, vanished with it to Noble Deathgrove.

Taxa sneered, "T'Yew Residence will not support you."

Of course not. "I repudiated it to Straif T'Blackthorn."

"True," T'Blackthorn said. "I so reported to Supreme-Judge Elder."

Ailim Elder nodded.

Lahsin shivered in relief. She reached desperately for other instances. There was only one, and Tinne had told her . . . but she had no choice. "I repudiated my marriage to Tinne Holly."

Lip curling, Taxa said, "I can see the HeartMate bond between you. He's your HeartMate, that doesn't count."

Thirty-four

❦

O*ne glance at* Tinne's *anguished face told* Lahsin *the* truth. He *was* her HeartMate. All this time he hadn't been honest, had misled her. About how much? Being in FirstGrove? Why he liked her? He didn't care for her for herself, for how she'd been and grown, but because she was his HeartMate. That was the only reason he'd helped her. Nothing more.

Her mind spun, struggling to understand. She swayed. Clute reached out and steadied her. Tinne held back.

Taxa was gloating again, whipping at Lahsin with her words. "You didn't repudiate my father, and you killed your husband. You'll die for that." She smiled, nastily. "Or, better, wear depressFlair cuffs for the rest of your life."

That drove a person mad, everyone knew that.

Lahsin repudiated her marriage within my hearing, Strother growled, trotting up to her and nudging his head under her hand. That steadied her. She breathed easier.

"You're her Fam. You don't count." Taxa spat the words.

Strother glared. *I was a feral dog when Lahsin repudiated T'Yew. Not her FamDog for days. That counts.*

"Indeed it does," SupremeJudge Elder said.

Ilexa bounded to them, sat and curled her tail around her paws, twitched her whiskers. *I was there when Lahsin T'Yew*

repudiated her marriage to the nasty man. I heard her. I am
her HeartMate's Fam, but that is all right in the rules.

"Agreed," Elder said solemnly. "Three neutral witnesses
state that the late T'Yew was not wed to Lahsin Burdock."
The SupremeJudge was serene, hands tucked in her opposite
sleeves.

Lahsin had never realized until now, when she wasn't
wearing one, how warm a heavy formal gown was with sleeves
made of thick material. Easier to think of that than Tinne or
T'Yew.

"I'll have your judgeship for this, Elder," Taxa said.

Ailim Elder shrugged. "More powerful people than you
have tried."

Taxa sent a withering look to the men who still held her.
They let her go. "She murdered my father, a FirstFamilies
GrandLord. She. Must. Pay."

Clute said, "An accidental death. I saw it all. T'Yew
grabbed my sister. He looked like he was going to kill her. He
had depressFlair bracelets for *Lahsin*, the gentlest person I
know." He shook his head.

Lahsin tried a smile, knew it was a travesty. "I learned being gentle was bad from T'Yew."

Clute scowled. "He was going to . . ." He squared his
shoulders. "I think he was going to rape her."

"She's his wife," Taxa screeched. "It's not rape."

"She was *not* his wife, and yes," Ailim Elder said, "it is
rape. I don't know where you get your primitive notions. A
girl, a woman *always* has the right to say no." Her eyebrows
raised. "I certainly can't imagine you submitting to rape."

"I saw everything," Tinne said. "The death was self-defense."

Tab Holly said, "An accidental burst of Flair due to recent
Passage in response to the threat of rape."

There was silence, and Lahsin could hear the wind. Now
she felt warm, hot from guilt and failure. She'd accepted yesterday during Passage that there would be more of both emotions
in her life, just didn't realize they'd plague her so soon.

Stepping away from her brother, avoiding Tinne's supportive gaze, but keeping her hand tangled in Strother's fur, she
met the SupremeJudge's eyes. "I killed T'Yew." Her mouth
tasted awful. "I didn't mean to. I didn't want him dead, I only
wanted to be free of him. I had my last Passage fugue yester-

day evening. I am an adult now. I'll accept whatever verdict you have of my actions." Her voice quavered on the last few words, shaming her.

Then she felt heat at her back, realized Tinne had moved to stand literally behind her, though she had not been able to look directly at him since the revelation that they were Heart-Mates.

SupremeJudge Ailim Elder swept the gathered FirstFamily Nobles with a stern glance. More had appeared, D'Sea, the mind Healer, T'Hawthorn, D'Grove.

The judge said, "I take the Words of Clute Burdock, Tinne Holly, and Tab Holly about the circumstances of this *accidental* death. Does anyone contest this?"

"I do!" Taxa shouted.

The SupremeJudge turned a look on her that sent a chill to Lahsin's bones. Taxa shut up. "You're emotionally overwrought."

"No!" Taxa spit.

"Anyone would be, under the circumstances." The mind Healer D'Sea glided up to Taxa, sent a glance to Lahsin. Lahsin was feeling numb. Probably not a good thing, but better than wretched betrayal or guilt or horror or . . . numb was better.

"My father was only taking Lahsin back to our Residence. For her own good."

Clute fired at that. "I don't believe that anymore. But you and T'Yew got what you wanted from my sister's marriage with him, didn't you? Got a whipping girl for years. Don't tell me you didn't, I can see that in my sister's face and yours. But Lahsin didn't produce a son for T'Yew, so now you're a FirstFamily GrandLady, and that's even better for you."

"My father is *dead.*" For the first time tears streaked down Taxa's cheeks, but she pushed away D'Sea's comforting arms.

"An accident he brought on himself," SupremeJudge Ailim Elder said. "After threatening a woman he'd previously abused." She focused her gaze on Lahsin, and Lahsin recalled that the SupremeJudge was a telempath and knew all the emotions going through everyone. She'd sense Lahsin's shock and the fear Lahsin had, might always have, of T'Yew. But Lahsin couldn't answer.

Tinne set his hands on her shoulders, and it was worse. She

wanted his touch, but wanted a friend's touch, not a Heart-Mate's. Lahsin couldn't prevent a sob.

The judge turned her stare to Taxa. "If you continue to press for a punishment for more than accidental death—which is letting the perpetrator live with the emotional hurt of the act for the rest of her life—then we must do a truthspell investigation of past events at T'Yew Residence."

"Impossible. You can't dare!" Taxa fumed.

Elder narrowed her eyes. "Most FirstFamilies have learned that the rule of law is superior to the rule of individual Nobles, or even the FirstFamily Council. Obviously some learn that lesson slower than others, D'Yew." The judge raised her brows. "But even if we judges did not have the right to question your Family and Residence about perversions committed there, there are more ancient ways. T'Yew submitted to the old rules when he was accepted into the FirstFamilies Council." Matching Taxa's glare, the judge said, "Six FirstFamily Lords or Ladies can vote to investigate one of their own."

"I'll vote for the probe," T'Holly said.

"And I," said T'Blackthorn.

"Me, too," said T'Ash.

"And I." Lahsin didn't recognize the voice, looked at the man. His cuffs showed him to be Saille T'Willow, T'Yew's enemy.

"That's four of six," the judge said. "Are you and your allies strong enough to stop another two from joining with these?"

"Don't do this, D'Yew," Vinni T'Vine, the boy prophet, said. "It's best that all consequences of your father's actions and Lahsin's reaction end here and now."

A vein throbbed red in Taxa's temple. "I don't need you to advise me. I'll never need you to advise me, you *child*."

White-faced, T'Vine bowed, then ranged himself with the older Lords. Tab Holly put an arm around the boy.

"Look to your alliances," T'Willow said, reminding every Noble there what was truly important. "Some ties made with your father expired with his death." His smile was unfriendly.

From the fleeting expression of surprise and wariness, Lahsin realized that Taxa didn't know her allies. Lahsin didn't think Taxa had made any alliances of her own.

T'Willow must have seen the same thing Lahsin had. "Sloppy," he said.

Of course T'Yew's life expectancy had been long. Lahsin felt sick again.

"I suggest you return to your Residence and set your affairs in order," the SupremeJudge said, not unkindly.

Taxa dashed more tears away. "I want to see my father in Deathgrove, prepare for his Transition ritual. His *unnatural* transition." She glared at Lahsin.

"Fate is entirely natural," Tab Holly said.

With a wordless cry, Taxa whirled away. D'Sea, the mind Healer, followed until Taxa rebuffed her.

"I hereby declare that the death of Ioho T'Yew is ruled as accidental and self-defense on the part of Lahsin Burdock."

"Rosemary," Tinne murmured. "Lahsin Rosemary."

"Lahsin Rosemary," the judge corrected. "And I state that I have come to this legal conclusion through observation, questioning witnesses, and through the use of my telempathic Flair. This matter is closed."

The Lords and Ladies gathered around T'Hawthorn and T'Holly to talk of politics and alliances.

"Lahsin, may I speak with you?" Tinne asked.

"You weren't honest with me. I always thought you were honest. Hon—orable." Her voice broke.

He came around to face her. His expression was strained, the skin tight against his face. "I was as honest as I could be." He hesitated. "Neither of us wanted a HeartMate. I wanted to get to know you." Another pause. "I wanted to help."

"But you've known all along."

"Yes."

"And you came to FirstGrove first to find me because I'd run away from T'Yew and was missing and I was your HeartMate."

He just nodded, turning paler, almost the color of his hair. His eyes were dark gray coals. He was beautiful, this man she'd taken as a lover. And he broke her heart.

"Lahsin, I learned something in the last few minutes." An ironic smile flickered on his lips, then vanished. "I always learned as much or more from you than anything you've learned from me."

As images flashed of their lessons, their talks, their sex, pain ripped through her.

His gaze was strong, level, serious. "I learned that I love you," he said.

She was still shuddering with sweeping emotions, couldn't cope with such change, so words just fell from her lips. "I don't love you."

His mouth thinned, but he showed no pain he might be feeling. She put her hands against her head to settle her spinning wits.

He nodded. "I will wait, Lahsin. We are HeartMates, and I will wait. Come to me when you're ready."

She saw that flash of anguish again. Her mouth dropped open, and before she closed it, he was gone.

D'Sea came up and wrapped Lahsin in a hug against her soft body, sending waves of calm, and Lahsin realized how stiff and hurt her muscles were, how cold she was. She began to quiver, then tremble, then shuddered and wept.

"You've been too isolated," D'Sea said, stroking her hair. "Going through all this on your own. Alone."

Strother barked. *I was with her!*

D'Sea didn't understand Lahsin's grief. It was because she *hadn't* been alone that she wept. Because her sanctuary had been perfect with a beautiful garden, great Fam, wonderful love, and all that had been an illusion. Tinne had only come to her, cared for her because she was his HeartMate.

That sounded strange, but she was too confused to sort it out and cried some more.

"Tell me where your hidey-hole is, dear, and I'll send someone to get your things." D'Sea patted her on her back. "You need a good place to stay."

The words brought Lahsin up short. D'Sea obviously believed she'd taken shelter in some deserted building in Druida. She hadn't. Lahsin had to keep FirstGrove secret and safe.

She drew away, swallowed tears, forced herself to speak calmly. "Thank you, but I'd prefer to do that myself."

D'Sea frowned, then said, "All right." She lifted a hand. "I'll get you an escort."

"That won't be neces—"

Tab Holly was there, taking D'Sea's hand in his own and bringing it to his mouth in a bow, then he let it go and turned to Lahsin. "Don't know if you recall that we've met. Tab Holly, Tinne's G'Uncle and mentor. Owner of the Green Knight Fencing and Fighting Salon." He held out a hand that was hard with calluses. "I'll accompany the lady," he assured D'Sea.

Lahsin eyed him. He probably knew a whole lot about what was going on. About Tinne, if she wanted to ask. She didn't. "Thank you," she said, taking his hand. Tab smelled a little like Tinne. Or because the man was so much older, Tinne smelled like Tab. Or they both smelled of the Green Knight Fencing and Fighting Salon.

No, the common scent was that of the ointment she'd first made for Tinne. Tears started again.

Tab gave her a huge linen softleaf.

Strother projected loudly, *I come. I am strong and tough.*

"I welcome your company," Tab said. He met D'Sea's gaze. "I think it's time that Tinne lives in T'Holly Residence. Gentle-Lady Lahsin Rosemary can stay at the Turquoise House."

D'Sea's eyes widened, then she nodded. "I agree."

"Good," Tab said. "Good with you, Lady?" he asked Lahsin. She didn't see any way out of it, so she sighed. "Yes."

"I'll inform Tinne of the change," D'Sea said.

When they'd reached the teleportation area, a rectangle of hard, dry earth, Tab said, "You visualize the coordinates, Lady, and send them to me. I think you'll find that we have a bond."

Because of Tinne. She gulped, nodded, wiped her face. Taking eight deep breaths to calm herself, she set the image of the northernmost door of FirstGrove in her mind. The dirty paved courtyard between the wall and abandoned warehouses. The light was *so.*

She sent it to Tab. He was right, there was a connection between them. He wrapped a sturdy arm around her waist, determined nothing would go wrong. That made her smile faintly. She held on to Strother's collar.

"On three," Tab counted down. "One, true HeartMates." Lahsin flinched. "Two, HeartBond dear, *three.*"

They arrived at the door without a sound, barely disturbing dust. Tab frowned. "I don't recognize this area. Where are we?"

Lahsin gestured to the wall to their left a few meters away. "The North Wall of Druida, near the northeast corner."

Tab frowned. "Still don't know." He turned in place, scanning the buildings, the brush, the narrow alleys, the wall. Then he nodded. "I'll find my way around."

I can help, Strother said.

"Appreciate it," Tab said. "How long will it take you to pack and return, GentleLady Rosemary?"

Lahsin said thickly, "Call me Lahsin, and not long." She wondered how many ructions BalmHeal Residence would make. She didn't know how much she could stand. But no one else could get her things. She really wanted a long soak in the Healing pool, to go to bed and hide under the covers but that wasn't going to happen.

I will wait here with Tab Holly, Strother said. She got the idea that he didn't want to be around the Residence, either.

Hands on his hips, Tab stared at the wall. "Looks concave."

"It is, it curves inward, not quite a triangle."

"Huh. Think I'll follow it along for a bit."

"It won't help you, you'll still forget."

He nodded. "Don' think I'll remember this, but may as well do a little explorin'. I've seen many an odd thing in m'life, this is jus' one more. Interestin'."

"All right. I'll be back as soon as I can."

Once inside the estate, Lahsin teleported to her bedroom. She still had too much energy, too much Flair, though she landed exactly where she'd envisioned, in the middle of the room.

"Residence . . ." She didn't know how to explain.

"I have heard of everything that has transpired since you left." BalmHeal Residence was subdued.

That surprised Lahsin. She got her few clothes and her thin sack from the wardrobe. "How?"

"I am now tied into a network of communication with other Residences. And the starship." It sounded sour.

"That's good."

"It's not enough. I know you're leaving."

"I had no choice. Tab Holly is waiting outside the walls to take me to another place."

"Hrumph. To that stup Turquoise House. I heard. Don't you forget your promise to me, Lahsin."

"I won't."

All the windows rattled. She wet her lips, thought of the lip balm and other jars and bottles of remedies she'd made. "I'd like to take my work that's in the stillroom."

"Take it, then."

She thought of something else. "I'd like to leave my HeartGift here. It's well placed in the greenhouse to get light and water. I've funded those spells for a few months. Could you look after it for me, please?" The little garden in the planter with sexual markings, the small holly sprigs twining into a heart shape. Her mind had cleared to let her know what it was, now.

"You would leave something so precious as your HeartGift with me?" BalmHeal sounded stilted, or choked. Lahsin decided not to tell the Residence how little her HeartGift meant to her.

"You'll keep it safe, and you'll have surety for my word."

It didn't deny that it wanted surety.

"Very well. I will watch over it for you and alert you should anything happen to it."

"Thank you." She'd finished gathering the other bits and pieces of her life. She'd put her drum at the bottom of the sack where she couldn't see it, but she couldn't leave it behind. Saying a spell to shield and strengthen the sack, she walked to the front great hall door and hesitated. "Thank you for your hospitality." She bowed. "Merry meet."

"Merry part," the Residence said.

"And merry meet again," she ended.

"We'd better," the Residence said.

Lahsin stopped at the stillroom building to pick up her jars and shoved them in the bag, then 'ported back to the door. She couldn't bear to look at the Healing pool before she left. Though from the way she felt, FirstGrove would open to her touch for a long, long time.

Tab and Strother were at the door, and they all teleported to the Turquoise House without a word. Tab opened the greeniron gates for her, and they walked through the short courtyard to the pretty pastel house.

"Tinne's already gone," Tab said.

Lahsin swallowed. "That's good."

"He didn't lie to you."

"He didn't tell the truth, either."

Tab snorted. "An' you were ready to hear he was your HeartMate? He wasn't."

"I can't talk about this now. Too much . . ." Her voice rose.

"Sorry," Tab said, then bent down and surprised her by kissing her forehead. "You've had a hard day. Rest. Take care of yourself. Spend time with your Fam. Don' let the Turquoise House talk your ear off."

That made her smile, but it faded when she saw his piercing stare fixed on her. "You be good to my boy, Lahsin Rosemary. And think on this, those who have HeartMates are blessed, and you're only seventeen. Got more'n a century to live. Don't throw away what you'll want later." Then he watched her open the door. When she closed it behind her, she sensed he was gone.

His words rang in her ears.

Tinne was gone, but his scent remained.

She dragged herself straight to bed—in a guest bedroom instead of the MasterSuite Tinne had used. Always a guest, never a good suite of her own, she thought tiredly. Only midday, and she needed sleep. The nervy energy from her Flair had vanished with the last teleportation, leaving her with barely enough to walk.

The Turquoise House, "TQ," was blessedly quiet, playing beautiful, soothing music. To "Recover from Passage and Emotional Events," it'd said in a wonderful male voice, almost crooning itself—himself.

Emotional events. She half laughed, half choked as she crumpled onto the bedsponge and drew an ultrasoft cover over her.

Tinne had left a faint imprint in here, too, as had his Fam-Cat. Tinne. How much of him was true and how much false? Was he friend or HeartMate? She didn't know. He'd deceived her, she didn't know him now.

She was adult and Flaired. She'd killed a man. She didn't know herself.

She felt betrayed.

Thirty-five

❤

T*inne arrived at the teleportation pad in the entryway of* T'Holly Residence a few minutes before his parents. His life had fallen to pieces once more, and he wasn't ready to deal with his HeartMate and her shock and rejection of him.

He *was* ready to deal with his Family who had controlled his life. He had let them, fearing falling, fearing failing, fearing change. Lahsin had become a woman, it was time he became a man.

T'Holly and his Mamá had arrived as soon as he'd flipped the switch on the teleportation pad to show it was free.

"You have a HeartMate! How wonderful. She'll change her mind soon about wedding with you! We'll make sure of it!" His Mamá rushed toward him and hugged him tight, and for an instant he allowed himself to love her unconditionally as he had all his life, to savor her warmth and her scent and her love. Then he stepped aside, back into his moving balance, not to be swayed again by them.

"No." He met his father's eyes. "I will handle my HeartMate and my love life and my whole damn life. By myself. As a man."

"Well, of course—" his Mamá started.

"No!" He made a cutting gesture. "You *will* listen to me. I have always preferred to follow your lead, take your instruction. Only when I had no choice, when you failed to listen to

me did I go my own way. That will stop now. I *will* conduct
my own life as I see fit. You *will* accept that."

Tears filled his Mamá's eyes, she stepped back and held out
her hand. T'Holly took it, drew her into his arms. She buried
her face in his chest. His face went stony. "I am listening,
I hear an 'or else'."

"Or else I move from T'Holly Residence permanently." He
didn't know where he'd go, since Lahsin was at TQ, but he'd
find a place. He knew how to live by himself, or by himself
and with his Fam. He glanced around for Ilexa and found her
sitting in a corner, claws spread, cleaning dirt from her pads.
She preferred living here, of course, but radiated support.

His father eased, and Tinne realized the man had been
braced for a threat to disinherit himself. Tinne shook his head
slightly and a corner of T'Holly's mouth quirked. He patted
his HeartMate's shoulder. "All sons must grow up, Passiflora."

Tinne's Mamá said a muffled, "My baby!"

He winced.

"Our fine son, a man to be proud of," T'Holly said. His
eyes were steady. "So?"

Tinne lowered from the balls of his feet. "So I want the
tower rooms. I've always wanted the tower rooms."

"But they're so far away—" his mother protested.

"I can play my drums in there and not have to muffle the
sound. Play 'em all night long if I want, and no one else will
hear them. You've kept those rooms filled with storage just so
you couldn't give them to me. Holm and Lark's child can
have my suite." Let them redecorate.

"But your HeartMate might not like the tower—"

"We will not discuss my HeartMate. Ever. Unless I bring
up the topic. You will *not* interfere in her life. Your Vows of
Honor on it."

Both flinched, so much had gone wrong last time they'd
given Vows of Honor and broken them.

T'Holly's eyes had gone steely. "Do you realize that except for my Oath of Office as Captain of All Councils, no one
has asked me for my Vow of Honor?" His smile turned ironic.
"As if I couldn't be trusted to give it again and keep it. Thank
you, son." He raised the hand that had been stroking his
HeartMate's back. "I solemnly swear on my Vow of Honor

that I will not interfere in my son Tinne Holly's life." He hesitated. "Without being requested by him to do so."

Tinne found his own lips curving, the man had to add a
qualifier. He gave a short nod and said, "Particularly with regard to Tinne's HeartMate, Lahsin."

"Particularly with regard to Tinne's HeartMate, Lahsin,"
T'Holly repeated.

"Good. Mamá?"

"Oh, very well." She turned in her husband's arms.
"I-solemnly-swear-on-my-Vow-of-Honor-that-I-will-not-
interfere-in-my-son-Tinne-Holly's-life-particularly-with-
regard-to-Tinne's-HeartMate-Lahsin," she said so fast that
he barely heard the words. Then she made a moue. "But you
know, we can help—"

"No, Mamá. She is young and finding her own way." Tinne
took both her hands and kissed them. "I'm older and finding
my way. We've both had great upheavals in our lives. Let us
deal with them ourselves and grow." He flashed a smile. "You
will have to limit yourself to interfering in the lives of the rest
of the Family. I think the cuz who's been my driver needs help."

Her face lightened. "Yes? Come, Holm Senior, let's go
find him."

"I have other plans." T'Holly lifted his wife in his arms,
and they disappeared.

"That was mean," Tinne's brother, Holm, said. He and his
wife, Lark, stood on the teleportation pad. "You never did forgive him for ferrying you around, did you?"

Tinne shrugged.

Lark walked to him, gaze searching. "How are you?"

The last thing he wanted was to tell a Healer, even his
sister-in-law, how he was feeling. He looked at his brother,
who just put his hands in his pockets.

Clearing his throat, Tinne said, "Shocked. Numb." He rubbed
his hand over his chest. "It's been a rocky few weeks."

"A lot of change," Holm agreed. He winked. "I have no
doubt that things will settle down for a while and in a few
months I'll be attending your wedding."

Tinne managed a choking laugh. "I don't know—"

Lark put her hands on his forearms, rubbed up and down
once. Tinne felt the infusion of Family energy, from her, his

brother, and even a tiny spark from the babe within. That awed him.

Lark said, "Everything has turned out well. Lahsin is away from that cruel T'Yew, has survived her Second Passage, and is an adult with Flair to control and mend her life. Tinne is free to HeartBond with her when they are both ready. And he is home." She rose on tiptoe to kiss his cheek. "With time, everything will straighten and smooth out." She sounded a lot more optimistic than he felt. "Now you go drum." Making a face, she caught Holm's hand in her own. "We need to survey your old suite for our child and see what colors and furnishings we might keep."

"He or she might like growing up in a Yule box," Tinne said helpfully.

Holm buffeted him on his shoulder as he went by.

"Welcome home, Tinne," said the Residence.

"Thank you, Residence. May I say that I missed you and will never take you for granted again? The Turquoise House is a good place, but exhausting, and BalmHeal . . ."

"Thank you, Tinne. The rest of us Residences are working with BalmHeal. Despite what you humans do, BalmHeal will not be forsaken and alone again." A note of exasperation came to T'Holly Residence's voice. "It was only its pride that kept it from reaching out for help until it was too late."

"A lesson for us all," Tinne said.

There was a second's silence. "Yes, a lesson for us all."

Then the Residence said, "But I would inform you that the tower rooms are now free of all storage items. The rooms are currently furnished with old pieces arranged in the way that you prefer. Between myself and the Turquoise House, we have moved the personal items you left there to that space, including your drums."

Tinne smiled and picked up the pace, until he was bounding up the stairs. "I'm glad I'm home, too. This calls for a celebration drumming." Better to say that than think of a despair drumming, or just plain drumming to let the pain out.

"I am sure that GreatLady D'Holly will realize that you were right to claim the rooms."

Jokes that Family understood. He was home. As a man.

* * *

Lahsin slept until late afternoon, rising just before sun-set. She and Strother and TQ had a good talk and dinner. She strolled with a cup of caff to the back window of the mainspace, which looked out on a flat grass yard of no distinction. She could . . . she found her shoulders had tensed and rolled them. No. She didn't want to rehabilitate another landscape that she'd leave. She'd been up front about that to TQ, and it had been cheerful about the comings and goings of occupants, unlike BalmHeal Residence. Guiltily she realized she liked TQ better already.

Guilt. It was like a huge, hard stone in her chest. There was no use pretending she hadn't killed a person. Again and again the moment when her hand hit T'Yew and he died replayed in her mind. SupremeJudge Ailim Elder was right. Living with that moment for the rest of her life would be punishment.

She felt even more guilt that she was glad the man was dead. She couldn't grieve for him, he'd been bad to her. Evil. Yet something inside her still told her it was wrong not to grieve for him. She shrugged again, shifting her shoulders, getting used to the lifelong burden of killing a man.

The Turquoise House coughed. It was a real cough, not some sort of soughing of wind through cracks in the house. "Yes?"

"There are many messages in your scry cache," it said.

Lahsin frowned. "Really?"

"Yes. Several from D'Sea. As part of your rehabilitation, the SupremeJudge has ordered counseling and mental Healing for six years or until you are through your Third Passage, whichever comes first." TQ sounded regretful.

Lahsin staggered to the couch. That was going to be expensive. She supposed she needed it, though. If she'd had counseling in the past, she might not be here, living with guilt. Might not have hurt T'Yew in the first place. She should have just run.

But she hadn't, and there was no going back. No matter how much she might regret her actions, there was no mending them.

"D'Sea would like the initial consultation tomorrow morning at WorkBell."

"Confirm," Lahsin forced herself to say.

"Confirmed with D'Sea Residence," TQ said.

"I'll need a map or teleportation visualizations."

"I'll take care of that," TQ said, then added, "your parents—"

"No!" Her voice was too sharp, she didn't care. "I don't want any messages from them." Surely, they'd had a hand in fashioning the events, as had T'Yew himself. The silence felt loud, and Lahsin thought she'd hurt TQ's feelings. "Thank you for telling me, but please erase all messages from the Burdocks unless it's my brother Clute." How was he feeling? Was he blaming himself for a bit of this tragedy, too? Or was Lahsin shifting guilt onto others? Thinking so much about the killing, because she was searching herself for more feeling than she had?

"Please inform T'Burdock Residence that I am considering disinheriting myself from the Family." Another tide of relief, that's what she wanted to do, whether or not it was "good."

"I'll do that," the Turquoise House said. "The next message is from HollyHeir, Holm."

Instant defensiveness. "Yes?"

"He has a banner Tinne Holly and I had requested for this space. Calligraphy." Holm probably wanted to talk about Tinne.

"He can deliver it tomorrow when I'm at D'Sea's."

"Very well."

Strother came in from the kitchen where he'd been testing the no-time food units. He crossed to Lahsin and put his head on her knee, looked at her with concerned eyes. *You are sad.*

"I don't know what I am."

The man attacked you.

"Yes."

You fought back, and he died. Why do you feel sad?

"He wouldn't have killed me." Not her body, but her spirit? Hadn't he wounded that already?

He would have hurt you.

"Yes."

Again and again.

"Yes."

Until you made him stop.

"Yes." She couldn't see any law, any FirstFamilies Council, any GreatLord or GreatLady preventing T'Yew from doing as he pleased with her.

Then what happened was inevitable.

"Yes."

So stop thinking about it.

"Easier said than done, but you comfort me. Will you come with me to D'Sea's tomorrow morning?"

Of course.

"Thank you. Turquoise House?"

"Yes, Lahsin?"

"I'd like to see a holo show. Do you have any recent ones?"

"I have *The Silver Hand*, starring the actor who gave me my voice, Raz Cherry," TQ said proudly. "It's very long."

Lahsin recalled that Raz Cherry was extremely handsome and not at all like Tinne Holly. "Let's see it," she said.

*T*inne spent hours drumming in his new sitting room. His memory of the day unrolled, and he pounded out his emotions as he'd felt them. Fury at T'Yew's attack; pride then shock when Lahsin defended herself and killed T'Yew. A slow thumping rising in volume and increasing in beat at the questioning.

His realization that he loved Lahsin was expressed with hard, joyful beats—the rhythm of a fast heart.

Her stricken look as she doubted him, understood that there were more circumstances surrounding his time with her than he'd told her.

Hurt. That look she'd given him as if he'd lied. Nothing with her was a lie, but he couldn't tell her that. She wouldn't listen or believe him.

Their link had narrowed again, through it he sensed her lost loneliness, her confusion, her own hurt at the way events had turned out, and he wasn't there to help her. Grief.

She wasn't here to help him. He repeated Lark's words over and over; they, too, became a drumming pattern. Lahsin would come to him. It was only a matter of time, but when?

Meanwhile he felt like he had a fatal wound but was still walking around, leaving a trail of dripping blood behind him.

Thirty-six
❦

O*ver the next two weeks counseling helped Lahsin.*
Strother did, too, as did Clute, who'd extended his time in
Druida. Her brother didn't press her to meet with her parents.
She thought he was mostly estranged from them himself.

D'Sea had not used distance Flair to set the killing far in
the past, that was something Lahsin would have to work
through herself, according to the SupremeJudge. But Lahsin's
memories of her marriage *had* been distanced, and much of
the emotional resonance removed. It seemed to have happened
to another person. She wasn't the same person she'd been before her Second Passage.

Lahsin had not spoken of Tinne or of her time in First-
Grove. Those memories came back beautiful or painful or
bittersweet.

T*inne drummed every night, and his Family commented*
on how pleased they were that he'd moved to the tower. They
left him alone and were supportive, and his father and brother
challenged him to sparring matches more often. He was glad
about that.

He'd consulted with Mitchella D'Blackthorn about decorating his new suite, and it became comfortable. Nothing re-

minded him of Genista. That hurt was an ache in the bottom of his heart.

Oddly enough, Mitchella had advised restructuring rooms just outside his tower on two floors to connect with it, making it into a suite for his HeartMate. She had plans for tinting the walls, murals and holos, furnishings, but Tinne told her to keep the decorating to a minimum, Lahsin would like to do it herself. He did approve restructuring a back room into a sunroom, opening onto an area that could be made into a garden.

He learned to live in the moment, one septhour at a time, focusing entirely on being the best he could for each septhour. He was at the top of his form and his energy and his Flair.

He still felt like he was leaking blood from a slow, mortal wound. But he had no more dreams of falling, and that was good.

One night when he'd settled down to sleep, sobbing filled his head. He sat up. *Lahsin?* Could she be as unhappy as he?

No answer. He opened the link between them and found her sleeping soundly . . . too soundly to be natural, and he saw the faint aura of a Healer's spell around her.

Ilexa was never sad enough to weep, besides, she was prowling the storerooms, choosing finishing touches for her room.

Sighing and rising to his feet, Tinne stretched, then marched over to the simple brass scrybowl. He ran a finger around the rim, "Turquoise House."

The water glowed blue green. "Here, Tinne. How can I help?"

It didn't sound as if TQ was crying. "How's my HeartMate?"

"Well. She chose a more feminine room than yours."

That hurt a little. He rolled his shoulders. "Thank you. Please take care of her, TQ."

"I will do my best." TQ throbbed with pride.

"Thank you. Later."

"Later."

He could still hear the crying. *Strother?* he projected, not quite sure of the strength of his bond with the dog.

Here, Tinne Holly.

Are you well?

I am exploring our neighborhood, an interesting area. I am very well.

Good to hear. Let me know if I can help you, or Lahsin, in any way.

Thank you.

Tinne rubbed his face, listened to the quiet weeping, checked every tendril to all his Family. Everyone was asleep.

Except him.

Finally, he found a big, cushy chair and sank into it, opening himself entirely. *Who cries? Who needs help?*

A choked gasp-sob, a tiny uncertain voice. *It is I.*

Tinne didn't recognize the person. *Who?*

BalmHeal Residence. It was a woman's voice, not the sour old man's Tinne was used to. *I have been abandoned again, and I will be forgotten again. This time I think I might die.*

No! Lahsin and I promised that will not be so.

You are not here. Now the grumpy oldster was back. *I even had a plan, and you did not listen.*

Events moved too rapidly.

BalmHeal Residence snorted.

Tinne stared at his very own bedsponge in his very own rooms and sighed. *I'll be right there.*

I will open my spellshields for you to teleport.

As soon as he'd landed, the Residence said, "I am alone again." The creaking of wood around him was a whispered despair.

"I'm here."

"But you will not stay. Not even for the night."

"No." He hadn't been back since the morning after Lahsin's last Passage. His body yearned for the heat and herbs of the Healing pool, his mind wanted the comfort of it, but his heart knew there'd be another wrenching blow if he went there. He'd see Lahsin in every shadow.

"You, *both* of you, said you would help me." The wind wept through the windows.

"Do you have any suggestions?"

There was a few seconds of silence. "You will help?"

"If I can." He'd learned that helping someone else eased his own pain, distracted his mind from repeatedly probing hurt.

"I told *the girl*"—obviously the Residence was having as much a problem as Tinne in dealing with Lahsin's rejection—"that I could call those who have taken sanctuary within the walls of FirstGrove to come back."

That pricked his curiosity. "Come back?"

"Come back to visit me, or meet to discuss how I can be appeased."

That didn't sound good.

"I can close the doors to FirstGrove, make the walls solid." More a whiney scold than a deadly threat.

Tinne kept his reaction cool. "That would be a great pity. FirstGrove is needed. *You* are needed."

"Then we should find a solution to my loneliness."

"I promised, so I will."

"Easier with many minds working on the problem."

"Many?"

"I sense twenty individuals beyond my walls in Druida City who were once within. Including the one-without-Flair."

"You can 'call' them?"

"I know their patterns. Four of them spent time within my walls. Three are old. I can send my wishes by Flair, or words on the wind. Most are powerfully Flaired."

"Let me think." Tinne paced the great hall. It was well lit, clean, beautiful, but he'd glimpsed its original appearance in Lahsin's mind. Grungy, gray with dust, deserted. "You have a good plan. Call and see who comes."

"When?" The Residence sounded apprehensive.

"What about dawn?" Tinne envisioned twenty people hovering by the four entrances. "Wait . . . people can't teleport in—"

"Lahsin showed me how to modify my shields for those without desperate need, within my walls only, they can't go into the estate. I can hold the teleportation pad open for a septhour or so. When I 'call' I can send images." It was more enthusiastic.

"You could tell them they could be disguised. Wear masks or something if they want. That might bring you some more."

The Residence sighed. "How many do you think will come?"

Tinne shrugged. "I don't know."

"I would like to see some of them again," it said wistfully.

The Residence hadn't been as comatose as he and Lahsin had thought. Not if the Residence controlled the estate. One more reason to keep it active. The more the house deteriorated, the more FirstGrove would close. Tinne was determined that Druida should have a sanctuary. What would have happened to Lahsin if FirstGrove hadn't been available? He hated to think of it.

"I'll come before dawn and be here when you 'call.' But now my Family is waiting for me, I must go."

"Merry meet," the Residence whispered.

"And merry part and merry meet again!" Tinne emphasized the words. Then he 'ported home. To T'Holly Residence.

At dawn, *Tinne was back in the teleportation room of* BalmHeal Residence, listening to the "call."

Come to me, I need you. I call all who were once here. Come. I will die if I remain alone and lonely and abandoned.

Dramatic, but BalmHeal Residence used all the desperation it so often felt from others and sent it with its call.

Come to me. Teleport here. An excellent image of the teleportation pad. *Come secretly, come disguised or not. Come!*

A loud bell rang throughout the house. Tinne jumped.

"BalmHeal Residence," the house said. Tinne looked around.

"This is the starship *Nuada's Sword*. My Captain requested we call you to say he is on his way by fast stridebeast. Please ensure there is proper stabling for the creature."

Tinne stared. There had to be stables, but he didn't know where, or their condition. He cleared his throat, but the Residence answered, "Tell the Captain to put the beast in the westernmost room of the clocktower building. It smells of dog."

"Understood. Done." The ship signed off.

"That's good." Tinne infused his voice with cheer he didn't feel. "The Captain of *Nuada's Sword*, Ruis Elder, always has a different viewpoint." Since the man had no Flair, suppressed others' Flair, Tinne foresaw an uncomfortable time.

There was a slight pop, and an old woman, dressed in wild purple night robes, appeared on the teleportation pad. She rubbed her nose, cackled. "It's too cold in here, Residence, turn up the heat!" Then her sharp black eyes fixed on Tinne. "T'Holly's youngest. Not surprising. Is there caff and food?"

He gestured to the hallway. "The parlor, second left door."

She sniffed, nodded, and without introducing herself, marched out.

The teleportation pad became busy with other men and

women arriving, most staring at the room in wonder, as if they'd never been inside the Residence. Three had come cloaked and masked.

Pounding thundered at the front door. Tinne hurried to the great hall, noting the twelve people who'd arrived had settled in the parlor, slurping caff, none of them attending to the summons. He opened the door to Captain Ruis Elder and Cratag Maytree.

"Saw this guy on my ride," Elder said. "Took him up."

Maytree flexed his shoulders, stamped his feet. "Don't have enough Flair to 'port." He grimaced. "Don't much like riding, either." He looked around. "Nice."

Elder nodded. "Yes. I knew the house was here but have never been in it. Last I saw, it was covered in brambles."

"The meeting is to the right and down the hall. Follow the voices," Tinne said.

Then he *felt* Lahsin arrive and stilled. This would be hard.

*T*he call had insinuated itself into *Lahsin's* dreams. Bad dreams of the past with overwhelming desperation. When she woke, her cheeks were wet with tears.

Reluctantly she dressed and teleported to BalmHeal Residence. It looked great. *She'd* done this, restored it.

She hadn't wanted to come, knew Tinne was here and didn't want to think about him, about whether she'd been unfair and dishonorable. She was confused.

But BalmHeal Residence had *called* with Flair that touched the blood in her body, and she could not decline. She'd promised.

The moment she'd arrived, the link between her and Tinne blew wide open. She suffered his hurt, the burden of her rejection, and she snapped the bond as narrow as possible.

Something else froze her in the spot.

She heard voices.

Others were in the Residence.

More than one person, more than her and Tinne.

Not far away. So she walked to the parlor and counted sixteen people, having flatsweets and beverages. They were an odd assortment: one boy younger than herself, the starship Captain, Ruis Elder, and the Hawthorn guard, Cratag Maytree, who'd given her the information about FirstGrove. He tipped his head when he saw her.

Most were older than she, and three were disguised in enveloping robes and full head masks.

Tinne stepped forward. "The Residence needs a caretaker, preferably a caretaker Family, more than one person."

She heard no BalmHeal grumbles in her mind and was grateful.

People protested, all wanted to keep the sanctuary secret, with no one on the grounds.

"As you heard in your call, if we abandon the Residence, Druida will lose FirstGrove forever. It is not well done of us to ignore and forget the place that sheltered us in a bad time."

More discussion, then agreement, but varying opinions as to what should be done. Finally Cratag Maytree said, "Perhaps it should be a family with nothing to lose."

"Are you thinking a cursed Family?" Tinne asked. "I'd never allow a cursed Family to besmirch this sanctuary."

The oldest woman creaked an amused sigh. "Wonder what would prevail, a cursed Family or a blessed sanctuary."

"Beg pardon," said Tinne shortly. "But I don't think you understand what you said."

"Beg pardon," the old woman mocked, "but I do. I am the last cursebreaker living."

That shut everyone up.

Lahsin glanced at Cratag, he was frowning as if fumbling for some concept. She offered him a flatsweet. He took it absently, bit into it. He said, "Not a cursed Family, but maybe a disgraced one?"

Ruis Elder stopped lounging. "What are you thinking?"

Cratag chewed, swallowed, waved the flatsweet. "Was thinking of the newssheets, the stories they tell." He looked at Lahsin. "A dim, runaway girl escaping her older husband. That smears a Family." He shot Tinne a look. "A Family with political aspirations and a divorce scandal, many past scandals."

Lahsin stared, but Cratag had judged Tinne's temper better than she. Tinne's jaw clenched, his hands curled white over the wooden arms of the chair, but he didn't move.

"A Family with a null in it," Cratag continued.

"Nulls aren't quite as disreputable as they were," Ruis Elder said coolly.

Lahsin prayed Cratag wouldn't mention thieves or murderers. He didn't. He merely took another bite of flatsweet. But everyone's attention was focused on him and no one else spoke.

"Thing is," Cratag said, "D'Yew's pride has been pricked, but she doesn't see herself as ruined. She's the head of a FirstFamily GrandHouse; the Hollys are a FirstFamily Great-House, as are the Elders; Captain Elder, here, is the Captain of the last starship. None of you are lowly enough to want to leave Druida, not even to rusticate."

"Certainly not in the winter," Tinne said.

"Scandals come and go, every Family has them," the old lady said.

"Exactly," Cratag said. "But a Commoner Family, or middle class, or even lower Nobility might not think that way. A scandal touching one member of the Family can affect them all."

"Unless they cast off the offending member."

"Yes. So we're looking at some characteristics here that might give us a Family who would care for the Residence and FirstGrove. A disgraced Family." Cratag finished his flatsweet, wiped the crumbs from his mouth with his softleaf.

"Honorable," Tinne said. "They—each member—must be honorable. Whatever the scandal attached to the Family name, it must not be one regarding honor. The sanctuary must be protected, they must be discreet and honorable enough to keep secrets." He smiled. "Even lie to keep the secrets."

"There are also perceived scandals, rumors, slanders, and beliefs about a Family that are untrue. A Family suffering such a fate would be an excellent choice," the old woman said.

"Flair," Ruis said. "The Family must have great Flair. Even now the Residence becomes uncomfortable at my presence, and spells will have to be rewoven." He dipped his head to Lahsin.

"I'll see to it," she said.

"If one of the members, or the Family itself had a Healing strain in their bloodlines, it would be good," said one of the cloaked ones, a female older than herself, Lahsin guessed. She wondered if that woman, too, had been abused. Were all three of the cloaked people abused women, or children now adult?

"A disgraced Family, of more than one member, a loving

Family who sticks together, a Family with great Flair, an honorable Family." The old woman ticked off the list on her fingers. "Each person to make a Vow of Honor of secrecy."

"I think," came a high voice of a man, another cloaked person, "I know such a Family."

"Who?" chorused several.

"The Mugworts."

Babel hit. "They are Cross Folk."

"They experimented with pylor."

"They might have had associations with the black cult!"

The man who spoke originally lifted a delicate hand with long fingers and well-shaped nails. "No! First, only the Lady is of the Cross Folk persuasion. Second, they had a couple of incense sticks with a trace amount of pylor in them, currently available from any candle shop." The man shrugged. "I'd imagine most of our households would have the same in a storage drawer. Third, GraceLord Mugwort was a circuit judge, this has ruined his career. The Family is in desperate straits and are packing to leave Druida, but they are not a wealthy Family." Lahsin thought she saw a flash of teeth. "They may show up here in FirstGrove."

"How many of them are there?" asked the old woman.

"The immediate Family? Four. The Lord and Lady and two daughters, one sixteen and one twelve. The Mugwort line itself is close to dying out, the Lord has no elders or siblings. GraceLady Mugwort's Family, the Ginsengs, have disinherited her."

"The Ginsengs have much old BalmHeal blood in them," the Residence said. "Good Healers. I would accept them if they have such Flair."

"All the Family has exceptional Flair. Tinne, you might ask T'Ash about the testing of the two daughters. The Lady and her oldest daughter have excellent Healing skills. The Lord is honorable. They are HeartMates, so the Lady is honorable, too, since that would be necessary for him. He has instilled high values in his children."

"You seem to know a great deal about them," the old woman said suspiciously.

The man shrugged.

There was murmuring, but no resolution.

Ruis Elder stood. "I must leave before I affect you all, the

Residence, and the estate with my nullness. Why don't we make inquiries in the next two days about the Mugworts then send a vote pebble to the Turquoise House cache box. White for approaching and accepting the Mugworts as a Family for the Residence, black for not." He bowed to Lahsin. "Gentle-Lady Rosemary will tally the votes and relay the information to GreatSir Holly." Now Elder bowed to Tinne. "Whom I thank for taking charge of this task."

Another cackle from the old woman, who grabbed a couple of flatsweets, stashed them in her cloak, and bit into another. "We'll cast our minds back to older scandals that might have impoverished a family." She munched the flatsweet. "One thing's for certain, if there isn't a scandal in the past, there's always one just around the corner."

Lahsin raised her voice in protest at having to deal with Tinne, but no one heard as they all gathered together and made their way back to the teleportation room, talking all the while.

Tinne looked at her with grief in his eyes. "You know it's illegal for me to inform you I'm your HeartMate, Lahsin."

She glanced aside, she'd forgotten that in her wallowing.

"I'm sorry I hurt your feelings. I wish I hadn't." He inclined his head. "But I have not offered you a HeartGift, or courted you, and I won't. Come to me when you're ready." He became brisk as he turned away from her. "Just count the markers and have TQ relay a message to me, but from what I've heard tonight, the Mugworts sound like a good choice."

Soon everyone had departed. Not even the Residence spoke to her. All was silent.

Thirty-seven

❧

*T*inne stood outside the gate of the Turquoise House and looked across the courtyard to where it glowed. It seemed satisfied with itself, growing into maturity. Just as Lahsin had. They suited each other, better than he had suited the place.

But he'd helped its development, had helped Lahsin. He could take pride in that.

He'd received a scry from TQ that the majority of those at the meeting had approved of offering the Mugworts the Balm-Heal caretaking position. Notes of research results had been included, testifying to the honor and decency of the Family, and not problems. Tinne had crafted a Vow of Honor for the four that Ruis Elder and his wife, SupremeJudge Ailim Elder, had approved.

He'd just come from speaking to the Mugworts under a secrecy spell. The relief that had flowed from them had been nearly overwhelming. They were pitifully grateful for the opportunity, and all had eagerly sworn Vows of Honor to care for BalmHeal Residence and safeguard it and the estate. They would interfere in no way with people who entered, unless those wished help.

Tinne had wanted to talk to Lahsin about it, missed discussing matters with her. Anything regarding FirstGrove and

BalmHeal Estate was not something he could speak to many about. Furthermore, she'd promised to key the spellshields individually to each Mugwort and the Family in general, so he'd wanted to tell her to meet them at the northern door at RetireBell.

But she wasn't here. TQ had excitedly told him Lahsin was out procuring supplies for a ritual to spellshield its House-Heart. So Tinne had left a message.

Lady and Lord, he hurt! Every minute was a struggle to endure. How could he have fallen in love again so fast? Except now that he looked back at his marriage, he saw that it had been over much longer than he'd believed.

He wanted Lahsin more than he'd ever wanted anything else in his life. More than he'd wanted to survive when the lifeboat had crashed. He'd had his brother then and had known they'd prevail. Now he wasn't sure he could make it another day without her.

Didn't that sound desperate! He snorted an ironic laugh. Here he was languishing outside his lover's, his HeartMate's, home. He wouldn't come back here, or go to FirstGrove.

Of course he wouldn't die without her. He'd continue to put one foot in front of the other, keep going until he found some emotional balance, then walk that tightrope of balance until he built habit and might someday find contentment in his daily life.

He would survive, live the best he could one septhour at a time.

But the agony wouldn't be going away soon.

*D*ressed in a flowing white ritual robe, *Lahsin* opened the hidden door that led to the Turquoise House's new House-Heart.

She'd assured Mitchella D'Blackthorn and the Turquoise House that she could work a full spellshield on it, and was told that even more was necessary. The House was willing to let her touch the HeartStones that held its personality and memory and being. She was to protect them and the new HouseHeart. It was a great honor that made her nervous. She'd boosted existing spells, revived and revamped the ancient BalmHeal ones, but had never created brand-new ones. This would be a true test of her Flair.

She walked through the passageway started by moles and finished by a machine from the starship. The moles probably knew where all the HouseHearts were located and didn't have much contact with people. The machine had no memory bank to keep any information about the project. The HouseHeart had already been decorated according to its own specifications by Mitchella D'Blackthorn. The HeartStones and space had been consecrated by the high priestess and priest of GreatCircle Temple. Lahsin would provide the spellshields. Both she and Mitchella had consented to memory-dimming spells. In a week, she wouldn't recall much about the House-Heart or details of the HeartStones.

For now she said a blessing and the simple opening spell before the door and took off her shoes. Then she stepped into the room and was impressed. Each wall had a different holosphere mural, which would eventually sink into the wall itself and become permanent. The north wall showed a profusion of exotic plants surrounding a turquoise pool where animals had gathered. "Gorgeous," Lahsin said.

"It is a garden in the Southern Continent," TQ said.

"Very beautiful." She smiled as she saw one of the animals was Strother. There was a small creamy pinkish tomcat and an elegant-looking fox. Then light brightened as if the sun rose, and flowers opened. Lahsin stood and stared. As she did, figures projected from the trees. She recognized Mitchella D'Blackthorn and her son, Antenn, several years younger than he was now. There was Tinne . . . and herself! Hand in hand. She swallowed.

"All my residents whom I can recall," the House said proudly.

"Ah, yes." Lahsin turned away.

The west wall showed the rolling tide on Maroon Beach south of Druida. As she looked at it, Lahsin became aware of the sound of the surf that permeated the room like its own pulsing heartbeat. The south wall was a huge stone fireplace, the opening nearly as tall as she. Crackling flames gave even more comfort. She went to the wall and touched a roughened stone slab. Real. Held out her hands to the fire. Definitely real. Near the right corner was a tall storage frame for the wood.

"I wanted a real fire," TQ said.

"You got it."

"Yes. Other Residences told me they have a special feature, most built by their Family to reflect certain characteristics or nature. Since I don't have a Family yet, I chose for myself."

"You did very well."

"Thank you. Mitchella said so, too, and she is the best at decorating. I have ambience and atmosphere."

"You certainly do."

"Or maybe it's atmosphere and ambience."

She turned and saw the wall that held the door. The wall was a pale silkeen of yellow with bright red and blue flowers, in each corner was a tree with branches flowing in a gentle wind. Chimes stirred gently. She stopped and stared.

"I saw this pattern in your head when you were talking to me mentally about BalmHeal Residence. I liked it very much," the Turquoise House said.

Lahsin swallowed. "I recognize the old paper in the great hall." How much could residential entities read minds?

"It was a strong impression," the Turquoise House said. "I liked it. And I wanted my own Fam."

"Your own Fam?" She still mulled over its previous words.

"Look closely." Humor laced the House's tones.

She studied the wall. There, off to one side, sat a holographic cat. It was a small gray and white tabby with some red and blue tinting to blend in with the pattern.

"My FamCat will be with me forever. I have already given her a little memory and information on cat habits. She may begin to move in a decade or two—"

The House certainly sounded like it had accepted the truths of its existence, had become an adult just as Lahsin had.

"—and right now she is the best of FamCats, she doesn't speak!" The house chuckled.

Lahsin smiled.

Then the fire died. She whirled. "Why—"

My HeartStones are in the corner of the fireplace.

"Oh."

The small round ones are my original HeartStones, the larger piece of obsidian Tinne gifted to me as a new Heart-Stone. It will contain much information and conducts thought well.

"Oh." Lahsin looked in, saw five pebbles and a shiny black rock with sharp edges that was roughly pyramidical.

They are not too hot. They are safe from the fire . . . and everyone else.

"Excellent deterrent."

Thank you.

She bent a little, the thick hearth was hot on her soles. Mind-speaking was more secure. *Can you cool this area so I can get your stones? Then we'll begin the shielding.*

Yes.

It only took a moment before the fireplace emanated a chill instead of warmth.

Thank you. After I shield the stones I can do more spells on the fireplace, then you can light the fire, and I'll work a spellshield to blend with the fire and the heat. So if a thief or intruder tries to harm you, you can burn them.

The House made a shocked noise.

"You are allowed to fight and hurt someone who is trying to hurt you," she said firmly.

I have already harmed one who harmed me. The words were barely a whisper in her head.

"So have I. We're alike that way, and we had no choice, did we?"

No.

She reached and scooped up the pebbles. When she grasped the obsidian it slipped a little and sliced her. She watched as her blood slicked down her hand and a couple of drops dripped into the corner.

Another odd sound from the House.

She said, *This will make my spellshields even more powerful*, but knew that memory of this place, gone or not, she'd be linked with the House as long as she lived.

The HeartStones felt odd in her hands, humming, alive. She swallowed again, went to the altar, and set them upon it. She prayed and drew on her Flair and bespelled them individually, then as a unit, then replaced them in their corner and put ash over them. The House sighed in her mind. Next she touched the inner walls of the fireplace, felt the blessing of the priestess and priest, smiled as she wove a spell to work with the blessing and safeguard the stones.

She stepped away from the fireplace, watched the fire ignite and rise again, put a couple of logs on it, and shielded the wall.

Finally it was time for the true test of her Flair, to fashion a spellshield for the entire House.

She had just enough Flair to complete the project. She drew in a long breath, leaned against the wall next to the door, and thought she felt the slight brush of the holographic cat's fur. Visualizing the layers of the spell that would shield the House from the inside out, with the strongest here in the HouseHeart, she set her hands against the wall and summoned her Flair.

She sent spells once, thrice, a dozen times through the House, until it was encased in a glittering diamond sheen in her mind's eye. Impenetrable, protected.

Lahsin let her knees collapse and crawled, panting, over to a large fat cushion by the fire and let the heat dry her skin.

"You have made me very, very beautiful!" the House sang. "Come outside and look!"

After she'd cleaned up and changed, she went out and stared at the House. The Turquoise House was permanently that deep color and shiny like it had been fired in enamel.

"Lovely," SupremeJudge Ailim Elder said, walking up.

Lahsin tensed and pasted a smile on her face. "Thank you."

A corner of Elder's mouth quirked. "I believe T'Ash has requested full Residence spellshields, too?"

"Yes."

"It will be interesting to see his reaction to having his pale yellow armourcrete Residence shiny as the inside of an egg."

"Maybe it won't turn out like this," Lahsin said doubtfully.

They studied the House, met each other's eyes, and chuckled. Knowing her duty, Lahsin said, "Please come in for a hot drink." The day was bright, but cold, another snowstorm was on the way.

Ailim Elder shook her head. "Thank you, no. I wanted to inform you that D'Yew contested my actions and verdict with regard to her father's death."

Stomach tightening, Lahsin wished *she* had a nice warm drink in her hands. Preferably with alcohol. "Oh."

"A panel of three judges examined the matter and agreed with me." Ailim smiled. "I know the law, and I'm a telempath, my rulings are rarely overturned. This is not one of those times."

Breath she hadn't realized she was holding whooshed from Lahsin.

The SupremeJudge's brows knit a little. "Then the First-Families Council got into the act."

"Of course. Politics. Alliances."

"Of course," Ailim sighed. "*They* scrutinized my actions, but they, too, are careful around me." Steel laced her tones. "The vote for accepting the verdict of accidental death was unanimous. D'Yew was not allowed to vote."

"Oh."

"D'Yew could be a vengeful, unpleasant enemy."

"I know." No one knew better.

"But I wanted to update you, especially since some articles will be in the newssheets."

"Thank you." She curtsied.

Ailim inclined her head. "You are most welcome." She glanced at the Turquoise House and shook her head, smiling. "Merry meet."

"And merry part," Lahsin said automatically.

"And merry meet again. You'll be getting an invitation to the annual open house and report on the state of *Nuada's Sword.*"

"Thank you." She didn't know if she'd go. Last year had been hideous.

"Better get in, the weather's changing," Ailim said, lifting a hand before she teleported away.

T*he next day Lahsin sat in a huge, soft chair looking out* the mainspace window at heaps of drifted snow. Neither she nor the House knew the proper spells for snow removal or patio and courtyard drying and maintenance. The House had dithered until Lahsin said that she liked the look of it. And the quiet.

She was more used to the quiet of her own thoughts now. Burdock Residence had been crowded and shabby and noisy, T'Yew Residence cold and quiet and formal, First-Grove empty.

If she extended her Flair she could sense the other minor Nobles and upper-middle-class people who lived in the large homes around her, or the passing of the PublicCarrier on the street. She liked the feeling of being among but not with others.

Under the sun, the snow was white and pretty and un-threatening. Pristine. Like her future.

She'd keyed the spellshields of FirstGrove to the members of the Mugwort Family with great success. Letting the spellshields of the estate walls flood her had been soothing, seeing the intricacy of their pattern was awesome. She'd never create such shields.

She was still allowed into the estate. She thought she always would be. Despite the mind Healers and the spiritual counseling and Healing of a priestess and priest of the Lady and Lord, she had a deep scar in her for killing T'Yew. She'd hated him and had killed him and couldn't know if her Flair would have been so strong in the blow if he'd been anyone else.

Though Taxa D'Yew hadn't openly called "feud" against Lahsin, hatred burned in her gaze, acid in her words. Lahsin had a deadly enemy for as long as one of them lived. The newssheets had wrung every moment of sensation from the story. Lahsin had the ironic feeling that now the scandal of the Burdocks and Yews might be as encompassing as the Hollys' recent problems.

She couldn't help but think of Tinne often. Now the shock had worn off and life had inevitably gone on, she knew her first thoughts of what he'd done were wrong. But she still couldn't bear to admit them. If she did, she'd have to decide to act on the HeartMate bond.

A bird chirped, and there was a whir of feathers. A flock scrabbled for purchase on a fountain rim Lahsin had filled with food last night. Snow made her footsteps vague dents.

The landscape outside was as pristine as her new life. Her brother had asked her to live with him and his wife, but Lahsin didn't want to move to Gael City. She could stay in the Turquoise House for five years, the payment for her spellshields.

She was still awed at the amount of gilt she could command. Her spellshields had been tested and withstood several attacks from FirstFamily GreatLords. Only when six had banded together had her weakest fallen—and she'd learned how to strengthen that weak point.

Since the FirstFamily Residences were sprawling manors or actual castles, Lahsin didn't have the energy to form shields on more than one a month, and her fees and stipend from the NobleCouncil reflected that. Three FirstFamily Residences a year were paid for by her annual NobleGilt. The rest of the Families would have to wait for next year—and show up on her doorstep at the first of the year to request the free services—or they would pay her or trade services with her.

T'Ash had been the first to ask for her, and she'd already spellshielded his home, and it hadn't turned out yolk yellow. Shiny, but not a deeper color. T'Ash Residence was much newer than most others. Only the size and the fact that D'Ash had occasional Fam Healing emergencies had made the job difficult. She'd done T'Ash's shop, too, and been paid for that.

In two years, when she finished all the FirstFamily Residences, she would be a wealthy woman, and no doubt would have allies, too. If she stayed in Druida, but the pressure of the FirstFamilies was on her to stay and shield their homes. Except for D'Yew Residence. It was a little nugget of pleasure to know that soon that mighty Residence would be the least secure of all the great houses. She'd heard Taxa was looking for a husband to ensure the Family line.

Great Residences and FirstFamilies and NobleGilt and a title of her own, when she decided who she wanted to be. GrandLady . . . what?

She didn't know.

Her thoughts cycled to Tinne. He'd finished helping the Mugworts with their move to their new Family home, Balm-Heal Residence. Their Vows of Honor were in place. The moment an individual broke that promise, the estate would banish them and knowledge of the location would disappear from their mind.

That Tinne could still easily enter FirstGrove was due to her, Lahsin thought. Another guilt laid upon her shoulders, one that shadowed her emotions about him.

She remembered his hands on her body, and a ripple of pure sensuality throbbed through her. If she followed her body's needs, she'd be 'porting to T'Holly Residence in a second. A chuckle caught in her throat. Her body had had no needs until Tinne Holly had awakened them in her.

The birds flew away, and the sun went behind the clouds, and suddenly the yard was cold and gray.

Thirty-eight

❤

Lahsin couldn't sleep. For three days she'd stayed inside TQ. She'd wanted to go out but hadn't wanted to talk with people. She was restless, couldn't settle.

Her body was achy. She'd been practicing the first patterns Tinne had taught her, and her self-defense moves, but she was sure she was doing some of them wrong.

He didn't scry.

He didn't come by to see her.

No one else's company would please her. She wanted Tinne. He'd shocked and misled and hurt her, but not deliberately. And wasn't she being a fool in not claiming such a lover?

But she hadn't wanted to go from parents' house to husband's house and never be independent. She was seventeen. If she went to Tinne, she'd be with him the rest of her life, live in T'Holly Residence.

Was loving him, being a HeartMate, a prison or true freedom?

She'd be part of a couple who'd die within a year of each other, that scared her, too. Did the benefits outweigh the problems? She didn't know.

She didn't know much, except that she was tired of herself, and if she was tired of herself she wasn't doing something right. It wasn't anyone's job to amuse her or please her or give her life meaning except herself. If she felt a lack, it was in *herself* and *she* had to fix it.

Except Tinne would amuse her and please her and give her life meaning if she went to him, just by being himself.

Muttering under her breath, she addressed TQ. "Do you have any divination devices here?"

"Of course. I have a bag of ancient runes; two sets of cards, holo and flat; a pendulum; and divination dice. I could call GreatLord T'Vine for a consultation?"

No, not Vinni T'Vine. What he said could be all too true, could not be ignored. "The dice," she decided.

"In the lower cabinet under the scrybowl."

"Thank you." She got the bag, deep purple and embroidered with sigils that were on the dice themselves. Luck. Inward. The Lady. Listen. HeartMate. The pouch hummed with Flair, the dice within were potent. "They're cleansed?"

"No one has used them yet," TQ said.

"Ah, all right."

"There's a spiritual cleansing bowl to put them in after each use. The one made of glisten with the proper symbols."

Lahsin got that and set it on a table. She poured the dice out. They were made of polished stones in all the colors of the rainbow. Gathering them in both hands, she sent them energy, whispered a prayer. "Lady and Lord bless these dice and this reading and me. Please be true. Tell me what to do."

She tumbled them from her hands. Three separated.

Be True to Yourself.

Change.

Follow Your Heart.

Strother came in and saw the dice before she could hide them. She didn't know if he understood them. He'd been dropping hints about Tinne for days.

Be true to herself. Who *was* she? Lahsin Rosemary, who had a great Flair for shields. What did she need? Tinne.

Change. The time spent in FirstGrove had been the only stable time she'd had lately, and even then she'd been in the midst of Passage. Continue to change? She hadn't finished growing, didn't ever want to stop growing mentally, emotionally, spiritually. The greatest change and risk would be to go to Tinne, accept him as her HeartMate and the Hollys as her Family. Lose her independence. Which she wasn't valuing right now.

Follow Your Heart. Oh, yes, she knew what that meant. Her heart yearned for Tinne. Time and again throughout the day she'd check their bond. She was ever aware of it.

She paced the mainspace. She could ignore the dice and her Flair that had imbued them. Or not.

Finally she swept the dice back into the bag, put them in the glisten bowl, and covered them with the top.

"Thank you, Turquoise House. For everything."

Strother yipped and wagged his tail.

She strode to her room and took out the scruffy, much-mended sack she'd escaped T'Yew Residence with. The only thing holding it together was her spellshields. She rubbed her hands on her trous legs, which were equally shabby. She hadn't gone shopping, hadn't thought of it. No one had seemed to care what she was wearing.

The bag held her drum, and she could see the shadow of it in the bottom, and her hands tingled. She still didn't have much to put in the sack. A change of clothes, the gilt T'Ash had given her for her wedding necklace. He'd told her he'd ship it to a shop in far Chinju across the ocean. Someone would buy it and bless it and cherish it. It only meant pain to her.

She'd need all her courage to walk up to T'Holly Residence and request admittance with only the sack containing a few possessions and her ugly but lovable Fam.

Your HeartGift. Strother panted beside her.

She hadn't forgotten it. Quite. She *reached* out, found it in the BalmHeal greenhouse, naturally invisible to everyone except her and Tinne. She 'ported there, felt the lustful heat of the HeartGift, slapped a spellshield on it, and murmured an anti-grav couplet. Then she 'ported back to TQ's pad, sat down hard for a couple of minutes, breathing raggedly. That had been a long trip, but had used up some of her nervous energy.

She hauled her HeartGift back to her bedroom—no, the bedroom she'd been staying in. What rooms would she have at T'Holly Residence? Would she share them with Tinne? She had to stop and sit and put her head between her legs for an instant at the thought. She clutched her fists between her breasts. This was the right thing to do, following her heart, but it was scary. Then she wrapped her other tunic over the pot, around the plants and the holly being trained over the heart-shaped lattice.

"You're packing," the Turquoise House said.

Though it had been said in a calm, adult tone, Lahsin winced. "Yes. I'm leaving, I'm sorry."

"I will be fine. I've had GreatLord Muin T'Vine here."

Lahsin shoved the last of her jars in her sack. "Really?"

"Yes. He did a prophecy for *me*." The House sounded justifiably proud.

She sat on the bed. "I'm fascinated, what did he say?"

"He said that though it might be many years before my true Family finds me, I will always have new and interesting people staying with me to amuse me and help me grow."

"What a lovely fate!" Her stomach knotted. She hoped she, too, was on her way to a lovely fate. She swallowed. How could she truly know? She stopped, thought, then carefully studied the glowing bond between herself and Tinne, examining it mentally, emotionally. It looked strong. She missed the House's words, though she caught the reference to Tinne. "What was that?"

"I learned from Mitchella that I was an entity in my own right, and how to be beautiful. I learned from Tinne how a young man lives and about honor and promises—"

"Of course." Lahsin wet her lips, "You learned from me?"

"Of course," it echoed. "I learned how a young woman lives and that I will not need Passages to grow strong in my Flair and that I will never be a victim again."

It was like a gong went off in her head. She *had* continued to act like a victim, allowed her past with T'Yew to define her, and destroy—no, postpone—her happiness. She had given his dead ideas power over her, had let Taxa's spite infuse her to the point of questioning herself. She stiffened her spine. No more.

She had survived her Second Passage and found herself. She had a lover, a HeartMate, a future with him.

"I'll miss you," she said to the Turquoise House. "But I'll come back to visit."

Strother yipped, grinning. *We go to T'Holly Residence now.*

"Yes."

Good.

"I will miss you, too, Lahsin Rosemary Holly. All my former people visit me. Except Antenn. But he will come someday."

She cleared her throat. "I'm sure."

"Mitchella told me what to do now. I am to call the All Councils clerk and tell her that I am ready for a new tenant and that they should send me some people to interview."

"You'll do great!" Lahsin jumped to her feet. "And so will I." She knotted her sack and slid it onto her shoulder, tangled her fingers into Strother's fur. "So will we."

When she opened the front door, the Turquoise House said, "Merry meet."

"Merry part," Lahsin said.

"And merry meet again." It closed the door after her when she left. With a shaky breath, she went to a corner of the courtyard and glanced down at Strother. "I think we can teleport to that area just inside Noble Country. All right with you?"

Yes. He turned his head for a last look at the Turquoise House. *An interesting place. Now we go to T'Holly Residence. We will have our own rooms?*

Her stomach began to pitch at definite plans. She clutched the sack. "I don't know, but I heard Tinne has moved into the small tower attached to the west wing. We'll have rooms there."

Strother heaved a sigh. *It will be difficult living with all those cats.* But his gaze was soft on hers, he licked her hand. *But I will manage. I love you.*

She petted him. "You're bigger than all of them, and I love you, too."

With one last mental check that the teleportation area was empty, she took them there.

*T*he walk to T'Holly Residence was long enough to have her nerves twanging. People stared, Lahsin heard snatches of comments—some condemnatory, some approving. She didn't like the attention, but it was a pilgrimage she thought she had to make. She'd run away and hidden for too long. That child was gone. Now she was a woman, an adult, and knew her own mind.

She wanted to be loved by her HeartMate.

She wanted a Family.

It surprised her that it would be a FirstFamily, but that's how the wheel of fate had turned.

Strother coursed ahead, and she smiled as she felt his great joy in being able to openly run and bark and play.

They turned down a street bordered by high walls, and Lahsin sensed scrystones recording them. She inhaled deeply and smelled the sea, but knew enough about T'Holly Residence that it didn't have an outlet to the beach. T'Yew's had, but they considered the beach dirty. Or only for T'Yew and Taxa.

As Lahsin and Strother approached T'Holly Residence, the tingle of old, strong spellshields slid over her skin. She'd make them the best on Druida. The greeniron gates were three times her height and very wide. When she and her Fam were a couple of meters from the gates, they swung outward and open.

All the way open.

Lahsin gulped but steadily walked through. The gates closed behind her. The gliderway was long. In the distance the tall, forbidding gray castle thrust into the sky, every stone proclaiming it a Warrior Family fortress.

They rounded the last curve of the drive, and Lahsin hesitated. There were three—three!—Gatehouses, and the Hollys that staffed them saluted then followed her. The whole Family had turned out, they stood staggered on sharply rising steps. T'Holly and D'Holly stood on the top step, holding hands. Just below them, also with fingers entwined, were Holm Holly and his wife, Lark. Holm wore a floral wreath on his head, and that made Lahsin blink. Then she sensed Lark had made Holm the wreath and her hold tightened on her own HeartGift. Interesting that she and Lark both had creative Flair that included flowers.

Her mind was gibbering. This was going to be more difficult than she'd anticipated.

But she had been the one to repudiate their love, so she was the one who had to bend her pride.

She just hadn't realized it would be before so many people.

Tinne stood at the bottom of the steps, waiting for her. Ilexa sat regally by his side, her tail curled over her paws.

Strother walked softly beside Lahsin.

Deep breathing. This is what *she* wanted. *Her* decision.

Keeping her eyes on Tinne, she marched the last few meters and stopped within his reach—she knew his reach exactly.

"I . . ." Her voice wobbled, and she hated that. Her throat tightened, and her mouth dried so that she didn't think she could speak at all. *Coward!* But she had the crazy notion that everyone would stay just as they were until she said something, and she didn't think she could do it.

But she could do something else. She unwrapped her pitiful tunic, showing the three-dimensional heart-shaped holly plant, rich with plump red berries.

A rumble of approval rolled from the crowd, making her shoulders tense.

She lifted the potted plant, met Tinne's gaze for the first time. His eyes were dark and showed hurt . . . and love.

Emotions spun between them. She let their bond expand, pulse with love.

With desire.

Heat flushed her, and more murmurings rose. She thrust the pot in Tinne's direction and found her voice. "My Heart-Gift!" Again a surge of Flair betrayed her. Her voice was so loud she thought all of Noble Country could hear her words. She lifted her chin. "My HeartGift for Tinne Holly, my HeartMate."

Cheers rang out.

But Tinne didn't move. He'd closed his eyes.

Her courage began to crumble.

She wouldn't let it!

This time her voice cracked, just like she'd known it would. "Please take it, Tinne."

He opened his lashes, and his eyes looked damp.

Clearing his throat, he took the plant in one hand, swept the other arm around her waist, and pulled her close. "I accept your HeartGift."

There was another cheer, and Lahsin sensed this sound, too, could be heard throughout Noble Country.

His arm trembled behind her waist, and he urged her up the steps, the Family parting for them.

Lark took Lahsin's limp hands. An immediate connection formed, a new friend, wives of the Holly sons. "Welcome to the Family, Lahsin," Lark said.

Holm kissed her cheek.

Then they stepped aside, and she was facing the older Hollys. The GreatLord and GreatLady themselves.

Her knees went weak, and Tinne's arm strengthened behind her. He was solid and wonderful.

Her HeartMate.

Tears rolled down D'Holly's face. "Oh, my baby's found his HeartMate." She pressed a hand to her chest. "Oh." Then she enveloped Lahsin in a fragrant hug.

T'Holly's eyes were wet, too. He kissed her. "Welcome to the Family."

Tab winked.

Everyone surrounded them, smiling.

D'Holly said, "I told you all that she was a wise woman and wouldn't wait too long."

People pushed forward, wanting to be introduced. Lahsin promptly forgot all their names. After a few minutes of milling around they still hadn't reached the great hall. Strother was being admired by many, given too much attention for Ilexa's taste. She sat on the sidelines and sniffed.

Finally, Tinne raised his voice. "Excuse me, do you think we could go and celebrate our HeartBond?"

Laughter rippled through the crowd, Lahsin flushed in embarrassment, but her nerves had settled. She knew herself, was accepting change, and had followed her heart.

Her body had heated since Tinne had touched her, instinctively readying for him. Her skin seemed too sensitive, and where his arm wrapped around her was pure pleasure.

He was pure pleasure. Why had she denied herself this?

Then she and Tinne were in the great hall, a moment later they'd teleported to a dim corridor and stood outside a door of ancient wood so hard and dark it appeared like stone. The hum in Lahsin's head grew louder, changed until it was a lilting melody.

"My Mamá," Tinne said. "Her tunes suffuse the Residence. I think it will sing for the rest of its existence."

"A blessing," Lahsin gasped, but barely heard what he was saying, what she herself said. She was on fire with passion. Heat pooled in her core. Need. Yes! "I *need* you," she panted.

His breath was unsteady, too. "I never thought . . ."

Her heart wrenched. "Is it too soon?"

He shook his head, his breath shuddered out. "You know it isn't. I don't understand how things happen, can only believe it's destiny."

She licked her lips, looked around the narrow corridor. "Where are we?"

"Outside the HouseHeart. I want you to learn about my Family, about me, here." He framed her face in his hands, and they were warm and calloused and wonderful on her skin. His eyes were a gleaming, intense silver. "Only you," he murmured, and it was her turn to shudder.

She wrapped her hands around his wrists, pulled them from her face to cradle them between her breasts. "I never dreamed I could feel so much. It's overwhelming, as powerful as Passage, but so much lovelier."

"I want to make love with you in the HouseHeart, Heart-Bond with you there."

"Yes."

Again he took her hand, faced them toward the door. "Listen, this is the rhyme to open the HouseHeart. My Mamá set it to music." He lifted his voice in a rhythmic song that was easy to memorize, the words simple and sincere. She touched her fingertips to the door, and sensation swept through her, the essence of the Residence itself—ancient, powerful. The door swung open.

With a Word, Tinne disrobed them, then lifted her into his arms. The feel of his bare skin against hers focused her entire being on him and the loving to come.

He carried her into the room, the door locked behind them.

He knelt with her, to lay her down. She clutched at his shoulders. "Don't. I want to come to you on my own two feet."

His gleaming gray eyes met hers, a smile touched his lips, and she had to touch them, too. She traced them with her finger, felt his smile widen.

"All right," he said and gently set her on her feet. Her bare toes curled in the rich permamoss. Tinne *listened* to her.

She drew back from him, looked around the HouseHeart. It was a small room with beautiful tapestries against smooth rock walls. The grass underneath her gave off a sweet scent. Tinne picked up her HeartGift and set it beside some other holly bushes along one wall, but they were different than hers. Ancient Earthan stock, like the low yellow light in the room approximated an ancient Earthan evening.

Tinne turned around and caught his breath. Tears welled in her eyes. He was the most beautiful thing in the chamber.

Slowly they walked toward each other. When they were close, they clasped hands, palm to palm. She opened all of herself to this man, gave herself to him. Accepted all of him in return.

Reality faded.

Lahsin's breath was swept away as they fell through gorgeous, star-studded darkness. So wondrous that she slowed their descent to see more than smears of bright white. Deep, deep black, like she'd never seen, stars of all sizes, pulsing to different beats. Fabulous.

She and Tinne danced. They played. They whirled gently toward the land below—blue green oceans and green earth— like a leaf on a lazy breeze. She sensed his surprise at her joy. "Beautiful," she said, squeezing his hands.

"Yes, it was. I'll tell you all about it later." He smiled, squeezed back.

Looking into his eyes she knew she'd learn and grow with this man beyond what she could comprehend now. She was whole without him, but would always be better, richer in mind, body, and spirit, with him.

They stood there for long moments, hands locked, emotions merging. Sexuality rising and rousing bit by bit, until all her skin felt warm and everything in her ached.

"Lahsin." Tinne's voice was a husky murmur.

"Yes, Tinne."

"Yes." He drew in a deep breath, and she felt it herself. "Accept me as your man, your lover, your HeartMate."

"I do."

"And you are my woman, my love, my HeartMate." Emotions swamped her, her love for him throbbing through their link, being returned, cycling, expanding. Tenderness. Gentleness.

Accept my HeartBond, he sent.

Her body heated more, desire twined tighter. HeartBonding, during sex—no, during *loving*.

Loving, he echoed. *Drop the shield from your HeartGift, Lahsin.*

She trembled. The instant she did that they'd feel only passion, their bodies would rule, explode. Her vision went blurry, but his gaze had sharpened. She released her HeartGift's spellshield.

Then she felt it, the HouseHeart cache opened and *his* HeartGift, a beautiful small drum, rolled out with a resonant thump. There was only desire.

"*I love you,*" she said mentally, sent through their bond, whispered aloud.

"*I love you,*" he returned with a lilting note, almost laughter.

They came together.

Enter the rich world of
historical romance
with Berkley Books . . .

Madeline Hunter

Jennifer Ashley

Joanna Bourne

Lynn Kurland

Jodi Thomas

Anne Gracie

Love is timeless.

Penguin Group (USA) Online

What will you be reading tomorrow?

Patricia Cornwell, Nora Roberts, Catherine Coulter,
Ken Follett, John Sandford, Clive Cussler,
Tom Clancy, Laurell K. Hamilton, Charlaine Harris,
J. R. Ward, W.E.B. Griffin, William Gibson,
Robin Cook, Brian Jacques, Stephen King,
Dean Koontz, Eric Jerome Dickey, Terry McMillan,
Sue Monk Kidd, Amy Tan, Jayne Ann Krentz,
Daniel Silva, Kate Jacobs...

You'll find them all at
penguin.com

Read excerpts and newsletters,
find tour schedules and reading group guides,
and enter contests.

Subscribe to Penguin Group (USA) newsletters
and get an exclusive inside look
at exciting new titles and the authors you love
long before everyone else does.

PENGUIN GROUP (USA)
penguin.com